P9-CDO-778

To my frie[illegible]
with best wishes
Bahman Sholevar

DEAD RECKONING

A NOVEL

by

Bahman Sholevar

Philadelphia

CONCOURSE PRESS

2009

Copyright © 2009 by Bahman Sholevar
Published by
CONCOURSE PRESS
a subsidiary of
EAST-WEST FINE ARTS CORPORATION
P.O. Box 8265
Philadelphia, PA 19101
www.ConcoursePress.com

All rights reserved. Except for brief passages quoted for criticism, no part of this book may be reproduced or transmitted in any form or by any means, electronic or mechanical, including photocopy, recording, or any information storage and retrieval system, without permission.

Manufactured in the United States of America
First edition, 1992
Second edition, 2009
Library of Congress Control Number: 2009922995
ISBN: 978-0-911323-27-6

Cover art work and design by Bahman Sholevar
Cover Photograph by Neil Pressley

Major Books by Bahman Sholevar

Poetry

- حماسهٔ مرگ ، حماسهٔ زندگی (Tehran: 1960)
- *Making Connection: Poems of Exile* (Philadelphia: 1979)
- *The Angel with Bush-Baby Eyes and other poems* (1982)
- *The Love Song of Achilles and other poems* (Philadelphia: 1982)
- *Odysseus' Homecoming* (Philadelphia: 1982)
- *The New Adam: Poems of Renewal* (Philadelphia: 1982)
- *Rooted in Volcanic Ashes* (Philadelphia: 1988)
- *Il Rimpatrio d'Odysseo/ Odysseus' Homecoming* (Italian-English Edition) (Philadelphia: 2009)

Novel

- سفرشب (Tehran: 1967)
- *The Night's Journey& The Coming of The Messiah* (1984)
- *Dead Reckoning* (English Original) (Philadelphia: 1992)
- *A La Deriva* (Spanish Translation) (Philadelphia: 2009)
- *Alla Deriva* (Italian Translation) (Philadelphia: 2009)
- *À La Dérive* (French Translation) (Philadelphia: 2009)
- بی‌لنگر (Persian Translation) (Philadelphia: 2009)
- سفرشب (Philadelphia: 2009)

Criticism

- *The Creative Process: A Psychoanalytic Discussion* with William G. Niederland (Philadelphia: 1984)

Translation into Persian

- *The Sound and Fury* of William Falkner (Tehran: 1959)
- *The Waste Land* of T. S. Eliot (Tehran: 1961, 1964, 2007)

DEAD RECKONING

A NOVEL

by

Bahman Sholevar

CONTENTS

INTRODUCTION

DEAD RECKONING is a realistic/symbolic novel in the best European tradition. It is a realistic novel in the sense that Tolstoy's War and Peace is: the saga of a nation in a dark moment in its history, as well as the saga of a family in its deepest crisis. It is a symbolic novel in the sense that Thomas Mann's The Magic Mountain or Albert Camus' The Plague are. It is a novel dealing with ultimate questions of value for the individual, as well as for the human society, where the individual's instinct to survive is pitted against his human bondage and his family and social responsibilities. It begs comparisons to such novels and holds its own. Even in its stylistic virtuosity and linguistic playfulness, such as exhibited in the chapters in Part VI, it is evocative of the best tradition established by European masters such as Joyce, Beckett, and Nabokov.

The realistic plot of the novel is simple enough. A young leftist rebel in a country under dictatorship has disappeared, presumably captured by the secret police, tortured, and killed. Nothing out of ordinary about that. It is an event happening routinely and daily in any of dozens of countries. But in this case, the rebel is the son of the country's Chief Justice, and the nephew of a Cabinet Minister, himself a turncoat former rebel. To add insult to injury, the family is ordered to make a public announcement that the victim has died in a car accident, and then bury an empty coffin with pomp and ceremony, and with full press coverage, to crush the rumors about the disappearance and death. The psychological action of the novel consists of the effects of this disappearance and death on the victim's family, the father, the elderly Chief Justice, the divorced mother, the uncle, and the sixteen-year-old brother, who is the ironic hero of the novel.

With his son's disappearance and murder, the old Chief Justice's world collapses around him. Disappointed in his marital life, and more than once, disappointed in his oldest son, who, sent to America to study international law and become a jurist, has become a football player and an insurance salesman, his only wish now remains to die, but first to get his youngest son to America, to a different America, to "Thomas Jefferson's America," "where the last battle would be fought," where human destiny would be fulfilled. What makes him wish to die is not only the tragic loss of his son, but the identity crisis which makes him question the meaning of his whole life.

The mother suffers and endures, as she has always done, as she did when she was "thrown out" of her home some fourteen years earlier, as she did when she lost the custody of her sons to her all-powerful husband, who still keeps her in awe, and whom she still loves. Her only solace is her meticulously performed religious rituals, and a strong denial, with which she hangs to the slim possibility that the disappeared never-buried son might one day miraculously reappear.

The uncle, the survival artist, survives this trial as he has survived every other. He lives, as the Chief Justice had predicted, long enough to bury them all. But he, too, pays a heavy price. His identity crisis is the deepest of all, despite his great talent for self-delusion. He, too, dies a broken man, facing his human condition, knowing that his life had not had much value, because he had 'never paid the full price for anything."

However, it is ultimately in the mind of the youngest son, Farhang, that the psychological drama and action of the novel fully unfold. He becomes everyone's point of reference. The boy whom everyone in the family had tried to spare, now all the evil forces outside try to entrap. For the next three years after the tragedy, he becomes a pawn in a game played between his father and the demonic forces that try to keep him from going to America, a pawn in a lose-lose proposition, where his life is the price for his father's silence, and his father's life the price for his.

"They will not let you go, son," his father bitterly tells him. "Not until they have made you into a snitch and a spy, and an informer, not until they have made you unfit for human company. That's what they did to me forty years ago."

"And is that what you want me to become, Dad?" the son asks, "A snitch, and a spy, and an informer, unfit for human company, in order to get a passport?"

"No son," the father replies. "I just want you to humor them for a while, until you leave. .. See whether you can find a place where you can be human without having to be ashamed of it. Hopefully, you will have a chance to do that, in America. A chance I never had here, not forty years ago, not ever."

Unable to absorb the full impact of the events happening to and around him, unable even to confront and properly mourn the death of his beloved brother, the young boy puts his own life, as it were, on hold. His mode of living becomes a "suspension of belief." He becomes an unimpassioned witness. Unable to live his own life, he is asked to take on his shoulders the sins of everyone else. The child who had been too innocent to know and choose for himself, finally becomes the judge and jury that will be asked to validate every other character's life experience.

When the novel begins, not on a Good Friday, but on a Friday the thirteenth, he is a thirty-three year old man who has been on a "seventeen year binge," with a seventeen-year gap in his life, filled by his other selves. And he has three days, until Monday morning, to put himself back together, to account for his own life, and, incidentally, to discover America. What he learns by Monday morning is that America is not a geographic location, but a personal experience, that America does not happen to you just by going there, that you must make it with what you bring with you when you go there.

For seventeen years he has waited for America to happen to him, just as he has waited for the news of his mother's death, his last "significant other." Finally, when that news arrives, at the opening of the novel, and as he had expected, on the anniversary of his father's death, which is also the anniversary of his brother's disappearance and death on his birthday, the now thirty-three-year old boy comes face to face with his own life as a man, realizing that America will never happen to him, unless he makes it happen, with tools he does not have.

"America," he says, "is a state of mind. America is an idea. America is what you bring to it with yourself. Dad never had an America. He never knew an America. He only had a dream, a vision, of America as a place where the future would be shaped, where the last battle would be fought. He never lived his America. He waited for others to live it for him. And they failed him. Alex had an America, even though he didn't know it. And he died for it. Cyrus came to America to sell. He sold America. I came to America to escape. I skipped America."

In this sense, the novel becomes also an American novel, in the sense that Huckleberry Finn, or Catcher in the Rye, or any of Henry James' or Hemingway's novels are American. The young boy has brought to America the radical innocence of his youth and the corruption of the old world. And he must choose upon which to build his America.

With the realization that he has never had an America, Farhang the protagonist's seventeen-year long binge ends and his experience of America, i.e., his search for America, begins: "Today," he says, "I know enough about myself to go looking for my America. I am going back to start looking where I began, where I missed the boat in the first place, where I lost myself. I came to America empty-handed. And I leave America empty-handed. I brought nothing with me, and I take nothing with me. When I come back, I will come with my arms full. And when the Lady with the Lamp, in the harbor, says to me, Give me your tired, your hungry, your poor. I will take care of them. I will say, No, Lady. You give me your tired, your hungry, your poor! I will take care of them. This time I have come back with my arms full.

Thus, America becomes not a passive vision of a Utopia, but rather an active and personal commitment to it. The protagonist goes in search, not of America, but of his America. In this sense, his becoming an American becomes more than an accident of geography. He becomes the embodiment of that search for value which was behind the original idea of America, and which has to be renewed by each generation, indeed by each individual, if the idea of America is to be saved. There is no longer "the Territory" to "light out for," as Huckleberry Finn had done. Huck's worst nightmare has come true, the whole world, the whole global village, has been "sivilized," and the only "Territory" left to go searching for is an inner space.

It is that inner space that the protagonist goes in search of, back where he had started from, and again, in Waterloo, Iowa. It is that same inner space, Alan Dugan, the American consul/poet goes to discover in Keokuk, Iowa, when he resigns from his post, echoing the American Indian's battle cry "It is a good day to die!" While issuing Farhang a visa to enter "Thomas Jefferson's America," his last official act as a U.S. Consul, he had warned him that "the jungle" Farhang was trying to escape did not end at the border of America.

"The jungle extends everywhere," he had said. "The only difference is that in America, the jungle is a patchwork, interspersed with small isolated 'colonies of the saved.' Out of those colonies come men like Thoreau, Hawthorne, Melville, Whitman. 'Isolatos,' Melville called them then, and Isolatos we still are. In America they let you get out of the jungle and stay out, if you really don't have the killer instinct, if you really want to go vegetarian, but only if you don't try to stop the jungle, to do something to stop it. You won't catch any big game that way. But then, if you are a vegetarian, you don't need big game."

"And if you try to stop the jungle?" Farhang had asked. "Then they crush you," Alan Dugan had said.

If Alan Dugan's discovery of America, of his America, came with the realization that he was a vegetarian mixed up in the "big game hunt" of carnivores, even though he was no more than "the guy who tends the mules," Farhang's uncle's discovery of America came with the realization that he was a vegetarian turned carnivore despite himself, just as Farhang's father's discovery that he was "the Chief Justice in a circus."

If Columbus had sailed west to discover east, in the last part of the novel the protagonist sails east to discover west. He heads back for the old world, for the heart of darkness he had escaped seventeen years ago, ostensibly to attend the funeral of his mother, but really to find the key with which he could open the door of America. He enters into the heart of a new darkness, a blacked-out war-ravaged city ruled by a new dictatorship, only to be immediately arrested, blindfolded, and thrown into a dungeon, to re-experience much of the fate of his disappeared brother, and by the same agents too, only to be saved from death by the money and influence of the billionaire uncle he has totally denounced.

Flown back to safety in Switzerland for reconciliation with the dying uncle, he admits that all he has learned from the trip is the knowledge of "how long a corpse can stay above the ground, unburied." The burial of the mother, which he did not even witness, finally puts into the grave the unburied ghost of the brother who has pursued him for seventeen years. He comes back to America empty-handed again, but the void in him has now been filled. He is no longer an "empty sack who cannot stand straight." He has found the key which will open the door of America.

Lighting out for the inner space of Waterloo, Iowa, he now means to rebuild the Garden of Eden on ten acres of bottom land, "a just portion for a just man." Accepting his human limitations, realizing that he is a man more sinned against than sinning, giving up his presumption of paying for all the sins of the world, he has managed to become Adam again. But his Garden of Eden is only a Noah's Ark, where he may still try to save the "sivilized world."

"And why animals for companions?" the dying uncle had asked him.

"Well," he had replied. "I've had a thought. Maybe we've had it all wrong all this time, going on the premise that human beings started as angels. So, we're so disappointed when we see them act like beasts. Maybe, if we begin by seeing them as beasts, and see how far they have to fall upward to become angels, we may get somewhere with them yet."

Robert Reed
Philadelphia, 1992

DEAD RECKONING

Doch der Tote muB fort

(But the dead man must go on)

Rainer Maria Rilke

Duino Elegies (The Tenth Elegy)

The world will soon break up into small
colonies of the saved.

Robert Bly

Those Being Eaten by America

PART ONE

CHAPTER ONE

FARHANG'S DIARY
Tehran
January 14, 1967

Mom came down this morning. Last night, when I could give no explanation for Alex's absence on his birthday, I finally had to let her know. That's the one day of the year he had not failed to spend with her for twenty-three years. On our birthdays all three of us have always belonged to her. That was part of the deal she made with Dad fourteen years ago, when she agreed to give up everything, including us. Dad doesn't believe in birthdays. It is all sentimental bunk to him. So, it was all very little sacrifice he was making.

She came at seven in the morning, on the first bus. She must have left at five to be here by seven. She came in through the garden gate, gave me a quick hug and kiss, and walked straight up the driveway, and up the stairs, into the drawing room she had given up fourteen years ago. She seemed so imperious, so distant, that I followed her without saying a word.

"Your father, son!" she demanded calmly, as she sat down on a wing chair. "Call your father! I will talk to him right away!"

She who had never demanded anything in her life, who had not demanded anything in fourteen years, now demanding that the man who had once driven her away, from himself, from her children, and from her home, present himself to her right away! And she sat there, as erect and as imperious, until Dad presented himself, all dressed up to rise to the graveness of the occasion.

"My son, sir!" she declaimed. "Where is my son?"

"I don't know, Madame," said Dad, sheepishly. "I'm sure I don't know." For the first time sounding helpless in front of this meek, mouse-sized woman, who barely filled the chair, whose shoulders barely reached the back of the chair.

"Fourteen years ago you divorced me and took my sons from me! Now I want my sons! Now I want my Alex!" I had never seen her so eloquent, so magnificent, sitting there like a queen, talking like a queen, too.

"I don't know where he is, Madame," Dad repeated helplessly. "I have tried to find him. God knows I have tried."

Dad stared at her, or maybe through her at something else, where Alex might be, what might have happened to him, what might be happening to him at that very moment. He had tried for three weeks now to do what Mom was asking him to do, to find Alex, to help Alex, to save Alex, if he could. It was three weeks since I had finally got sick worrying about Alex and had let Dad know that he had disappeared.

Alex had a habit of going away for several days at a time, without telling Dad. But he always told me where he was. Dad had got used to not seeing him around the house much. I was their channel of communication. "And what's that brother of yours up to now?" he would ask plaintively, if he hadn't seen Alex for some four or five days. "He's mountain climbing," I would say. That was always a safe answer. Alex was an avid mountain climber. He was the first man having climbed Damavand summit, and from two different slopes. Dad would shrug his shoulder. "It would be nice to have him at the dinner table once in a while," he would grumble. You could tell that he missed him. I certainly did.

Eight weeks ago, Alex suddenly packed almost everything he had, his mountain climbing gears, his personal things, a few books, all his cash, and left without telling me where he was going. "Mountain climbing," he said. "That's all you need to know. And that's all you need to tell Dad, or Mom, or Uncle J., or anyone who must know." It was not unusual for him to go mountain climbing for an indefinite period of time, but this time I knew something was different. The way he hugged me and kissed me again and again, it seemed like he would be gone for a long time. It seemed like forever.

"I'll call you every few days," he said, "just to say hello, to let you know I'm all right, and to see whether anybody has been looking for me. You know what I mean. If I come back to see you, it would be probably some late night, in secret. No one must know. If I can't call you, someone else will, to say I'm all right. If something happens to me, someone may call to let you know. If you hear nothing for two full weeks, that means something has happened to me. Tell Dad then, not before. And take care of Dad and Mom until I get back. Call Mom every day to see that she's all right."

He left some code words. If he asked how my poems were going, he was asking whether strangers had been looking for him. If strangers had been looking for him, I should then answer "Not too well." At that moment I knew this was not an ordinary going away. "You are coming back again, aren't you," I said, tears running down my face. "Maybe not for a while," he said. Then he said what he had not intended to say. "I'm going underground." I had a scary feeling that I may never see him again, the scariest feeling I had ever had in my life. I don't think I have ever loved anyone as much as I have loved Alex.

I helped carry his stuff to the car, even though he didn't want me to. There were two other young men in the car, who made a subtle but deliberate attempt to turn their faces away from me. Alex hugged me again and quickly sent me away.

For the next six weeks I could do nothing but wait for his phone calls. I got two very short calls in the first two weeks. He asked how I was, how Mom and Dad were, how my poems were going, and said he was all right. Again, he wouldn't say where he was. In the second call, he said I would not see him for a long time, and then showed up at my bedroom door like a cat burglar at midnight that very night. I wasn't asleep yet. When I heard shuffling of feet, I hoped it was Alex, and it was. He hugged me and kissed me a few times, asked about Mom and Dad, and told me he would not see me for several months. "I don't know how I will keep in contact with you," he said, "but I will. Remember the two weeks. If you haven't heard from me or about me for two full weeks, then tell Dad."

In the third week I got a short call, but not from him. The maid answered the phone, before I could get to it. "It's for you," she said, handing me the receiver. I grabbed it and was disappointed not hearing Alex's voice. It was the voice of a stranger: "Alex is all right. Sends his love," he said, and hung up.

In the fourth week I heard from another stranger, a woman this time, saying the same thing. "Farhang?" she asked, as I picked up the phone. "Yes," I said, realizing that it was not Mom's voice. "Alex is all right. Sends his love," she said, and hung up.

I heard no news in the fifth week. I walked around dazed like a sleepwalker all week. Dad must have sensed something was wrong with me, because he asked a couple of times whether I was sick or something. I pulled myself together and smiled, not letting on.

The sixth week was a nightmare. That made it the second week I had not heard from or about Alex. And I was scared to death that something had happened to him. I counted the days, then the hours, then the minutes, until the two weeks were up. In fact, I cheated. It was still four hours short of the full two weeks, when I broke down and let Dad know that Alex had disappeared. We were about to begin the dinner, when I felt I could wait no longer. There was no way I could go through another dinner counting the minutes, keeping to myself what was killing me.

"I have to tell you this, Dad!" I spurted it out, impulsively, anxiously. "Alex has disappeared."

The spoon fell from Dad's hand, hitting the edge of the dinner table and dropping to the ground. He froze, looking at me in deadly silence, while a strange look came over his face.

"He has not been mountain climbing. He went underground six weeks ago," I almost babbled. "He visited one late night. He has been in contact every week, until two weeks ago. He said if I didn't hear from him for two full weeks, that meant something had happened to him, and only then I should tell you all this."

"And you had to wait two full weeks!" Dad said, his eyes letting me feel the full weight of my guilt. "You have to do everything exactly as he tells you, don't you, even when his life is on the line?" I couldn't speak. I felt the tears running down my face. Dad had already left the table for the telephone. He called Uncle J. and asked him to drive over immediately. "It's about Alex," he said. "It seems he has disappeared. Yes, yes. By all means. Make a call right away. See what you can find out. Call me back right away. I'll be waiting."

Uncle J. called back in half an hour, which seemed like an eternity. Dad had been pacing back and forth all that time, while I had been watching the hands on the grandfather clock. He grabbed the phone even before the first ring. I ran to his bedroom and got on the other receiver to listen. "They've got him, all right," Uncle J. said. "They've had him for three days. It's bad news. I'll do what I can. But it seems like very bad news. I'll come over right away."

He got there in less than half an hour, without his chauffeur, driving his private car. He sat down and asked me for all the details. He wanted to know when Alex had left, exactly what he had taken with him, who was with him when he left, when the contacts had been made, and by whom, and every word that had been said. I told them everything I knew, but it didn't seem to be of much help.

"Did you talk to the General?" Dad asked anxiously.

"Yes," said Uncle J. "But even he may not be able to help. He says this is a real bad case. They think Alex has been the leader of an armed group called The Revolutionary Army that has been attacking gendarmerie stations all over Geelan Province for some time. They have taken a lot of arms from those stations, and a few gendarmes have been killed. He says the group members usually die under torture, before they can be made to talk. And if they think Alex is their leader, you can imagine how much worse that would be for him. Even talking probably wouldn't save his life. And the General himself is very weary of meddling in the case. He says he may be the number two man in the Savak, but he has many enemies who are always on the lookout to trip him. He's looking out for himself and I can't say I blame him. Alex apparently is in the hand of their worst what they call 'specialists.'"

"What's that?" I couldn't help asking.

"You don't want to know," said Uncle J.

"I just wish you had told us sooner," said Dad.

"It wouldn't have made any difference," said Uncle J. "Not the way it sounds. We wouldn't have known where to look for him."

I thought that should make my guilt less, but I didn't feel any better. And I didn't care whether anybody thought I was guilty or not. All I cared about was Alex.

"Would they let me see him?" Dad asked, helplessly.

"I don't think so." said Uncle J. "He is in their most secret place, and by now he is probably in such a shape they wouldn't want anybody to see him, least of all his father. Don't forget, you're still the Chief Justice. What would happen if you decided to talk?"

"Would they let you see him?" Dad asked. He was almost begging.

"I doubt it," said Uncle J. "Unless the General could persuade them that if I saw him, he might talk. They are probably under pressure to get him to talk before his group can re-organize and find new hideouts. That would be the only reason they might let me see him, and only if the General is willing to stick his neck way out."

"Would you do your best?" Dad begged.

Uncle J. nodded. "I did try to warn him," he said, sadly. "I tried to steer him away, but he wouldn't listen. He had to go it alone. He wouldn't even trust me. This is not just underground party work, printing underground papers, writing slogans on the walls. This is armed resistance. I could tell he was involved in something real dangerous. It's bad news. He can't be saved. It might even drag all of us down, the General included."

I hated him at that moment for what he said. I didn't care if it dragged him down. I didn't even care if it dragged Dad down. I didn't care if it dragged the whole world down, if Alex was in that much trouble. I could no longer stand it. I ran to my room, threw myself on the bed, hid my head under the pillow, and sobbed a long time, until I fell asleep. I had nightmares all night long.

And now after three weeks, Dad was not any closer to finding or saving Alex, than he had been then. Two weeks ago, Uncle J. had managed to see Alex with his General friend, had come back very upset and angry, and after a private talk with Dad, had washed his hands of the whole case, leaving Dad to his own devices, to try helplessly day after day, to help Alex, but with no luck. Dad wouldn't tell me what shape Alex was in when Uncle J. had seen him, or what had happened.

Now, not even looking at Mom, as if talking to no one in particular, Dad repeated himself. "I have tried to find him. God knows, I have tried."

"You haven't tried hard enough, Sir, if you haven't found him!" Mom thundered at him again. "You find him! You hear me? You find my Alex and bring him back to me! Today! You will find me sitting here on this chair waiting, when you come back, with Alex!"

Dad now turned to go, his hat in his hand, on his seemingly futile quest, as he had done every day for the past two weeks. "I will try again, Madame!" he said sheepishly. "I will try!"

"You didn't sound so sheepish fourteen years ago," Mom declaimed again at his turned back, "when you drove me away from my home and my children! You let me know then who you were, and what you were! Now you let them know who you are, and what you are! You are the Chief Justice! Let them feel the weight of all your might and power, the way you let me feel it then!"

Was she ironic? Had she sensed that the matters were already beyond Dad's power? Or was she just wishing, for her own sake, for Alex's sake, even for Dad's sake, that Dad would be all-powerful now? Dad stopped for a moment without turning, precariously balanced on his left tiptoes, frozen in the gesture of reaching for the door handle, his right knee bent motionless in midair as in a film clip. Then his frozen form resumed its motion and he hurried out, gently closing the door behind him.

Mom motioned to me to go and sit by her side. I sat on the carpet next to her chair and let her pull my head down into her lap. I could not see her face, though I was expecting her to break down any minute and start sobbing. Her left hand firmly held my head down in her lap, while she tensely combed my hair with the fingers of her right hand. When she heard Dad's car start, she let go of me.

"Your school, son!" she said firmly, without any emotion. "You will be late for school."

It was then I looked at her face and noticed that she had not shed a tear, not one. I asked her to let me stay with her.

"Your education is the only consolation I've had," she said resignedly. "I submitted to fourteen years of suffering, fourteen years of loneliness, fourteen years of separation from you, because I thought he could give you a better education, better than what I could either afford or offer. Don't let him ever say that I kept you from your school."

Dad was waiting for me, with the motor running. He must have known that Mom would not hold me back, although on that day, he probably would not have cared if I missed school. He might have even been glad to let her have me for a day, whatever little consolation that was for Alex's disappearance. Once I was in the car, I felt much relief that she had not let me stay with her. I could not have sat there for hours, with my head in her lap, or watching her glued to that chair, feeling sorry for her, for Alex, for Dad, for myself, and for the whole rotten world.

Dad drove so absentmindedly that several times I thought he would hit another car, or run over some pedestrian. We did not speak a word throughout the long drive, although I would have given anything to hear Dad say that Alex would be all right. When he dropped me off in front of the school, I felt his mind was miles away. As I shut the door, I could not help saying, "Good luck, Dad!" He nodded. He had tears in his eyes. And so did I. He told me not to expect him to pick me up.

I daydreamed through all my morning classes. A couple of times teachers picked on me, but gave up when they saw how out of it I was, and how funny I seemed to the rest of the class. At lunch time I felt like taking the bus back home, but I didn't, knowing Dad wouldn't be back yet, and knowing that I couldn't face Mom alone. After the first afternoon class I couldn't wait any longer and I decided to skip the last one and go home. I was so anxious to know whether Dad was back. I was so anxious to know about Alex. I missed him so much. I had never been away from him for so long. Eight whole weeks.

The porter tried to stop me from leaving, threatening to report me to the principal. He was surprised to hear me say that he and the principal could both go to hell, as far as I was concerned. I was not one of the guys who talked that way. I climbed the locked gate, jumped down into the alley, and ran away, all the way to the bus stop. I jumped on the back of a double decker, just as it was pulling out. I was glad I had left early. If I had waited until the schools were out, I would have had to wait in line for a long time.

I nervously cracked my knuckles all the time I was on the bus, the longest bus ride I had ever had. It made every stop. It took forever to get home. I ran all the way home from the bus stop, praying, I didn't know to whom: Please let Alex be home! I would do anything if Alex was already home! Then it occurred to me that I had to pray to someone, even though I had stopped believing in God again. So, I began addressing my prayers to God: God! Please! Let Alex be home now! I would do anything for you. I would do anything for anybody. How happy would I be! How happy would Mom and Dad be! How happy would everybody be! We could have a birthday party for him right away, with Mom and Uncle J. and everybody there. Dad wouldn't mind it, I am sure. He would be so pleased, he would love to have a party for Alex.

I still had his present to give him, all wrapped up from eight weeks ago. It was a hardcover copy of Steinbeck's *Grapes of Wrath.* He would like it, I bet, though it is funny the way he reads novels. He reads them like they were dictionaries, beginning with the first page and going on until he gets bored, then jumping to the last page and reading backward until he gets bored again. Then jumping back to the beginning and reading another page, skipping five or ten, reading another page, skipping, reading, skipping, reading, skipping, reading, until the book is finished. If he ever finishes any novel. He is even worse with poetry. He doesn't believe in literature much. He says it doesn't do anything for a hungry stomach. But what does it matter whether he likes literature or not? Who cares what he thinks of poetry? I just miss him so much.

I reached home at four, awfully disappointed not seeing Dad's car in the driveway. That meant he wasn't home yet. And that certainly meant Alex wasn't there. I was fearful of facing Mom alone, of having to look her in the eyes, though I could see no self-pity there, no emotions whatsoever. Her eyes looked hard as rocks. She still sat on that chair, as erect as before. The maid said she had not moved since the morning, and had refused to eat all day. She had had nothing but two glasses of water. I tried to get her to eat something, but she insisted that she wasn't hungry. I hadn't eaten all day either. I was hungry. But I did not want to eat. I decided to wait until Dad was home. He couldn't be long now.

Dad returned at four thirty-five. I ran out to meet him as soon as I heard the car. Alex wasn't with him, of course. I tried to read his face, but he wouldn't even look me in the eyes, walking right past me as if I wasn't even there. He looked so fierce, so resolute, walking so hard as if he wanted to dig holes in the ground, clenching his teeth and looking straight ahead, as if there was one thing and only one thing in his life which he was determined to do, and damned be anyone who got in his way. There was a package in his right hand, badly wrapped in coarse brown paper. He went to his room and stayed there for a good ten minutes, while Mom and I waited for him in the drawing room. When he finally came in, he looked as fierce, with his right arm hidden behind his back, apparently holding something. Looking cold-blooded and steely- eyed, he stood against the picture window, facing Mom and me, silently grinding his teeth, as if in a loss for words. "Madame!" he said finally, fiercely, suddenly bringing forward and holding up whatever it was he was holding, a wide brown belt with a shiny brass buckle and a black Russian hat, Alex's. "This is as much as you will ever see of your son again!" And just as I was about to fly in his face with a choking rage and squeeze his fat neck, he continued with a voice that gradually lost its fierceness and its cruelty and its arrogance and approached the helplessness of a moan: "This is as much as I will ever see of my son again!"

It was only then I knew why. He had to be so cruel to Mom, to be able to speak of his own grief, of his own helplessness. He had to be so cruel to be able to speak at all. As he turned toward the door, his hands joined behind his back again, holding fast to that hat and that belt, his fingers digging cruelly into them. Then, as he slowly stepped towards the door, little by little the grip of his fingers eased, until finally, almost absentmindedly, he let the belt and then the hat drop to the floor, just before he walked out. Had he already forgotten them, I wondered, he who had never believed in the sentimental value of anything, anyway? Or was this a sacrificial gesture to this woman whose very life he had sacrificed fourteen years ago? Was he now trying to compensate for all her losses, by giving up his claim to a hat and a belt?

Only at that moment I became aware that Mom was clutching my hair, that she had been clutching my hair all the time, ever since Dad spoke. And only then I realized why she had made me sit next to her on the rug, and put my head on her lap again, just before Dad came in. For support! For sheer physical support! I was the last piece of the shattered raft of her life to cling to, to save her from sinking, to pull her ashore. Was she aware that she was gripping my hair that tightly? Or had she suddenly been struck dead and what I felt was only the grip of a dead hand?

I sat there staring at that hat and that belt, unable to move. When I desperately tried to turn my head and look at Mom's face, to see whether she was still alive, she finally let go of my hair, but only as a dead woman's grip would have let go. I ran and picked up the hat and belt. It was the hat Alex had let me wear so often to keep me warm, when we had gone hiking or mountain climbing. It was the belt we had often played with. Once, when climbing rocks, I was caught at the bottom of a boulder, unable to move forward or backward, he had come around from above, hung this belt down for me to grab, and pulled me up. Then I had realized why he wore belts long enough to go almost twice around his waist. He had even hit me with that belt once. The memory of that belting seemed so precious now.

I looked up then and saw Mom's right hand already reaching out for them in a silent command and I knew that I too had to give up all claim to them, as Dad had just done. I realized then that Alex had been theirs, before he was mine. How long had I taken it for granted that Alex belonged to me before he belonged to anyone else? I crawled back on the rug and reluctantly handed over my treasures. A terrible thought came to me: I would inherit that hat and that belt when Mom was dead.

January 14, 1967
8:00 p.m.

Mom left an hour ago, refusing to stay overnight, as Dad had insisted, and also refusing to let me go with her, as Dad had suggested.

She walked out of here in such a daze, as if she didn't know who she was or where she was. I am so very sorry for her, even more than I am for Dad, or for myself. I am so terribly worried about her, although her strength is surprising me. The first danger seems to have passed, but maybe the truth hasn't hit her yet. Maybe she is only in shock. She has not shed one drop of tear. As if suddenly removed from the world around her, some awesome aura has surrounded her. I felt I had to offer her some hope, something to hang on to. I told her I would call her as soon as I had heard more about Alex from Dad. But the way she nodded, it seemed as if she didn't care any longer, or didn't understand.

January 14, 1967
9:00 p.m.

Dad has locked himself up in his room since he spoke to Mom. The only words he has spoken since, through the locked door, are when he told me to ask Mom to stay for the night, or if she refused, to offer to go with her. The maid has knocked on his door several times to ask whether she should serve the dinner, but has received no response. I have knocked once myself and there has been no answer. We are both scared to try again.

The maid served my dinner in the kitchen, although I felt guilty eating it. I felt guilty being the only member of the family who hadn't lost his appetite. But I was so hungry. I hadn't eaten all day. I am so worried about Alex. I am so anxious to talk to Dad. He couldn't mean that Alex is dead already. Wouldn't they have sent us the body, if he were dead? Has Dad been able to see him? If they let Uncle J. see him two weeks ago, why wouldn't they let Dad see him today? Where is he? Where are they keeping him? What are they doing to him?

I probably won't be able to speak to Dad until tomorrow. The lights in his room haven't come on since he locked himself in. I doubt whether he is asleep, though. He hasn't been sleeping much since Alex disappeared. I have watched the light in his room come on and go out so often in the middle of the night. What frightens me most is that he doesn't want to talk, that he doesn't want to face me. It makes me suspect the worst has already happened. I know I won't be able to sleep all night.

January 15, 1967

I did not sleep all night. Dad's words about that hat and that belt being all he and Mom were ever going to see of Alex again, kept pounding in my head. I wondered all night what Mom was doing and whether Dad was really asleep. His light didn't come on even once during the night. I have been snooping around his bedroom since six this morning, hoping to catch him and talk to him the minute he comes out, to go to bathroom maybe, before he can go back in and lock himself up again. I even dared to try his door quietly, to see whether he might have unlocked it during the night.

What if something has happened to him too? A stroke or something. What would I do then? His high blood pressure might have got worse. What if he has died during the night? Just when I was getting myself all worked up, I heard his bed squeak. That means he is at least alive.

....

Dad finally came out at ten this morning. He looked frightening. His bloodshot eyes looked like two red blobs. His face was all red and swollen. Had he been crying all night? I never thought he could cry, any more than I could fly. He couldn't have been drinking. He doesn't keep any liquor in his room, and he never left his room all night.

He stood in the middle of the hall looking bewildered, staring at me as if I was a stranger. Finally, as if he had just recognized me, he asked why I was not at school. I mumbled something, being taken by surprise, not having even thought about school. But he wasn't expecting an answer, not even listening, as he walked absentmindedly to the drawing room, as if expecting to see Mom still sitting there on that wing chair, then to the living room, then to the kitchen, and ended up going to the bathroom.

I stood in the hall, waiting for him. When he came out, he again asked why I was not at school. This time I found my tongue and said that I had to talk to him, about Alex. He waved me away impatiently. "Later! Later!" he said, and hurried back into his room. I saw the maid running after him with an ice pack. "It's for his head," she whispered to me confidentially. In a minute she came out, fanning the air with erratic and pitiful motions of the hand, and I heard Dad's door lock behind her. That meant I would not be able to talk to him again today, to ask about Alex. I had then a sure feeling that I would never see Alex again, and suddenly felt a terrible urge to run, to run out of the house and keep running, forever.

When I stopped running, when I even realized that I had been running, not knowing how long, not knowing where to, I found myself quite out of breath, on the foothills above the Haunted Valley. I threw myself down on a rock and began to sob uncontrollably. I cried a long time before I felt calm enough to head back home.

January 16, 1967

Dad came out of his seclusion this morning and we finally talked. What he told me left me numb. Alex is still alive, but he is doomed. Nothing can save him now, except a miracle. And Dad doesn't believe in miracles, and neither do I. But for Alex's sake, I am ready to hope that there might be one. If there is a God I'm sure he can't help hearing Mom's prayers. She has been His faithful servant if there has ever been one.

January 17, 1967

I talked to Mom on the telephone today. She sounded like a ghost. She asked whether I had heard any more about Alex. He is alive, I said. We only know that much. But they won't let Dad see him. They won't let anyone see him. I didn't tell her that Dad had said that Alex was doomed. I gave her hope. I had to. I have to keep her going. I am glad she hasn't given up yet. She wouldn't last a day if she did. I must go see her.

January 18, 1967

Dad has not left the house since that day and rarely leaves his room. He spends most of the time behind the locked door, God knows doing what, probably playing with his books. I have not been back to school yet, either. The principal has called twice and the maid has told him that I am very sick. I spend most of the time in Alex's room, going through his books, his clothes, his pictures, anything I can find. Dad and I see little of each other, now that we no longer have our meals together. Dad eats in his room, if he eats at all, and the maid leaves my meals behind Alex's door, having been told not to disturb me when I am there. I look for food behind the door, only when I get terribly hungry, which is not very often.

January 20, 1967

I have run out of things to do in Alex's room, having gone through everything two or three times. And there's nothing else left to do at home. I don't even think about school. The whole idea of going to school now seems so absurd. What good did going to school do Alex?

I have decided to go hiking or climbing, to the places I used to go with Alex.

January 22, 1967

I have spent the past two days by the Twin Waterfalls, where Alex and I used to hunt for river crabs. I have brought two of them home today in a can, not knowing what I intend to do with them. Alex and I once brought a couple of them back from the river. I don't remember what we did with them then either. I think they crawled out of Alex's knapsack and got away along the way. I am desperately reaching out, for anything that would still connect me to Alex.

January 23, 1967

I had a nightmare last night. I dreamed that the river crabs had gotten out of the can and were crawling up my legs, inside my pants. Before I could stop them they had reached my testicles and were devouring them. I was going mad with fright. I felt such a relief when I woke up and realized that it was all a dream. I have killed the crabs and buried them in a flower bed under Alex's window.

January 25, 1967

Dad and I had breakfast together today, for the first time in many days. He seems so calm and yet so broken, as if he had aged ten years in less than two weeks. He has lost so much weight that his shirt looks a couple of sizes too large for him. The skin of his neck hangs loose under his chin and his cheeks look so flabby. There are big bags around his eyes. It's strange what less than two weeks can do to a man. We spoke only two sentences each. He said it was time I went back to school. Then he asked when I had last talked to my Mom. I am surprised to find him so concerned about her in the midst of his own grief. Is he feeling guilty? He wants me to go and visit her often now, to spend time with her, to look after her. He reminded me that with Cyrus away, I was all that she had left in this world. He did not even mention Alex.

January 26, 1967

I saw Mom last night. She seems completely transformed. Paler than ever, she looks so impassive and calm. If it was not for the extreme sadness in her eyes, you would think she were an angel. Whatever her suffering, it has sunk so deep that nothing shows on the surface. Even the sadness in the eyes does not seem to be up front, but rather somewhere deep in the back, as on the far end of a telescope. Her face seems like a frame around a static picture of frozen grief, the focus of which are her eyes. I have the feeling that this woman will never again be able to cry, that the only tears she might ever shed would be tears of joy at seeing Alex in her arms once more. If anything, the shock of that might kill her then.

January 28, 1967

The unsayable thing has happened and I am too sick to speak of it. I did some real drinking last night, more than I had done in all the sixteen years of my life, that is, a glass of wine at dinner now and then with Dad, and an occasional glass of vodka with Alex and his friends on outings. I started drinking at home, out of Dad's brandy bottles, while he was visiting his doctor, then went to town like a madman, having a shot at any bar that came my way. I can't clearly remember everything that happened between seven, when I left home, and whatever time it was I made it back, miraculously on my own two feet.

The events of the first few hours are vivid in my mind. Then everything becomes hazy. I remember stopping at many bars, drinking many shots on the run. I remember walking down dark empty alleys singing Hafiz and Rumi poems at the top of my voice. I remember fighting a husky queer fellow trying to hustle me in an alley next to a bar, in a fight that might have taken forever, before I knocked him out. I remember stopping at another bar, where a kindly Armenian bartender told me that my face was bloody, that I had drunk enough for one night, and that I had better get myself home before my folks worried themselves to death about me. I remember washing the blood off my face in a dirty bathroom, and checking my bleeding lip in a very crooked mirror, before finally setting out for home.

The next vivid thing I remember is sitting up in my bed, throwing up in a washbasin held by the maid, while Dad stood at a corner of the room watching. He did not look angry or even upset, but rather extremely sad. I knew what he would say if he ever opened his mouth: "There is no excuse for this. No matter what you are going through, there is no excuse for this." But there was an excuse, and a damn good one, too. I had thought of not telling him, at least of not showing him the picture, to spare him more grief. But seeing him standing there watching me like that, I felt so ashamed. I felt I had to let him know that I would not have done it otherwise.

Just as he was about to leave the room, without having said a word of reproach, I pointed to the low dresser in the corner, where the paper was. First, he did not understand. Then he saw it. He walked slowly toward the dresser and stood there looking at it, but not touching it. From up there, maybe he could make out the picture, but he certainly could not read the caption. Yet he took such a long time, as if he was actually reading the caption. He did not pick the paper up to bring it closer to his eyes. Nor did he sit down. He just slowly bent over for a closer look.

Was the picture telling him everything, and so vividly, that he had no need to read the caption? Or was he scared to read it, scared to touch that piece of paper, as if it were some explosive that could blow him up sky high? Could he read that faceless face as well as I could? Wasn't he curious to know what those little holes were all over the body, the ash not showing in the picture? The rest wasn't hard to guess. Not hard to guess at all. My God! What beasts! Now I knew what Uncle J. had meant by their "worst specialists," and why he had thought I had better not know what that meant.

Dad finally reached out with a trembling hand and picked up the paper. It was the first time I had seen his hands tremble. He looked at it for a long time, reading, if that's what he was doing. He examined it, first with and then without his glasses. I knew he could not see well without his glasses. So, why was he even trying? To persuade himself that the fault was with his eyes, a trick of refraction and not with what he saw? He put the paper back on the dresser and slowly collapsed in the chair, his elbows coming to rest on the dresser, his forearms propping up his head, his hands covering his face. I could not even feel sorry for him. I had no more sorrow left to give, and I was sick to my guts.

I don't know how long he sat there like that, certainly long enough for the maid to carry the washbasin out and come back with a wet towel to clean my face. I could hear a barely audible inhuman moan, and for a minute I thought it came from Dad, until I realized that it came from the old maid. Did she know? She couldn't read. But if she had seen that picture, what the hell did it matter whether she could read or not? Didn't the picture tell everything? Couldn't she guess whose body it was? Or was she only so grieved to see me drunk for the first time, to see Dad watching me like that, to see what Alex's disappearance was doing to me, was doing to us?

I had propped myself up on two pillows against the wall, feeling so weak and nauseated. I felt like throwing up again, but I knew there was nothing left in my guts to throw up. There was more stuff in that washbasin the maid took out than I could have possibly swallowed all day. I had been bringing up some bitter golden yellow stuff, pure gall probably. I leaned my head against the wall and closed my eyes for a few seconds, trying to calm down my stomach.

Finally Dad looked up after a long time, looking like he had just woken up. So he wasn't struck dead! How sturdy this family is turning out to be! How could all these people get a hold of themselves so fast, I will never know. Where the hell do they find all the strength? He picked up the clipping again, looking at it so calmly.

"Is that him?" he asked casually, resignedly. "Can you tell for certain?"

Didn't he really know? Couldn't he tell? Or was he hoping that I would say no, that I would contradict the testimony of his eyes? No, of course he could not tell. How could he, with the face almost totally gone? How many times in the past ten years had he seen Alex's bare body? I was the only one who could be sure, if anybody. Wasn't I an authority on Alex? Hadn't I seen his naked chest and body a thousand times, in the bathhouse, in the gym, in the river, on the beach? And with the face gone, could even I be certain, absolutely, beyond any shadow of doubt? Or did I also need my denial, my need to hope against all odds, that the picture was not that of Alex? Hadn't I sat down for a long time and examined every line of the head and the hair and the neck and the chest and the abdomen, while guzzling brandy out of Dad's bottles?

"Yes," I said.

"Are you sure?"

"I wish I were less sure than I am."

"Where did this come from?"

"Out of a paper someone slipped under the gate. I burned the rest of the paper."

"Did you see who it was?"

"No. By the time I got to the gate and opened it, he was gone."

Then he said something that surprised me.

"It's a good thing you didn't see him. It is better that way," he said, and walked out.

Now I was glad that I had told that lie. Could he tell that I had lied? I *had* seen the guy's face. He was Alex's friend. I had seen him once before too, with Alex, the last night he came back from the woods to see me. He was standing guard for Alex at the gate. I was not supposed to go to the gate when Alex left. But I did. And then I saw him, through the crack in the gate. He didn't know I had seen him.

This time, I happened to be near the gate, when I saw the paper slipping in under it. I ran and opened the gate, surprising and frightening him, facing him as he straightened up, quickly retrieving the paper and trying to hide it inside his coat.

When he saw that it was me, and that I had recognized him, he asked in a whisper whether there was anybody behind him in the alley. I told him there was no one. "Get in quick!" he said, pushing me in and getting in after me and closing the gate. He asked whether my father was at home. When I said he was not, he shoved the paper into my hands. "There is something in this paper you and your father would wanna see," he said. "It's about Alex. I know how much you loved him, and I know how much he loved you. I have risked my neck to get this paper to you. Burn it the minute you've read it. They'll kill you if they find it on you. And don't tell anybody where you got it, not even your father. Tell him you found it under the gate."

I nodded.

I had watched Alex burn papers like that at the sink before, first making sure that no one was around, not even the maid. He would never let me read them, though. "What you don't know wouldn't hurt you," he would say. "You will know soon enough. In the meantime, don't let anybody say that I risked my kid brother's neck." He was talking about Dad. He had made him some kind of promise about me. Everybody always made everybody promises about me.

He made me look out and make sure that nobody was in the alley, before he left. "Remember!" he said emphatically. "You never saw me! Not now, not ever! And you never saw who slipped that paper under the gate! For your own sake and your father's sake, more than mine!"

I nodded again, gratefully. I never knew his name.

January 29, 1967

I could not sleep a wink last night, and I spent most of the day in bed today, being still sick. Standing up makes me dizzy and nauseous. I am dying to sleep, but I can't. I can't eat, either. I have had nothing but a bowl of hot soup all day. The maid tells me that Dad has locked himself up again. Soon this house will be nothing but a few solitary prison cells, and we a bunch of isolated invalids who are spoon-fed by a kind old maid.

CHAPTER TWO

FARHANG'S DIARY
Tehran
February 23, 1967

At nine this morning a military Jeep stopped in front of our house and the maid rushed into Dad's room to let him know that two men wanted to see him. They would not give their cards or their names. Dad took a few minutes to respond, probably looking out of the window to examine the men and the kind of car they drove. He then told the maid to let them in. I watched through my window as two tall thin men in dark brown suits and sunglasses came up the steps and were led into the drawing room. It didn't seem like good news. They were obviously from the Savak. They looked like the men who had come around once or twice before, to talk to Dad about the sham funeral for Alex.

Was Dad in trouble now? Had they come to arrest him? Hadn't Uncle J. warned that the Alex affair might drag them all down? But why arrest Dad? He had done everything they had told him to do. He had said everything they had told him to say. He had put the ads in the evening papers announcing that his son had been killed in a car accident on the Chalus road. He had gone along with that sham funeral, burying an empty coffin with pomp and ceremony and with full press coverage. He had not breathed a word to anyone, including Mom. So why should they want to arrest him now? I felt furious and helpless.

Dad went to see them in his dressing gown. It was unusual for him to receive anyone, specially strangers, in his dressing gown. But it was unusual for strangers in a military Jeep to visit him unannounced at nine in the morning on a weekend. Especially now that he did not attend Court sessions and hardly went down to the Ministry of Justice. It couldn't be that they were here to make him resign his post as the Chief Justice. Dad no longer wanted it, anyway. He had tried to resign, and had been told by the Minister that it was His Imperial Majesty's wish that he should stay on. If he resigned now, the Minister had said, it would seem as if he were unhappy. His resignation might lend credibility to those false vicious rumors about his son, the rumors fueled by those fantastic stories published in illegal terrorist papers, and spread abroad by international Communist propaganda.

Now, the Minister had rambled on, even the BBC had got hold of those illegal scandal sheets, and the Ministry of Foreign Affairs had done their best to kill the stories through diplomatic channels. Not to mention anything about those jokers who call themselves Amnesty International or whatever, infiltrated by Communists and Socialists, who tried to stick their big nose into the internal affairs of any country, who would try anything to attack His Imperial Majesty's Government. We did not need any busybodies to meddle in our internal affairs, thank you. We had our own system of justice, which was one of the best in the world, and which was working fine. Can you imagine what a juicy story that would give them, the son of the Chief Justice, etc., etc.? They would do their damnedest to denigrate the whole country, try to make us look like a bunch of savages and barbarians.

Dad had nodded at everything the Minister had said. He had agreed to stay on, if he was not asked to conduct any more official business until his death, which he sincerely hoped and wished would not be too far away. Nonsense, the Minister had said. The Chief Justice had at least another twenty years to live. "And for what?" Dad had asked. And the Minister had become silent. If anybody now wanted him to resign, they wouldn't send those two apes. The Minister himself would come down. These were Savak lackeys. They had some more dirty work for Dad to do. He probably would have to put some new ads in the papers, to contradict the new rumors. Maybe they were here to warn him about giving any interviews to foreign journalists.

After Dad went in, I ran to the hall and listened behind the closed door. There were the usual loud greetings and then suddenly inaudible whispers, which I couldn't make out. Then I heard Dad's angry shout: "But he's only sixteen!" So, it was me they wanted, not Dad. They began whispering again. I ran to my room, suspecting that Dad would be coming to see me soon, and not wanting him to know that I had been eavesdropping. When I heard the drawing room door open, I got back in bed and reached for a book, pretending that I was reading.

Dad knocked gently and came in. He was trying to seem casual and undisturbed, first making small talk. He asked whether I had just woken up. Had I slept well? What was I reading? Then he became more serious and looked very disturbed. He asked a lot of questions. Had I talked about Alex to anyone? Had I said anything to Mom about the whole business? Had any strangers approached me asking about Alex? Had I heard of a group called Amnesty International? Had anybody talked to me about BBC? Was there anything about Alex or his friends that I knew, which I had not told him. Had I said anything to anyone about the man I saw putting the newspaper under the gate? Had I ever learned his name? Had I ever seen him again? With each question his voice became more anxious, his tone more urgent. After I had said no to all his questions, he threw up his hands in despair.

"Get up and put on your clothes!" he said. "There are two Savak monkeys out there, who want to take you in for questioning. They'll probably ask a lot of questions about Alex and his friends. They'll probably show you a lot of pictures, asking whether you know or have seen any of them. Tell them everything you know. Tell them everything they want to know. Do everything they tell you to do. They are killers, my boy! They are worse than killers! They are the lowest creatures on the face of this earth. I don't have to tell you. You know. You know what they did to Alex."

Tears were running down his face. I jumped out of bed and hugged him, crying myself, as he stroked my hair. "Promise me to do exactly as I told you," he said. I promised.

"Did you tell them anything about the man who put the newspaper under the gate?" I asked.

"No," he said. "Why?"

"If his picture is among those they show me," I asked, "is it all right if I say nothing?"

"Let's hope you have forgotten his face," he said. "These men have ways my son, of making people say what they don't want to. They have ways my son. They are the lowest creatures on the face of the earth. I met them when I was a young man. I experienced them when I was a young man. I wasn't always the Chief Justice, you know. But I didn't have Alex's courage, his stubbornness. I can't say I am not proud of him. But I do wish he had saved himself. For my sake, for your sake, if not for his own."

What was Dad telling me, I wondered. Had he been a Revolutionary as a young man, too? Had he also been jailed and tortured and broken down? Is that the price he had paid to one day become the Chief Justice, the way Uncle J. had made an about-face to become a cabinet minister?

"Remember what you promised me, my boy!" said Dad, as he let go of me! There was no sign of tears in his face. I made my promise again. "And now, wipe off your tears. Don't let those dogs know you are afraid! No heroics, mind you! I don't need another dead hero for a son. But don't let them know you are afraid." Dad stood there and watched me put on my suit. I asked him whether I should wear a tie. "No," he said. "You look fine. Just do what they say. Don't argue with them. If they insult or humiliate you, bear it patiently. These men have no shame. Remember that."

As the two men led me down the driveway toward the Jeep, Dad shouted at them: "Remember he is only sixteen, and he knows nothing!" I was surprised at the strength of his utterance. There was no sign of weakness or fear or grief in his voice. He sounded every bit the Chief Justice of the land. Was he bluffing them? Or was he threatening them, to let them know that he would not put up with it one more time, that they could not do to me what they had done to Alex?

"He'll be all right Mr. Chief Justice!" one of the men shouted over his shoulder. "Just a few questions, that will be all. I promise you!"

I sat in the back of the Jeep and we headed down the road for Tehran. After we had passed Mahmoodieh, the car stopped abruptly in the middle of nowhere. They took me out of the Jeep and led me to a black van that had apparently been following us all along. There were two more men in sunglasses in the van. I was made to sit between them. When they told me they were going to blindfold me, I began to be scared. I remembered Dad saying that these men were killers. But I also remembered him telling me not to show that I was afraid.

Now I couldn't see anything. I could smell the two men sitting next to me. They didn't smell good. I wondered whether they were the same men who had taken Alex in, except that Alex wouldn't have gone in like this so sheepishly. They probably had shot him first, before they could even capture him. They probably had to drag him into the van, in handcuffs and leg irons. I suddenly felt an intense hatred for those men.

I was squeezed tightly between them. No matter how small I made myself, I felt their thighs pressing against mine. It gave me a very uncomfortable feeling. One of them, the one on my left, laid his hand on my thigh once, just for a few seconds, and then removed it. I felt a sense of disgust. I was so relieved when he removed his hand. But then he did it again, and this time he let his hand stay there. I felt a shudder run down my spine. I remembered what Dad had said. "They are the lowest creatures on the face of the earth." I also remembered his saying that if they tried to insult or humiliate me, I should patiently bear it. Could this be what he meant?

I remembered the stories I had heard from Alex and his friends, about the terrible things that were done to the political prisoners. There were stories of impaling them on bottles and on blackjacks. There were stories of raping the women and the young men. There was even the story about a bear Savak kept, which was trained to rape the women. Were these the rapists? Were they going to rape me? Is this what Dad meant about bearing the humiliation? Had they raped Alex before torturing him? Had they impaled him? Is that why Dad was crying, not for what had happened to Alex, but for what he was afraid might happen to me? If I had a choice, I'd rather they tortured me than raped me. I could bear the torture. Didn't Dad say he was proud of Alex? But I couldn't bear being raped. I would be so ashamed. I hated those men with all my heart. Dad was right. They *were* the lowest creatures on the face of the earth.

The car turned into a driveway and then into what must have been an underground garage. I heard an automatic door open and close behind us. I was led down a flight of steps and then left standing there in my blindfold. Were they staring at me now? Were they sizing me up? Were they watching to see whether I was trembling? I would do just what Dad had said. I wouldn't try to be a hero, but I wouldn't let them see I was scared either. Though I was scared. I was plenty scared.

They finally took my blindfold off. I was in the middle of a very large dark room, more like a basement, without any windows. The first thing I saw was the glare of a powerful light on a desk in a corner, covering the face of a seated man, apparently smoking, whose feet were propped up on the desk. There were three other desks in the other corners, with three shadowy men standing next to them in the dark. The seated man, whose face was covered behind the light and whose feet were propped on the desk, seemed to be in an army uniform, but I couldn't be sure. "Sit down!" he shouted. He had a harsh mean guttural voice. Only then I noticed there was a chair right behind me. I sat down.

"What's your name?" he shouted again. I decided he was an army officer. He barked like one.

"Farhang Shadzad," I said. I was surprised how timid my voice sounded. I had intended to speak loud and clear, sound as Dad had sounded when he had shouted, "Remember he is only sixteen!" But my voice had come out small and scared, misjudging the length of the room.

"Can't hear you!" he shouted again.

I repeated my name louder, not sounding so timid this time.

"That's better," he shouted. "Do you know where you are?"

"No," I said.

"What?" he barked back.

"No, sir," I said. Was he trying to intimidate me? Well, he had done that. I had not intended to say *sir*, but I had done so.

"That's better," he said. "You mean your father didn't tell you where you were going?"

"He said I was going for questioning."

"Questioning by who, the City Sanitation Department?"

"I think he said the Savak."

"That's better. Questioning about what?"

"He didn't know. He thought it might have to do with my brother Alex."

"So you know about your brother Alex? What else did your father tell you?"

"He told me to do whatever you asked, to answer all your questions, to tell you the truth about anything I know."

"He is a wise man, your father. I can see His Imperial Majesty has picked a wise man for His Chief Justice." He said it with obvious sarcasm, looking around the room at the men standing in the shadows. "And are you gonna do what your father told you?

"Yes, sir!" I said.

"Good boy!" he said. "Do you always listen to your father?"

"Yes, sir!" I said.

"Good!" he said. "You are a good boy. I don't think we'll have any trouble with you."

"Gentlemen!" he said to the faces in the shadows, as he got up from behind the desk. "We have a good boy here. I don't think we'll have any trouble with him at all. He is going to tell us the truth and he is going to tell us everything he knows."

As he slowly walked toward me, I could see that he was an army lieutenant colonel. His uniform collar was open and he wore no tie. The three men in the dark corners also began walking toward me, at the same time, and at the same pace. They were not in uniform and they also wore no ties. I had the feeling that the room was closing in on me. The colonel had a prominent Prussian style mustache with the ends twisted upward like a handle bar, giving his mean face an even more sinister look. He was looking at me with an amused lascivious smile.

"Isn't he a nice boy?" he asked the other men, gently pinching my cheek. I felt a shudder. They nodded, smiling.

"Good-looking, too," one of them said. I looked at him. He had shiny greased hair and a sleazy smile on a mustachioed face. Four gold teeth at the center of his mouth, matched up and down, gave his smile a sinister look. As I was studying his face, his mouth opened even wider into a more hideous smile and he gave me a lecherous wink. I turned away from him impulsively, as if in disgust, and looked at the other two men. One of them had a butch crew cut, like an army sergeant, and a missing front tooth that looked like a dark hole in the middle of his smile. The third man was not smiling. He just looked plain mean. I remembered what Dad had said. "They are the lowest creatures on the face of the earth." Had he seen these faces, too? Were these the faces Alex had spent his last days with in intimate quarters? How lonely he must have felt.

I felt I was sharing something with Alex now. Knowing that Alex had been here, made me feel less lonely, less afraid. They couldn't possibly be as hard on me as they had been on Alex. I was only sixteen, I knew nothing, and I had done nothing. But would that be enough? Would they even believe me?

"So, you know about your brother Alex?" the colonel asked again, blowing some smoke in my face. He had his right foot on a chair that one of the men had quickly got for him. He obviously outranked them by far. They couldn't be more than corporals or sergeants. "What do you know about your brother Alex?"

"Not much," I said. "I know he is dead."

"How did he die, my boy?" he asked.

I felt a shudder run down my spine. I wished he wouldn't call me "my boy." That was what Dad called me, and I loved it when he called me that. I felt this man was dirtying those words for me forever.

"He died in a car accident," I said.

All four men laughed simultaneously, a long, mean, dirty laugh. The colonel's laugh lasted the longest, and died down slowly in a decrescendo fashion. They seemed to share such an intimate knowledge of Alex. Had he pinched Alex's cheek too? Had he called him "my boy," too? Suddenly I was no longer afraid. I was just very very sad. I felt like crying. But if I cried, if I showed any tears, they would take it as a sign of fear. These were not the kind of men who would understand tears of sadness or of love. That helped steel me up. I was equal to them now. I was equal to anything now. I could take anything they could dish out.

"Who told you that?" the colonel asked.

"My father," I said.

"Your father told you that, of course," he said. "The Chief Justice! That was very wise of him to tell you that." He turned toward the other three men. "Don't you think that was very wise of the Chief Justice, boys?" They giggled. I looked at their faces. Now they were all looking at me with sleazy smiles. The man with the gold teeth gave me that lecherous wink again. I felt such a disgust just looking at him.

"Did you see your brother's body, when he was buried?"

"No," I said.

"How come?" asked the colonel.

"There was no body," I said.

"How come?" he asked again.

"The body had been too smashed and burned in the accident to be recognizable," I said.

"And who told you that?" he asked again.

"My father," I said.

"Your father, of course," he said. "The Mr. Chief Justice."

Were they after Dad now, I wondered. Were they trying to pin something on him, to drag him out here? Were they trying to get me to say something that would give them the excuse? They would never succeed in that, I was sure. Unless they tricked me into saying something. I had to be even more on my guard now, for Dad's sake.

"That is true, my boy. He was very badly hurt. He had to have many operations. These gentlemen here are the doctors who operated on him. They are our specialists. Let me introduce them to you. This is Dr. Hosseini." He was pointing to the man with the gold teeth, who smiled and winked at me again. "This is Dr. Azodi." He pointed to the man with the missing tooth. "And this is Dr. Azizi."

So, these were the men who had tortured Alex to death. Alex had told me that the Savak torturers called themselves *doctors*. They told their victims that they were sick, and that they were being cured of their sickness by these methods. I was surprised that instead of anger, I now felt a sense of gratitude. I felt I had been given the privilege of sharing Alex's last days and last moments with him. As the colonel introduced the men, I felt like someone looking at the last mementos of a loved one; as if someone was saying, "This is the bed where he last slept. This is the window he last looked out of. This is the room where he last felt forlorn and doomed."

"Do you wish for these doctors to give you a report of their operations on your brother?" the colonel asked.

Strangely enough, I felt I did want to hear the details of what they had done to Alex, painful as it would undoubtedly be. I wanted to share Alex's pain and loneliness and fear during those last days and hours. I wanted to know whether the rumors were true, whether the story in that underground paper was true. I had to know.

"Yes," I said. "I would appreciate that." I was afraid they were only teasing me, that they would not go through with it, that they would be too ashamed, even though by now I had the feeling that they were trying to scare me, to psyche me out, so that by the time they asked their questions I would be too frightened to lie.

They all laughed.

"Well," said the colonel. "This *is* a nice innocent little boy. He would *appreciate* hearing about his brother. Well, boys, let's gratify him, let's give him a report."

Now I knew they would tell me all, not only to scare me, but because they were proud of what they had done. There was no danger of their feeling ashamed. Dad was right. These men had no shame.

"First he was very thirsty and hungry," the colonel continued. Apparently he enjoyed too much telling the story himself to share the pleasure with his assistants. Or maybe he was the only one of the group who could make sentences. Maybe the other ones only knew how to giggle and smile and wink and rape and torture. "He couldn't eat or drink. He hadn't been able to eat or drink for three days." So, it was true. They had starved him first.

"He was badly smashed, badly beaten up. We could not feed him through his mouth. His mouth was bent out of shape, his jaw was broken, his teeth were broken. So we had to tube-feed him. We could not feed him through the veins, because we couldn't find them. So we had to feed him through the rectum. Dr. Hosseini here is our resident proctologist. He was in charge of that. He would tube-feed him three or four times a day, through the rectum. He is a specialist in feeding through the rectum. He has the most expertise and the best equipment for that. Isn't that true boys?" They all laughed that same dirty laugh.

So, that was true too. They had raped him repeatedly, after they had broken his jaw and smashed his teeth. Poor Alex. I wasn't afraid for me any longer. I could take anything now. I looked at the man with the gold teeth. He smiled and winked at me again. I felt an urge to spit in his face, to spit right in his winking eye. But I held myself back. I didn't want to interrupt the story. I didn't want to give them an excuse not to continue. They had no idea how much they were gratifying me. They didn't know how precious knowing those details about Alex was to me, no matter how shameful their acts. I wanted to hear it all. As I was studying the man's face, he winked at me again. No doubt he would be glad to do as much for me, as soon as the colonel gave the go-ahead. How absurd of me to have thought that they couldn't do that to me, because I hadn't done anything. Neither had Alex. He had done nothing that would deserve those animals.

"Between the tube feedings," the colonel continued, "we had to bottle feed him." So, they had impaled him, too. The stories I had heard from Alex and his friends were all true. I had read in a newspaper about Ottomans having been the initiators of that method of torture, using it on Serbian prisoners. "We had to leave the bottle in place, so that the wound wouldn't close, until the next tube feeding. Dr. Azodi here is our specialist in bottle feeding." He pointed to the man with the missing tooth, who gave me a sick smile, like a schoolboy who has just been commended on his excellent penmanship.

"When that didn't cure him, we had to apply electroshock, to the testicles." I felt a shiver like an electric current run down my spine, and the muscles of my eyelids began to jump. I remembered my dream about the river crabs. "Dr. Azizi here is our board-certified, electroshock specialist."

"When that didn't cure the patient, we applied the cigarette therapy. You know that therapy? You don't. Well it is simple. Since we are short of ashtrays in this place, sometimes we use a patient's body to put out our cigarettes. It makes a lot of holes in him, but they are not too large and they are not too deep. They don't look pretty though, like a lot of nasty little pockmarks."

The colonel stopped and studied my face for effect. This was the first straight statement he had made that was not couched in dubious medical terminology, that could be understood even by an idiot. He wanted to make sure that I had been following his meanings through his admirable phraseology and figurative language. He wanted to make sure that he had not wasted his sick metaphors on me, that I was fully appreciative of his literary talents. Maybe he had expected me to scream with pain by now, begging him to stop. That might have been the clue to tell him that I was now *primed to tell the truth.*

"Do you follow me, boy?" he asked, now somewhat maliciously.

"Yes, sir!" I said. "I do."

"Do you want me to continue?" he asked.

"Yes, sir!" I said. "I do."

"You don't have a weak stomach, do you?" he asked.

"I don't think so, sir," I said, preparing myself for the worst, if the newspaper account was totally correct.

"You won't get sick on me, will you? We still have questions you have to answer."

"No, sir! I won't get sick on you."

"Well, we have a strong-stomached boy here," the colonel announced to the room. "He wants to hear it all! So, we will tell him all."

"We had to *amputate*," he vouched emphatically, addressing me again. I felt my stomach turn. So, it was all true. "His legs and arms weren't any good to him any more, you know. So we had to amputate them, to *cut them off*."

He studied my face for effect again. I must have looked awfully pale, since I was beginning to feel sick. But I thought I could control myself. I had felt sick on the airplane once, flying to Abadan to visit Uncle J., and had been able to control myself during the two-hour flight. There was a young girl seated across the aisle, watching me with a sadistic smile, waiting for me to throw up any minute, eager to see me shame myself. She seemed so proud of herself for not being airsick. Just to spite her I wouldn't, I had thought to myself, just to disappoint her. I was too ashamed to be sick, when she wasn't. I was thirteen then. Maybe I would be as lucky this time.

"You're sure you won't get sick on me?" the colonel asked again. I only nodded, avoiding his eyes, not being sure at all now.

"We had to amputate his arms and legs, *one at a time,*" he walked to the right and left in front of me, trying to keep eye contact, nodding to the beat of his own words. "These doctors had to take turns operating. It was too much work for any one of them. Now you must understand, we are not well equipped here. We are out in the middle of nowhere. We do not, for example, have anesthesia. So we have to operate without it." I was getting sicker.

"We do not have all the latest surgical equipments," he went on. "So, we have to use a bucksaw to operate. It hurts a little, of course. The patient screams a little. So, we have to stuff his mouth to keep him from screaming too loud. These doctors have very sensitive ears. They would lose their hearing, if we didn't stop the noise pollution."

I had closed my eyes and had clamped both my hands on my mouth. I was fighting very hard, but it was no use. I began vomiting into my closed mouth and swallowing it back.

"Well, our boy is sick after all," I heard the colonel say, with relief. "His stomach isn't as strong as he thought it was. Somebody had better give him a bucket. We don't want him to throw up all over the floor and then have to clean it up. It isn't a nice job for a nice rich boy like him. The Chief Justice's son."

I heard a bucket being dragged on the floor and felt a hand on my shoulder. I opened my eyes, so that I wouldn't miss the bucket, and let go of myself. I kept throwing up and retching, and retching and throwing up, for a long time, until I began tasting the bitter taste of pure gall in my mouth.

"Do you feel better, my boy?" asked the colonel kindly, as he bent over and looked into my eyes, his hand still on my shoulder. I nodded, no longer avoiding his eyes. "I warned you, my boy," he said. "But you were stubborn. You wanted to hear it all. I have had more experience with these things than you. I know nice boys like you get sick hearing them."

So, I was not the first sixteen-year-old they had had down there. Nor was I the only one given the privilege of hearing Alex's case, or similar cases. The colonel was so proud of himself, the way you heard him talk, that he must have recounted this "textbook case" of his to many of his visitors. That is probably how the story had got out, to the underground papers, to the BBC, to the Amnesty Whatever. At first, when he began telling me freely of their exploits, I thought I would never get out of there alive. But then I wondered whether he did not really want to spread the word, to scare people out of their wits, before they even got there. That would make his job easier with his other "patients." Maybe he would even get more "referrals."

Or maybe he was disappointed in Alex, for being one of their "treatment failures," for making them go to the bitter end without spilling his guts, without naming names, without revealing secrets. Maybe that's why they wanted me now, to give them the satisfaction Alex had denied them, to finish his unfinished business for them, even though I knew no secrets. Alex had tried to protect me against this day, suspecting that it would come, and knowing that it would take more than will power and loyalty and courage to get through it in one piece. Well, the colonel had won this one with me, by making me throw up. But he probably had not succeeded in making Alex do that. If he had, he would have got him to spill his guts, too, telling them whatever it was they wanted to know. Alex must have proven stronger than all the colonel's "specialists." I was so proud of him. Even Dad admitted, despite himself, that he was proud of him.

"Are you now ready to answer questions, my boy?" the colonel asked.

"Yes, sir!" I nodded.

The feeling I had for him and his men at that moment was incomprehensible to me. It was something beyond hatred. It was something beyond anything human I had ever experienced or could think of. It was a sadness beyond despair, that no amount of anger could express. Now I knew what Dad had felt all these weeks and months. Now I knew why he had wanted to die. I felt I wanted to die, too. And I felt that the men around me were irrelevant to what I felt at that moment.

"Do you want to wash your face, my boy?" the colonel asked. I looked at him and nodded.

Now there seemed to be some genuine compassion in his face. Was it conceivable that this man, at this moment, really felt some sympathy for me, that he had not told me all those gory details because he enjoyed tormenting a sixteen-year-old-boy, but because he would rather nauseate than torture me into telling what I knew? Had he got so used to his profession that he could no longer feel the pain of his victims? Or did he conceivably believe that he was inflicting those horrible punishments on his victims for the greater good of the society, the way the Holy Inquisition burned heretics to save their souls? Should I be grateful that he had not personally raped and tortured Alex, even though he could have? Was it possible that he too had a sixteen-year-old son, whom he called "my boy?"

They led me to a sink in a dark corner and let me wash my face. I even gargled to get the bitter taste out of my mouth. At the moment, it hit me as absurd that I should be gargling, as if I was getting ready for breakfast. I recalled having read somewhere about a man on his way to the gas chamber, who had asked to brush his teeth. That had hit me as absurd, too. But somehow I felt I could face these men better, if I had no bitter taste in my mouth.

They took me to the colonel's desk for questioning. They turned on some more lights. The colonel asked me whether I wanted some Coca Cola. I said yes. I drank a gulp and felt better. What did it matter that I was accepting a drink from such men at such a time? He asked what I knew about Alex's activities. I told him I knew nothing, that Alex had kept me in the dark about what he did, to protect me, and because he had promised my Dad and Mom to keep me out of politics. He said if anything ever happened to him, I would be jailed and tortured, and thought it was better that I knew nothing of what he did. What was it I thought Alex and his friends did, the colonel asked? Something illegal, I said. Like printing illegal newspapers, or writing slogans on the walls. I had seen him burn newspapers. He wouldn't let me read them.

For how long had I known they were attacking gendarmerie stations? I had no idea they were doing that, I said, if that's what they were doing. Where did they keep their firearms? I had no idea, I said. I had no idea they had any. Had I not seen Alex with any firearms, pistols, shotguns, rifles? No, I said. Where did he keep his arms? I had no idea he had any, I said. Who were his friends? I didn't know, I said. He had stopped seeing his old school friends, and his new friends we didn't know. We didn't even know who he went mountain climbing with, except for when their pictures were in the papers. When there was anyone with him, he wouldn't let me follow him to the car, or made sure I wouldn't see their faces, or know their names. Didn't I think that was strange, the colonel asked? I suspected they were doing something they shouldn't be, I said. Why didn't I tell my Dad about it? I didn't want him to get angry at Alex, I said. And then he was gone, anyway. We hadn't seen him for six weeks. I suspected he would never come back. What kind of messages I passed on for him during those six weeks? None, I said. What kind of messages I received from him and his comrades? Some short calls, I said. Either from him or from strangers, only telling me that he was all right.

How much did my Dad or uncle know about Alex's activities? I said Alex wouldn't trust either one of them with his secrets. So, I thought. They were trying to pin something on Dad and Uncle J. Had my Dad or uncle ever tried to persuade Alex to stop, he asked? Many times, I said. But Alex wouldn't listen. And he denied he was doing anything. So, they both gave up on him. How often and how long was Alex gone from home? Quite often, and as long as a week at a time, I said, after he quit college. Didn't my Dad wonder where he was gone? Mountain climbing, we all thought, I said. He was a well-known mountain climber. His picture had been in all the papers. My Dad had got used to not seeing him around the house. So he didn't think much of it. How much money did he get from my Dad or uncle, he asked? He got fifty tomans a week allowance from my Dad, I said. Nothing from my uncle. He had even stopped taking the gold Pahlavi my uncle gave all of us kids on the New Year's Day. Why? he asked. He said he didn't want to be beholden to him, I said.

Again he asked which one of Alex's friends I knew. His tone was much more menacing now. He warned that if I lied, he would spot it immediately, because they had had our house under surveillance for months, and he knew everyone who had been visiting us. Was that why they had not sent for me earlier, watching our house, hoping that some of Alex's friends would come by to contact me? Luckily, none of them had, except for the man who brought the newspaper. Was that why even Uncle J. had stopped visiting? He must have known about the surveillance. The colonel was obviously bluffing about everyone who had been visiting us.

I told them about a man who had slipped a newspaper under the garden gate. They showed me the newspaper. Was that it? I nodded. What did the man look like? I said I had hardly seen his face. It was evening. It was dark. He wore a cap that was pulled down over his nose. A scarf covered half of his face. I happened to see the paper sliding in under the gate. I ran and opened the gate and surprised him as he stood up. I only got a glimpse of his face in the dark. He said, "There's something in this paper you and your father should see. It's about Alex. You've never seen me, if anybody asks. Not even your father. You just found that paper there." He told me to burn it as soon as I had read it, and then he left.

It was true, what I told them. If they had got the man, there was no point in keeping this a secret. If they hadn't, this wouldn't give them any clue. What I didn't tell them was that I had seen the face well enough, that I would recognize it anywhere.

The colonel asked whether I showed the paper to my Dad. Yes, I said. But only the part about Alex and the picture. I had already burned the rest. Did I think that was Alex's picture, he asked? I couldn't tell, I said. With the face gone, it could be anybody's picture. Did my Dad believe that was Alex's picture? He couldn't tell any more than I could, I said. What did my Dad do with the paper? He gave it back to me, I said. Where did I send it then? Nowhere, I said. I burned it. The man had said that I would be killed, if I was caught with it.

He asked about the man again, making me repeat everything. Now I noticed they had been tape-recording me. Again he asked what the man looked like. I told him again I had not seen his face well. It was dark. How could it be dark, he asked, when there was a light right over the garden gate? I told him that Alex had broken the light bulb long ago, to keep the gate dark. Dad had replaced it once, Alex had broken it again, and it had remained that way. That was true, too. I noticed the colonel looking at one of the men, the one with the mean serious look, the one he had introduced as "Dr. Azizi, the electroshock specialist." The man nodded slightly. Did that mean they knew about the broken light bulb? They wouldn't go after Dad for not having replaced the bulb, would they, I wondered.

"Did the man have a mustache," the colonel asked.

I found it safe to admit that he did. That wouldn't give away anything, either. Almost all of Alex's friends had a mustache. Alex used to joke that you could tell a revolutionary by his mustache and a Savak agent by his sunglasses.

Would I recognize the man's picture? I didn't think so, I said, but I could try. I thought that was clever of me to volunteer, having already been told by Dad that they would be showing me pictures to identify. And I was curious to see what pictures they would show me. I didn't know for sure which ones of Alex's friends were his comrades.

They brought me several big boards with many pictures on them. I went through them carefully. I saw some faces I had seen in Alex's underground papers, with captions stating that they had been killed under torture. I picked those faces and said that they looked familiar. That was also a safe thing to say. Had I seen them face to face? I didn't think so, I said. They just looked familiar. Could I have seen them in papers, they asked? It was possible, I said. I thought I was being awfully clever. What papers, they asked? I said I had discovered some newspapers in Alex's room, after he disappeared. They seemed to be illegal papers. What had I done with them, they asked? I had burned them. Why? Because I didn't want my Dad to find them and get upset. He has high blood pressure and his doctor has said he shouldn't get upset. He had warned Alex many times that he shouldn't bring those papers home.

Then I saw the picture of the man who had brought the paper. I didn't let on. I quickly glanced at it and moved on. Azizi was watching my eyes as I went over the pictures. I didn't think they would catch me, and they didn't. I wondered why his picture was there. Had they already caught him? Or were they looking for him? Were all those people dead, were they being tortured right now in some other dungeon, or were they out there somewhere hiding or fighting? Alex's picture wasn't there.

"You seem like an honest boy to me," the colonel finally said. "It doesn't sound like you are lying. You don't look like a traitor, like your brother was. Can you imagine how much your family owes this country and His Imperial Majesty? Imagine, the son of the Chief Justice turning traitor. And His Majesty has allowed your father to keep his job, instead of letting us drag him down here and kick his ass."

It hurt me to hear him talk that way about my Dad. A lieutenant colonel, and that kind of a lieutenant colonel, and my Dad being the Chief Justice and all. I had seen with what awe and respect people in the Ministry of Justice talked to and of my Dad. I had seen how the Minister himself deferred to him. But I had also seen how helpless he looked all these weeks. It was all a joke, that Chief Justice business, when it came to dealing with the Savak. Even Mom had seen through that, naive as she was in these matters. I thought it was pointless for me to try to explain to the colonel that my father had tried to resign from the post, and that it had been His Majesty's wish that he should stay on, in order to quell the rumors about Alex, rumors that by now had reached even the BBC and the Amnesty Whatever.

"And your Uncle," the colonel added, "the arch-traitor and Communist, the former Provincial Secretary of the Tudeh Party. His Majesty should have let us drag him in here and cut his balls off. If we had done that, maybe your traitor brother would have thought twice before starting his own 'Revolutionary Army.' But His Imperial Majesty is very kind. Instead of having your Uncle hanged, he makes him the Chairman of the Planning Organization, with the rank of cabinet minister, and this is the gratitude he gets back from your family. Remember that. And remember your brother. Let his case be a lesson to you, in case you get smart ideas."

I was quiet. There was nothing I had to say in reply, or wished to say. It was useless. The man's mind was made up. He seemed quite ominous now. But I was no longer afraid, at least not for myself. I was somewhat worried about Dad. I remembered what Uncle J. had said that night: "You're still the Chief Justice. What if you ever decided to talk?" Did that mean that they might make Dad disappear, too? Maybe arrange a real car accident for him? Was that why he did not leave the house any more? Was that why he was so unwilling to go to the hospital for tests, why he did not want to see anyone but his own family doctor, whom he had known for many years, since his school days? I wasn't too worried about Uncle J. I remembered Dad saying that Uncle J. was a survivor, and that in time, he would bury them all.

"You have a lot to be grateful for," the colonel said, shaking a finger at me. "And a lot to make up for. And your father and your uncle, too. Believe me they are not as safe as they think they are. One false move, and I will personally drag them down here to answer for it. I guarantee you that. And you know how I make people answer. This time, even His Majesty won't stop it. Two traitors in one family are quite enough. Do you want anything to happen to your father and uncle?"

"No," I said.

"Good! Do you want anything to happen to you? Do you think you have the stomach to take what your brother took?"

"No," I said.

"Good! At least you are honest with yourself. Will you cooperate with us?"

"How?" I asked.

"By helping us round up the rest of these traitors in your brother's gang. You will report to us if you see any of these faces. You will report to us anybody who contacts you. And if I suspected that you were even thinking of lying, you would be down here for the real treatment. And the Mr. Chief Justice would be down here for the real treatment. And who knows, maybe even Mr. Chairman and Cabinet Minister would be down here for the real treatment. They should have stopped your traitor brother or reported him to us a long time ago and they failed to do so. They failed His Imperial Majesty and His Majesty will not forget that. They are traitors."

The colonel let me know that he was finished with me for the time being only. He gave me a telephone number I should contact, if I saw or was contacted by any traitors. They made me go over some of the pictures again, of those who they thought might contact me, or that I might run into. The picture of the man who had brought the paper was among them. I felt glad they had not caught him yet, at least. He had risked his neck bringing me that paper and I would have felt awful if they had caught him because of that. At last I was told I could go home. They blindfolded me again and took me to the van. I felt so exhausted I could go to sleep on my feet. In the van, from the smell of the two men next to me, and the way they pressed their legs against mine and kept their hands on my thighs, I could tell I was accompanied by the same men. Unless they all smelled bad and they were all pederasts. But now, after all I had seen and heard in that basement, I couldn't even care that they touched my legs. I just wanted to go to sleep. And I did fall asleep in the van.

I woke up when they took off my blindfold. We were in front of our house. The men holding my arms and leading me out of the van were different ones. So, they all wore sunglasses and smelled bad and were pederasts. I ran up the driveway and all the way up to the top of the steps, straight into my Dad's waiting arms. He must have been watching the gate from his window all day long. I saw tears running down his face and I too began to cry.

"Did they hurt you, my boy? Did they physically hurt you?" he asked.

"No," I said. "Not physically. But you were right. They are the lowest creatures on the face of this earth. They told me all the horrible things they had done to Alex, all that was in that paper, and much worse. They were so proud of themselves. You should have seen them."

"I have seen them, my boy."

"They said they would do all that to me too, if I didn't cooperate with them."

"Then you must not give them the excuse, my boy. I can't afford to lose you, too. You're all I have left now. You're all your mother has left now. I am grateful that Alex kept his promise to me and spared you. I am glad you know nothing to tell them."

"But they want me to report to them any of Alex's friends that came to talk to me," I said.

"Has any of Alex's friends come to talk to you in the past three months?" he asked with amusement.

"No," I said.

"You think they will be foolish enough to do it now, even if they weren't all caught? Alex didn't talk, but that doesn't mean no one else did, either. They are testing you, my boy. And they are trying to scare me, to keep me silent, after what they did to Alex. They are worried that I might talk to foreign reporters or leak something to them, to confirm the stories about Alex. They are reminding me how much more I can still lose, if I talked."

"Yes," I said. "The colonel said they would drag you down there and do those horrible things to you too, if you made one false move."

"The colonel would like to do that, wouldn't he? But the colonel is just the dog. He will have to wait until his master has sicced him, not before. And his master will not do that yet. To keep me in this position will serve their purpose for a while, for as long as they fear world opinion. In good time, they'll probably arrange something for me, too. A real car accident, maybe. Even though that might not look too convincing. The Chief Justice and his son both dying in separate car accidents!"

"He called you a traitor," I said.

"He is right, my boy!" said Dad, with a sigh. "But not for the reasons he thinks. Not to the cause he thinks. I made a false move forty years ago. I should have chosen to die then, as Alex did. But I made the choice that kept me alive and in the long run made me the Chief Justice of the land. And the ultimate irony is that this should happen to Alex, when I am the Chief Justice. Alex somehow knew this, too. Although he didn't plan it that way, he somehow knew that his death would make me take a close look at myself. He wanted to open my eyes, and he did. I have been living in self-deception for thirty years. His Majesty doesn't need a Chief Justice. The only Justice in His Majesty's land is the Justice of the Jungle, handed out by those beasts you saw. I deserved what I got. I closed my eyes when it was happening to other people's sons. I thought it would never happen to me. But you don't have to worry about me. The only way they can hurt me now is through hurting you. And you have to make sure you won't give them the excuse. You have to promise me that."

"I promise," I said. "I won't let them hurt you through me, ever."

"That's my boy!" he said. "Then you'll have to do anything they tell you, until I find a way of getting you out of the country, if I can. Send you to America, maybe. I never thought much of Cyrus. But maybe this one time he won't disappoint me."

"They are after Uncle J., too," I said. "They are watching for him to make a false move, too. Do you think we should warn him?"

"They have been doing that for a long time my boy," Dad said. "They would have got him, if they could have. Your Uncle J. lives a charmed life. They will never get him. He is already beyond their grasp. He is already too big for their net. They are just barking at him. You don't have to warn your Uncle J. How long is it since you have seen him come around?"

"A long time," I said.

"Smart boy! Don't worry about your Uncle J. You just do whatever they tell you. Anybody who comes up to you for the next three months, talking about Alex or revolution, or tries to recruit you for a cause, is their agent. Report him with a clear conscience. But we'll talk about all that later," he said. "You must not have eaten all day. You must be starved."

"Yes," I said. "What time is it?"

"Five," he said. "You have been gone all day. I was afraid I had lost you too. I am glad at least they didn't physically hurt you."

Then Dad told the maid to serve the lunch. He hadn't eaten all day either, waiting for me.

CHAPTER THREE

Waterloo, Iowa
Friday, January 13, 1984
9 p.m.

I began this diary on a bleak day, seventeen years ago. I last wrote in it on another bleak day, fourteen years ago. And I take it up now on this bleak day, not having looked at it for years. It has been seventeen years to the day, and reading it now, it all seems like yesterday. And not only because I have been away.

That Mom should die now, on this anniversary day, in her sixty-fifth year of life, on Alex's fortieth birthday, is understandable. She must have set herself this goal on that day: to endure until she was sixty-five, until Alex was forty, to wait seventeen more years, and no more. Wait for what? For Alex, of course, to come back, to reappear: *I am Lazarus, come back from the dead, to tell you.* Now she would have to look for him in the other place, *death's other kingdom.* That she should die on Alex's birthday, was always predictable, as it had not been in the case of the man, the man in her life, the only man in her life, Alex's father.

By fourteen years she survived him too, by fourteen years to the day, that meek mouse-sized woman. *Fourteen years ago you divorced me and took my sons away from me. Now I want my sons. Now I want my Alex.* She who had never confronted him, never questioned him, never demanded anything, from him or from anyone, now demanding a son, from him. *Madame! This is as much as you will ever see of your son!* As if he had to break her, to keep himself from breaking. I watched her, waited for her to be struck dead with those words. In my concern for her, I did not even feel the ache in my own heart. When she survived that, I knew she would survive anything this side of hell. By fourteen years to the day she survived that.

He couldn't think of her. Not then, not ever. For him she had never really existed, as if he could not understand that we were her sons too. And yet, who would have thought he would croak first? Big and strong and cruel as he was. Standing there with his back to the picture window, holding that brass-buckled belt and that black Russian hat high in the air: *Madame! This is as much as you will ever see of your son!*

By now she probably did not remember that he too had died on the anniversary of Alex's birthday. Under other circumstances, Dad's death would have been the most significant event of her life. She might have chosen to die on that day, just because he had died on that day. She had waited for reconciliation for fourteen years, even though Dad had married and divorced twice more in that time. With each new divorce she had waited for him to go back to her. And when that did not happen she still waited. Then the Alex business came about, and only then she stopped caring about Dad. She considered it somehow his fault. He had taken her children away from her, to take better care of them, and he hadn't done that. Cyrus was away, had been away for nine years, not ever coming back. Who knows what he was doing? Who knows whether something terrible might not happen to him too? And now Alex was gone. And I was only a kid of sixteen. Who knows what could happen to me, now that even Alex wasn't there to look after me?

By then, of course, I don't think she was really thinking of me either. True, I had been her baby. I had been her favorite. She always commented on how more and more I looked like Dad. People said she was partial to me, because I looked like Dad. As if she could love him all over again in me. But after that happened to Alex, I don't think she cared for Dad any longer. She probably hated him by now. And if I reminded her of him, then so much the worse for me. Now Alex was her baby. Sometimes I would catch her caressing his framed picture on the mantelpiece and mumbling "My baby! My baby!"

So Alex became the new center of her life. She forgot about the other man. Now he could live or die, and she couldn't care less. He was responsible for what had happened to Alex. He was responsible for what had happened to her. He was responsible for what had happened to everybody. He was the Chief Justice. He was responsible for justice. And under him no one had received justice. So, when he died, on Alex's twenty-sixth birthday, Mom's mind registered the event as an incidental one. For her on that day Dad was an "also ran," an extra in the action. His death became a footnote to history, soon to be forgotten. The day had been Alex's birthday. There was no way it could now become Alex's birthday and the anniversary of Dad's death. It remained even that way for me. And even now that she herself had chosen to die on this day, she had seen to it that her own death be forgotten, that the day remain inviolably Alex's birthday.

On that day, she also forgot about Cyrus, if she had not done so sooner. Now Cyrus's letters would remain unopened for days. There was nothing in them to interest her. It didn't matter now that Notre Dame had retired his uniform number. And she forgot about me, too. It is true that I was indispensable to her during those initial years. But I was indispensable in the sense of being her attendant in the rituals relating to Alex's cult, of which she was the Priestess. I was there as an altar boy, to run the errands, to light the candles, to blow them out. I was significant to the point that I reminded her of Alex, to the degree that we had Alex to share. I had been Alex's baby brother. I had been her baby once. But now I was more Alex's baby brother. She had made Alex promise to take care of me, to keep me out of trouble. And now that he was gone, who would do that? We celebrated Alex's birthday together. We celebrated Alex together. Only the two of us could share him, each knowing what he had meant to the other.

I watched her put the candles on Alex's birthday cake, the numbers growing year by year, twenty-four, twenty-five, twenty-six, until I was no longer there to see them grow on a dead man's cake, dead but not buried. I watched her put them on patiently, then ask me to light them, then sit down and stare at them in silence for a long time, stare at the flickering flames, as if she saw Alex flickering there, dancing upon the cake like a genie out of *The Arabian Nights.* Watching her staring at whatever it was she saw there, each year I wondered whether that would not be her last vigil. And when she finally asked me to blow them out, the way she would have asked Alex, but now with no trace of joy in her voice, I would hesitate. I was afraid that with that same act I would blow out the flame of her life, or rather the last spark in the cinders that were left of her life.

Each time, after I had blown the candles out, I would look at her face, searching for some sign of life, something in her dead stare at the dead candles to tell me that she was still there; alive. But there was no such sign. She sat there and stared at the candles with the same frozen face that had stared at that brown brass-buckled belt and that black Russian hat: *Madame! This is as much as you will ever see of your son!* Until she would finally reach for my hand, caressing it, pulling my head down into her lap with her other hand, gently running her fingers through my hair. And only then I would know that there had been a reprieve, that she had been spared one more year, that she had endured one more year, that she would wait one more year, until the next birthday when, who knew, Alex might burst into the house with his loud exuberant laughter, lift her tiny body into the air, and waltz around the room with it.

When the midnight bell rang, she would ask me to go to bed and take a nap. We had to get up early the next morning, for the long day. I would go up to my room, lying down in bed, seeing her in my mind's eye sitting up all night, staring at that cold cake. Once or twice I would tiptoe down, pretending to want to drink some water, to peep at her through the half open door just to make sure. She never looked up.

She was with Alex then, somewhere, in some ethereal world, in some eternal meeting place, she believing in Heaven, and not knowing what I knew.

Early at dawn, after her morning prayers, she would come up to ask what I wanted for breakfast before we set out, knowing full well that neither of us would have any. Then we would leave, with me carrying the cake box, and she hanging on my left arm. We would stop at the flower shop to pick up the wreath she had ordered. Then she would let go of my arm, to pick up the wreath, and we would be on our way. Shopkeepers would stop their work to look at our little funeral procession. Customers would stop picking at tomatoes and cucumbers to watch us march down to the bus stop, for the long ride to the graveyard at Shah Abdol Azim Shrine, she carrying the wreath with so much care, as if it were a baby sleeping in her arms.

At Alex's grave, while she knelt down in silent prayer, counting the prayers on her rosary and blowing them over the grave, tears rolling noiselessly down her gaunt pale cheeks, I would count the beggars gathering around, trying to avoid looking at Alex's sham tombstone, that dumb cowardly tombstone! At what it said, or rather did not say, telling myself it did not matter. It wasn't Alex's tombstone anyway. It wasn't Alex's grave. He wasn't there. He was somewhere down in the kingdom of the fish, doing his dead man's float.

When her prayers were over, she would ask how many beggars there were. While I cut the cake, she would take the money out of her purse, Alex's birthday money, all in new one-toman bills, which she had taken from the bank the week before and laid between the pages of the family *Koran* until this morning. She would take the pieces of the cake, putting each on a napkin and covering it with a bill, and take them around to the barefoot beggars, one to each, man, woman, and child alike, serving them with the humility of a scullery maid serving a gathering of princes.

If there were more beggars than there were bills, the children, starting with the youngest, would get only a piece of cake each and no money. If there were more bills than beggars, she would pick out a couple of women with babies in their arms and slyly pass the extra bills to them, trying to keep it a secret from the others, to avoid a riot. We were not allowed to return anything home.

We would have the long bus ride back home, without a word. She would not hear of my going away until she had stuffed me with some food. There was always the whole roast turkey or goose or chicken, which she had made the day before, just as she had done every year on our birthdays, first when Cyrus and Alex and I were all there to celebrate, and later when only Alex and I were left.

Usually by around three o'clock, I would become a free man at last, ready to celebrate Alex's birthday by myself, my Alex not hers. My celebration and my vigil always came a day too late, one day after I had watched hers, celebrating it not with cake, not with *funeral baked meat*, but with wholesome booze, hitting every bar in Tehran, alone, until I was drunk on my ass. Chasing Alex's ghost from bar to bar and from street to street, until all the drunks had safely made it home, all the streetwalkers had shut off their meters for the night, and the street cleaners had started sweeping the streets before the next sunrise.

Even these fourteen years that I have been away, I have still followed the same routine, keeping vigil with her on Alex's birthday across some ten thousand miles, in my mind's eye, following her around the house, watching her light and blow out those candles by herself, as scared as I was then that with the putting out of the candles her life's flame might also be put out; waiting every minute for the Western Union man to arrive with the news of her death; while at the same time continuing with her vigil, watching her at her morning prayers, watching her lug the cake box and the wreath on the bus, all by herself, counting the beggars, all by herself, cutting the cake, all by herself, and taking that long bus ride back home, all alone.

And each year when the Western Union man did not come, I knew that there had been another reprieve. One more year to go. Until now, the sixty-fifth year of her life, the fortieth anniversary of Alex's birth, the fourteenth anniversary of Dad's death, as if people should all die on round numbers or on anniversaries. Unless she had set this as her goal on that very day, that she should endure sixty five years and no more, that she should give Alex until his fortieth birthday to come back and no more.

....

I am desperately trying to impose some kind of order on my mind. Everything there has been scrambled into a well composed abstract painting: Uncle J.'s telegram, Clare's letter, Cyrus's phone calls, Alex's birthday, and *The Disturbing Muses* on the wall. And the bourbon isn't helping any to keep them separate. I have to find a way of taking all the pieces of the puzzle apart, dealing with them one by one, and then putting them all back together. It has suddenly become very cold. Out the window I can see a blizzard in the making. I take it for an omen. The elements are still with me. I have a feeling that before this night is out, I will be rushing out into the storm like mad old Lear.

I pick up Uncle J.'s telegram and read it again. It seems the easiest piece to deal with: *Your mother died Friday point Funeral Saturday point All will be taken care of point Uncle Jalal.* It is so self-contained. Mom is dead and that is that, and neither the Devil nor mighty little Jesus can change that. Whatever surprise that news might have once had for me, has been dissipated through such a long anticipation. I probably could not make it for the funeral, even if I tried. I would not be needed for it. Uncle J.'s message is clear. *All will be taken care of point.* I then read the copy of my own telegram. *Postpone funeral until I arrive or you hear from me otherwise point Farhang.* I don't know whether I will go, but until I do, the dead will have to wait. The dead will have to wait until the living have made up their minds, until they have put their own house in order.

CHAPTER FOUR

Waterloo, Iowa
Friday January 13, 1984,
10 p.m.

That Mom should die on Alex's birthday was inevitable. That she should die on this particular birthday was logical. That Clare should choose this night to do what she is doing, even though she has as yet no knowledge of its new significance for me, is ironic. And yet the two events fit so perfectly in my mind. Each makes the other at once easier and harder to bear. Each at once adds to and subtracts from the reality of the other. I cannot quite determine the exact purpose and meaning of the letter. She not only has to let me know what she does, and who she does it with, but also where she does it, and when.

I pick up the letter and read it again, more to distract myself than to discover any new meaning in it. *I have to learn to stand on my own feet. I have always leaned on someone. First there was my Dad, then Jamie, then Johnny, then you. That's why I've got to do it. Don't you see? I've got to free myself. From everyone. Even from you. Especially from you. And I no longer care whom I hurt. At least not yet.* Right on! First there was Dad. Then Jamie. Then Johnny. And then came Apollo the Tiger. The deputy sher'ff, Sheepshit County, Ioway. An outdoor type with bow and arrow. A local Apollo with a blonde goatee.

Don't you see why I have to do it? Deep down I am still that little girl from that little Midwest town with a hell of a lot of hang-ups. I've got to get over my hang-ups. I've got to do it. O.K. O.K. But why with him? Why with a worthless bastard like him? *Exactly because he is a worthless bastard. Would you rather I did it with a bastard like you, whom I might fall in love with? And don't tell me you never slept with a worthless bitch. Or should I say with dozens of them?* Right on! She sure knows how to hurt a man. A woman gotta do what a woman gotta do! It is her destiny. She too will dance herself to a standstill.

I should have imagined she was free enough. The way she positively would not get out of the car, if I opened the door for her. *I can open my own goddamn car door, thank you! Opening the door is just another excuse to patronize us women. You men pretend to put us women on a pedestal, so that you can treat us like whores. Lady is just a euphemism for slave.* Right on!

The way she marched into that country courtroom. *If it is cause they want, I'll give 'em cause. They want adultery? They'll get adultery!* How magnificent she looked, facing all that Harper Valley PTA crowd. *Yes, Your Honor!* she said. *I have committed adultery.* Not *sotto voce,* but blaring it out without shame. *If that's what Johnny wants, that's what Johnny will get. If he can stand being called a pimp, I can stand being called a whore. It is his hometown too, you know!* Oh, what a magnificent bitch she looked! Anna Karenina would have been proud of her. Hedda Gabler would have been proud of her. Uncle Nathaniel would have been proud of her. *And if you love me as much as you say you do, you'll stand next to me in that courtroom, when I call myself a whore.* And I stood there in that courtroom with a hangdog face, though not next to her, looking and feeling every bit like a goddamn reverend Arthur Dimmesdale, worried that any minute they might drag me to the dock to let them all see what a gook fornicator looked like, not even knowing whether that was a deportable offense or not. Now she has got the wanderlust. Another woman ruined by Isabel Archer. Join the Army and see the world.

I bring her picture album and start looking at the pictures. Clare at five, looking like a Shirley Temple. Clare at seven, walking in her Dad's boots, with a towel wrapped around her head, playing the gypsy. Clare at nine, sitting on the gigantic shoulders of her grandfather, who voted for the prohibition and on the way back home bought a case at the local friendly bootlegger's. Clare at fourteen, the town tomboy, fishing and hunting with her Dad, climbing trees with that delicate waist and those shapely hips, raising a calf for the Four H, singing in the church choir on Sundays. How lovely she looked and how loving and trusting. How did she grow to so mistrust and hate men?

Clare at fifteen, the freemartin. Thought she could never have children, after having watched a movie about a young girl who thought she could never have children. Now she doesn't want children. Thinks it is unfair that women should be yoked with the burden of childbearing. Thinks they should all adopt children instead, which makes logic irrelevant.

Clare at nineteen with long blonde hair, looking like an angel. *Love her! Love her!* Kneel to her. Kneel to her and pop the overwhelming question, make it a deliberate study of your life to love, cherish, and adore her. Oh, how easy it would have been to love, cherish, and adore her! If it wasn't for my ghosts. Is it my fate to always fall for such loveliness and innocence? And yet what happened to her dreams of love and freedom and joy? Dragged into filth in a country courtroom in front of a country judge.

I go back to the letter. It would be superfluous to say that she wants to make me jealous. It would be silly to suggest that she wants me to step in and stop her. What she is doing is probably larger than all that. She is probably trying to make me face the unreality of my life, to come down to earth and start feeling what other people feel. She is trying to show me that she also is capable of shrouding the simple daily affairs of men and women in universal philosophical trappings, that when we come right down to it, all the talk about existential lucidity does not stand up to the simple human feelings of love and jealousy and betrayal. I have no right to be bitter. When I had my chance, if I did not encourage her, I certainly did not try to stop her. I would have been a hypocrite if I had. And I would be a hypocrite, if I tried to stop her now.

But is that what she wants? For her sake as well as mine? Is she giving me another chance to stop her? To show that I love her, not in large universal terms, not in ideal trappings, but the way a simple man loves a simple woman. To show that I care, the way ordinary human beings care. Is she testing me again, to show me that despite all my highfalutin discourses on ideal love, I am nothing but another simple jealous lover, who would not come to his senses until he is about to lose his love object? Isn't that what happened with Beth? Isn't that what happened with Shay? Isn't that what is happening with Clare? Am I not just another simple jealous lover?

And if I am, what am I supposed to do? Get my .22 and go down there, making a fool of myself with the deputy sherr'f, the way Jamie did with me? Or am I supposed to call her, pleading, using my poor mother's death as an excuse? Would she not hate me later when she finds out that I had the perfect excuse to call and stop her and I did not? Would she not hate me later, knowing that I endured this night as I am doing, not calling for help? Wouldn't that prove that I am what she says I am, what my analyst says I am, a narcissist, unwilling to share even my sorrows with the world?

I scan the letter again. "If you have to reach me for any reason this weekend, we will be in Room 216, Holiday Inn." I like that *we* there. Not "I will be" but "we will be." That's so subtle. "I'm sure you can get the telephone number from the information, should you need to talk to me." And why should I need to talk to her? What would I want to tell her so urgently that could not wait until Monday morning? Unless it were, Please, Clare! My mother is dead. And Sam will probably go through with it tonight. I need you now. I am an orphan. So young and so orphan. So, don't do it, Clare! For the love of God don't do it!

For the sake of my poor poor dead mother, dead but not buried! For the sake of poor orphan me!

And what if I tried and could not stop her? Wouldn't that be a blow? If she just said, "I can't talk now. I'm in the middle of something. I'll see you Monday." What would that signify? That an erect penis has no conscience? Nor an aroused vagina? I am being disgusting again, of course.

"I will be thinking of you. You know you're still the one I love." I like that *still*, too. It is so tentative, so precariously balanced in the middle of the sentence, so vulnerably. As if to say, I still love you now, but by Monday morning, who knows? Anything can happen tonight. And what if by tomorrow she loves him? He may be an ignoramus deputy sheriff. But what if he has got a schlong as big as a horse and knows how to make a woman swoon? But for the time being at least, I am the one she loves. I am still number one. Number A 1. You hear that, Sher'ff? You hillbilly Apollo? Eat your heart out, bugger! I'm still number one. You gotta try harder, much harder. You gotta bust your ass tonight, while I take it real easy.

Here's looking at you, kid!

....

I have concluded that Clare's letter is an ironic sentimental gesture, asking for nothing more than an ironic sentimental gesture on my part. To show that I also am capable of such a gesture, I have written out a little scenario, which will be acted out tomorrow at Room 2l6, Holiday Inn. The action will begin at ten a.m., which in my experience is a short break between the first and the second morning delight, while the loving couple are still abed. At this time there is a knock on the door and a delivery boy delivers a dozen red roses to the bed of fornication, along with a card and a letter. The card is a birthday card for the lady's new birth, inside which is written the lesson of the Master: *Go woman and sin some more!* The letter contains excerpts from Miss Clarissa Harlowe on the topic of virginity and ruined maidenhood, such as:

> Thou pernicious caterpillar, that
> preyest upon the fair leaf of virgin
> fame, and poisonest those leaves which
> thou canst devour!
>
> Thou fell blight, thou eastern
> blast, thou overspreading mildew, that

destroyest the early promise of the
shining year! that mockest the laborious
toil, and blastest the joyful hopes of
the painful husbandman!

Thou fretting moth, that corruptest
the fairest garment!

Thou eating canker-worm, that preyest
upon the opening bud, and turnest the
damask rose into livid yellowness!

If, as religion teaches us, God
will judge us, in a great measure, by
our benevolent or evil actions to one
another----O wretch! Harlowe you are and
harlowe you shall be, to our shame!

and a little poem, as follows:

It was not jealousy, my love!
It was grief; that you should
Be a common feast and I
The only townsman not invited.
I would not have minded the others:
Your bounty could have feasted us all.

Here's looking at you, kid!

....

I pick up Uncle J.'s telegram and Clare's letter and tack them on the wall on both sides of *The Disturbing Muses,* to remind me of my Scylla and my Charybdis. Now there is nothing left on my desk other than my diary, the bottle of bourbon, and the two glasses for Alex and me. I put on a record and listen to Jimmy Buffet singing:

My head hurts, my feet stink,
And I don't love Jesus.
It's that kind o' day.
Really, it has been that kind o' night.

I fill the two glasses for Alex and myself and sit down and gaze at *The Disturbing Muses* on the wall, trying to focus my thoughts. I know I will not be able to come to a decision about anything, until I have properly celebrated Alex's birthday. And by then I would be too drunk to be able to come to any decision whatsoever.

Happy birthday, kid! Here's looking at you.

PART TWO

CHAPTER FIVE

Waterloo, Iowa
Friday January 13, 1984
11:40 p.m.

Cyrus just called, for the third time today. He asked by what right I kept postponing a dead woman's burial. I said by the right of being the only suffering bastard in the dead woman's family. If you measure a man's suffering by his drinking, he said, you sure must suffer a hell of a lot.

He wanted to know whether I really intended to attend the funeral. I said I wouldn't know until sunrise Monday morning. Why the hell would you wanna go to the funeral, he asked? Haven't we had enough funerals in this goddamn family, with or without the stiff? You wanna risk your goddamn neck to watch them put a stiff in the ground? Besides, you'll never make it for the funeral. They have to bury the stiff before it begins to smell, you know. It's not the funeral I'm thinking of, I said. Then what the hell are you thinking of, he asked? What the hell do you wanna go back to? Two full graves and an empty one, I said. Besides, I am going to collect my inheritance: a brown brass-buckled belt and a black Russian hat.

Maybe I would like to look into her eyes before they put her in the ground. Maybe I'll find something there, something I must have lost, something I must have left behind. The only one of my significant dead I'll ever see actually buried. Alex refused to be buried. And Dad wouldn't let me stick around until he died. He wanted me out of that hellhole before he was pronounced dead. He was afraid they wouldn't let me go afterwards. The only satisfaction he would take to the grave was seeing me leave, out of the one eye that could still see.

To America my boy! Now! Before I die! Promise me that! The last words I heard out of his mouth, out of half of his mouth, the half that moved, while the other half, the paralyzed half, the speechless half, mocked me and mocked the world. The mad intense stare in his left eye goaded me on to God knows what, while his right eye sneered at the ceiling. *To America my boy!* Done father! Rest in peace! The promise and the price the dead extract from us.

I tell you what you'll find there, said Cyrus. A bullet with your name written on it. It's a zoo there now. They shoot people for crossing the street, for breathing. Don't tell me not to worry. You're all I've got left in this world, kid! You're my goddamn kid brother. I'm the only thing *you*'ve got left in this world. I've got to look after you. *Put money in thy purse. I say, put but money in thy purse.* I knew I was being unfair to him again. Maybe I'm just jealous of his success. Maybe I can't stand people who earn a living, instead of living off the dead.

The problem with Cyrus is that he left home too early, before the shit hit the fan. He saw nothing. He heard nothing. He knew nothing. He felt nothing. And when he finally knew what had happened, it was so long after the fact that it no longer mattered. No longer mattered to him, at least. He was never the type to brood over things. He is the type that forgets easily. When all those things were happening, he was writing us about getting into the football team at Notre Dame. Sending Mom those padded pictures of his, which Mom put on the mantelpiece. *My son Cyrus, from America. He is on the football team.* And she would say it to strangers, with that impassive look, not knowing what it meant. Her whole mind was on Alex now. She had no room for anybody else.

And when he became the team's Quarterback, he sent a telegram. Two telegrams. One to Dad, and one to Mom. My son, the quarterback, she would say, not having the faintest idea what a quarterback was. He got Americanized too fast. First with football, then the business school, then the money racket. He got into that racket too soon, too. And to think that Dad had wanted him to study law. Constitutional law. To become, not a lawyer, but a *jurist*. Dad had done that, studied constitutional law. At the Sorbonne. Which is why he wanted Cyrus to do the same. The son of the Chief Justice carrying on the family tradition. Dad wouldn't have him in the law racket back there. But maybe Cyrus could be luckier. He could end up in an international forum. The President Judge of the World Court at Hague, maybe. Dad didn't know when to give up.

It was all a joke now, anyway. I sent my son to America to become a jurist, he would moan, and he has become a salesman. See what America has done to my boy. But that was not true. America hadn't done that to Cyrus. Cyrus was born like that. He was a born salesman. I never remembered him giving Alex or me anything. He swapped. He bartered. He loaned. We could never touch anything of his. He would raise hell if Alex or I even wore his sandals around the house. He would raise hell if we used his toothpaste. It was his. He had paid for it with his own money. Even though I was just a little kid, and he was my big brother. If he had stayed back there, he would have ended up in the Bazaar. Dad never understood why Cyrus did not turn out the way he had planned it for him. And with Alex he didn't even try. Alex was in a world of his own.

That's why he had to plan it all over again for me. He had to plan another America. A different one. *To America my boy!* He didn't know that America is a state of mind. You bring to America what you are. Did Cyrus have an America? Yes, the one he has got now. *Put money in thy purse. I say, put but money in thy purse.* And Alex? What America do you have out there in the water, my boy? *Only the total sincerity, the precise definition.*

....

He called again, two hours later. For the fourth time. He wanted to know why it was taking me so long. I told him I was celebrating Alex's birthday. Sure, kid, he said, sure! Get drunk on your ass again. Like you have done all these seventeen years, on or off Alex's birthday. Don't kid yourself! You aren't gonna solve your problems that way. You can't hide from the reality forever. It will find you out. There is a world out there. And the sooner you come out to face it the easier it is gonna be for you.

Uncle Sigmund right out of the horse's mouth. Translate it into his jargon and it means come out to New York and sell life insurance. He can set me up there. *Plenty of dough in it, kid. I know you always thought money stinks. But one of these days you'll have to earn your living like the rest of us chickens and you'll stop acting so high and mighty towards people who have always had to work. You can't hide in school forever. You can't hide behind the dead forever.* Maybe not. But I can try.

He could never forgive Dad for leaving everything he had in a trust fund for my education. He felt cheated. Dad felt cheated too, because Cyrus never became a jurist. To Dad business was not an education. It was something you learned in the Bazaar. To stick it to the other guy, before he could stick it to you. To buy cheap and sell dear. The only line of Shakespeare he ever knew, or cared to quote. Cyrus didn't have to go to America, to waste all that time and money, to learn business. He could have done it right here in the Shoemakers' Bazaar. And as for football? He considered it a primitive activity at best. He would tear up Cyrus's football pictures as soon as they fell out of the envelope.

Sending his son to America for that? Football and business? He had no idea of America.

Cyrus didn't think that was fair. All his life he had tried to please Dad. He had done his best. Any other father would have been proud of him. At least he didn't go get himself killed, like Alex did. And for nothing. And he didn't turn out useless like me. He felt cheated out of his inheritance, no matter how meager. He should have got half of whatever was there, Alex being dead. Alex being dead, couldn't of course care one way or another. But Cyrus didn't need the money. Bullshit he didn't need the money, Cyrus would say. He could always use money. He was always short of ready cash to invest. He had two teenage kids to raise and send to Wharton. And Dad leaving everything to me.

It confirmed what he had always known. I was always Mom and Dad's pet. They even preferred Alex to him, his being the firstborn notwithstanding. And Alex and I always stood together against him, conspired against him. And to think of it, it was really he, Cyrus, who had to raise us, after Mom left. He practically had to toilet train me, spoon-feed me, help me swallow my own spit.

Yes, he could set me up in the insurance racket. Or maybe I preferred the real estate racket. I could become a land developer, maybe. Live off the fat of the land. Or go into the stock market and become an investor. Live on *unearned* income. A true aristocrat. For the seventh time chosen a member of the President's Millionaires' Club. That's Metropolitan Life's President, not the other one. Now shooting for the President's Billionaires' Club. With that silly picture of his in their magazine: *OUR MAN FROM . . .* A gook who has done well for himself in America!

Why waste your life on that literature crap? There's nothing in it. There never was. Come here where the ball game is. He *would* call it that. To me the whole world is a stage, and to him a ball game. No thanks, Coach. I would stick to my Wilhelm Shagespeheare and Geoffrey Chaucer of Monmouth. Will be an expert in all the seventeen cants (cunts?) of Christendom, and in Ovid's *Amatory Arse.* Will waste my life in search of Aristotle's Golden Mediocrity and Emerson's Perfect Hole. Never mind I almost flunked German 101 and Chaucer because I thought *eine gute Fahrt* meant *a good fart* and *Goddes' privitee* meant *God's privates.* He sold two million dollars worth of life insurance last year, and got ten percent of that.

Why waste time on that drama crap? This is where the money is, kid! Life insurance. And today money talks. It always did. He has learned their jargon well. It isn't for nothing he is their prize salesman. Yes, Dad sent him here too soon. He missed something back there. It would have been quite an education for him. Although he never had a mind for the abstract.

Suppose you got a Ph.D., kid. What is that worth? You would have to kiss a lot of asses to land a twenty thousand-a-year job. How much do you think I made last year? How does two hundred thou grab you? And I'll give you another tip. Inside dope. In five year's time, every university in this land will be bankrupt. Broke. Finished. Every blasted one of them. Even the ones with big endowments. Even the ones with money-making football teams. Think o' that!

I *have* thought of that. *Put money in thy purse. I say, put but money in thy purse.* All his trophies. The salesman of the day, of the month, of the year, of the century. A nation of salesmen. Is this what Dad had in mind for me? Was this his America? You bet there is a world out there, but what the hell does Cyrus know about it? We live in two different worlds.

Where the hell was he when Alex disappeared? Where the hell was he when I stood on that goddamn grave and watched them bury an empty coffin and put that fake stone on top of it? He was sending us telegrams, telling us that Notre Dame had retired his football number. Where the hell was he when Dad busted his heart and his brain? Where the hell was he all those years, when I watched those goddamn candles grow on Alex's birthday cake, lighted them, blew them out, each time expecting to see Mom's life go out with them? Where was he when I lugged that cake all the way to the graveyard, counted beggars, fed them cake, watched Mom kneel and cry over an empty grave, and then marched her back home to *funeral baked meats*?

I tell you where. He was selling life insurance, to anybody who didn't need it or couldn't afford it. He was bribing the janitor at the UN to let him pose for that phony picture, to put in that phony magazine, to send to Mom and Dad to impress them. Just six weeks before Dad busted his pump. As if Mom and Dad were in a condition to care for that kind of crap. But God knows I am trying not to hold it against him. I keep telling myself he couldn't have known what was going on, he being the only realist in our family, the only pragmatist, the only salesman, the only ten-percenter, if we leave Uncle J. out of it.

He wanted to know how long the dead could wait while I was making up my mind. They could wait, I said. Oh, yes, they could wait. They've got nowhere to go. I have waited for the dead long enough. They can wait for me for a change. I'll have an answer for him by sunrise Monday morning. I'll have an answer for him, all right. I'll have an answer for all of them. For the time being, I am still celebrating my brother's birthday.

Here's looking at you, kid.

....

Cyrus called again. For the fifth time. He is trying the high-pressure sales technique on me. He is going to flood out all my defenses, before I am too drunk to hear. Booze has that effect on me. Makes me go deaf. As I was talking to him, it occurred to me how little we knew each other. He was my oldest brother, by now my only brother. I was his "kid brother," by now his only brother. And yet how little we knew each other. How little we had seen of each other. How little we had shared over the span of years.

Cyrus left home when I was only seven. I remember when he left, when we all went to Mehrabad airport to see him off. Dad and Mom and Alex and me. Dad and Mom were polite and distant to each other. It seemed like a very somber occasion. Cyrus laughed a great deal to lighten things up. "For God's sake," he exclaimed. "This is not a funeral. It is supposed to be a happy occasion. I'm going to America to study, not to be buried." When it was time to board, Dad reached out to shake hands with him. But Cyrus pushed his hand away and hugged and kissed him several times. That was Dad's style. In public, he always reached out to shake hands with us. Francophile that he was, he was self-conscious that European men, even fathers and sons, did not hug and kiss. But when we did hug and kiss him, despite his mild protests, he was pleased.

Mom kept Cyrus in her arms for a long time, silently crying. "Who knows whether I'll ever see you again," she whimpered.

"For God's sake, Mom!" exclaimed Cyrus. "I'll come to visit. America is only a day's journey away by jet. We are not in the Middle Ages, you know. People don't travel by horse and buggy any more, you know."

"Who knows what God has in store for us from day to day, son?" Mom whimpered again. "I might die tomorrow."

"Don't start on that again, Mom!" said Cyrus.

Mom hugged him again and held him, until Dad politely touched her on the shoulder and reminded her that Cyrus was getting late. Then she let go. Mom's instinct had been right. She never saw him again. He never came back. Once or twice he wrote Dad for a ticket to come home and visit. But Dad wrote back and told him to stay put until his studies were finished. Home could wait. Dad thought of the expenses, of course. He wasn't a very rich man. No honest judge was, even if he was the Chief Justice. Cyrus's education in America cost every penny he had. All he had to his name was the house, which he was willing to mortgage, or even sell, if needed, until Cyrus's education was finished.

But Cyrus's education was never finished. As far as Dad was concerned, it never even began. Cyrus never made it to the law school. Maybe he never even tried. When he changed his major from pre-law to business, he didn't even bother to tell Dad. But as he kept sending those pictures of his in football uniform and helmet, Dad suspected that Cyrus was not studying law or pre-law or anything like it. "A law student," he grumbled, "wouldn't have time for such foolishness, even if he was brighter than Cyrus is."

Dad had never considered Cyrus specially bright. No one had, including Cyrus himself. He was big and muscular and handsome and easygoing. He could climb trees better than a cat. Sometimes just watching him on a small branch on top of the walnut tree in our garden made me dizzy. He could kick a ball so high that it would almost disappear in the clouds. And that was before he became a football player, in America, and a quarterback for the Notre Dame.

As a child, I remember how I bragged about my big brother Cyrus, about how he could kick a ball and climb a tree. I took his helmeted pictures to school and showed them off to the kids. As they fought each other to see the pictures, I basked in the sun of my big brother's glory. He was, not only studying in America, which was distinction enough, but also the quarterback for the Notre Dame football team. They couldn't get over the shape of the ball. I would explain to them about American football, mouthing off what Cyrus had written me. What we called football, they called Soccer. This is what they called football, this egg-shaped ball. It is something like rugby, I would say. Even though none of us had ever seen rugby played, either. They would look at Cyrus's picture with fascination. Wow, they would say! Isn't that awesome!

When he wrote Dad, saying that he was graduating from the business school with a B.B.A., Dad was highly disappointed, but not surprised. It seemed as if he had always known that Cyrus would disappoint him. Then he got a job, selling life insurance in New York, and Dad felt that his obligations to Cyrus were over. He considered his education finished, aborted was more like what he thought. Now he could concentrate on worrying about Alex's education, and mine.

When Cyrus sent home that picture, asking permission to get married, more like announcing that he was getting married, Dad's reaction was one of disinterested befuddlement. He no longer seemed to care what Cyrus did. As soon as he unfolded Cyrus's letter, a picture fell out. It was a colored Polaroid picture of a girl in her mid-twenties in a house dress. Cyrus was good with Polaroids. He had always been handy with cameras. Alex used to tease about Cyrus having some Japanese blood in him, some dominant picture-taking genes. The girl in the picture was standing next to an avocado-colored refrigerator in a kitchen, her right hand grabbing her waist, her left arm raised and leaning against the refrigerator. She was about five two, had plump rosy cheeks, and a healthy peasant look. She smiled at the camera with sweet self-confidence. On the back of it Cyrus had written, "My future wife," not even naming her, probably to keep Dad's interest going.

After reading the letter, all you could say about her was that her name was Patsy. He had met her at a cocktail lounge in New York, where she was waitressing on her summer vacation from college. She had a B.A. in home economics and had been a cheerleader at Rutgers. In fact, she had also attended Notre Dame at one time, for one semester only. She was from Trenton, New Jersey, even though her family had originally come from a little Pennsylvania town called Intercourse. They used to have a Mom-and-Pop store there. Now they had a gas station in Trenton. She was four years older than Cyrus. The minute they had met, they had known that they had the right chemistry for each other. They had so much in common. And now Cyrus was asking Dad's permission to marry her. They would like to do it on Valentine's Day, which was only two months away, if that was all right with Dad. Patsy had this thing about Valentine's Day. She was very sentimental about it. Their first date had been on a Valentine's Day, you know.

As Dad read the letter, he seemed to be in a daze. He kept mumbling certain words to himself, as if he had difficulty understanding them. Words such as *cocktail waitress, cheerleader, Trenton, Intercourse, chemistry, permission to marry, Valentine's Day.* After he had finished, he stopped for a moment, staring into the space with a blank look. Then he reached over to me with the letter. Read this, he said absent-mindedly. See if it makes any sense to you. It doesn't to me. There must be a joke there somewhere, which I fail to appreciate. As he said that I remembered how Cyrus used to laugh and what Dad used to say about it.

Cyrus didn't really laugh. He let out a peal of laughter in a crescendo fashion. And he laughed before and after anything he said. And as he laughed, he got red in the face, as if he was embarrassed. His laughter had nothing to do with anything being funny. Even as a child, I could tell that. At first, I always wondered why Cyrus laughed any time he spoke. But after a while I understood. That was just Cyrus. But Dad never did. He always thought there was something unnatural or disrespectful about Cyrus's laugh. "I fail to appreciate the joke!" he would say to him. "Is there any?" And when Cyrus assured him that there was no joke, he would say, "Then why the laugh?" Once in a while Cyrus would lose his cool and shout, "For God's sake. Can't I even laugh in this house, without having to explain why?"

And now, when Dad asked me to read Cyrus's letter and see whether there was a joke in it somewhere, I almost heard Cyrus's laughter, as if he had tried to say in person all that he had said in the letter, laughing that crescendo laugh with each word. He wouldn't have been able to finish the story. Probably he wouldn't have been able to speak any of it. What nobody seemed to realize was that, despite his easygoing ways, his bravado, his loud cursing, and that crescendo laughter, Cyrus was basically a very shy person. He was genuinely in awe of Dad, the Chief Justice. He was afraid of the weight of every word Dad uttered, as if everything he ever said was a judicial pronouncement.

Of course, Cyrus had written all about Patsy to me separately, telling me to keep it under my hat. And there *was* a joke somewhere in his letter to me. He had told me that his future wife was a "witch." Honest-to-goodness, he wasn't kidding. This wasn't fairy tale stuff, he wrote. There were people in America today, who considered themselves witches, descended from a long line of witches going back to those who were hanged in Salem a couple of hundred years ago. Patsy's mother, he wrote, was a card-carrying witch. And she raised both her daughters, Patsy and Elma, as witches. They used to have blood sacrifices as kids. Their mother would cut the head of a squirrel, or a rabbit, or a pigeon, pour the blood in a bowl, and burn candles around it all night long.

Patsy and Elma had to follow their mother and the bowl of blood around the room for almost an hour, repeating her gibberish words. They kept the whole thing a secret from their Dad, who is not a witch. They did this only when he was away for the night. Of course, looking at Patsy, the way she stood there smiling sweetly and leaning against that refrigerator in her house dress, you wouldn't guess that she was a witch. She looked like any cute normal housewife. But Cyrus said that sometimes even he felt she was a witch. She was a mighty powerful woman, who could make anybody do anything.

She said she had bewitched him on their first date, to marry her. And she had succeeded, hadn't she? She had told him not to worry about Dad not giving his permission. She would bewitch him, so that he would have no choice. Just between us, he said, he had had his first sexual experience with Patsy. And that sure was a mighty powerful stuff. Patsy wasn't a virgin when they met. She was *experienced.* But Cyrus was glad to have been broken in by an experienced woman. Imagine the both of them not knowing what the hell they were supposed to do. Of course, he trusted I would keep this confidence, and not breathe a word of it to Mom or Dad, especially to Mom. I shouldn't mention it even to Alex, although knowing how close I was to Alex, he suspected I would tell him anyway. But if I did tell Alex, I had to make him swear that he wouldn't breathe a word of it to Mom or Dad.

So, as Dad looked so befuddled reading the letter, and especially when he reached over with it and said something about a joke, I was afraid that Cyrus had spilled the beans in that letter, too. But as I read it, I realized that he hadn't, that to Dad the whole thing was a joke. A bad joke. Maybe to Dad Cyrus himself had been a bad joke. After Cyrus, I think he learned not to expect too much from any of his children.

He wrote back to Cyrus and gave him permission to marry "his future wife," the way you tell a passenger on the bus, Yes, he may sit down next to you, knowing that you are just returning a meaningless courtesy. He assumed she was already pregnant. Otherwise, why such a hurry? After that he hardly ever mentioned Cyrus by name. Now he was always "that boy." And he never even tried to learn Patsy's name. She remained forever "that woman." And poor Cyrus, worrying about Dad learning that Patsy hadn't been a virgin. As if Dad could care less what Patsy was.

Cyrus kept trying to win Dad's good opinion of himself. He kept trying to impress him with his achievements in salesmanship, sending us Xerox copies of his accomplishments. The one about his membership in the President's Millionaires' Club caught Dad's attention for a few seconds. He thought that referred to the President of the United States. For an instant, I thought maybe he could forgive him after all. But as soon as he realized that it was the President of the Metropolitan Life Insurance he meant, and that all Cyrus had done was sell a million dollars worth of Life Insurance, his contempt for him seemed to increase. Gimmicks, he mumbled. Only an idiot like that boy would fall for that kind of gimmick.

After that he would only scan Cyrus's letters. Words had lost their meanings there: The Seven Million Dollar Club. The Fifty Million Dollar Club. The Billion Dollar Club. When he wrote that he was now an Insurance Underwriter, that he had actually become a millionaire, his assets amounting to slightly over a million, I don't think Dad even realized what he read, let alone be impressed by it. When he sent the Metropolitan Magazine, where they had featured him as the Salesman of the Year in Manhattan, along with a Policeman, a Fireman, and a plumber, Dad flipped the pages the way he did the advertisement pages in a magazine. First I thought he had missed Cyrus's life-size picture. Then I realized he hadn't. When he saw his picture in the empty UN auditorium, behind the flag and the name plate of Iran's Permanent Representative to the United Nations, his face was distorted by visible pain.

"He could have easily been that, if that was the limit of his ambition, if I had had my way," he mumbled. "He would have sat in that seat, instead of taking a fake picture there to impress idiots like himself. Any idiot could have his picture taken like that for fifty cents."

When he wrote that his first son Jonathan was born, six pounds and three ounces, Dad took three weeks to write back a two-line letter of congratulation. That is all he ever did for Jonathan. When he wrote that his second son, David, was born, Dad did not even write back to congratulate. That, of course, was after the Alex business. By then Dad probably thought it highly inappropriate that anybody should still be fathering children. Patsy, of course, never counted. Her witchcraft apparently did not work with Dad. She never wrote to the family and the family never wrote to her. Only Mom would mention her in her letters to Cyrus. Mom's letters always ended with, "Say hello to Patsy," and rarely with, "Give my love to Patsy."

After Dad's death, when he left everything he had in a trust fund for my "education," Cyrus felt doubly betrayed. He felt Dad was being vengeful, even after his death. All his life he had tried to please him, and for what? He was a great success. Everybody knew that but Dad. Everybody acknowledged that but Dad. He had been in the newspapers. He had been on the television. He was the only Insurance Underwriter who was a member of the Rotary Club in Hoboken, New Jersey. He was a respectable member of the Republican Party of the State of New York. He had been asked to organize all the Iranian Americans in the United States into the Republican Party, with himself as their leader. Think what a power base that could give him. He had Senators and Congressmen for clients. He had had his picture taken with the Governor of the New York State. He had once been a speaker on a platform in Washington, where earlier in the day the President of the United States had inaugurated the National Convention of Life Insurance Underwriters.

You would think that his own father, the Big Man, the Chief Justice, would once, only once, acknowledge any of his son's accomplishments before he died. No, not him. Everything had to be his way. If Cyrus hadn't become a lawyer, a *jurist*, that meant he was no good. And even now, after his death, what did he get from him? Nothing. A kick in the teeth. Not that he needed the money. He was a millionaire, thank you! Dad's whole estate didn't add up to fifty thousand bucks. It was just the symbolism of it. Just to have acknowledged that he existed. Even if he had left him only his dirty underwears, an old sheepskin coat, a pair of worn-out socks. Nothing. He never even acknowledged that he had two grandsons. And what did his other two boys do for him? Alex got himself killed, for nothing, for some pinko revolutionary bullshit, so that he could send the old man to an early grave, in disgrace with King and Country. And Farhang turned out a no-hitter, a boozing bum, a scared little kid hiding his head in a hole, a dime-a-dozen actor, a *permanent student.*

Even Mom hadn't given him his due. She had hardly acknowledged Patsy as her daughter-in-law and seemed barely aware of the existence of Jonathan and David. They were always "the boys." "Say hello to the boys!" "Give the boys a kiss!" Maybe she never even learned their names. And after Alex died, they stopped even hearing from Mom. For her the whole world died with Alex, although she was not even supposed to know for sure that he was dead. Cyrus had never received justice from anybody in the whole family, with the exception of Uncle J. He was the only person who seemed to understand and appreciate Cyrus's accomplishments, the boy from Sang-e-laj, who had done well in America!

And now he was calling to know why I wanted to go back for a stupid funeral, not knowing whether I could get out again, not knowing whether I would be jailed, tortured, shot, or sent to the front to fight a stupid war, and maybe get myself blown up that way. "You wanna kill yourself?" He was screaming on the phone. "Well, do it right here! Save the plane fare. And we'll have the best funeral in the world for you. You know, America is famous for funerals. Dogs get better funerals here than people do in other countries. We will put you in a gilded mahogany box and have a two-hundred piece band play over you. It would still be cheaper than the plane ticket. Now I would understand it if we were talking about going back to a civilized country. Hell, I would go back myself. She was my mother too, you know. But we are not talking about a civilized country no more. I don't know what has got into those people, but they are eating each other alive. They use each other for target practice.

"I bet you I wouldn't even recognize the streets. And neither would you. You have been away fourteen years, don't forget. And that was before the mullahs took over. They have done more damage to the country in four years than all the Shahs did in four thousand years. Now if Uncle J. hadn't arranged for the funeral and everything, like we know he has, if the stiff was sitting on the ground with dogs chewing her ears off, I could still understand why you would have to go back and take care of things. But the way things are, you will only mess everything up, interfere with all the arrangements Uncle J.'s boys have made. Don't forget, I was his oldest son. I still am. And I have a say in how things are going to be done."

"But not about whether I go to the funeral or not," I said. "All I have asked is for them to hold off three days. I don't care about any other arrangements."

"And what is it you want to do in three days?"

"Make up my mind."

"About what?"

"About everything."

"Look, kid!" he shouted again. "You haven't made up your mind about *anything* in thirty-three years. What makes you think you'll make it up about *everything* in three days? And how the hell are you gonna make up your mind by getting drunk on your ass, as I know you're doing at this very minute? I can smell the booze on the telephone. Using Alex's birthday as an excuse, as if you needed an excuse to get drunk."

"You would be surprised," I said, without defiance or mockery, "how much booze can help you concentrate sometimes. Try it! Booze and black coffee."

"Don't give me that shit!" he said.

"What difference does it make to you, anyway?" I asked, genuinely curious.

"What difference does it make to me, anyway?" he shouted with disbelief. "God damn it! You are my kid brother! You are my only brother! You are the only family I have left in this fucking world. You are the only uncle my kids have."

Suddenly what he said hit me as strange. In the fourteen years I had been in America, I had seen Cyrus twice, once by myself and once with Uncle J. and Aunt Sarah. I had seen his wife and kids once, when I visited their home and stayed overnight. He had never visited me. I still remember all the details of the night I stayed over. I had driven up to New York on a whim, with a friend from college who was going to a wedding, with the excuse of helping him drive. I called them from a public telephone. Jonathan picked up the phone. I gave my name, which he did not recognize. Then I gave my rank and serial number. "I am your Uncle," I said. "Your Uncle Farhang." He passed the phone to someone, saying, "There's this weird guy, says he is my Uncle Somebody." I heard Patsy's voice. I gave my name to Patsy again.

"This is Farhang," I said.

"Yes?" she said, clearly indicating that more information was needed.

"Farhang," I repeated. "Cyrus's brother."

"Yes?" she said again, still waiting for the punch line. I realized that the problem was not with recognizing my name, or who I was, but with perceiving the purpose of my call. Was somebody dead? Was somebody mentioned in a will? Did somebody want to borrow money? Did somebody want to buy a life insurance?

"I'm in New York," I said. "I thought of giving you a call."

"Well, that was nice of you," she said, still waiting for some crucial information which apparently I was failing to produce.

At this time I heard Cyrus's voice across the room, asking impatiently who it was. "It's for you," she said calmly, passing the telephone to Cyrus.

"Farhang?" shouted Cyrus with disbelief, blurting out his crescendo laughter. He was genuinely pleased. "I can't believe it. It's Farhang, my kid brother Farhang!" he announced to the family, with another peal of crescendo laughter. Then it occurred to him that his family should have recognized this sooner, should have given it more weight and significance.

"That's your Uncle Farhang, Jonathan, you Dodo," he shouted at his son, a shout interrupted by a peal of crescendo laughter. "What the hell do you mean by saying, 'There's this weird guy, says he is your Uncle Somebody?' Didn't you hear him say he was your Uncle Farhang?"

"He said he was my Uncle Something," Jonathan defended himself. "I didn't know who the hell that was."

"Jesus Christ!" shouted Cyrus again. "He is your Uncle Farhang, my kid brother, the only uncle you've got in this world."

"Oh!" said Jonathan with disinterested surprise. "Is he the one who sent us the ten-speed bicycles for Christmas?"

"No! That's Uncle J.," said Cyrus laughing. "He is *my* uncle. This is *your* uncle, Uncle Farhang, my brother, my kid brother."

"Oh!" said Jonathan again, with as little enthusiasm.

A woman in a nasty voice was telling me my time was up and I had better put in another quarter if I wanted to continue.

"What did you say?" Cyrus got back to me.

"Nothing," I said. "It was the operator. Was telling me to put in another quarter."

"Where are you calling from?"

"Here in New York. Somewhere on Forty-Second Street."

"Forty-Second Street?" he echoed me. "Here in New York? I can't believe it."

He announced the news to the whole family again. "He is in New York. I can't believe it. He is in New York."

He must have got a very unenthusiastic look from Patsy. By now he must have figured out that I might have given Patsy that news before.

"Did you know he was in New York?"

"Yeah, he said so," said Patsy, with irritation.

"So?" asked Cyrus.

"So?" echoed Patsy.

"Then what was all that 'Yes?' 'Yes?' 'Yes?' 'It was nice of you to call' business? Jesus Christ! Here's my kid brother coming to New York in a coon's age, and is this all the welcome this family can give him?"

"Pardon me for living," said Patsy. "What was I supposed to do? Call a parade? I don't even know who he is."

"Jesus Christ!" shouted Cyrus again. "He's my brother. He's my kid brother. He's my only brother."

"I still don't know who the hell he is," Patsy said casually.

The voice was telling me to put in another quarter. It was lucky I had a handful of dimes and quarters on me. I had got them out of my laundry jar before we left. That was almost all the money I had left, too. I hadn't got my monthly check yet.

"What was that?" Cyrus asked again.

"Nothing," I said. "The same old lady. Wanted me to feed her another quarter."

"Where are you staying?" he asked.

"Nowhere yet," I said. "We just got in. This friend I have, was driving up to New York for a wedding. So I thought I would come along, help with the driving, and say hello to you."

"That's great news," he said. Cyrus always liked to exaggerate. "He's here for a wedding," he announced to the family.

"Not me," I said. "I'm not going to the wedding. My friend is."

"When are you coming over to see us?"

"I don't know," I said. "It depends. We are heading back for Waterloo tomorrow, right after the wedding."

"What's the big rush?"

"Well, my friend is going back. And I've got to go with him. He's the one who's got the car. And he's got classes on Monday. We just came for the weekend."

"I can't wait to see you," he said. "When are you coming down?"

"Well, I can come down now, if that's O.K. with you. I can ask my friend to drop me off, if you give him the directions."

"What the hell do you mean if that's O.K. with me? You're my kid brother, aren't you? Your name is Shadzad, isn't it? Have you had dinner yet?"

"We munched something on the way."

"Good! We can have dinner together. Patsy will put another plate on the table. We have meatloaf. Patsy makes a terrific meatloaf. We eat at seven, sharp."

As he was giving my friend the directions to his place, it turned out that they did not live in New York after all, but in Hoboken, New Jersey.

We made it there at a quarter of seven. As we pulled in the back, I saw Jonathan and David playing basketball, shooting into a hoop over the garage door. The first thing about them that hit me was how tall they were. Jonathan was six foot, if an inch. And David was already taller than I was. As I watched them from the car window, I could easily tell they were Cyrus's boys. Jonathan had his swagger, especially every time he scored, and David's lower lip sagged in the left corner, the way Cyrus's did.

I waited in the car for some kind of acknowledgment from them. There was none. I got out and walked toward them, thinking that we would be hugging and kissing, good old-fashioned Persian style, as soon as they had made the next basket. That's the way it was with me at fourteen, when an uncle, a half brother of my mother, had dropped by. He said he was my uncle and we immediately hugged and kissed. I remember how glad I was to meet him. And he seemed equally delighted. But after a couple of more baskets, it became clear to me that Jonathan and David weren't about to stop their game, uncle or no uncle. I stood beyond the asphalt, where I assumed was the limit of their makeshift ball court.

"Hey, guys! I am your Uncle Farhang." I shouted.

"Right!" said Jonathan, and they both went on playing, without as much as a glance in my direction. I remembered I was just this weird guy who had said he was Uncle Something or other. I gave up on them. I rang the bell and Cyrus came to the door. We hugged and kissed several times. He was very glad to see me. And I was glad to see him. "I can't believe it," he kept saying, laughing his crescendo laugh each time.

"Let me look at you," he said again, when we were inside. "You know, you were this big when I left home. Remember? How old were you, seven, eight? I remember I carried you on my shoulders at the airport. Remember? You always loved that as a kid. You said it made you feel like a giant. Remember?"

He kept laughing the same crescendo laugh after each sentence. He hadn't changed much, except for his hair that was much thinner, especially in the front, and gray, especially on the sides. There was now a slight stoop to his posture, but he walked with the same swagger. Patsy's welcome was correct, distant, and unenthusiastic. She seemed different from that old picture of hers I remembered. There was none of that confident carefree look about her. She had aged. Her face looked petty, betraying a muffled rage at the world. She was setting the table with bored impatience.

When the grandfather clock in the corner chimed the seven o'clock, Cyrus hollered the boys in for dinner. I thought how proper it was for

Cyrus to have a clock that chimed the hour, the half hour, and the quarter of an hour, and also how proper that they should eat by the chiming of the clock. Cyrus was always big on order and timeliness. He had learned that from Uncle J. They were both big on that. That was one thing in Cyrus Uncle J. always commended. They would both rather be three hours early for a flight, than risk having to run through the airport to catch it. Alex and I were just the opposite. We always did things on the run. We got a big kick out of that. We loved to jump on the train, the minute it started moving. Cyrus thought that was dumb and dangerous. Uncle J. was horrified by the idea of it.

When the boys came in, Cyrus said, "Hey, boys! This is your Uncle Farhang! My kid brother!"

"Right!" said Jonathan again, heading straight for the john. David just slumped into the nearest chair at the kitchen table and didn't bother to look. There was a moment of silence, while the only noise came from the john, Jonathan's mighty and steady stream hitting the water in the bowl. Cyrus was visibly embarrassed. "I wish you would teach that son of yours to close the door when he pees. It's embarrassing."

"You teach him honey," said Patsy, impassively. "He is your son, too."

"Sure he is," said Cyrus. "When he wants money. Then he remembers who brings the dough home. Any other time, I would have to beg for some respect from him."

Patsy just shrugged her shoulder. The conversation on that topic was finished, as far as she was concerned. And so was Jonathan's peeing. He came back and slumped in another chair, across from David.

"Wouldn't you boys like to wash your hands at least?" asked Cyrus.

"They're clean," said Jonathan. David said nothing. He was slumped down and resting on the nape of his neck. He didn't have to take any risks. He was a "me too" guy. He would second anything Jonathan said or did.

"What do you mean they're clean?" said Cyrus with irritation. "You guys have been playing with that dirty ball for an hour."

"We are using forks and knives, aren't we," said Jonathan defiantly. "It's not as if we were gonna eat with our hands." "Besides," said Cyrus, "you just walked out of the john. Don't tell me you washed your hands in there."

"How do you know I didn't?" asked Jonathan.

David was sneering in a self-endearing manner.

"How do I know?" said Cyrus with more irritation. He didn't laugh. I noticed that when he talked to Jonathan, he usually didn't laugh. "The way you leave that goddamn door open, even the neighbors can hear what you do in the john. We sure as hell didn't hear the water running, except for the flushing of the toilet. Unless you washed your hands in the toilet bowl."

"Can we please change the subject?" said Patsy, with only slight irritation. "We are supposed to be eating."

"Right!" said Cyrus. He looked around the room for a new subject to talk about.

"So, how do you like New York?" he asked, when his eyes met mine. I didn't bother to point out that we weren't really in New York, but in Hoboken, New Jersey.

"So far, so good," I said, remembering the joke about the man who had fallen off the Empire State Building. As he was passing the forty-second floor, some guy in the balcony had asked him how he liked it. "So far, so good," he had replied. I chuckled.

"What?" asked Cyrus.

"I just remembered this joke about a guy who fell off the Empire State Building," I said. I told them the joke.

"That's funny!" said Cyrus, laughing his crescendo laugh. Nobody else laughed. The boys were busy stuffing their faces with meatloaf.

"Isn't that funny, honey?" Cyrus asked Patsy.

"I guess so," Patsy said.

I remembered I was the boy who had cheated her husband and her out of their inheritance. That would have been twenty-five thousand dollars, at least. They could have bought a new car with it, a station wagon maybe, a new washer and dryer, a self-cleaning oven, put a new floor in the dining room.

"So," said Cyrus, rubbing his hands between feedings. "My kid brother visiting us after all these years. What do you think of that, David?"

"It's alright, I guess," said David, examining the meatloaf on the tip of his fork.

"Sure it's alright," said Cyrus. "It's terrific." He always went for the overkill.

After dinner, the boys headed for the television in the family room to watch football. Cyrus helped Patsy clean the table and wash the dishes. I offered to help, but Cyrus turned me down. "You just sit back and enjoy yourself," he said. "You're my kid brother. I gotta take care of you. Watch some football with the boys." As he was washing and drying the dishes, he kept shouting "What happened?" every time the boys wowed. When they wouldn't answer him, he would come to the family room, with the dishes in his hands dripping soap water over the carpet.

"I wish you would stop doing that," Patsy would shout at him.

"Right!" he would say, running back to the sink, standing sideways and watching the game in the cupboard glass across the room.

"I've got the perfect thing for you," he intimated to me, when he finished. "The genuine twenty-four-karat hundred proof double-fired raisin arak from Tehran. Brought for me special order by this general I know." He loved to show off about the important people he knew. The guy was probably an ex-major, or maybe a rug merchant.

We drank arak together for the next two hours and ate pistachios and dried sour cherries. It was a pretty hot evening and we were both sweating visibly. Several times he said something about turning the air conditioning on, but then he talked himself out of it. He felt guilty about it, though. He kept bringing up the topic and then saying something about how much the central air conditioning cost, if you kept it running the whole evening and the whole night. And if you weren't going to run it the whole evening and the whole night, you might as well not run it at all and just open the windows.

Seemed like a reasonable argument to me. And I didn't care about it being too warm. But he kept asking my opinion about it and was only too glad to take my silence as a sign of consent. By ten-thirty I noticed Patsy wheeling around us and fidgeting with things, as if giving me a hint that the party was over. Cyrus seemed to have noticed it too. After a few minutes of beating around the bush, he asked when my friend was coming back for me.

"Not until tomorrow afternoon," I said.

Cyrus was about to say something, but he quickly stopped himself and said something else. I think he was going to say, "Then where are you staying tonight?" when he suddenly realized that I might have expected to stay with them. Instead, he said, "Then you can stay with us tonight."

"I suppose I could," I said, playing with the dimes and quarters in my pants pocket, trying to figure out how many nights I could stay in a hotel on that, even in Hoboken, New Jersey. The whole conversation hit me as being extremely preposterous. I noticed Patsy had stopped fidgeting around. She was standing straight and looking at us. Her mouth was slightly open and there were no emotions in her eyes. She was just looking at us.

"You might as well open the sofa bed in the living room then," Patsy said casually, sounding as enthusiastic as a cold pizza in the morning. "I'll get a sheet and a pillow."

"Right," said Cyrus. "Where are your bags?"

I sheepishly looked at the old briefcase standing lonesome in the corner of the room. Cyrus and Patsy exchanged a knowing glance. I felt that some kind of explanation was in order.

"It was one of those things," I said. "My friend said, 'How's about going to New York with me?' and I said, 'Hell, why not? I got a brother there.'"

"Sure you do, kid!" said Cyrus.

"So I threw in a change of underwear, a pair of socks, a toothbrush, and a book for good measure."

Patsy looked like she was going to say, "Can we change the subject, please? I don't want to hear about your underwear. I hope they are clean at least." But she turned around instead and walked out of the room.

I slept well that night, having had only catnaps in the car the night before on the road. We had driven all night, taking turns. The next day, being Sunday, everybody got up pretty late. We ate breakfast together more or less in silence. Cyrus tried some of his showmanship and adlibbing with plenty of crescendo laughter. But we could all tell that the life had gone out of the party. After breakfast Cyrus and the boys decided to play basketball and Cyrus asked me to join, knowing that I wasn't much of a ball player. I said I preferred to go for a walk. I came back just about in time for my ride back to Waterloo.

That was the last time I saw Cyrus and his family. We rarely talked on the phone. We didn't have much to say to each other. And I couldn't afford long distance calls anyway. So, it was surprising that Cyrus was suddenly showing so much interest in whether I went back for the funeral or not. Maybe he felt guilty that he hadn't tried to see me or talk to me more often. Maybe he felt guilty if I went back for the funeral and he didn't.

It now struck me that Cyrus had missed every funeral in the family. Alex's, Dad's, and now he would miss Mom's. I had been present at least at Alex's sham funeral. I had been one of the star attractions, one of the major bereaved parties. And I would have been present at Dad's, if he hadn't driven me away, insisting that I should leave the country before he died, and making me promise. He died only three days after I left. And now I might be the only family member at Mom's funeral.

Was Cyrus now in rivalry with me, as he had been with Alex? And whose affection would he compete for, now that both Mom and Dad were gone? Uncle J.'s, maybe? But we both knew that Uncle J. was in his own sphere, way above us both, and above Mom and her funeral. Mom's funeral was something for his "boys" to attend to. He certainly wasn't impressed with my playing with the idea of attending the funeral. It would be interfering with his boys. The family had always depended on Uncle J.'s boys burying our dead. They were the ones who bought the best graves and got the best headstones money could buy. And Uncle J. always paid for them.

Cyrus couldn't be worried about being cheated out of any inheritance due him from Mom's estate. Mom really didn't have an estate. We all had taken it for granted that she had been living from hand to mouth, ever since Dad divorced her. And whatever her share in her father's home was, if not already deeply mortgaged, couldn't come to much. The way she had run her life since Alex's death, it would be a miracle if she didn't owe her brothers and sisters a fortune. Even if she had anything that could be sold, with the inflation and the war and all that, the money you got wouldn't be worth the paper it was printed on. That's why I was now so broke, because the monthly check from Dad's trust fund, once exchanged into dollars in the black market, wasn't enough to tide me over for ten days. That's why now Uncle J. wanted to "do for me" more than ever. That's why the "princesses" Mini and Mo assumed that Uncle J. was now "doing for me" more than ever, and expected me to kiss their cute fat asses or else.

I had to take it at face value that Cyrus was genuinely worried about me. Unless Uncle J. had asked him to try to persuade me to stay put and let the dead bury the dead, or at least let Uncle J.'s boys bury the dead. Sure, something could easily happen to me there. I could die of a million causes, none of them good. And Uncle J. wanted me alive. He still had to win with me the argument he had lost with Alex. I was Alex's proxy. I was the one who was going to vindicate him, restore his seal of orthodoxy as a bona fide revolutionary and intellectual, re-validate his sincerity and integrity, which had been called into question. Cyrus, of course, didn't know, didn't understand any of this.

If Cyrus had told Uncle J. that he "would talk to" me, that he "would try to put some sense into" me, it was now a matter of honor with him, a matter of "winning". To Cyrus honor and winning were the same. As in his college days, if he promised the Coach "to win this one for him," it was a matter of honor to do so. If you lost, you lost your honor. He had to succeed, especially in the eyes of Uncle J. He was trying to win with Uncle J. what he had lost with Dad.

Uncle J. was his absolute idol, the man who had made it in a very big way, beyond Cyrus's wildest dreams. He was a man who understood business, understood the world, understood the world of business, and the business of the world. He was a man who knew that becoming a judge or a jurist was not the only way to be a success. He probably bought judges and jurists the way he bought Mercedeses, a dozen at a time. For Cyrus, it was an honor to be asked by Uncle J. "to talk to" me. He was given a chance to "prove himself." Not many people "got a chance" from Uncle J. Uncle J. didn't have to give chances. He had his "boys" to depend on. That was probably why

Cyrus was now calling for the fifth time in twenty-four hours, more times than he had called me in my whole life.

"Let's start all over again, kid," he said. "Why do you wanna go back?"

"I want to find myself," I said.

"Are you drunk?" he asked.

"No," I said. "Why?"

"You talk like you were," he said. "You don't make sense."

"I would probably make better sense, if I were drunk," I said.

"O.K. Let's get serious. Why can't you find yourself here?" he asked, genuinely baffled.

"Because this is not where I lost myself," I said.

"Can you cut the bullshit, please?" he begged me. He could probably tell already that he could not keep his promise to Uncle J., that he could not win this one for the Coach, that he could not save his honor.

"You are drunk," he said. "We'll talk tomorrow, when you are sober."

"I would probably be more drunk tomorrow," I said.

"Are you proud of yourself for that?" he asked.

"No," I said. "I'm neither proud nor ashamed. Just drunk."

"Do you hate success?" he asked.

"Depends on what you call success," I said.

"Do you hate money?" he asked.

"Money is like toilet paper," I said. "You need enough of it to keep yourself clean. But sure as hell I wouldn't wanna fall in love with it."

"Do you hate it?" he asked again.

"Well," I said. "If I must choose between loving or hating it, the answer is, yes, I hate it."

"Why?"

"Because of all the things people are willing to do to get more and more of it."

"Don't you like to eat good expensive food, wear fine expensive clothes, live in a nice expensive house?" he asked.

"I like good cheap food," I said. "I feel guilty eating expensive food."

"Why?" he asked.

"It would remind me of all the people who are hungry and can't afford to eat," I said. "And expensive food doesn't necessarily taste good either."

"And you hate expensive clothes, because it reminds you of all those people who are cold and can't buy clothes?" he said in an ironic tone.

"Right!" I said. "You got it."

"And you hate living in a nice expensive house because it would remind you of all the poor and the homeless?"

"You got it!" I said.

"And you want to go back and get yourself killed because that would help all the hungry and poor and cold and homeless people in the world, right?"

"Wrong!" I said. "I wanna go back to find out what the hell was it I ran away from, in the first place. Or rather what the hell was it people told me to run away from, when it didn't even occur to me that I could have a voice in deciding what I did."

"I tell you what you ran away from," he said. "Turn on the television news at six-thirty, and you will see it in color. And if you weren't so dumb and so drunk, you could see it right away, without having to go there and get yourself killed for it."

"But I am so dumb and so drunk," I said. "Besides, why do you buy tickets to the Notre Dame football game each year, instead of watching it on the tube?"

"But they don't shoot at me at the Notre Dame football game, they don't throw bombs and rockets at me. You are impossible to talk to, sober or drunk. I don't know why I even waste my time on you. You wanna commit suicide, go ahead. What's one more stiff in this family, anyway, right?"

"Relax, Cyrus," I said. "You're taking the whole thing too seriously."

"You're right," he said. "I don't have your gift of clowning. I don't make a fool of myself and the whole world and call it a profession. You know, some of us have to work for a living."

"Besides," I said. "I haven't even decided to go. This is only Saturday. Maybe by sunrise Monday morning I'll decide to stay. Maybe I'll decide to come to New York and sell life insurance for you."

"Yeah, go ahead. Make fun of me. Make a fool of me. But it is not only me you're making a fool of. You're making a fool of Uncle J. too. You're making him wait too. And he won't like it. Now, I wouldn't try to make a fool of Uncle J., if I were you."

"So," I said. "That's the real reason. I had guessed right. You have promised to win another one for the Coach, haven't you? This is just another football game to you, isn't it?"

"You hate Uncle J. too, don't you?" he asked. "After all he has done for you. After all he has done for this family. You hate him, admit it!"

"I didn't say that," I said. "You did."

"Yeah! You hate him alright, because he is very rich, and because he is very successful. Dad hated him for that too. You can't stand successful people. Dad couldn't either. You think it is a badge of honor to be poor and miserable and a failure. Admit it!"

"O. K.," I said. "I admit it, if that makes you happy."

"Well! I'm washing my hands of you. If you wanna go get yourself killed, be my guest. And I'll let you do your own explaining to Uncle J. One of these days you'll need help and you'll find out you're like the fox who needed clean soil for his sore eye and he found out he had not left one hill unsoiled in his whole territory."

"I'll drink to that," I said. He hung up. He will not care for my answer on Monday, one way or another. That's one guy I won't have to worry about disappointing.

PART THREE

CHAPTER SIX

FARHANG'S DIARY
Tehran
March 1, 1967

Today, as I walked to school from the bus stop, a tall thin man in his twenties caught up and kept pace with me. "Keep walking and listen, without attracting attention!" he said in a hushed, conspiratorial tone, without as much as turning his face toward me. I did as he said, trying not to show my excitement and anxiety. He said he was one of Alex's comrades and they needed my help. With what had happened to Alex, I was now an important symbol for the whole revolutionary movement, a rallying point around which they could recruit many young people. Would I be willing to help, for Alex's sake? I thought of what the colonel had said, and what my Dad had said, and said "yes." He told me to turn into the next alley on the right, walk to the mosque on the left, and wait. Another comrade would meet me there.

"But I would be late for school," I said.

"School can wait," he said. "How could you worry about being late to school, after what has happened to Alex?" He talked like Alex. He didn't look like a Savak agent. I wondered whether Dad had been right. But I thought of my promise to him and did what the man had asked.

In the alley, I easily found the mosque. There was no one there. In a few minutes I saw someone approaching from the opposite direction. He walked very cautiously and constantly looked over his shoulder. As he got closer and I saw his face, I startled. It was the man who had put the newspaper under the garden gate. That meant the other guy was on the level too, was really Alex's friend. And I had taken him for a Savak agent, ready to turn him in, with all his friends, so that they could do to them what they had done to Alex. Suddenly I was angry at Dad. He didn't know everything, after all.

The man walked back in the direction he had come and told me to follow. We walked up the alley, until we reached a point where there were no shops and no houses. It seemed he wanted to make sure that no one could eavesdrop on us. I was confused. What would I do now? I either had to betray Alex, or break my promise to Dad. Maybe I could discuss it all with Dad in the evening and then decide what to do. They didn't expect me to report things immediately on a public phone, did they? I didn't have any coins, anyway. But I had to warn this guy, to let him know that I had to report anyone who contacted me, and then ask him to tell his friends to stay away from me.

"Do you know me?" he asked.

"Yes," I said. "You were Alex's friend. You are the guy who put the paper under the gate."

"Do you trust me?" he asked.

"Yes," I said.

"Why?"

"Because you were Alex's friend."

"That doesn't prove anything. Alex is dead. I am alive. How do you know what I had to do to stay alive?"

"What are you trying to tell me?" I asked.

He ignored my question. "Do you know my name?" he asked.

"No," I said. "But I know they've got your picture."

"Who is they?"

"The Savak. They took me down there. They told me all about what they had done to Alex. Everything in that paper was true. They had done all that, and much worse."

"You don't think I know that?"

He sounded very irritated, as if I had said or done something wrong.

"They showed me a lot of pictures," I said, "including yours. They wanted me to finger Alex's friends. They wanted me to finger you, but I didn't. I told them about the paper you had put under the gate, but nothing about you. I gave them no clues. When I saw your picture, I didn't let on. I said I hadn't seen your face well. I said it was too dark, your face was half covered by a scarf, you had pulled your cap too far down. I said I couldn't tell what you looked like. I didn't finger you, I swear."

He looked at me with a sad expression, his irritation beginning to subside.

"That was dumb of you," he said. "Why didn't you? You know what they would have done to you if they knew you were lying? You want to be another dead hero like Alex?"

I still could not figure out why he was so irritated with me. Did he want to get caught? Did he want me to turn him in?

"I couldn't have done that to you. You were Alex's friend. He loved you. You loved him."

"How do you know all that?" he asked.

"Because you wouldn't have risked your life, bringing me that newspaper."

"How did you know I was risking my life? How did you know I wasn't a Savak agent? How did you know bringing you that paper wasn't part of a plan to get your trust, so that I could use you later? What good was that paper, anyway? Alex was dead already, wasn't he? What was easier than sending that paper around, to sucker you? Who would have been dumb enough to risk his life for that, when he could have guessed that your house was being watched?"

What he said certainly made sense. It could have well been true. I was beginning to realize how naive I was in all this. And I had thought I could outsmart that colonel and the whole Savak organization, just because I had read a few books. I remembered what Dad had said about the ways these people had to make you do what you didn't want to. At the time, I thought he was talking about torture. Well, he was talking about that. But he could have meant these tricks too.

But even Dad hadn't suspected that the guy who brought the paper might be an agent. Would he be telling me all this if he was? Maybe he was just testing me, to see how naive I was. Maybe this was my first lesson in revolutionary tactics. He was already educating me. But I had an advantage of him that he wasn't aware of. He didn't know that I had seen his face before. He didn't know that I had spied on him through the crack in the gate, that late night when he came with Alex, when he kept watch for Alex. Didn't that prove that Alex trusted him?

"But I had seen you before," I said. "I knew you were a good friend of Alex. I watched the two of you that late night, when Alex came from the woods to see me. I promised I wouldn't follow him to the gate, but I did. I saw the two of you together. I could tell you had been keeping watch for him. I could tell he trusted you. I saw the way the two of you hugged, before you went different ways, so that both of you couldn't get caught at the same time. When you said you knew how much Alex and I loved each other, I could tell that he had talked to you about me, maybe made you promise to come and see me if anything happened to him. I couldn't have done that to you. I couldn't have fingered you." I almost shouted at him. "That would have been like fingering Alex. That would have been like betraying Alex."

I saw a drop of tear running down his face.

"I would have fingered you if they had asked me," he said. "I wouldn't have risked my life for you."

"And for Alex?"

"I wouldn't have risked my life for Alex, either. I would have talked rather than die."

Suddenly, I remembered what Dad had said. "Alex didn't talk, but that doesn't mean nobody else did, either." Had he talked? Had he betrayed Alex? Is that how they had got Alex? But it couldn't have been. When he brought that newspaper, Alex was already dead.

"Why did you follow that man?" he asked, again with irritation. "Why did you do what he asked you to?"

"Because he said Alex's comrades needed me, that I was now a symbol around which the whole revolutionary movement could recruit people."

"And you believed him?"

"No," I said. "Not at first. Not until I saw you."

"Why did you follow his instructions, then?" he asked again, with irritation.

I felt terribly embarrassed. I had come here, ready to snitch, to inform, to turn in whoever was there, just because Dad thought they would all be Savak agents. If it hadn't happened to be him waiting there, I would have turned them all in, all Alex's friends. Just because of what Dad had said. Dad didn't know everything. Or maybe he had lied to me, so that I would turn everybody in, just to save my own miserable hide, to spare him more agony.

"I am embarrassed to tell you this," I said. "I promised the Savak colonel to cooperate with them and report any of Alex's friends who contacted me. I didn't intend to do it, though. I thought they would send agents to test me for a while. I was going to use my judgment and only report those I thought were agents. Of course, it would be terrible if I made a mistake either way, wouldn't it? Then my Dad told me to report everybody. He said Alex's comrades wouldn't come near me now. He said anybody who approached me for the next three months would be a Savak agent. So, I assumed this guy was an agent too, and came here ready to report him, and ready to report whoever was waiting here."

"And now?" he asked.

"Well, my Dad was wrong. Obviously everybody who approached me could not be a Savak agent. I was dumb enough to believe him. Maybe he just lied so that I would report everybody, to spare me the risk of torture, and to spare him more agony."

"Or," he said, with an amused smile, "maybe you were dumb enough not to believe him, when he was right. Oh, how Alex loved you! How hard he tried to protect you. And see where that has got you." A few more tears rolled down his face, as he put his arm around my shoulder, the way Alex would have done. We started walking again.

"You mean that guy is an agent?"

"Right!"

"Then he can send them after you, can't he?"

"Maybe he thinks I am an agent, too," he said.

"You mean you could be a double agent?" I asked. I remembered Alex telling me that once the Tudeh Party had many double agents inside Savak.

"Why not?" he asked with an amused but sad smile. I felt so green, so stupid. I felt he was playing with me, the way a cat plays with a mouse. I still trusted him, though. The way tears ran down his face every time he mentioned Alex, he must have loved him.

"So," he said. "Are you going to report him?"

"Shouldn't I?" I asked. "If you say he is an agent."

"He is," he said. "You should report him. And what about me? Will you report me, too?"

"Of course not," I said. "I can say you weren't there. I can say I didn't go to the mosque."

"And what about when they take you back to that basement for the 'treatment,' will you stick to that story? You think the colonel told you all about Alex to amuse you? You don't think those men are capable of doing the same thing to you, just because you are sixteen?"

I remained silent. I felt so naive and dumb and confused. I had no idea what I would do under torture. I remembered how I had thrown up just hearing about it. I wished Dad was there, so that I could ask him. But I knew what he would say. I wished Alex was there. I didn't know what *he* would say. And this man who had been Alex's friend, what was his advice? Hadn't he just told me that he would have turned me in rather than risk his life? Would he now advise me to report him? Was he really a double agent? Was he outsmarting the whole Savak organization?

"Do you think I should report you too?" I asked, the way I might have asked Alex.

"Can you take torture the way Alex did?" he asked.

"I don't think so," I said. "I am not very strong."

"Are you willing to join the revolutionary movement, go underground, pick up a gun and take to the woods, the way Alex did?"

"No," I said. "Alex knew what he was fighting for. I wouldn't know what I am fighting for. Alex had a cause he believed in. I don't. At least not yet. I just believed in Alex, and in what he did, because I loved him so much."

"Then you have no choice but to report me," he said. "You don't think they followed you to see whether you would come to the mosque or not? You don't think they are waiting right now somewhere along the way, to see how long you spent talking to me?"

I realized again how naive I had been, and how hard it would be for me to outsmart the Savak with no risk to myself or Dad. This was a dirty business there was no getting out of, once you had got involved, no matter how innocent or how smart you were. How naive of Dad and Mom and Alex, to think that if Alex didn't get me involved in politics, I would be safe. Nobody was safe. Dad was not involved in politics, he was the Chief Justice, and he wasn't safe. Uncle J. had given up being a revolutionary, he was a cabinet minister, he played poker with the Shah, and he wasn't safe. I had never got involved in anything, and I certainly wasn't safe.

"And if I report you," I asked, "what would happen to you?"

"That would be my problem," he said, "not yours. You would do well if you just saved your own skin."

I wandered how he could keep so cool about the whole thing. He talked as if he had all the time in the world and nothing to worry about.

"Are you a double agent?" I asked.

"Would I tell you all this, if I were?"

"No," I said. "But why aren't you worried then? Why aren't you in hiding? You said that man is an agent, and he certainly knows where you are right now. They will catch you. They know who you are. They have your picture. I saw it."

"How do you think they got my picture? Out of a candy box?" he asked with a bitter smile.

"You mean they've already caught you?"

He nodded, suddenly looking terribly guilty and embarrassed, as if he was ashamed for not being dead, as Alex was.

"And you talked?"

"And I talked," he said, tears running down his face. "We all didn't have the mettle Alex had," he added in a harsh angry tone, as if he was angry at Alex for being dead. "You know, we can't all be dead heroes. Some of us have weak stomachs, throw up easily. We can't all die. Somebody gotta stay alive, or soon the world will be an empty place." Tears kept running down his face.

"Did they torture you, too?" I asked.

"Oh, yes!" he said. He took his cap off and showed me some deep scars in the middle of his head. Then he pulled his shirt up and showed me some bizarre-looking scars on his belly. "You wanna see more?" he asked.

"No," I said, with embarrassment. Now tear were running down my face.

"And the worst is not what they do to you," he said. "The worst is what they do or could do to those you love dearly."

I thought of my fears for Dad, and of his fears for me, and I understood what he meant. Listening to what they had done to Alex, I had thought I could have suffered all that for Alex, only if he would have been spared. I had thrown up not out of fear for myself, but because of what they had done to Alex, though I really didn't know what I might do, if I had to go through all that myself.

"You know," I said. "I threw up when I heard all they had done to Alex."

"Don't feel bad," he said. "I threw up, too."

"They did all that to you, too?" I asked.

"Short of the bucksaw. That's when I spilled my guts. I was glad Alex was already dead though, so I couldn't hurt him any more. His screams had stopped the night before. At least I didn't betray him. Most of our comrades seemed to have been caught already, anyway. They already knew an awful lot about us. Somebody must have talked. Anyway, I hope nobody was caught or killed, because of what I said. I held out long enough to make sure what I said wouldn't do them any good."

Suddenly I felt so sorry for him.

"Was it that lieutenant colonel and those three apes, one with the gold teeth, and one with a missing tooth in the middle?" I asked.

"Yes. They are their worst 'specialists,'" he said. "Once you are referred to them, your case is past hope. I thought they would kill me for sure, even after I had talked. The reason they haven't yet is that a few of our comrades are still in deep cover. I am the bait to catch them with. So are you."

"You have pledged to work with them too, haven't you? And you knew that I must have done the same. That was the reason for all those questions, wasn't it? To see whether I was on the level with you?"

He just looked at me.

"I'm dead either way," he said. "And as for you, give up trying to figure out who is on the level and who isn't. You are too innocent for this dirty game. Thinking that anybody who was a revolutionary once couldn't be an agent now! How green you are. Former revolutionaries make the best agents. Some of the top men in the Savak are former high-level members of the Tudeh Party."

I thought of Dad and of Uncle J. They had been revolutionaries once. They weren't Savak agents, true. But one was the Chief Justice, and the other a cabinet minister.

"But why don't you run away?" I asked.

"They've got something of mine," he said.

He made a long pause, as I was trying to figure out what could he have so important that he would risk his life for it by not running away.

"They've got my younger sister," he finally said. "I love her the way Alex loved you. Talking about the cost of mistakes. If I don't report a contact who I think is on the level, and I am wrong, it wouldn't be just my skin, but my sister's too. Although, I don't know whether even she cares to live any more. I certainly don't.

"That's how they got to me in the first place. They brought her in when they had me. They raped her before my eyes. They tortured her before my eyes. I couldn't stand hearing her beg me to do something, to help her. I didn't think either one of us would get out alive anyway, even if I talked. So, I didn't talk even then. But something in me snapped already. I began throwing up and kept throwing up and throwing up. But I still didn't talk. Then Alex stopped screaming, and I knew he was dead, and I felt so lonely. As long as I could hear his screams, and I knew he could hear mine, it was still bearable. But now suddenly nothing seemed to matter. I felt dead already. I felt dead inside. They didn't know it, but I would have probably talked even without the bucksaw."

Now I felt so guilty. I felt that I had got away scot-free, while everybody else had paid a terrible price. Maybe if they had done to me what they had done to his sister, now Alex would be alive, too. Had they spared me because I was the Chief Justice's son? But, then, so was Alex. And that didn't do him any good.

"You know, Alex was lucky." he said, as if he had just read my mind. "I wonder how well he would have taken it, if they had raped and tortured you before his eyes. Who knows whether he might not have snapped, too. And they would have done it to you too, if your Dad didn't happen to be the Chief Justice. In a way, Alex was the luckiest of us all. After I talked, I wanted to die, more than I wanted anything else in the world. When they let me go, I had already planned to kill myself. Then I found out they had kept my sister. Now I have to buy the blood of my sister with the blood of my friends. I wonder what Alex would have done in my place?"

I honestly couldn't answer that question. Maybe he was right. Maybe Alex was the luckiest of us all, of all the three of us, of all the four of us, if we counted my Dad too.

"When did you get caught?" I asked. "Before or after Alex?"

"They caught us the same night," he said. "We were on the same team, and on the same mission. We fell in the same trap. He got shot in both legs, trying to escape. I didn't even get a chance to run. They worked on him sooner than on me and more intensely. He was the bigger fish, the biggest, and they knew it. Someone else had talked, just before dying."

"And when you brought that newspaper," I asked, "was it their idea?"

"No, it was mine. I had promised Alex I would try to see you, if anything happened to him and I remained alive, but only when it was safe. And he had promised to do the same for my sister, if I got killed and he remained alive. I was as safe then as I would ever be. And I wasn't risking the life of any of our comrades. I had cooked up a story to tell them, if they caught me at it, that this was a ploy of mine, to get your trust."

I was relieved to hear that bringing of the paper and the news of Alex's death was what I had thought it was, a pure gesture of love, for Alex. I was so glad now that I had not identified him, regardless of whether there was any risk in it for him or not.

"What are we gonna do now?" I asked, tears still running down my face.

"They are testing both of us. We have to pass the test. We have to report exactly the same thing, the same conversation, almost word for word. Let's say I asked you to join us, to go to the woods with us. And you said you couldn't, because that would literally kill your Dad. We'll say we talked about your visit to the Savak and the story of Alex's torture and death. But you've not heard a word about my having been caught, my torture, my talking, and my sister. "You know, you have something in your favor. You are the one thing they can buy your Dad's silence with, short of making him disappear. If he ever got a chance to speak to the international press, or to the UN, or to some group like the Amnesty International, that would be the greatest embarrassment for them. He is still the Chief Justice, if only in name. That's why they won't touch you for a while. And for God's sake, after today, report word for word anybody who contacts you. The only comrades of Alex who are still alive, will remain in a deep hole for a long time. Even I couldn't find them now. Your Dad is right. Anybody who contacts you will be a Savak agent."

When we parted, I felt like hugging and kissing him on the cheeks, the way I would have done with Alex. He must have felt the same way. We did exactly that. As I started walking away, I realized I had never known his name.

"What's your name?" I shouted back.

"Sufi," he said.

CHAPTER SEVEN

FARHANG'S DIARY
Tehran
August 15, 1967

I graduated from the high school this summer and, complying with Dad's wish, applied for a passport. I took the University Entrance Examination, not because I wanted to, but because Dad wanted me to. He wants me to have the option of going to the University here, if they don't let me leave the country. Otherwise, he says, they will draft me, and once I am in uniform, they can do anything to me they want, without him or anybody else ever finding out.

I don't want to cross him in anything. I am so worried about him. His high blood pressure has been getting worse, despite all the medication. The doctors say if he doesn't take care of himself, sooner or later he will have a stroke. He doesn't even care about that. He says he wants to live only until I'm safely out of the country, out of the hands of these "butchers and pederasts," as he calls them. He is not sure they will let me leave, as long as he is alive. And he doesn't know what they might do with me once he is dead.

He knows they have other ways of silencing him, by putting him in jail, or by doing away with him. "Another car accident maybe," he says with a chuckle. But he doesn't think they can afford that for a while. With all the rumors about Alex spreading inside and outside the country, they can't afford to make Alex's father, the Chief Justice, also disappear. It would be too embarrassing to them, just at the time when His Majesty wants to show the world what a safe place for investment his country is. They do not want to add to the international dimensions of the scandal. And they do not want to make Alex even a bigger hero for all the leftist and nationalist groups, than he has already become.

Dad's complicity would be necessary to hush and discredit the rumors about Alex, not to mention all the other torture stories by Savak already buzzing around the world. With shame and bitterness, Dad now recalls that once before he also had consented to be part of a cover-up of mass torture of political prisoners, during the visit of an international observer team. With full knowledge that the bodies of the political prisoners allegedly killed under torture had been switched and replaced by anonymous dead bodies, along with appropriate death certificates forged by the Coroner's Office, Dad, in his capacity as the Chief Justice, had led the international team in a sham examination of those anonymous dead bodies and an official tour of "the Halls of Justice." That, of course, was long before the Alex affair.

Dad is under strict orders not to give any interviews, or receive any visitors, unless they have been cleared by the Savak. Many people want to interview him. There are reporters from British, French, Scandinavian, and even American newspapers and television networks, all eager to call on him. The BBC team is the most insistent. So are the representatives from the Amnesty International. The rumors about Alex's death must have had some impact. The son of the Chief Justice killed under torture! The Government's best defense, of course, is that if the rumors were true, would the Chief Justice be still silent. But they don't want the risk of having him face to face with even one foreign reporter, all his "loyal" past service to His Majesty's Government notwithstanding.

He is also under strict orders not to leave the house, except when escorted by Savak agents. He does not want to leave the house, anyway. The doctors visit him at home. Rarely, when he has to go to the hospital, he can go only in an official Savak car, marked with the insignia of the Ministry of Justice, driven by a Savak driver, and accompanied by two armed agents. The official excuse, of course, is to protect the Chief Justice from the terrorists. But we know better.

Our house is watched around the clock. Relatives and friends are routinely stopped and searched before entering or leaving the house, and they are questioned in detail about the purpose of their visits. They even have been stopping my Mom and asking her whom she has been visiting and why. When she says she has been visiting her son, they ask whether she has also visited the Chief Justice, and why, and what messages she is carrying from the Chief Justice, and for whom.

Dad is not allowed to talk to any strangers on the telephone. Regularly, we get a visitor from the Savak who questions me and the maid, trying to intimidate us into reporting any telephone calls from any strangers, even though they know that we know that our telephone is bugged. Our standard response to all callers is that the Chief Justice is too sick to receive any visitors or calls. Dad prefers that, anyway, to having to tell people himself that he cannot talk, or worse, to lie and confirm the official version of Alex's disappearance, protecting his murderers.

I also am watched and followed, whenever I leave the house, just as I was watched when I was in school. The principal was under orders to keep an eye on me at all times, to report any time I was late to school, or absent, or was visited by strangers. They don't trust me a bit, even though, complying with Dad's wishes, I have pledged to cooperate, to report, to snitch, to inform, and do anything they ask. I have done everything they have asked me to do. I *have* reported and snitched and informed. Thank God, almost everybody contacting me has been so obviously a Savak agent that I have been able to keep my word to Dad without any pang of conscience.

All our mail is censored, incoming and outgoing. They are especially keen on censoring our letters to America, that is, to Cyrus, and his letters to us. Sometimes there has not been even an attempt on their part to re-seal the opened letters. They are so dumb or shameless about monitoring our telephone calls that, sometimes after our call is finished, they ask if we are done, before they hang up. They have warned us about saying anything on the telephone, even to Cyrus, that might be interpreted as a coded message. Cyrus still doesn't know the real story about Alex, still believing that he was killed in a car accident, unless he has heard the rumors. But Cyrus does not read the newspapers that publish that kind of rumors. He probably only reads about stocks and bonds.

I have had a rather good summer. I immersed myself in the works of Shakespeare. I translated *Timon of Athens* and we performed it at the Fine Arts Theater. I played Timon, and my performance was received well. I don't mind if I have to do this for the rest of my life. Dad thinks it is a good hobby, but he warns me against wanting to make acting my profession. It is an undignified profession, he says, and I will die penniless. I don't want to contradict him. I don't want to say anything that might upset him. I give in to all his wishes.

If I can get a passport, if I can get a visa, I will go to America, just to please him, though I don't want to. I would rather stay here and take care of him. He says they may give me a passport and then make it impossible for me to get an American visa. Then, he says, we can hope for some help from Cyrus. As an American citizen, he can help from the other end. But that is provided that I can get a passport first. That is why he wants me to cooperate with the Savak in any way they ask. I can regain my honor and dignity, later, he says. In America.

"I can't be your conscience my boy," he says. "No more than I could have been Alex's. I can't ask you to deliver one innocent boy or girl into the hands of those butchers and pederasts. Not any more. Not after what they did to Alex. But if you do not report a contact, make absolutely sure the fellow is on the level. And then warn him to stay the hell away from you, and tell his friends to stay away from you. I can't imagine there are still such innocents left in the world. If you are wrong in your assessment, remember what risks you will be running. It won't be just a question of not getting a passport then. You heard it from their own lips, what they would do to you. And there would not be a thing I could do to help you, just as there was not a thing I could do to help Alex."

"His Majesty is kind," he says, "to allow his dogs to buy my silence with your life. It is kind of him to spare an old judge the pain of jail and torture and death. Even though there is nothing now I want more than dying. But it is not all kindness, either. They know if they do away with me, they will be fueling more rumors. What has kept those dogs in chain is their fear of world opinion. His Majesty does not wish that the world think of him as a barbarian. He wants to claim for himself the six-thousand-year-old grandeur of the Persian Empire. He likes to be thought of as an enlightened benevolent dictator. After I die, if you are still here, I don't know what they will do to you. I tremble to even think of it. Why would they want to leave a live witness to their butchery and beastliness?"

After several years of silence, Dad has written to Cyrus, asking him to do his best to get me to America, even if for a short visit. If we can really convince them that a short visit means a short visit, he tells me, there might be a chance that they let me go. He doesn't care if he has to put up the house, which is all he owns, for surety that I will return, and then lose it. But he doesn't want me to ever come back, once I have set foot out of the country, no matter what I have to do to stay out. Cyrus has sent me an official invitation to visit him for three months. The summer vacation, however, is already over, and I don't have a passport yet. So, America will have to wait.

They have been giving me a great deal of difficulty in the passport office. First, they would not process my application, because I was not of legal age, even though Dad had filled and signed and notarized all the necessary forms, as my guardian. Then they wanted Dad to come down in person. When we tried to get permission to take him down, someone from the Savak called and told them to accept the Chief Justice's signed forms. Then, they told me I could not apply for a passport, because I had not done my military service, even though they agreed that I was not old enough for the draft. I am barely seventeen. Then, they agreed to let me file the forms, but told me I had to have clearance from the Savak, to be able to leave the country.

Hearing that I had to go back to the Savak made me tremble. I dreaded having to go back to that horrible basement and face those dreadful men again. But Dad assured me that I would not be going there, that I would not be seeing those men, not for the passport. He reminded me that they were their "specialists," and that luckily my illness did not require their services, yet.

I was sent to a Savak office in a very nice building on Shahreza Avenue. I was received by a very polite, well-dressed, well-spoken, full colonel in uniform. He asked why I wanted to leave the country, and why I wanted to go to America. I said I wanted to visit my brother who lived there, and to see my sister-in-law and my two nephews whom I had never seen. Why at this particular time, he asked? I said I couldn't have done it earlier, because I was still in school. And I won't be able to do it later, because I would be either in college or doing my military service. What if I didn't come back, he asked? I said my father would put up his house as a surety that I would come back.

"A house?" he shouted with amazement. "Is that what the Chief Justice thinks we are talking about? A house?"

"I thought that was the law," I said, "to put up a property as bail. And the house is the only property my father has."

"The law?" he shouted again with amazement. "Is that what the Chief Justice thinks we are talking about? The law?"

I then said the only thing I could think of, that my father would personally stand surety for me, that I would return from America.

"The Chief Justice is a very old man," the colonel said. "He may die any day. And when he dies, then who will stand surety that you would return from America."

The thought that Dad may indeed die any day, brought tears to my eyes and a burning sensation to my nose. The colonel was right, callous as it was of him to talk about Dad's death that way. For the first time I noticed the insignia on his uniform. He belonged to the legal branch of the Army, which meant he was a graduate of the Law Faculty. He must have been Dad's student at one time or another. He couldn't have gone to the Law School and not have taken a course or two with Dad. And for him to speak that way of Dad's possible death, as if the only significance his life had was as a means of ensuring my return into the trap!

"But, Colonel," I said, in a tone that was meant to admonish him for his callousness. "If my Dad dies, don't you think I would return for his funeral?"

"Well," he said, "the question is neither here, nor there. But we'll leave it aside for the time being."

Obviously, that whole line of argument did not seem satisfactory to him. So, he began a new one by asking whether going to America was my father's wish or mine. It was my wish, I said, and my father had reluctantly agreed with it. The truth, of course, was the other way around. But I knew where the colonel was coming from and where he was headed. For whom, he asked, would I be carrying any messages from the Chief Justice? No one, I said. Would I be going through London? I didn't think so, I said. I would fly directly to America, unless there was no direct flight. Whom in BBC did I have an appointment with? I said I didn't know what he was talking about. Whom in the Amnesty International did I have an appointment with? Again, I said I didn't know what he was talking about. He said he could see that my father had coached me well. I said my father had done no such thing.

The colonel then delivered a long speech about how much my family owed the country and His Imperial Majesty, and how ungrateful we had been after all the favors His Majesty had showered on us. First, he began counting, His Majesty had given my father the highest judicial position in the land, and had let him stay in that position despite manifest acts of treason by the members of my family. Then, he had pardoned my uncle who had been a confessed Communist traitor and had given him the rank of a cabinet minister. Then my brother had turned traitor and he would have been put in jail and severely dealt with if, luckily for him, he had not been killed in a car accident. And now my father and me and the rest of the family were not doing our best to quell the vicious false rumors spread around the world by an international Communist conspiracy to discredit His Imperial Majesty's Government.

As I watched the colonel delivering his monologue, pacing back and forth between his desk and the wall, while maneuvering around the empty chairs, his hands clasped behind his back, his head bent at a stiff angle, his eyes fixed on an invisible spot in front of his nose, I had the feeling that I was auditioning an actor, a ham actor, acting a scene from a play which I was somehow familiar with, but the title of which escaped me. The man was genuinely impressed by his own performance. And I sometimes wondered if he did not really and truly believe what he said. When he finished his monologue and straightened up, I almost applauded impulsively. Luckily for me, I returned to reality in time to check my enthusiasm and look serious and genuinely affected.

I reminded the colonel that my father and I had done everything we had been ordered or asked to do. He had stayed home and refused to receive any visitors or telephone calls, or give any interviews. He had carried out the funeral as ordered, to the letter. He had the ads published in the newspapers, as ordered, denying and denouncing all the rumors about the circumstances of my brother's death. I had done everything I was told. I had fully cooperated with the Savak, reporting and informing on anyone who had contacted me. And I thought it was rather unfair of the colonel to accuse me and my father of lack of cooperation or of treason.

"You have done everything you have been *ordered*, you say?" the colonel shouted back, as if he had finally caught me on a fine point of law. "That is my very point. Why should you have to be *ordered* to do your duty? Doesn't the Chief Justice know the duties he owes His Imperial Majesty and the country, after thirty years of judicial service, to do these things on his own, without having to be *ordered* to do so? And why were you not brought up properly, to know that it was your patriotic duty to report and inform on traitors, without having to be ordered to do so? And why did not your father stop your traitor brother from his traitorous acts in the first place, before he was caught and killed in a car accident? Does your family take pride in breeding traitors?"

"My father didn't know what my brother was doing, Sir!" I said, almost tempted to point out to the colonel that he had just made a slip of the tongue. "He had already left home and disappeared, we didn't know where?"

"That is no excuse," the colonel said. "Your father had twenty-three years to bring up your brother properly and instruct him in his patriotic duties and he failed to do so."

I had nothing to say. So, I said nothing.

The colonel embarked on a different argument after a long pause, still walking back and forth between his desk and the wall, still maneuvering around the empty chairs.

"Who," he suddenly shouted, as he came to a halt behind a chair, his right hand raised, with the index finger pointing to the ceiling. "Who," he repeated, "will stand surety for you, if we allow you to leave, that you will behave and talk properly while you are outside the country? You know what an object of propaganda you can be for those people who want to discredit His Imperial Majesty's Government?"

"My father will, Sir," I said, sheepishly.

"Ha!" the colonel chuckled. "And who will stand surety for your father, that *he* will behave and talk properly, once you are outside the country?"

"*I* will, Sir!" I said, as if by reflex, before I discovered the absurdity of my answer.

The colonel turned his head at a bizarre angle that made him look definitely cross-eyed, and gave me a strange and puzzled look, as if trying to figure out whether I had intended to mock him by that answer.

"You don't think I would risk my father's life, sir, do you?" I hurried to say, trying to let him know that I was too aware of the possible risks to my father to be mocking the colonel.

"Nobody wants to risk your father's life, if that could be helped," he said. "His Majesty would be very unwilling to let us drag your father down here and teach him some proper lessons. And it would not look good for the image of the country, if the Chief Justice had to disappear without an explanation. There would be more rumors. And we don't want that."

"I promise you, colonel!" I said, trying to further re-assure him. "I will not say anything inside or outside the country that would be embarrassing to anyone, so as to get my father in trouble."

"Ha!" the colonel chuckled again, resuming his walk at a slower pace, apparently re-assured at least that I had not intended to mock him. "The promise of a traitor's brother! And how good would that be?"

"Well, we've got nothing else to offer, Sir!" I said, in desperation. "We've got only our house, my father's word, and my word."

The colonel gave me that same cross-eyed look again. Then, as if feeling sorry for our destitute situation, he nodded several times.

"We'll see what we can do," he said. "Everything now will depend on how well you will perform your duties and prove your patriotism to us. You are not only a good propaganda object for the subversives, mind you! You are also a good bait for us. You can help us uncover and infiltrate all these subversive groups. If you do that well, we *may* give you a passport. Mind you, we *may*, I said. I'm not making any promises."

So, I thought. Dad was right again. He knew these animals inside out.

"They would not let you go, son," he said to me. "Not until they have dirtied you, not until they have made you into a snitch and a spy and an informer, not until they have made you unfit for human company. That's what they did to me forty years ago."

"And is that what you want me to become, Dad?" I asked. "A snitch, and a spy, and an informer, unfit for human company, in order to get a passport?"

"No son," he said. "I just want you to humor them for a while, until you leave. I want you to outsmart them. Thank God that wouldn't be hard. They are not only so low. They are also so stupid. They could not be so low, if they were not so stupid. You know, if I thought you had the stomach to take up a gun and head for the woods, the way Alex did, I wouldn't try to stop you now. I didn't try hard enough to stop Alex, either. But he had the stomach for that kind of thing. You and I don't. Neither does your Uncle J. I admitted what I was, a long time ago, and then became what I am. Your Uncle J. never admitted what he was. He still doesn't. He likes to think he is what he really isn't. Only Alex among of us was what he thought he was. And see what they did to him. Just outsmart them, son! Do it for me, for a sick old man who doesn't have much longer to live."

"I never told you this before, Dad!" I said. "But I did throw up when they told me about Alex down there!"

"Don't feel ashamed, son!" he said. "I threw up, too. Forty years ago. It was a different stage and the actors were different, but the story was the same, and the theme was the same. It is not our fault if we cannot stand that kind of beastliness. Don't be ashamed of having been human."

"And what am I to do after I have outsmarted these beasts?"

"See whether you can find a place where you can be human without having to be ashamed of it. Hopefully, you will have a chance to do that, in America. A chance I never had here, not forty years ago, not ever."

CHAPTER EIGHT

FARHANG'S DIARY
Tehran
September 1, 1961

I passed the University Entrance Examination, against my own expectation, and in the top hundred. Dad is very proud of me, for being in the top hundred among twenty-four thousand. But he still insists that I should follow the business of getting a passport, no matter how long it takes. I told him I would rather stay and go to the University here, and look after him, as long as he was alive. But he is adamant that I should go to America, if they let me. The maid can look after him, he says. They'll hire a nurse. He is even willing to let Mom come back and look after him, if I agree to go. I don't want to leave him, but I want even less to contradict him. His high blood pressure gets worse, whenever I argue with him.

Being in the top hundred means that I can enroll in any Faculty I want. Everybody assumes I will enroll in the Faculty of Medicine, since only the top three hundred can get in there. My friends think it would be stupid of me not to do so. Nobody among the top three hundred ever chooses anything but medicine. Mom also thinks I should go into medicine. Uncle J. thinks I should pick engineering, or go into finance. But Dad still insists on my enrolling in the Faculty of Law. He still hasn't given up on another jurist in the family, a constitutionalist.

"Law," he says, "is the highest point in that human endeavor we call civilization. Plato in his *Republic* put the Lawgiver above everyone."

"Plato in his *Republic*," I say, "would have banished me as a poet, to say nothing of his recommending beating of wives."

"You mustn't take him literally there. He was just railing against the poetic excesses of the time, which attributed licentious behavior to gods."

"So I am to become a Lawgiver, am I?" I ask.

"Why not?" he says.

"A Chief Justice, maybe?" I say, quite innocently.

But he takes it personally. "Just because some of us have prostituted ourselves," he says with extreme sadness, "it does not mean that Justice is a prostitute. She will shine in her purity long after all these Majesties and Chief Justices are buried. Maybe you have to find a better place to be a Chief Justice in. Here they don't need a Chief Justice. They need a circus master to keep His Majesty's clowns and dogs in check."

So, it is to the Law Faculty I will go, to keep Dad happy. I have to do my acting and my writing in my spare time. I will be an amateur gentleman-artist, as befits the son of a Chief Justice.

September 30, 1967

I have been refused enrollment at the University, being among the top hundred notwithstanding. I have been referred back to the Savak office for clearance. No student, I am told, can register without a Savak clearance. And I do not have one.

At the University Savak office, I am told that my case is a complicated one. What is normally required of any student with political record, is to sign a form denouncing his past traitorous activities, have a "confession" published in the two evening papers, expressing repentance and humbly begging His Imperial Majesty's pardon, and sign a "pledge" to cooperate with the Savak. I point out to the man that I have had no record of any political activity, whatsoever. He asks me whether I am not the brother of Eskandar Shadzad, alias Alex Shadzad. I admit I am. "That is plenty record," he says. "Anyway, your problem is bigger than that. You must see someone in the Headquarters." He scribbles a telephone number on a sheet of paper.

To my surprise, I leave the office with a great sense of relief. Maybe now I won't have to go to the University, after all. Maybe now I can stay home and read and write, and act on the stage in the evenings. Maybe Dad will finally give up the idea of another jurist in the family. But I am wrong. Dad points out the alternative to me. If I don't satisfy them, he says, and enroll in the University, they will draft me next, as soon as I turn eighteen. And if I like this circus, I would love the other one. In the army, he points out, I would be lucky if they let me off with the stockade and solitary confinement. Soon enough, I would give them a reason or two to shoot me.

"You have seen these men, son! Once you fall into their hands, for whatever suspicion, you are doomed. What they do has nothing to do with guilt or innocence, with what you might or might not have done, by commission or omission, in deed or in thought. They are a bunch of mangy dogs, who enjoy humiliating and harming and torturing innocent souls. They will use you as a piece of meat, any way they can. And there is no way you can outsmart them there. If you prefer that to going to the Law School, you have that choice."

So, it is back to the Savak, back to the building on Shahreza Avenue, and my Ham-actor Colonel. He asks whether I am willing to sign a "confession and declaration of repentance" and have it published in the evening papers? I say I am. He lets me sign the form. It is very simple and very stupid. I declare that I had been misled by traitorous and godless Communists into betraying my country and His Imperial Majesty and I am now repentant and humbly beg His Imperial Majesty's pardon. Apparently, I should have refused to be born into a family that might one day breed a revolutionary traitor.

"On second thought," the Colonel says, "maybe it is not a good idea to publish your confession. Maybe it is smarter not to let the other fish know that you have been caught once and thrown back into the water."

His fish metaphor reminds me of Sufi. "I'm the bait," I recall him saying, "and so are you." But I try to look surprised and totally baffled by the knowing look on the Colonel's face.

"You can be more valuable to us in a different way," he adds knowingly, quite pleased with his own cleverness. "Will you sign the pledge to cooperate with us?"

I remind the Colonel that I have already signed "the pledge" and have been cooperating with them for a long time.

"But your cooperation hasn't borne fruit," he says. "Everyone you have informed on so far has been one of our own agents. Either the traitors have got wind of it that you are working with us, or you are smart enough to figure out whom to report and whom not to report."

I assure him that I have reported everybody who has contacted me. I remind him that I am only seventeen years old, that I have had no experience with politics, no training in intelligence or counter-intelligence, espionage or counter-espionage. I do what I am told. Maybe those guys stay away from me, because they don't trust me, because aside from being a traitor's brother, I am also the son of the Chief Justice and the nephew of a cabinet minister.

"Hmmm!" the Colonel mumbles significantly. "Maybe. Maybe so. Or, maybe you are smarter than you seem. But if you are, I assure you we will catch you sooner or later. And then it would not be simply a question of not getting a passport, or not enrolling at the University. Do you get my drift?"

"Yes, Sir!" I say, trying to look scared, but not overdoing it.

"I'll give you one more chance," he says with magnanimity. "We'll let you enroll in the Faculty of Law. You will report any political activity you observe, and any political comment made in the classroom by any student or instructor. Remember that your reports will be double-checked, and triple-checked. There are at least three students in each class reporting. Remember that."

"I will, Sir!" I say. "And I am grateful for the chance you are giving me."

"You have to do more than that!" he shouts, while shaking a finger at me. "You have to do more than being grateful! You have to produce results. You have to join and infiltrate underground student organizations. There are many of them. There are the Communists, there are the Socialists, there are the Nationalists, there are the fundamentalists, there are the Islamic Marxists. Do you pray?"

"No, Sir!" I say.

"How come?"

"I guess I wasn't brought up right, Sir."

"Do you know any lines from the *Koran*?"

"One. *In the name of Allah the Compassionate, the Merciful.*"

"How come only one?" he asks.

"I have had a faulty education, Sir," I say. "My father is not a religious man. He says he abhors religious fanaticism even more than other kinds of fanaticism."

"Hmmm!" he mumbles again. "No wonder your brother became a godless Communist traitor."

"My father doesn't love the Communists any better, Sir!" I protest casually.

"That's no excuse for not having a religion," he says. "Anyway, I'm afraid you won't do well with the Fundamentalists and the Islamic Marxists. They won't let you within a mile of them, if you don't pray five times a day and are not a hand at quoting the *Koran*. You just look for the Communists and the Socialists. They are your best bet. Not knowing your *Koran* would be a credit with them. You'll make a good bait for them. They have made such a big hero out of your brother, whether he belonged to them or not."

I remain silent. I feel that anything I say now may be used against me. The Colonel apparently interprets my silence as another act of treason. Maybe I should have said something about how terrible it was of my brother to have allowed the Communists and the Socialists to make a big hero out of him, by having been caught and killed in a car accident. Something like, *He should have died hereafter;/There would have been a time for such a word.*

"You have to do much better than you have been doing," the Colonel says. "The burden of proof is on you. We want results, not promises. You must prove to us that you are not a traitor, like your brother was. University education is not a right, but a privilege. Remember that! Only His Imperial Majesty's loyal subjects are entitled to that privilege. And so is a passport. We can't allow traitors to go to the University and corrupt the innocent minds of the youth. Nor can we allow them to travel around the world and give the country a bad name."

He is overacting again. Both his hands are now flying all over the place, as if he were shooing flies. And the spot before his nose, which he stares at when he declaims, has shifted slightly to the left, giving him even more of a cross-eyed look. I wonder what role we could cast him in. He would fit some character in Shakespeare. Maybe the Duke of Cornwall in *King Lear: "And what confederacy have you with the traitors/Late footed in the kingdom? Wherefore to Dover? Let him answer that."* I only wish he would let me give him some proper lessons in acting.

I walk out of the office with my commission in my hand. I am now His Imperial Majesty's unpaid official snitch, spy, and informer, committed to the Freshman class of the Law Faculty. Now I am entitled to an education in Law.

At home Dad tries to cheer me up. I don't have to worry about anything, he says. There is nothing I can report that could get anybody in trouble. No instructor with the slightest unorthodox tendency is allowed to teach at the University. All the professors and instructors with any political record were purged long ago. And the remaining ones have signed oaths of loyalty and pledges of cooperation with the Savak, to be able to continue teaching. Even the full professors with life tenure, especially the full professors with life tenure, were forced to pledge themselves to work with the Savak or else. That was when Dad had used the excuse of overwork at the Court and resigned from his academic position, a timing which had not escaped the attention of the authorities.

As for reporting on the students, he continues, the real political activists would know better than saying anything in the classroom that could be reported. And if a politically naive student without any tie to any organized group said anything, they would take him down and slap him around a few times, until he cried and asked for his mother, and then they would let him go with a promise of good conduct in future. That would be the best education in law and democracy he could get. "Just getting to know those animals for the price of a few slaps would be worth the education, don't you think?" he asks.

"Yes," I say. Dad can make anything sound right. Once he starts reasoning, there is no way you can walk away unconvinced. What a pity that all his talent is wasted on being the Chief Justice in a circus.

"As for infiltrating the underground organizations," he adds, "if *you* could do that, anybody could. If you could infiltrate them, they haven't got a prayer. I tell you what your best protection is. Be overzealous in trying to infiltrate them. Be an overeager revolutionary. That will mark you in ten seconds as an informer and a snitch. Everyone will stay clear of you then, except for the Savak agents. Report them all wholeheartedly then and pile up a lot of credit with your lawyer-colonel. Do you want to do that?"

"Yes," I say, suddenly sounding enthusiastic. "That's a wonderful way of doing it. It would be ham-acting, like the Colonel."

I wonder how Dad came to know all these things. Had he gone through it all himself? What was the price he said he had had to pay forty years ago, to become His Imperial Majesty's Chief Justice someday?

"There is only one thing," he says, as if he has just read my mind. "Remember you will pay a price. You will become an outcast. Your fellow students will avoid you as if you smelled of garlic. You will be lonely. And when you see a fellow student spitting on the ground as you walk by, you will be hateful. For a second, you will even think of revenge, of exerting your hated power, of reporting him, of getting him in trouble, of getting even. But just for a second, until you come to your senses again, until you remember why you chose to be an outcast. Can you live that kind of life? Can your pride take that?"

"Yes," I say, with full conviction, already enjoying the prospect. "I prefer that kind of life to having to send one boy or girl to those butchers and pederasts, as you call them."

"Good!" he says. "Then you are ready for your education in law. You have just received your first lesson." He has tears in his eyes, as he turns to leave the room.

"Dad!" I call after him. "Did you have to go through all this, too?"

"Now you know, my boy!" he says, without turning to look at me. "Now you know the road that in the long run leads to the office of His Imperial Majesty's Chief Justice. But you have an advantage of me. You know something which I didn't know then. And you may have a proper place to know it in. So, when you have a passport, you will have a choice."

CHAPTER NINE

FARHANG'S DIARY
Tehran
August 15, 1968

Almost a year has gone by since that last conversation with Dad. I have finished the first year in the Faculty of Law. Things have gone exactly as Dad foresaw they would. I have taken massive notes in the classroom and reported them to the Savak. I have driven them up the wall. I report anything that has to do with politics. And in the study of law, the way I see it, almost everything has to do with politics. They have kept asking me to "cut down, cut down." The Colonel has said to me that if he had wanted a note-taking service, he would have hired one. He said he had already taken these courses once and passed them. He did not need "to be spoon-fed the same intolerable lectures, after they had been digested in my guts." I have finally been told to forget about what the instructors teach and just concentrate on reporting what the students say.

Outside the classroom, I have been a resounding success. My over-enthusiasm in *becoming* a "Revolutionary," my overzealous ham-acting *as* a "Revolutionary," my over-eager seeking out *of* "Revolutionaries," has made mine a dirty name in *all* political camps. I am considered the number one snitch in the whole school. In the classroom, no matter where I sit, I find the seats on my right and my left empty. People avoid me like plague. They shout the words "snitch" and "spy" at my back, as I walk down the street. On snowy days, I am the number one snowball target of armies of fellow students. There are so many people spitting on the ground as I go by that I have stopped keeping count.

I am on the lookout for the first time when someone might try to spit in my face. When that comes, they'll find me ready, to cover my face with my hands faster than they can spit. I have no friends. The few students who occasionally talk to me, out of sheer pity, are the sons and daughters of some army officers and top Government officials, among them probably my two fellow informers. They belong to a small clique, who are themselves shunned by the rest of the class. But since I avoid the small clique as well, I have become a clique by myself, a majority of one.

On the romance side, there is only one girl who pays me the slightest attention, telling me how sorry she is for me, seeing how obviously lonely I am. She is the daughter of an army major general, herself not very popular at all, being neither very attractive, nor very intelligent, nor very humble. It is possible that she has a crush on me. But, receiving no encouragement from me, even she has finally begun to give up.

What surprises everyone is the cheerfulness with which I bear all my indignities, as if I enjoyed my outcast state. And that indeed I do. What surprises me is that I do not feel lonely at all. I feel that Dad is with me every step of the way. I feel I am reliving his younger days. With every humiliation, with every insult hurled at my back, with every snowball hitting me in the face, with every spit on the ground, I feel I know him a little bit better. And Alex too. Sometimes, facing a young man staring at me with sheer contempt and hatred, I feel I'm facing Alex. I begin to worry about him, imagining him cornered in that dark basement with those four animals. Would he be throwing up like me, or would he be looking out of swollen eyes, as Alex had done with Uncle J., saying, "They got you to do their dirty work for them again, didn't they?"

But I don't feel I am doing anybody's dirty work. I am getting an education in law. Most of the education I get, however, is outside the classroom. Dad was right again. I do have a choice. I know for certain now that I will never be a Chief Justice. I know for sure that I will never be a cabinet minister.

July 14, 1969

Finally, I have been given a passport, a token that I have proved my loyalty to my country. I have paid part of my debt to His Imperial Majesty for all the traitorous acts of my family. And I have applied to the American Consulate for a visa. I have had my grades translated and notarized and have applied for admission to different colleges in the United States. I have taken the student foreign language test and have passed it with high distinction. After Shakespeare, the questions on the test seemed like a joke. Today I actually received an acceptance from an American college, from a state college in Waterloo, Iowa. Sounds like such a wonderful place for me to go to. To have my Waterloo. The fifth element, the mud, said Napoleon.

I continue my studies in law, even as I prepare to leave. I am finishing the second year in the Faculty of Law. I have passed my exams with flying colors, as befitting a Chief Justice's son. I have become brilliant in arguing subtle points of law, especially of constitutional law. Maybe the Chief Justice will have his wish after all and the Shadzad family will produce another "constitutionalist." I would almost hate to leave this place now.

My outcast state has not changed. I have become less enthusiastic about trying to infiltrate underground organizations, as the Savak has more or less given up on me, as the most inept informer and infiltrator they ever had. I walk around lonely and cheerful, so cheerful some people can't stand it.

"What the hell are you so cheerful about?" asked a girl once, shaking a fist in my face. "Where's the wonderful news?" Another one told me, "I'd like to wipe that smile off your face!" The female students take more liberties with me. They think it less likely that I will report them, even though no one can cite a single case where I have reported anybody or got anybody in trouble. It is even likely that they are beginning to see through me, seeing me for what I am, somebody who is no good at anything, including spying, on purpose; a deliberate failure.

September 1, 1969

It has been five weeks since I applied for an American visa, and no news yet. I have gone to the American Consulate almost every week, for the past five, as Dad has insisted that I should. At first it seemed that with the invitation and affidavit of support from Cyrus, with my college acceptance form, and with my very high grades on the English test, it would be a matter of days before I received my visa. But no dice as yet. Dad says he smells a rat somewhere. As he had foreseen, he suspects that they have given me the passport, but they will see to it that I do not get a visa.

October 10, 1969

Finally, I am told at the Consulate that I will not be given an American visa after all. The woman at the desk cannot give me a reason. I ask to see the Consul, as I know Dad would want me to. I am told that he is too busy to see me. I go home.

Dad sends me back the next day to insist on seeing the Consul, a vice consul, a consular officer, or anybody who can give me a reason. "They must give you a reason," he says. "I know that much about the law, even their law. They must give you a reason, in writing. Insist on that!" He is very upset.

I go back the next day and insist on seeing a consular officer. I am told everybody is too busy to see me that day. I ask for an appointment for another day, for any day. They give me one for the following week. I go back the following week and manage to see a vice-consul. He flips through my file and then informs me that according to the authorities of my country, I am a subversive. That is the ground for rejecting my visa. I ask if they could give me that reason in writing. I get a negative response. I try to argue, as I know Dad would want me to. How could I be a subversive? I ask. I don't even know what the word means. I am only eighteen years old. I have never been involved in politics. I have never been arrested. I have no records of any kind. The vice-consul politely lets me know that I am arguing with the wrong party. That is something between me and the authorities of my country, he says.

"We must depend on the information supplied to us by your security officials," he says. "We do not gather information ourselves. If the Savak says you are a subversive, we cannot let you into the United States." He gets up and politely lets me know that the interview is over.

I am satisfied, but Dad is not. I can stay here. I can read and write and act, and still study law. Waterloo can wait. But that's not the way Dad sees things. I must go back to the Savak, to my "lawyer Colonel," as he puts it. I am to tell him that he is a double-crosser. I am to tell him that they had better change their report or else.

"Tell him they can't play with me like that!" he shouts. "I may be a Chief Justice in name only. But, dammit, I am still the Chief Justice. I'll talk. I'll talk to the BBC. I'll talk to the Amnesty International. I'll talk to the UN. I'll talk to the World Court at Hague. Let them come and drag me to jail and torture and kill me, so that the world can see them for the monsters they are."

After he has calmed down, he revises his strategy. He tells me to hold off on saying all those things. If it came to that, he says, he would talk first and let them find out afterward, when it would be too late for them to do anything. For the time being, a veiled threat would do. I am to call the Colonel and tell him that I have something very important to report, in person, to make sure that he would see me right away. Then, I am to tell him that I have a message from the Chief Justice, that they had better clear the misunderstanding or he would petition His Imperial Majesty. "Tell them I said I mean business. They will know what that means."

I call the Colonel and he agrees to see me right away. He is very eager at first, but becomes disappointed after hearing me out. He had expected to hear about a major revolutionary plot of some sort. However, he is conciliatory. He wants me to assure my Dad that the Savak has lived up to their end of the bargain, that it is the American Consulate that is lying. It is they, he says, who do not want to give me a visa, because of "the Alex situation," and they are blaming it on the Savak.

"We are a good scapegoat," he says. "Ask the Chief Justice to reason it out for himself. With all the rumors about Alex's case, does he think the American Consul would be eager to have Alex's brother on an American college campus confirming those rumors? Not that the rumors are true, mind you. But suppose someone managed to persuade you that the rumors were true. Can you imagine what kind of a star witness you would make for some of those guys, the Amnesty International or whatever. The next thing you know, you would be testifying in front of those Communist members of the American Congress. Does the Chief Justice think that the American Consul wants that? If that ever happened, His Majesty would have our heads, including that of the Chief Justice." For the first time I notice that the Colonel is not ham-acting, and I wonder whether he is not telling the truth.

October 11, 1969

Yesterday, when I reported all this to Dad, he sat patiently in a chair and listened, nervously fidgeting with his cane. "Liars and cheats and double-crossers all," he said, once I was finished. "Now we will never know the truth. The Consulate will blame the Savak, and the Savak will blame the Consulate. Either way that means no visa for you. Shameless liars that they are, this time the Colonel may be telling the truth. The Americans may be more afraid of Alex's story now than these dogs. They are their dogs, anyway. Their President just gave the top dog here his vote of confidence. They might have to explain to their people why these murdering thieving dogs here deserve the American taxpayer's support." "I have seen their visa applications," he added, after some musing. "It hasn't changed since my days. It asks whether you have ever known a Communist, fed a Communist, sheltered a Communist, made love to a Communist, lent money to a Communist, but not a word about whether you have known a Fascist, fed a Fascist, sheltered a Fascist, made love to a Fascist, lent money to a Fascist. They must have missed the boat somewhere. Is it all right to be a Fascist in America? Is that the impression they want to give the world? Does Justice Douglas know about those applications and does nothing to change them? For my money six of one, half a dozen of the other. I don't care whether I perish under Hitler's tyranny, or Stalin's, or His Imperial Majesty's. They are all Fascist dogs. And if I begin to talk, so much the worse for both of them, the Colonel and the Consul."

Suddenly, he asked me to get Cyrus on the telephone. He seemed quite excited, as if he had found a way out. "We have one more shot," he said, "before I pull all the stops. We have seen how our law works. Now let us see how their law works. We have seen the King's justice, now let us see the President's justice."

It took two hours before we could reach Cyrus in New York. They kept saying the line was busy and Dad kept telling them to try again. "Tell them it is Mr. Chief Justice who wishes to speak to New York," Dad shouted from across the room. "That oughta make those dogs a little bit curious."

Finally, the operator rang back and said that New York was on the line. It was Cyrus. Dad grabbed the phone out of my hand. "Cyrus!" he shouted. "I'll give you one more chance to redeem yourself, to regain your standing with me. I have seen all your certificates, Salesman of the Day, Salesman of the Week, Salesman of the Month, Salesman of the Year. Now I have one piece of salesmanship for you, and if you can deliver on that, I'll give you the credit due to you, even though you have disappointed me in everything else."

On the other phone, I could hear poor Cyrus's voice trembling and choking with excitement and awe and gratitude. "Anything, Dad, anything!" he kept saying. Dad hadn't talked to him on the telephone for years. And now he was suddenly overwhelming him. "First, give me a straight answer! And I mean straight! Are you or are you not an American citizen?"

"I am, Dad!" said Cyrus, his voice cracking. He was probably crying with joy. For years he had tried to keep this a secret, in case he came back for a visit. Iran did not recognize dual citizenship, even though some of our diplomats and top government officials themselves had it. The authorities' memory worked only selectively. They would remember the regulations, only when they wanted to get somebody in trouble. But Cyrus was so eager to please Dad at this time that he couldn't care less.

"Then I want you to write and call your Congressman and your Senator and ask them to put all the heat they can on their Consul here, to explain why he is denying your eighteen-year-old brother, who has never had any political involvement in his whole life, an American visa."

At this time there was some clicking on the telephone and Dad thought they were disconnecting him. He shouted at the top of his voice, "And don't you Savak dogs dare disconnect my phone while I am talking. This is Mr. Chief Justice speaking."

The telephone line, through sheer awe, got connected again.

"Hello, hello!" came Cyrus's voice again. "Are you still there, Dad?"

"Yes, my boy!" said Dad, gently. "These dogs and monkeys were fooling around with my phone. But I straightened them out. Don't forget, the Congressman and the Senator, and any other influential person you know. I want an answer out of the Consulate here. They are passing the buck back and forth between them and their dogs here, about who doesn't want Farhang in America."

"I'll get on it right away, Dad!" Cyrus shouted back again, his voice still cracking with emotion and gratitude. "I'll go down to Washington today and see them in person."

"That's my boy!" said Dad and passed the phone to me. I just said hello to Cyrus again and asked how he was and hung up. Dad was stumbling towards his bedroom and I ran to hold his arm, to make sure he would not fall. He was totally exhausted with all that excitement. I was sure his blood pressure had shot up again. He got to bed and slept for the rest of the night.

CHAPTER TEN

FARHANG'S DIARY
Tehran
November 1, 1969

Last week I received a registered letter from the American Consulate, informing me that I had an appointment with the Consul for today. Dad was so pleased and excited. "Good boy!" he said, referring to Cyrus. "He has done his piece of salesmanship. Now we must do ours. At least, we'll find out which one of them is the lying dog, the Colonel or the Consul." He was so excited that he wanted to accompany me to the Consulate. With great difficulty I was able to talk him out of it. I promised him that I would be as eloquent, as persistent, and as persuasive as he could ever wish me to be.

"And I want you to tell the Consul everything," he shouted at me as I was leaving. "And I mean everything. If he knows it already, it wouldn't hurt. If he doesn't, it was high time he did. He must have an answer now, if not for you, then for those dogs that Cyrus has sicced on him."

I went in at 10:00 a.m. and was immediately taken to the Consul. He was a man in his early forties, rather tall and trim, polite and pleasant. He surprised me by introducing himself in flawless Persian. He said his name was Alan Dugan. He asked whether he could call me by my first name. I said he could. He asked whether I preferred to talk in English or in Persian. I said I preferred to talk in English, although I congratulated him on his flawless Persian. He congratulated me on my English, but asked why I preferred to talk in English rather than in my mother tongue, being a poet and all. I was surprised he knew I was a poet. I said it was easier to be less formal in English. The formal Persian was too stiff for me. He smiled and said he understood.

He asked whether we could get right down to business. He said he had received some inquiries from some American citizens, which had prompted him to personally review my case, to see whether my visa request had been justly denied. And then he had found my case extremely intriguing. He was prepared to take some time with me. He had left his morning free to deal only with my case. How much time did I have? I said I had all the time in the world and nothing else to do. He asked what I had done concerning the rejection of my visa, since my meeting with his Vice Consul.

"I visited the Savak," I said, "to ask why they had given the Consulate a false report on me."

"And?"

"They said they hadn't. They said the Consulate didn't want to give me a visa and was using the Savak as a scapegoat."

"They did, eh?" said the Consul, with an amused smile. "And who is they?"

"The Colonel I have been talking to," I said.

"Is that Colonel Sobhani?"

"Officially I have never been told his name. But once I did hear someone refer to him by that name."

"And did you believe Colonel Sobhani?"

"I no longer know what to believe, or whom to believe," I said.

"I understand your feelings," he said. "I would have felt the same way, if I were in your shoes." And after some silence, "Why do you want to go to the United States?"

"It is my father's wish," I said.

"It is not your wish?" he asked.

"I can stay here or go there. It doesn't make much difference to me. Actually, I would rather stay here and look after my father. But I also want to do what he wishes. He is a sick old man, and I will do whatever pleases him. And it pleases him that I go to America."

"Why does it please him that you go to America?" the Consul asked.

"Well! He has this thing about America. He says America is the last best hope of mankind. He says the last battle will be fought there."

"What battle?"

"I don't know. He hasn't said. And I haven't asked. Of course, that's not the real reason. He wants me to be near my older brother. He is worried about what might happen to me here after his death."

"What is he worried about?"

"I don't know. He is afraid I won't be able to survive here. He says I lack jungle instinct. And he considers here a jungle. He says I am too innocent."

"You are a poet, a playwright, and an actor, I understand. You have translated Shakespeare. You act Shakespeare. Is that true?"

"That's why my father thinks I lack the jungle instinct required to survive here."

"But this is the land of poetry. It has always been the land of poetry. That is why I asked to come here. That's why I learned Persian. I am a great admirer of Hafiz and Rumi."

I looked at him with disbelief. No wonder he spoke such a flawless Persian. First I had thought he was one of those six-week wonders of their State Department, their audio-visual language prodigies, who know little beyond daily amenities and pleasantries. But Hafiz, Rumi?

"I see I have shocked you," he said. He reached back to his bookshelf and grabbed a small collection of Hafiz lyrics in English, along with Ghazvini's *Divan of Hafiz*, and Arberry's *Mystical Poems of Rumi*.

"These are my favorites," he added. "I was a student of German literature at first, at Columbia, when I discovered Hafiz through Goethe's admiration for him. Then I began studying Persian, read Hafiz in translation, worked my way through a few of his lyrics in Persian with a lot of help, and fell in love with the man. Later, when I went into the diplomatic service, it was always with the thought of coming here some day, 'the land of flower and nightingale.' I finally asked to be transferred here a few years back. And have found it difficult to leave since."

He looked at me still sitting dazed and surprised. "Have you got over your shock, yet?"

"Yes," I said. "Come to think of it, it is really no stranger than my falling in love with Shakespeare when I was fourteen. I would stay up all night, reading him with excitement, looking up the words in Concise Oxford Dictionary, and then dozing off through all my classes the next day. That's when I actually began translating *Hamlet*, at fourteen, although it didn't get published until I was seventeen."

"Yes," he said, "I asked to see that when I became interested in your case. Your translation of *Hamlet*, I mean. I read it with great interest, last night. You have done a very good job. I wish I could translate Hafiz into English like that."

"But Hafiz is much harder to translate than Shakespeare," I said. "Most of his lyrics, most of his 'metaphysical' conceits are untranslatable."

"I agree with you," he said. "God, I would much rather talk about Hafiz and Shakespeare than about passports and visas, wouldn't you?"

"Absolutely," I said. "That's why I said it doesn't make much difference to me where I am, as long as I am allowed to have my Hafiz and my Shakespeare with me."

"But your father may be right," he said. "You may not be able to survive as a poet. It is not only a question of earning a living as a poet. You may find yourself in a place where they might make it impossible for you to write and read poetry. I have lived in such places. It is hell, even if you are there as a tourist."

"It is that way here," I said. "Not a word can be published until the Savak says it can be published. That's why my father wants me to go to America. He thinks I could find a place there, where I would not have to be ashamed of being human. That's the way he puts it."

The Consul looked at me sadly and in silence. "I know," he said. "I write poetry too. Maybe later we will have more opportunities to talk poetry. But today I have to deal with the matter of your visa. Not only for your sake, but also because I have two telegrams to respond to, one from a Congressman and one from a Senator. Your brother in New York is a very effective lobbyist."

"He has to be," I said. "He is the best insurance salesman America has."

We both laughed.

"Will it be easier for us now to talk frankly and honestly to each other?" he asked.

"Absolutely!" I said.

"Would you feel comfortable calling me Alan?"

"If you please," I said.

"Can we be friends?"

"Yes," I said, unequivocally.

"Good! On your visa application you have said you are not and have never been a subversive, a Communist, or a leftist. Is all that true?" Alan asked.

"Yes, it is!"

"And you have never had any political affiliation or persuasion or activity?

"None whatsoever," I said. "The only thing remotely resembling any political activity is what I have had to do for the Savak in the past two years, not because I wanted to, but because they told me I had to, and because my father told me to cooperate with them."

"And what is that?"

"They would not let me enroll in the University or get a passport, unless I agreed to report and inform on other students, on the faculty, or on any political activists who approached me for any reason. They wanted me to infiltrate various underground student organizations."

"And did you do all that?" he asked.

"I tried. I went through the motions. Unfortunately, the only people who were dumb enough to approach me were other Savak agents, whom I reported. Besides, any organization that I could infiltrate, Savak wouldn't have to worry about."

"If you did all they asked you to do, then why is the Savak unwilling to give you a clearance?"

"But they deny that. They say they have given the Consulate a visa clearance for me. They say it is the Consulate that doesn't want me to go to the United States."

"Did the Colonel say why the Consulate does not want you to go to the United States?"

"He said it is because of the rumors about the death of my brother Alex. That I may become a source and a witness to confirm those rumors.

"How did your brother Alex die?" the Consul asked.

"Do you really want me to tell you?"

"Yes, if you please."

"Tell you as Alan Dugan, my friend, or as the Honorable Mr. Dugan, the Consul of the United States of America?"

"As Alan Dugan, your friend," he said.

"According to the official reports, my brother died in a car accident."

"And according to the unofficial reports?"

"According to the unofficial reports, he drowned in a river. That is, he drowned in a metaphoric sense."

"How could you drown in a metaphoric sense?"

"He had forgot to take his arms and legs with him, to swim with, when he jumped into the river. And he was dead before he jumped in, anyway."

"Let me see whether I get your meaning correctly. You mean someone tortured your brother to death, mutilated his body, and then threw the mutilated body in a river, to make it look like he had drowned?"

"No, to make it look like he had been killed in a car accident."

"But how could a drowned man look like he had been killed in a car accident?"

"The State Coroner never addressed that question. But he did officially certify that my brother had been killed in a car accident."

"What did the body look like?"

"There was no body. We were ordered to publicly confirm and advertise the cause of death as car accident, and then bury an empty coffin with pomp and ceremony, and with full press coverage."

"So, if there was no body, how can you tell that he was tortured to death and mutilated and the mutilated body was thrown into a river?"

"Underground papers reported it that way."

"But Savak says those are rumors, fabricated by Communists, and published in illegal Communist papers"

"They might have been rumors to me too," I said, "until one day nearly three years ago, when I was taken away from my father's house in a military Jeep, blindfolded, and taken down to a Savak dungeon for questioning. I sat in a steamy Savak basement for two or three hours, while a Savak lieutenant colonel in uniform and three torturers, took pride in giving me minute details of how they had tortured and mutilated my brother to death. Their account confirmed every detail of the reports given in the underground papers and more."

"Why would the Savak want to tell you those details?"

"To scare me, so that I would tell them whatever I might know about my brother's friends, and help them round up those who they believed were still in hiding."

"Would it be too painful for you to repeat to me those details about your brother's torture and mutilation?" Alan asked.

"At this time," I said, "they would probably be more painful to you than to me. I have lived with them for nearly three years now. If you wish, I will repeat them for you. But I warn you, when I first heard them I threw up. And I kept throwing up."

"Can you give me a brief idea?" Alan asked.

"Yes," I said. "They had starved him, beaten him up, broken his jaw, smashed his teeth, repeatedly raped him, impaled him on a bottle for long hours, burned cigarette holes into his flesh, and then sawed off his limbs with a bucksaw until he was dead. This is where they mercifully stopped their story, because I was throwing up. The rest of it I have by rumor, by third party testimony, by the underground paper reports, that they defaced him beyond recognition and threw the defaced body in a river, where it was allegedly fished out by the underground organizations."

Now it was Alan who looked dazed. His face was pale.

"Have I shocked you now?" I asked. "If I have, I am sorry."

"Don't be sorry," he said, reaching over and touching my hand. "I, too, had to know. I was prepared to take the risk of throwing up, even though he wasn't my brother."

"Then you might also want to know that not only they threatened to do all that to me, but to my father as well, the Chief Justice of the country."

"What was the lieutenant colonel's name?" he asked.

"I never knew," I said. "His three accomplices, the men who had personally carried out the torture, he introduced as *Doctors* Hosseini, Azodi, and Azizi. But I am sure those are not their real names."

"Would you recognize them, if you saw them again?"

"Anywhere, any time," I said. "Down to their handlebar mustaches, the gold caps of their teeth, their missing teeth, their lascivious winks, and their lecherous smiles. Until I began throwing up, I spent time painfully studying their faces. I was desperately trying to determine where on the ladder of human evolution I was related to them."

"Was your brother a Communist?" he asked.

"I don't know," I said. "I never heard him give his politics a name. I know he did not believe in the Communist Tudeh Party, or in the Stalinist Russia. He talked about a vision of a just world, where people would not be hungry, or cold, or oppressed. He was against tyranny, in any form, and anywhere. I know nothing about the armed group the Savak says he was leading. I had never known him to possess a firearm. I had never known him to use a firearm. Now, of course, every group has appropriated him as one of them. The Communists, the Socialists, the Nationalists, the Fedayin, the Mujahedeen. He wasn't related to any of the groups who are embracing him now, as far as I know."

"Did you approve of what he did?" he asked.

"I don't know what he did," I said. "The Savak says his group attacked gendarmerie stations. I don't know that. That's what they say. No courtroom testimony said that. No judge or jury said that. The brother I know was a young idealist, believing in a possibly impossible Utopia, but devoted to what he believed. Dogmatic and doctrinaire, maybe. But an idealist, nevertheless."

"Did you approve of his politics?"

"I didn't really know his politics well. I probably would not have approved of his methods. His ideal world had little room for poetry. It was too obsessed with bread. And maybe he was too optimistic about attaining his Utopia. He underestimated the psychological, the human weakness, the human potential for beastliness. I tried to get him to read Shakespeare's historical plays, to see how ends became corrupted through means, how champions of democracy became the new tyrants. But he said that was literature, and for him literature had little to do with the real world."

"Was he a Marxist?" he asked.

"I am not sure," I said. "At first, maybe. But probably not later. He had read Marx. He had his books. If he was a Marxist, he was probably a very modified Marxist. He was much less dogmatic than the Marxists I have known. He was probably some kind of a Socialist."

"Did you approve of him?" he asked.

"I loved him," I said. "And I know one thing. Whatever he was guilty of doing, no matter how misled, could not have possibly deserved those four animals he spent the last weeks of his life with. Whatever he did, could not have possibly deserved what they did to him. That much I am certain of. I would not have minded any sentence they might have given him in a court of law. I would not have minded it if a judge had sent him to the gallows or to the firing squad, after a proper trial, and with no torture. And my father could have lived with that, too."

"Have you talked to anyone about your brother's case?" Alan asked.

"No," I said. "To what purpose? I haven't talked to anybody, except for my father. Even my mother doesn't know what happened to Alex. Even my brother Cyrus in America doesn't know what happened to Alex."

"Have you talked to anybody in your judicial system?" he asked.

"Are you kidding? My father is the Chief Justice. I have talked to him. Or rather he has talked to me. He knows. He knew it before I did."

"And what has he done about it? Has he talked to anyone else?"

"He tried to save the life of my brother when he was being tortured. But it was useless. He knows that when it comes to dealing with the Savak and the Army, the Chief Justice is a joke, the Ministry of Justice is a joke, justice itself is a joke. He hasn't talked to anybody since, not only because he is under official orders not to do so, but because he doesn't see any use in it, either. All he wishes for now is death. And the only thing that has kept him alive this long, is his wish to see me safely out of this country, before he dies."

Alan stood up and turned to the window. He stood there in silence for a long time.

"Are you familiar with Tennessee Williams' *The Night of the Iguana?*" he finally asked, in a sad gentle voice.

"Yes," I said. "Quite familiar."

"What was the name of that defrocked priest who was gathering evidence of man's inhumanity against God?" he asked.

"Shannon. Reverend L. T. Shannon. And he claimed that he was not defrocked, that he was only locked out of his church by his own congregation."

"Yes. He also felt like dying, didn't he?. Well, that's the way I feel at this moment. Do you ever feel that way?"

"Quite often!" I said. "That's exactly the way I felt when I heard what they had done to Alex, that is, after I stopped throwing up. But you know, there is also an unhealthy part of me that doesn't want to die, that wants to stick around maybe a few thousand years, to see how the world turns out."

Alan turned around and looked at me with a gentle sad smile.

"You think it might get any better?" he asked.

"I don't know," I said. "That's what I want to find out. You think it could get any worse?"

"You know," he said, "before I came here, I was posted in a Latin American country. I won't give you the name. Once I saw a man thrown out of the third story of a security police building over live wire. I don't mind telling you that I also threw up. And I kept throwing up. I then asked to be transferred, because I could no longer take it there. I asked to come here, naively hoping that it would be a little bit better here. We consular officers don't always know all the dirty business that goes on around us. And to think that we support these governments, in the name of democracy, in the name of fighting Communism! Could the people we are fighting do possibly worse than these people we support?"

"My father would be delighted to hear you say that," I said. "That is what he always says. You know, he is a great believer in Constitutional Democracy. He admires your Constitution. He is always talking about the First Amendment and the Fifth Amendment to the American Constitution. Listening to him, you wonder whether he is the Chief Justice in America or here."

"I am a believer in our Constitution, too!" said Alan. "But at this moment I can almost see Thomas Jefferson turning over in his grave. And I can hear Toynbee's words, that when we adopt the methods of our enemy, our enemy has conquered us."

"Do Americans know what their Government supports abroad?" I asked.

"Interesting question. There are those who know and condone. There are those who don't know and condone. There are those who know and don't care. There are those who don't know and don't care. And there are those who know and try to fight it and do not succeed. These last ones are still dreaming Jefferson's dream. Have you read any Jefferson?"

"No," I said. "But my father has a shelf full of his works. He greatly admires him. He says when he speaks of America, he speaks of Thomas Jefferson's America. It is to Thomas Jefferson's America he wants to send me."

"Your father is an enlightened man! You should read Jefferson," he said. "Sometimes I wonder how far we have strayed from his dream of America."

"So the jungle doesn't end at the American border?" I asked.

"No, unfortunately not!" said Alan. "The jungle extends everywhere. The only difference is that in America, the jungle is a patchwork, interspersed with small isolated colonies of the saved. Out of those colonies come men like Thoreau, Hawthorne, Melville, Whitman. 'Isolatos,' Melville called them then, and isolatos we still are. In America they let you get out of the jungle and stay out, if you really don't have the killer instinct, if you really want to go vegetarian, but only if you don't try to stop the jungle, to do something to stop it. You won't catch any big games that way. But then, if you are a vegetarian, you don't need big game."

"And if you try to stop the jungle?" I asked.

"Then they crush you," he said.

"And are you a vegetarian, Alan?" I asked. "Or are you after the big game?"

"Funny you should ask that," he said. "I had been in the big game hunt without even realizing it. You live in a dream for a long time, and then you wake up in a nightmare. You dream of the ideals of the Jeffersonian democracy and you wake up in the nightmare of social Darwinism. You eventually realize that your life has been a paradox, that you have wanted to be a vegetarian and still catch the big game, become an ambassador, the Secretary of State, the President. But to stay in the big game hunt, you have to have the killer instinct. There is no room for vegetarians there.

"The toughest revelation comes, when you face the fact that even though you have not been doing the killing yourself, you have been eating the others' kill, neatly packaged and put on the supermarket shelf for you; when you realize that until you have weaned yourself from those neat convenient packages, you are still part of the world of killers. For years, I had thought that as long as I had given up on the big jobs, as long as I was not doing the dirty work that was going on all around me, I was clean, I was home scot-free. I am just a Consul, I said to myself. I am a poet at heart. I am a vegetarian. Latin America opened my eyes. Here I fully woke up. I may be the guy who tends the mules in the big game hunt. But that makes me as much a part of the world of killers as the guy who pulls the trigger."

"So the Savak Colonel wasn't really lying," I said.

"Let's say he wasn't totally lying," Alan said. "Yes, we do pass the buck back and forth. My ambassador is as afraid of you ending up in front of the Senate of the United States, testifying about your brother, as those Savak colonels and generals are. If that happens, somebody back in the States will have my ambassador's head, and the Shah here, will have the head of those colonels and generals."

"So, what do we do?" I asked.

"Nothing," Alan said. "Everybody lies. Everybody passes the buck. We make you the guilty party. Your brother has not been killed under torture by this 'democratic government' we support. It is all Communist propaganda. And you, too, are part of that Communist propaganda. We pile the sins of your brother, whatever they were, on your head. That way nobody gets hurt."

"Great!" I said. "Let's go for it. Pass me the cup!"

"But," said Alan, "there is a new twist in the plot. We have to deal with your brother in America, who as a citizen can make noise. He has already made some noise, even though he himself doesn't know what the stakes are. He has already been able to get two telegrams to my ambassador, from a Senator and a Congressman, and not from Delaware, but from the State of New York. Not form letters either, mind you, but personal telegrams, indicating that they have more than a routine interest in the case of your visa."

"Now what do we do?" I asked excitedly, feeling like Dr. Watson playing the straight man to Alan's Sherlock Holmes.

"Either we lie through our teeth to everybody," said Alan, "including the Senator and the Congressman, make you a totally dangerous and subversive villain, and keep you out of the United States, so that we won't run the risk of having unfriendly American groups getting hold of you, and using you for propaganda against the government here, and against our Administration there."

"Or," I said, mischievously.

"Or," echoed Alan, "the Savak can get rid of you here, another car accident, which means they would also have to get rid of the sick old Chief Justice, who might not stand for the disappearance of a second son. That, of course, would be an internal matter for your government and would not really concern us. But then there would be more noise from your brother in America and his friends, which *would* concern us.

"Or, we give you a visa on the promise that you will never say a word about the whole thing in the United States. And how could we then guarantee your compliance?"

"All you have is the word of a traitor's brother, as Colonel Sobhani would put it," I said with amusement.

"Or," said Alan again, as if he had not heard my interruption, "we just give you a visa and take our chances with the liberal Senators and Congressmen and the Amnesty International and all the liberal and leftist groups in the United States, who want to see us drop our support of the Shah."

"So, which one is it gonna be?" I asked.

"Are you asking me, or are you asking my ambassador?"

"Whom should I ask?" I said.

"Yours is a big case now. The decision will be made by the ambassador, who I am now sure knew the whole dirty business all along. He would rather keep you here and tell the Senator and the Congressman that you are a dangerous subversive and a Communist. And even if he lets us give you a visa, then the Savak will find other excuses to hold you back, or to get rid of you, altogether, which would again be an internal matter for your government and no concern of ours."

"So," I said, "it seems the only purpose of my coming here was your education and mine. And now we can both head back for the jungle with clear conscience."

"Not so fast!" said Alan. He stood there looking silently out of the window for a long time.

"I don't know about you," he said finally, "but I can't. You know, the American Indians had a war cry when they went into battle. 'It's a good day to die,' they would say. And for them often it was exactly that. You know, to me, the saddest and the most shameful page of our history is what we did to the American Indians. That is even sadder and more shameful than what we did to the black slaves. When I feel I need courage, I think of those Indians and say to myself, 'It's a good day to die.'"

He turned around and looked at me with clear blue eyes. I had never seen eyes that clear and that blue. I did not want to interrupt him. I knew he was not finished making his point.

"My wife comes from a little Iowa town called Keokuk," he continued. "It has less than ten thousand population. It's the kind of town where they roll up the sidewalks at night. My father-in-law has a corn processing plant there. He always tells me that when I retire from the State Department, after I have been an ambassador and everything, I can retire there and be the manager of his plant. I don't think he ever thought I would take him up on his offer. He thought of it as a family joke. But this morning I feel like saying, 'It's a good day to retire,' and go to Keokuk, Iowa, and become the manager of a corn-processing plant. And the last official act of this Consul of the United States is that you will have a visa to enter Thomas Jefferson's America.

"I may be the guy who tends the mules, but I am still the Consul of these United States. And I am satisfied that you deserve an American visa and a chance to look for a place for yourself in Jefferson's America, where you would not have to be ashamed of being human. And if my ambassador tries to overrule me, or if they try to stop you from leaving this country, or if they try to make you disappear, it will be I who will be testifying before the Senate of the United States. Then, let them try to arrange a car accident for me too."

"Well," I said, "it seems like I might have my Waterloo, after all. But with you in Keokuk, and me in Waterloo, you think Ioway can take all the vegetarians headed that way?"

"Why not?" he said. "There is enough corn in Iowa. We are the bread basket of the world."

"Isn't it funny," he added after a moment, as he was putting his seal on my passport, "that with all the pain that goes with our being human, we still manage to get our laughs?"

PART FOUR

CHAPTER ELEVEN

Waterloo, Iowa
Saturday, January 14, 1984
1:30 a.m.

Uncle J. just called; from Paris. He wanted to know what my telegram to Tehran about postponing my mother's funeral meant. He had already taken care of things, he said, when my telegram arrived and created a confusion. Uncle J. is a man who takes care of things. Everything. We depend on him.

He said his "boys" in Tehran had already taken care of things, when my telegram arrived and created a confusion. Mind you, Uncle J. doesn't take care of things himself. His "boys" do that. They are most reliable. They have to be. Uncle J. depends on them. We all depend on them. Somebody in the family dies. The word gets to Uncle J. Uncle J. gives the word. And his "boys" see to it that the dead man gets a proper funeral and a proper headstone, and that his widow and orphans get some ready cash to tide them over, until things are settled. He is a generous man, my Uncle J. is. And his "boys" are everywhere: Tehran, Paris, London, Istanbul, Hamburg, New York, Riyadh, Addis Ababa, Kuwait, Honk Kong, Kuala Lumpur.

He is rarely at the funerals himself. But his wreaths always arrive on time, in one of his Mercedeses, whether he is in them or not. He has a Mercedes in every town. He has great faith in Mercedes. I have never known him to drive anything else. I have never known him to drive a rented car or ride in a cab. Wherever he jetsets to, a Mercedes is waiting for him. If it is a town where he doesn't keep a Mercedes, his boys see to it that one is waiting for him, anyway. All his boys have Mercedeses. They are very well paid and loyal. They wouldn't dream of quitting him or working for anybody else. I have never known any of them who has done it. They treat Uncle J. like their own father.

I have known nobody that Uncle J. has ever fired. Well, almost nobody. There was one man, a parking lot attendant who worked for his company in Tehran. He apparently was not very reliable. Sometimes, he might disappear for fifteen minutes without an explanation. Now, that's one thing Uncle J. cannot comprehend, doing things without an explanation. To him everything is explainable, or should be. There are no mysteries in life. So, if something cannot be explained, somebody is at fault. People who have unexplainable things cannot be relied upon. So, the parking lot attendant "had to be let go." That's the way Uncle J. is. He would never fire any one. He would just "let them go." He would feel bad doing it any other way. He would feel guilty. And to show you how generous he is, he called the man up, gave him a thousand-toman bill, and told him that he was really sorry, but he "had to let him go."

The man was confused. He did not know what was happening. But luckily for him, and for Uncle J., he was very happy to see that thousand-toman bill in his hands. His face beamed with happiness, he shook Uncle J.'s hand that was offered in a gesture of farewell, bowed way down with gratitude, and left. He seemed glad to have a thousand tomans in his pocket and nothing to do for a while. He was that type of man. He would probably loaf around for a few weeks, eat high on the hog, and be happy, not worrying about a thing, until his money ran out. That is why he was unreliable. That is why he "had to be let go." He was not appreciative of what he had, a regular job, a good salary, paid vacation, sick leave, bonuses and tips. And he was not one bit worried about losing it all. You cannot depend on a man who does not worry about losing his job, who does not worry about or plan for the future, as long as he has enough spending money for a few weeks. That is the kind of man Uncle J. could not abide.

He suspected that the man would realize what an opportunity in life he had missed, as soon as he was broke, and then would return to ask for his old job. Of course, it would be too late then. At the time of "letting him go," Uncle J. was ready to do some explaining, telling the man that maybe he was not happy there, that maybe this was not the right job for him, that maybe he would rather work for someone else, someone not as demanding about time, about reliability, about loyalty. He wouldn't use the word "loyalty," of course. He might not even think it. But to him loyalty and reliability were almost the same thing.

If you did not worry about losing your job, you could not have loyalty to it. If you did not have loyalty to your job, you could not have loyalty to your employer. And, of course, the better your job and your pay was, the more loyalty you felt. Uncle J. didn't consciously think all this; he instinctively knew it. Only someone who planned his life well ahead, who knew what he wanted to do and where he wanted to work, for the next so many years, could be trusted. That was the kind of man with whom you could have an accommodation, an understanding, that if you were kind and generous to him, he would be loyal to you, indefinitely, until he retired, or until he died.

That is why Uncle J.'s companies all over the world had the most generous fringe benefits and pension plans. In Tehran, he set up pension plans and life insurance programs for his employees, long before anybody had heard of such things. A private company having a pension plan? Pension was something a government paid, if you had worked for it for thirty years. And life insurance? Somebody paying somebody just because you died? Unheard of. It was an act of God. Allah giveth, Allah taketh away. Making money out of an act of God? Incredible!

But, of course, Uncle J. was a man well ahead of his time, even before he was exposed to all those Western ideas from his parent companies. He saw physical things almost metaphysically. His emphasis on reliability, for example, did not stop with death. To be reliable, a man had to be able to plan his future even after death. There had to be guarantees. Hence, life insurance. In short, how could you depend on a man who could not depend on you, even after death? Of course, Uncle J. never really figured on any of his employees dying on him; that is, before they retired. For him, even death had to happen in an orderly and predictable fashion, allowing him time to plan for it in advance. He could not forgive people who died on him suddenly. This, possibly, had to do with his mother having died on him suddenly, when he was a child of ten. But that is another story.

Whatever the reason, he could never forgive people who died suddenly, without a notice, say, in a car accident. That always implied carelessness on their part, even if the accident was not their fault. They should have driven more slowly. They should have driven more "defensively." He was a great believer in "defensive" driving. You could understand that feeling in a man who had driven for thirty years in cities such as Tehran, Ankara, Istanbul, Rome, Paris, Tokyo, and New York, without ever being in a car accident. That's my Uncle J. And how could you help but admire such a man?

Another thing about Uncle J., he could never trust a man past the age of thirty, who was not married. Not that he was a puritan about sexual morality. Nor did he have any known religious convictions that might explain his great belief in the institution of marriage. This, again, aside from the fact that he himself had married at age thirty, had to do with his ideas of order. Marriage was another ingredient in a well-planned life. It gave things an aura of predictability. You could depend more on a married man, you could foresee his moves better, you could count on his needs, and you even had a better excuse to be generous to him.

In his subtle, unconscious way, he was always pressuring his employees to get married and to stay married. In conversations with his unmarried employees, quite unawares, he would be always making references to "when you are married and settled, etc." With his married employees, he was always considerate enough to ask about their wives and families. He would never miss an opportunity to endear himself by doing them small favors, by sending the wives small gifts. If a couple wanted to separate or divorce, he was always against the one who wanted out. And he would make it known. He never trusted a man who had divorced his wife. A woman divorcing her husband, he considered unthinkable. Everyone knew that even the announcement of an intended marriage was an invitation for Uncle J.'s favors. Handsome wedding gifts from him were a certainty, whether he attended the wedding or not. The unmarried people working for Uncle J., on the other hand, always felt that they were missing out on something, that they were being shortchanged, that they were not favored.

But to get back to our young parking lot attendant, and to show you what a keen insight Uncle J. had, the man returned three weeks later, broke and repentant, looking for a job. Obviously, there were no jobs for him. He asked to see Uncle J. Now, you would expect that a company president as important and as busy as Uncle J. was, would have no time to see a parking lot attendant, whom he had personally fired only three weeks earlier, especially when he had no intention of offering him another job. But that is not my Uncle J.

He saw the man, not because he has an aversion to being disliked, although that he does, and not because he needs to be liked, although that he does, too. He saw the man, because it did not occur to him not to see him. You should know something about my Uncle J. He is the type of man who, when checking into a five-star hotel, not only tips handsomely, the doorkeeper and the porter and the bell captain and the bellhop, but shakes hands with every one of them, giving them the distinct feeling that they are his friends and equals, that they have just done him a great personal favor that he will not forget. He wants them to remember him, and he hopes to remember them, next time when he comes around.

He is full of such personal touches. And what is more, these touches come to him naturally, with no ostentation or showmanship. So, it was quite natural for him to see the young man for a few minutes, express regret that his old job was filled, and that there were no other jobs to offer him at the time. Yes, he said, if there were any openings in future for a parking lot attendant, he would think of him. But, obviously, that was not a promise. His obligations to the man were finished and done with. This was simply a matter of being polite and pleasant. Uncle J. was nothing if not always polite and pleasant. No one had ever heard him utter an unpleasant or impolite word, not even when he was angry. But then no one had ever seen Uncle J. angry.

At times he had been seen getting pale, awfully pale, usually when his wife, in a fit of rage, had called him every dirty name in the book. But even then, after he had swallowed hard once or twice, and had allowed the color to return to his face, he would amaze every one by showing what a cool head he had. He would make an utterance that would send his shrewish wife up the wall; some comment such as, "My dear, you are being quite unreasonable again," or "There is no point arguing with you when you are in one of your moods." And then, he would surprise whoever was a witness to the indignity put on him, by smiling pleasantly and saying, "I was warned before I married her that she was the moody type." If his children reported to him some disgustingly abominable conduct on the part of someone they knew, something that would have sent any father into a fit of rage, my Uncle J.'s response would be, "Obviously, these are not the kind of people we should associate with."

So, when Uncle J. had said to the young man that, yes, he would "think of him," every one in the room, including the man himself, had taken it for what it was, a non-promise, a mere civility. What the young man did not know was, that if he ever returned in future with some new facts about himself, indicating that he had changed, say, that he was married, that he had a child, that he realized that his past life had been irresponsible, unreliable, unpredictable, wasteful, he might still have a chance with my Uncle J. Uncle J. believed in the perfectibility of man. But he was not about to give the young man a clue as to how to go about correcting a past mistake. That wouldn't do. To get the credit, the man had to do it on his own.

He had had his chance, three weeks ago, to ask for an explanation, and he had missed it, being pleased to accept a mere trifle, a tiny separation bonus, a poor exchange for a lifelong employment. Uncle J. would have been only too glad to give him a piece of advice then, about his character and demeanor. He might have even agreed to keep him on, a while longer, on probation, if he promised to improve himself. In fact, Uncle J. enjoyed giving advice and was flattered when his advice was asked for. But, if his advice was ever not heeded, or met an argument, he would suddenly clam up and become impervious. And never again that person would have the favor of his counsel.

Anyway, to get back to Uncle J.'s telephone call, my telegram asking that my mother's funeral be postponed until I arrived, or until they heard from me otherwise, had confused Uncle J.'s boys. They were not used to getting instructions from the likes of me, in fact from anybody other than Uncle J.; especially instructions that contradicted his. They had called him from Tehran, asking for further instructions. Mine obviously were not good enough. I had no standing with them, son or no son. Their boss had told them to bury a dead woman, and that was exactly what they were going to do, unless they heard otherwise from him. It might have seemed to them quite ungrateful of me, to try to countermand Uncle J.'s orders, instead of calling him in Paris or London or Tokyo, or wherever he happened to be at the moment, to thank him. Nobody, but nobody, countermanded Uncle J.'s orders.

The purpose of Uncle J.'s call was really to "understand" me. Uncle J. was a good one for "understanding" people. It was incomprehensible for him that I should even be considering going back to Tehran at this time, the funeral notwithstanding. No one in his right mind would do that. Didn't I know what was happening there? Hadn't I been following the news? There were more men hanging from the trees than fruits. They were shooting people for crossing the street. They were whipping people in public for smelling of beer. They were executing people for smoking during the fasting hours in the month of Ramadan. They had just executed a physician for doing that, at a time when physicians were rarer than gold, when all but a handful of them had left the country. They were putting men in jail for wearing ties. They were imprisoning women for having their faces uncovered. They were trying to take the country back to the Dark Ages.

To say nothing of the war with Iraq, about which nothing good could be said. One didn't even have to mention the Iraqis' use of chemical weapons, or the fourteen-year-old boy-soldiers sent running barefoot across the mine fields to clear them. There were more homey horrors at hand. There was a shortage of everything. You had to buy everything on the black market, even toilet paper and kleenex. There was a nine-hundred per cent inflation of the currency. People had to stand in line for hours or days to buy a chicken at extravagant prices. Even on the black market, you had to bribe someone to get what you wanted. The mullahs were running roughshod over everybody and everything. His boys were bribing the butchers to the tune of one-thousand tomans a day, each, to be able to get all the meat they wanted.

Now, what did I expect they would do with me? What did I have to recommend me to them? After fourteen years in America, what was I taking home that would endear me to them? If they whipped people in public for smelling of beer, what would they do to those smelling of whiskey, never mind that I couldn't even find rotgut arak there, let alone whiskey. If they were shooting doctors for smoking, what useful profession I was bringing them to expect a better treatment? Did I intend to read them some of my irreverent poems, that they would no doubt consider sacrilegious. Would I offer to act my Prince Hamlet in their passion plays about the martyrdom of Imam Hussein? They would hang me from the nearest tree.

Was I prepared to be jailed and tortured and hanged as the agent of the Great Satan, or as Alex's brother, whom they probably considered a godless Communist? Was I prepared to die for being the son of the Shah's former Chief Justice, to pay for what they considered my father's crimes, what had happened to Alex notwithstanding? (He wouldn't of course make any reference to my being the nephew of the Shah's former cabinet minister, confidant, and poker partner. Uncle J. did not believe in cluttering details.)

Was I a hand in quoting the *Koran*, did I know my daily prayers, was I a teetotaler, that I thought I could go with impunity into the lion's mouth and come out alive? Were my studies such a resounding success that they would have no choice but to let me return to them after the funeral? And what were my feelings about being drafted immediately and sent to fight a senseless war, along with barefoot thirteen and fourteen year old peasant boys, who had not even been given a proper two-week training in the use of firearms?

Didn't I know all this? Of course I did.

What I had always admired about Uncle J. was his systematic way of thinking and presenting ideas. As he was shooting these questions at me, one, two, three, with an impassive steady voice, I was struck by their orderly and progressive logic, even more than by the justness of their content. With each indisputable reason offered I expected the next, and when it was offered, I could not help admiring Uncle J. for his logical and orderly mind, and admiring myself for having foreseen what was coming. This systematic and logical thinking of Uncle J., no doubt, had its roots in his early Marxist training.

Yes, Uncle J. had been that, a Marxist, a revolutionary, in his younger days, long long ago. But, mind you, he is not an ex-Marxist. He would be greatly offended if you called him an ex-Marxist. If you called him a Marxist, he would equally deny it. At least in public he would. In fact, in public he would avoid any discussions that might touch on his past political leanings. He would avoid any hobnobbing or involvement with any former friend or associate, who was still avowedly a Marxist, a leftist, a revolutionary, or a radical, for the fear of guilt by association. In private, however, if you called him a Marxist, he would not argue with you. Rather, he would be flattered. But, even in private, the only people he would discuss his personal politics with were his fellow non-ex-Marxists, with whom assumptions could be made without having to make definitions explicit. And of these, there were plenty around Uncle J. Some of his "boys" were exactly that.

In such discussions, he would say that he still held the same political convictions as he always had, except that he would no longer act upon them. People like us, he would say, have a split personality. We believe a certain way, but we live a different way. This apparently easily solved the dilemma of being a Marxist in conviction, but a billionaire capitalist in fact. In such a logical system, one apparently could be neither a Marxist, nor an ex-Marxist, nor a capitalist, and still be all of these. It was a new dialectic, in which the opposites were merged in a higher non-truth, which was not a synthesis, but a split duality coexisting in exactly a non-synthesis.

Of course, with Uncle J. one has to be careful not to talk in Hegelian terms. He doesn't like Hegel. He likes Marx. He hasn't read Hegel. He has read Marx. He doesn't know Hegel. He knows Marx. And when you talk dialectics with him, you have to be sure you are not talking Socrates, or Plato, or Hegel, but Marx, or Lenin. For Uncle J., the history of philosophy begins with Marx and ends with Lenin. In fact, Uncle J. is contemptuous of philosophy. He would probably be surprised if you called Marx a philosopher. If you called him, Uncle J., a philosopher, he would dismiss it with a smile, but he would be flattered. He knows that would impress others.

With Uncle J. you have to be very careful what you call him. He is a very touchy man. Aside from the unacceptable Marxist-ex-Marxist-revolutionary-billionaire-capitalist definition, which is not a well-rounded identity, anyway, you are hard put to come up with an acceptable definition of his identity. By education he is an electrical engineer, allowing people to address him with the traditional title of *Mr. Engineer*. But he is so divorced from either engineering or electricity that if you asked him how you change a light bulb he would say you call an electrician. Calling him an engineer is like calling a Catholic priest, who could never father anything, Father.

If you call Uncle J. a millionaire, a multimillionaire, or a billionaire, he would consider it a put-down, without arguing about the factuality of it. Of course, no one, not even his wife, knows exactly how much he is worth. That is a jealously guarded secret. With his wife, he would like to pretend that he is not that rich, merely to discourage her extravagance. On rare occasions, when he does question her extravagance, and immediately retreats under the barrage of insults such as "lowborn, lowbred, miserly, beggarly, upstart, nouveau riche," you hear him sheepishly mumble in protest that his riches are not illicit gains, but the result of hard work. But once the insults start pouring out fast and furious, his concern is no longer with her extravagance, but rather with getting out of harm's way as fast as he can. Even though it is common knowledge that his wife's fits of rage are usually faked and intended to intimidate him, that has never diminished his awe of them, genuine or fake.

If you call Uncle J. an industrialist, he tolerates it. If you call him a businessman, he gets offended. If you call him a merchant, he gets very offended. He couldn't really argue with you that what he does is business, even though what that business is, is not certain. It is import and export. But import and export of what? Well, import and export of anything that needs importing and exporting; anything legal, that is, that word being very loosely interpreted. For example, is bribing a government official to get a contract legal? Well, of course. That is the only way to do business in over half of the world. Is padding the accounts and making payoffs legal? The answer again is, Yes. Do in Rome as Romans do. And remember Marcus Aurelius: "And when I say Rome, I mean the world."

What if what you do is legal in one country and illegal in another? Well, then you go by the laws of the country where it is legal, and do whatever you have to do to circumvent the law in the country where it is illegal. That is the advantage of being a multinational. The concept of law becomes very relative and very dispensable. It is buying where buying is cheap, and selling where selling is expensive. It is marrying in California and divorcing in Las Vegas. It is marrying Catholic and divorcing Unitarian.

People have done that sort of thing ever since time began. States have done it. Churches have done it. Annulling a marriage with six offspring. Who could call that wrong? As long as you did it for Princes only. The excuse? The woman you had married and pumped for the past twenty years, and who had borne you six children, had been originally intended as the bride for your dead brother. Hence, you have been living with her in sin. And the children? Bastards all. When did you find all that out? Oh, you had known it all along. It just started bothering your conscience now. Hence, annulled. Morality is for the poor, who can afford it. And who are the princes today? Well, the Captains of Industry, the Robber Barons, the multinationals. Those who make the laws, those who break the laws.

What about when country A says it is legal to export commodity A to country B, but illegal to export it to countries C and D? Well, you arrange for your boys in country A to export the commodity to country B, while your boys in country B re-export it to country E, and then again re-export it to countries C & D, at even a higher price. Simple high school math. Just as the Prohibition was only good for the bootlegger, legality and illegality in international commerce can only make the businessman richer.

What about the concept of morality in business? Well, Shakespeare defined that once for all time. A merchant, he said, is one who buys cheap and sells dear. And if the average businessman had any qualms about his personal morality, Uncle J. didn't really have to worry about that. All that was so bourgeois. As a split Marxist-capitalist, who still believed in all the precepts of Marxism, but lived by all the precepts of capitalism, he didn't have to worry about any of that. Any business principle would not square with his imagined ideological Marxist identity. Hence, his embarrassment at being called a businessman.

My preferred occupational definition for Uncle J. is a ten-percenter. What is a ten-percenter? Well, someone who gets ten percent. Ten percent of what? Of whatever he buys and sells. What would he buy and sell? Well, anything that paid ten percent. From whom would he buy and to whom would he sell? Well, anybody who paid ten percent. And if you bought and sold the same thing over and over and over, you would get first ten per cent, then twenty, then thirty, then forty, then fifty percent, and so on and so forth. Ten percent was the minimum, and anyway, you counted ten percent at a time.

What laws would you abide by, divine or human? Well, forget about divine laws. How many divisions does the Pope have, asked Stalin? Of course, that was the wrong question. Rather, he should have asked, how many Bulls has the Pope sold lately? Or, how many Vatican banks have been caught at it, again? Before you have divisions, you should have money. If anybody understands business, the Church does. They were selling cardinalships to three-year-old cutthroat princes during the Renaissance. For a price, of course. Always for a price. Even Julius II did it. One cardinalship sold to finance his wars, another to buy marble for Michelangelo.

And human laws? Well, man's judgment is fallible, and his laws are all relative, tied to a time and to a place, which could and should be circumvented. Become a criminal in one country, and you would be a hero in another. Especially, if you were rich. One man's crime is another man's sainthood. Those who made the laws, could break the laws. Those who paid to make the laws, could pay to break the laws. Hence, what personal dictum to follow? Get rich and get rich fast. Get money and you will have power. Get power and you will have money. And, by all means, stay out of jail. There is always an island country to buy.

What about identity? Well, that's another story. Of course, Uncle J. admits that he has a split personality and a split identity. And he says this with such self-congratulatory nonchalance, as if he was talking about a split banana ice-cream. Sir! I would have liked to say to him.

Sir! Your identity is your soul! It is like water in the palms of your hand! The smallest crack, and it drips away, never to be restored again! Something like that. Sir! You would not drink out of a cracked cup. You would not eat out of a cracked plate. Why would you want to walk around with a split identity? The human vessel is not a pot of dirt, that can split and still hold the soul. It is a glass bubble holding a vapor. The smallest crack and it will fly away. It is a balloon full of air. One little pinprick is enough to empty it.

But that is philosophy. And Uncle J. is innocent of philosophy. Or, rather, that is poetry, and Uncle J. is innocent of poetry. Well, that is not quite true. Uncle J. knows all about philosophy. He has read Marx. And Uncle J. knows all about poetry. He got an A in composition in high school forty three years ago. He once memorized Sa'adi's *Orchard*, copied it in longhand, word for word, for high school class assignment. And he got an A for literature, an A for penmanship, and an A for effort. That is another thing Uncle J. is, a master in penmanship. All the relatives ask him to pen a line of Sa'adi's verse for them, to hang in their parlors. He is flattered by that. That is usually good for ten brownie points with him.

To suggest that someone who penned Sa'adi's *Orchard* forty- three years ago does not know literature, that copying verse is not the same as understanding poetry, is sacrilege, to Uncle J. and his family, Aunt Sarah his wife, and his daughters "princesses" Mini and Mo. To say that Sa'adi was really a versifier, a rhetorician, rather than a poet, is heresy. It takes a certain kind of personality not to have read any Hafiz, not to have read any Rumi, and to have read only Sa'adi, to be more exact, to have copied Sa'adi's *Orchard*. And that is the type of personality Uncle J. has. That type is always good in penmanship. That type is always good with money. That type does good and that type does well.

Anyway, you can now see why my type always confuses Uncle J.'s type. Think of it. Here I am. Thirty three years old. I haven't got a pot to piss in, and I am unlikely to ever have a pot to piss in. I haven't finished my education, and I am unlikely to ever finish my education. I am past age thirty, am not married, and I am unlikely to ever get married. I have never planned anything in my life, and am unlikely to ever plan anything in my life. I have read all of Hafiz and all of Rumi, but haven't read much of Sa'adi. I like poetry, but I don't like verse. I understand philosophy, but not logic. And I am an atrocious penman. Compare that with Uncle J., who is so logical, and so systematic, and so orderly, that he probably planned his own being born; and who is a billionaire; and who knows all about philosophy, because he has read Marx; and who knows all about poetry, because he has read Sa'adi's *Orchard*; and who has beautiful penmanship.

Take this phone conversation. How could I sit there for an hour on the long-distance phone from Paris, and agree with the justice of every statement he has made, and the logic of every word he has uttered, and at the end still not know whether I am going to attend my mother's funeral or not? What is it I want to decide on Monday morning that I cannot decide now?

What is it you want to do there for your mother's funeral that my boys cannot do, he asks? Nothing, I admit. What is it that you can do for her now, when she is dead? Nothing, I admit. Have you suddenly got religion, have you suddenly started believing in afterlife, do you believe her soul is watching you from Heaven, and that she would be displeased not to see her son at the funeral? No, I admit. Then why do you want to go there?

I want to go there not for her, but for me, I say. I want to go there not to do something for her, but to do something for me.

And what is it that you would be doing for you, may I ask?

I don't know yet, I say. I don't even know for sure whether I will be going. But if I do decide to go, I will go because I will be doing something for me, and not for her.

That blew Uncle J.'s mind. For the first time in my life I actually heard him get upset. He said he did not know why he bothered to discuss anything with me, why he ever tried "to do for me." That is Uncle J.'s phrase. He "does for people."

I tell you what you will be doing for yourself, he said. That's another thing Uncle J. is good at, telling people what they are doing, instead of letting them find out what they are doing. He doesn't tell you what you should do, mind you. He is not that type. He just tells you what you are doing. Analyzes it for you, if you please. That's another thing he is good at. Analyzing everything for you. Making you *see* what you're doing.

I tell you what you will be doing, he said. You will be getting yourself killed in a hurry. And if that is what you want to do, why not do it right here? Why travel ten thousand miles to kill yourself? Why not do it right where you are and save everybody the trouble? That way everybody can come to your funeral, at least. Just put a bullet in your head. It is easier, faster, cleaner. Don't you agree? You won't be starved, you won't be tortured, you won't be humiliated. You are a proud man, you know. The hardest part won't be when they torture you, but when they humiliate you.

That is probably true. Uncle J. knows how to hurt a man.

Do you want to go start a one-man revolution against the Mullahs, he asked? Hardly that, I said. Do you want to go work with them, work for them? No, I said. Then what do you want to do there? I want to go and see what is going on, I said. Well, I can tell you what's going on, he almost shouted. I can tell you what's going on, much better than you will ever find out on your own. I get a day-to-day report of what's going on, from people who are there, who have always known what's going on, who know what to compare with what. People like me, who have been through it all once or twice before, who have survived it all once or twice before. You won't last there for twenty-four hours. They'll cut you to ribbons.

He was probably right there too. Uncle J. was nothing if not a survivor. And he had been through it all once or twice before. As a young man, he had been a member of the underground Communist Tudeh party. There had not been a more dedicated Marxist-Leninist party member than him. And he had risen up through the ranks fast, to become very important. He was the Party's First Secretary for the oil-rich Province of Khuzestan, which with its massive labor force was one of the most politically important provinces. He had managed to stay out of jail and torture chamber longer than any of his comrades. So much so, that some of his rivals, out of envy or sibling rivalry, had started rumors that he must be in league with the Shah's secret police Savak. Three days only in jail in twenty years of important party work that included the membership of the Executive Committee and the First Secretaryship of the most crucial Provincial Party? Incredible! Nobody was that lucky.

Of course, the rumors were not true. What had helped Uncle J. beat the odds was his system, his methodical application, and his easy-going and charming personality. No doubt he had been lucky, too. He had many friends in all walks of life, and in all ideological camps, not out of any conscious motives of self-interest or self-preservation, but simply because he was a well-liked man, and because he liked to be a well-liked man. He instinctively would not say anything bad about anybody. If he had nothing good to say about you, he would say nothing. Sometimes, when his comrades spoke with heated bitterness about a political adversary, Uncle J. would make a perfectly cool remark such as, "Well, what do you expect from a general?" or "What do you expect from a mullah?" or "Does that kind of behavior in a Savak torturer surprise you?" This would make his comrades throw their hands up in despair. They had nicknamed him "cucumber," for his coolness.

He was as devout a Marxist as any in the party, but he never came across as a fanatic. He did not throw around words such as *bourgeois, petit bourgeois, capitalist, intellectual, lumpen,* as terms of abuse, as many of his friends did, but rather applied them with a kind of scientific objectivity, without any personal animosity or rancor. His most heated political arguments lacked the acrimonious tone common to such disputes, though none of their conviction. It was not unusual for him to end a heated discussion with an adversary on a mild note such as, "Well, obviously we are rooting for different sides." And when somebody added, "Does that mean if your side wins, you won't hang me?" his response would be, "Not at all. It only means I will do it without any hard feelings or personal animosity. But then I am sure you would do the same for me any day." This cool wit endeared him to almost everyone and infuriated some.

More than once, on the way to a secret meeting of the Party, he had got a call from a friend, an acquaintance, an admirer, in the Government camp, warning him to stay away. Often, this meant that the Savak had got wind of the meeting and was about to raid it. Uncle J. would pretend this was a joke, would deny any knowledge of any meeting or party, but immediately would go to work to avert the danger from his comrades. A number of times, when he had failed to warn his comrades in time, and had only managed to save his own skin by not attending, had convinced the Savak that he couldn't be really that important in the party hierarchy. And this had helped keep him out of dungeon and torture chamber. But, it had given ammunition to his detractors, who suspected his complicity with the Savak. A number of times, when he had succeeded to save his comrades, only one step ahead of the raid, had discredited his rivals and confirmed his leadership. Although, it had not kept his more persistently jealous detractors from whispering that those raids were staged by the Savak to increase his credibility.

He had tons of stories of his cool-headed bantering with military provincial governors, police chiefs, military prosecutors, and Savak agents. He knew how to impress them, how not to protest too much, how to throw in a few touching details at the right moment to throw them off the scent. One military governor had once told him contemptuously, upon his arrest: "You don't look like much."

"Did I say I did, General?" He had responded in a bantering tone, and with equal coolness.

"But they say you are the Provincial First Secretary of the Party," the General had protested with excitement.

"Did you ever hear *me* say that, General?" Uncle J. had asked.

The General had admitted, rather reluctantly, that he had never heard him say that.

He had been picked up many times for questioning, at the time of the oil workers' strikes, or during the leftist demonstrations, but he had always succeeded to somehow convince the agents that, although he had some leftist sympathies, the rumors of his being the First Secretary of the Provincial Tudeh party was at best a vicious joke, started by some real smart First Secretary, who was now having a big laugh in a basement hideout at the expense of both him and the Savak.

Once, while being interrogated, he had made an extremely smart move that had not only benefitted him then, but also for years to come. During the questioning, while under a barrage of insults and threats of torture and death, he had calmly noticed that the colonel's hair was too closely cropped for an officer. He had ventured a guess that the man was a very devout Moslem, having just returned from a pilgrimage to Mecca on the Feast of Sacrifice a month earlier, where shaving of the head is part of the ritual. With feigned piety and humility, he had abruptly asked whether the interrogation could be stopped long enough for him to say his late afternoon prayers before the setting of the sun. It had worked like a charm. The colonel had quickly and reverently led him to his own office, lent him his own prayer rug and Imam Hussein's prayer seal and rosary, showed him the Mecca direction, and waited patiently in the other room for him to finish his prayers.

Suspecting that the room might have a one way mirror and a hidden microphone, Uncle J. had shown utmost meticulousness in praying correctly, bowing down and prostrating himself with absolutely correct timing, as if his life depended on it. It did. He even took the risk of praying in a loud whisper, loud enough to pass for the extremely devout, but not so loud as to seem ostentatious, hoping not to make any mistakes, pronouncing his *th's* in the correct Arab fashion, the way the pupils of Koran schools or Madrassah seminarians did.

His suspicion was well founded. There was a one-way mirror and a hidden microphone in the room. The colonel, unsuspecting at first, had begun to harbor some doubts, once he had got over his initial surprise that a godless Communist should ask to say his prayers punctiliously on time, before the sun went down. He had then watched like a hawk and listened like an owl, on the lookout for the slightest telltale sign that someone was trying to pull a fast one on him, already half jubilant about the punishment he would dole out to Uncle J., if he turned out to be a false pilgrim.

First, expecting to witness a silent prayer, the colonel had whispered the prayers under his own breath, to monitor the correct timing of the bows and prostrations, the only way he could tell whether Uncle J. was really praying or just going through the motions. When he had realized that Uncle J. was praying audibly, he had been delighted. Now, there was no way that he could put one over on him. He had leaned back in a comfortable armchair, lightly hitting his officer's pointer against the palm of his left hand, like a mullah in a Koran school watching a pupil recite the daily prayers, ready to pounce on him at the slightest mistake or mispronunciation and beat the daylight out of him.

As he had begun to despair about Uncle J. making any mistakes, as he had heard his pedagogical pronunciation of the Arabic words, especially his *valathalleen's*, as he had watched the concentration on his face, as he had remembered that he had been about to order his torture to begin, when he had asked to pray, his mind had drifted away to the martyrdom of Imam Ali, the Lord of the Faithful, the first Imam, the son-in-law and successor of the Prophet; how he had drunk the nectar of martyrdom while saying his daily prayers; how he had divined that he would be stabbed in the back while praying, but had refused to postpone his prayers; how he had heard the footsteps of the assassins behind his back, but had refused to interrupt his prayers to save himself, his two-edged sword Zolfaghar lying at hand next to the prayer rug, where he was prostrating himself to his God. If anyone was so depraved as to stab Allah's saint, the Prophet's chosen Caliph and successor, in the back, in his prayers, then so much the worse for him, and so much the better for the martyr, who would be dispatched to Heaven instantly.

The colonel had become aware that with all his own piety and devoutness, he had not observed that the time of the afternoon prayers was passing, while this prisoner about to be tortured, possibly killed, had remembered his duty to his God. And even now, he was maintaining his concentration and composure in his prayers, without a hint of being disturbed by what was in store for him, while he himself, the Colonel, the Hajji, who had just returned from his third pilgrimage to Mecca and the House of Allah, instead of taking the prisoner's request as a reminder to say his own prayers before the setting of the sun, sat there watching him like a hawk, hoping to find him false, hoping to catch him at a blunder, so that he could pounce on him and torture him even worse.

And what if he *had* made a blunder? What if he had missed a word here or there? What if he had counted wrong the number of bows and prostrations? Would that be anything to wonder at, with the terror he must have felt, having been driven blindfolded and bundled up on the floor of a military Jeep, to an unknown place, to a windowless dungeon, not knowing whether he would ever see the daylight again, not knowing whether his tortured, mangled, and disfigured body might not be thrown into a river to rot?

The colonel had looked at the pointer in his hand hiding a slender dagger. Was he a Shemr, a Yazid, the assassin of Imam Hussein? Was he the assassin standing behind The Lord of the Faithful Ali's prostrate back, ready to stab him as soon as his prayers were finished, but not a second sooner, so as to deprive him of the privilege of being dispatched to Heaven instantly? And what if the prisoner had not asked to pray? What if he had silently borne his torture, not giving a sign of being a true believer until the end, saying *I witness there is no Allah other than Allah* only at the moment of his death? All these years he had appeased his conscience by telling himself that he only tortured or killed those godless Communists, who were against God, King, and Country. Had he martyred any other faithfuls like this man, who was now kneeling in prayer before Allah, unawares that an assassin's eyes were watching him like a thief, coming between him and his God?

The colonel had suddenly found himself sobbing and shedding tears of repentance. What was he doing there anyway, in a dungeon in the middle of nowhere? Was he getting too old for this kind of work? He had been waiting for his retirement, hoping that he would land a brigadier's star before he retired. But those bastards in the Personnel and in the Joint Chiefs' Office kept giving him the runaround. This was the third year he was promised a brigadier's star and then disappointed. He had paid off those bastards in the Personnel fifty thousand tomans, three times in three years. They kept saying his name had been submitted three times for His Majesty's signature, but had been crossed out each time. And who knew whether they were telling the truth? They just wanted to milk him dry before they delivered. And how much did they think he made on a colonel's salary, to pay them fifty thousand every year. They must know we guys in the Second Department don't make any money on the side. Who would pay us off? These hungry godless Communists, who would die under torture rather than give us the time of day?

But we've got power, they say. Everybody is scared of us, they say. And a lot of good that has done me. They call us spies and SS and Gestapo and what not. Sure they are scared of us. Sure they watch their steps around us. But that isn't helping much with my promotion, is it? They kiss the ass of the general staff and give us colonels the runaround. They milk us for whatever we are worth. And I am not one of those young fancy pants officers of the Imperial Guard, who stand behind the royal princesses' bedrooms with their dicks in their hands, ready to serve on a minute's notice. *They* sure get their promotions fast. They don't even have to finish the War College before they are handed their first, second, and third stars one two three. But here I am, finished War College ten years ago, first in a class of hundred and ten, serving His Majesty in a dungeon for ten years, torturing misled young men. And for what?

I hope His Majesty appreciates the work I do for him. If there is a revolution, I will be the first one to hang from a tree, while His Majesty and the Imperial family will fly to Switzerland or Los Angeles to live happily ever after. God knows how much money they have stashed away in those numbered Swiss bank accounts. Amir said he couldn't believe his eyes when he saw the zeros on those checks. He was the military attaché in Switzerland for two years. He had to do their dirty work. He had to open some of the accounts for them, with fake ID's.

We have to do their dirty work for them. They wouldn't trust anybody but us dumb loyal Second Department officers. And what do we get for it? We are called spies and SS and Gestapo by those fancy pants officers who wear canary-yellow aglets and hang around cabarets and whorehouses. And everybody says we've got power, that those boys in the Personnel wouldn't dare postpone our promotions, that nobody crosses our names off the lists, not even His Majesty. Maybe that's true after we get our second star. But I doubt if I ever see my second star. I doubt if I even see my first star. I will always remain just a colonel, His Majesty's loyal butcher.

The colonel's thoughts were interrupted only when Uncle J. had finished his prayers, had sat down cross-legged and recited a few optional *Say That He Is The One and Only Allah's*, counting them on the colonel's rosary, had kissed the Imam Hussein's prayer seal and rosary three times, before folding them away in the prayer rug and putting them on the top shelf with genuine reverence. The colonel had again been struck by Uncle J.'s extreme piety and had thought that he, expecting the worst, was preparing himself for martyrdom. He had burst into the room, embracing Uncle J., calling him "my son" and "my Moslem brother," kissing him heartily on the cheeks, begging his forgiveness in the name of their common ancestor the Prophet, blessings of Allah be on him and on his descendants, while shedding infantile tears.

Uncle J. had also been overwhelmed and had burst into genuine tears, responding to the colonel's embraces and kisses with equally honest affection. While praying, he had temporarily forgot himself, and forgot that his praying was a sham. He had thought of his dead father and his dead mother, both devout Moslems, both descendants of the Prophet's line. He had remembered his first prayers at age six, standing behind his mother's veiled back, knowing and reciting only the first line of the prayers, *In the name of Allah the Compassionate, the Merciful*, bowing down every time his mother did, and prostrating himself every time she did.

The whole thing had seemed funny to him at first. But after his mother had assured him that this was quite an acceptable method of praying for a boy of six, until he was old enough to learn the whole text of the prayers; and that as long as his heart was in it, he would get the full credit with God, he had begun taking the thing more seriously. Besides, being with his mother, sharing the ritual with her, and seeing how happy this made her, were enough to lend the action a feeling akin to reverence, which he never felt as a true believer. In fact Uncle J. stopped believing in God immediately after his mother's death, when he was only ten years old, as if any religious feelings he had ever felt were directly related to the bond he had had with his mother. If anything, his mother's early death turned him against God, whom he somehow held responsible for it.

When Uncle J. began his sham prayer, he had to stifle a strong inner urge to keep repeating *In the name of Allah the Compassionate, the Merciful*, imitating the motions of a vision of his mother planted three feet ahead of him, in a flowing white polka dot body veil, bowing down and prostrating herself at fixed intervals. He was dragged back to the real world, when he remembered where he was, who was probably watching him from behind a one-way mirror, and what was possibly in store for him once his prayers were finished. As his mind drifted again to his early childhood memories of his mother and his father, what kept him on course and helped him avoid any fatal mistakes, was the harsh discipline of those few years spent in a Koran school in Tabriz, under the mean beady eyes of Mullah Mostafa, and the canings he had got for every little mistake or mispronunciation, especially of the word *valathalleen*.

He had finally become so good in pronouncing that word that he was often called upon by Mullah Mostafa to be a model pupil and an expert witness, for the purpose of instructing the other boys. Every time a boy had stumbled on that word and had got his ration of caning, Mullah Mostafa would turn his face to the blackboard and his tall straight back to the class and shout "Jalaaal!" When he had heard Uncle J. jumping to his feet and saying "Yes, Excellency Mullah!" in a surprised and terrified tone of voice, he would say calmly, "Show him how it is done." Then a comical routine would follow behind the Mullah's still turned back, with Uncle J. and the miscreant boy facing each other in the middle of the classroom, Uncle J. spitting slowly *valathalleen*, and the other boy spitting back *valazalleen*, with each boy in the class quietly whispering the word to himself, before his turn at caning came.

The Mullah would patiently stand there facing the blackboard, squeezing the cane in both hands behind his back, and in full view of the class. He would usually not turn around until the boy had got it right. If by the third round of spitting he had not got it, the Mullah would abruptly turn around with each wrong pronunciation and give him a hard whack on the butt. If by the sixth round he still had not got it, and that rarely ever happened, the boy would get a fresh round of caning, five hits on the left hand, while the right one had hardly stopped hurting. Mullah Mostafa's system was so consistent you could set your clock by it. And maybe that's where Uncle J. learned his methodical ways, his system.

Of course, a good many of the boys in the class, through guilt by association, had started hating Uncle J., as if he was partially responsible for their woes. Maybe he should not have learned to pronounce *valathalleen* as well as he had. But then, they remembered that Uncle J. had been caned often enough before he became the expert. Others would bait him constantly by spitting *valathalleen* in his face, every time they passed him. And when anybody got in an argument or a fight with Uncle J., the handiest insult to throw at him was *Mullah's* pet, even though Uncle J. hardly ever fought anyone, and all things considered, he always had more friends than he had enemies.

Much as Uncle J. had reasons to thank Mullah Mostafa's cane on that day and for many years to come, the credit for that success was not wholly due to that great man. Nor was it all luck that had saved Uncle J.'s skin; nor a brilliant observation alone. Even here there was evidence of Uncle J.'s methodical planning in life. Those brief years of study at the Koran school in Tabriz so many years ago, would not by themselves have been enough to ensure Uncle J.'s flawless performance that day in that Savak dungeon.

Ever since age ten, when he had stopped believing in Islam and in God, he had resisted regression to an earlier state of mind. In the middle school in Tehran, he had fought back an impulse to shine in Arabic courses. In fact he had semi-consciously seen to it that he would do rather poorly in Arabic, so as not to invite the epithet *mullah's son*. That was an abhorred epithet to most middle school boys then, at the end of the Late Shah's reign, who were part of a new intellectual wave discovering Western culture, nihilism, and then Marxism, in that order. Since quite a few of them who were from the provinces had, at one time or another, no matter how briefly, attended the Koran school, and since most of them had seen at least one or two pictures of their fathers or grandfathers in a robe and turban, the customary garb for a great sector of the population before the Constitutional Revolution of 1906, they all felt vulnerable to that epithet.

In his middle thirties, hearing the Muezzin's melodious call while passing a mosque or a minaret, though he had not prayed for over twenty years, Uncle J. would sometimes catch himself mentally repeating the words of the Muezzin. He would then stop and harshly censure himself for not being rid of the dead hand of his regressive past. He would berate himself for being the offspring of generations of mullah-ridden petit bourgeois ancestors and as such not yet a true-blue Marxist revolutionary. But at some point in his life, and he could not exactly fix that point in time, he lost his aversion to Arabic language, to the Muezzin's call to prayer, to the Moslem cantor's chanting at the funerals, and he began again mentally repeating the words of the *Koran*, whenever he heard them. And at some further point, he made a deliberate decision to re-memorize the five daily prayers.

Who knew when they might come handy, considering that eighty per cent of the population, especially in the provinces, were still basically illiterate and deeply religious and superstitious? Who could tell what his kismet was? One day on the run from the Savak, he might have to hide in a robe and turban and pass as a mullah. He could even make a living that way, going from house to house as a cantor, or chant the *Koran* at the funerals, or even act passion play scenes from the martyrdoms at Karbala on the Martyrs' days. That would, indeed, be easy living. If those illiterate mullahs could do it, any idiot could do it. He could preach sermons that would make mullahs turn green with envy, maybe work some Marxism and liberation theology for the masses into them, rubbing in the misery of the poor and the evil of the rich. After all, the whole history of the martyrdom of the Shiite Imams was nothing but a revolutionary struggle against tyranny and corruption and greed. Opium of the masses or not, maybe Marx and Lenin had missed the potential opportunity of using the symbolism of the religious struggle against evil as a tool in modern revolutions.

Of course, Uncle J. was too much of a votary to ever seriously deviate from the orthodox party line or theoretical dogma. In the weekly party Doctrine or Self-criticism classes, he was always the *bon élève*, the exemplary student, the Mullah's pet who could pronounce *valathalleen* even better than the Mullah himself. Even when he became the Mullah, the teacher, the Provincial First Secretary, it hardly ever occurred to him to deviate from the dogma. But maybe because some even older dogma was still operating in the depth of his unconscious, he found enough plausible reasons to go back periodically and re-memorize the daily prayers and the common Koranic phrases. And if he had not done that with an eye on such a day, when he might have vital need to pray, his life that day in that Savak dungeon would not have been worth a spit in the wind.

That afternoon prayer not only saved his skin on that day, but it caused an item to be entered in his Savak file that he was a devout Moslem, and as such unlikely to be or to have ever been a devout Communist, as rumored. Years later, when he jumped camp and joined the Shah's party, that item helped his credibility more than anything else in his thick file. Even when the Shah's regime fell and the Ayatollah's turbaned army took over, Uncle J.'s old Savak file came to his help, as well as "his" old Colonel, now a general, who as a devout Moslem was transferred lock, stock, and barrel, to the Ayatollah's Islamic Secret Police, Savama. If Uncle J. wasn't really a Communist for the Shah's Savak, he couldn't be really a Communist for the Ayatollah's Savama either. But that is getting ahead of the story. Getting back to that prayerful afternoon, from that day on Uncle J. and the Savak Colonel became very good friends, which made his detractors in the party even more suspicious that he was an undercover agent.

Of course, that kind of rumor was nothing to sneeze at. If the party really thought that he was an undercover agent, he could be done away with. It had happened. Uncle J. knew of cases where it had happened. But he also knew that kind of thing would not happen without orders from the highest level of the party, especially if it was a matter of doing away with a Provincial First Secretary. And the party had enough agents in the Army and the Savak to check the files and find out that he was not an undercover agent. Unless somebody in the Savak wanted to do away with him by the hands of the Party itself, in which case they could plant false information in the Savak files. But then, if Savak really thought he was that important, they would do their own dirty work much easier and much faster and get a lot of information out of him under torture besides, they hoped.

CHAPTER TWELVE

Uncle J.'s real test of survivability, however, came a few days before the August 19 Coup in 1953. On August 16 and 17, after the first two coups by the army against Prime Minister Mosaddeq and the Parliament had been foiled, and the Shah had fled to Baghdad, and the Tudeh Party's Central Committee had decided to sit that one out and wait, Uncle J. had a feeling that things would go from bad to worse. He figured that there were more coups to come, and that one of them would succeed. With his reputation in the Khuzestan Province, he had no doubt that he would be one of the first to be killed by the military government. And if they didn't finish him off, his jealous underlings, too eager to succeed him, probably would. It was to Uncle J.'s credit that, even though he knew that his rivals would eliminate him if they had a chance, he would never try to stick it to them first. He treated the rumors of his own being a double agent as an honest mistake on the part of some over-zealous comrades.

It is also possible that Uncle J. was losing his fire for the good fight. He was past the middle of his life, he had been married for several years, and now had an infant child. Whatever it was, on August 16, after the first foiled coup attempt, he put his wife and infant daughter on a TBT night bus for Tehran and waited, marking the time. On August 17, after the second coup had been foiled by the Mosaddeq loyalists, he fled town, dressed in a mullah's robe and turban. He left behind a sealed envelope containing his resignation from his position of the Provincial First Secretary, his membership of the Executive Committee, and the general membership of the Tudeh party, which envelope his eager assistant and arch-rival promptly found and turned to his own advantage. He arrived in Tehran and waited again. On August 19, the hour the fourth military coup succeeded, Uncle J. mailed a letter from the Central Post Office in Tehran to his Savak colonel in Abadan, using the post office box address he had once been given, "just in case he had any information to report." With his methodical knack for not discarding anything, he had kept this address, not knowing why, sure as he was that he would never have any use for it.

He pre-dated his letter by two days, to make it coincide with the time that the news of the Shah's escape to Baghdad had been made public. By mentioning in the letter that he was dropping it in a mailbox, and then having it postmarked two days after the alleged date of the letter in the central post office, he could persuade the Colonel of the correctness of that date. In the letter, he confessed that in his youth he had been misled by Marxism and had joined the Tudeh Party, and that he had remained a member until recently. Then he gave the reasons for his change of heart and his resignation.

As a devout Moslem, he wrote, for years he had been misled to believe that Marxism and Communism were not incompatible with Islam, as they all sought to establish a just and equitable society. But gradually, he had discovered the godless nature of Communism and the enmity it held towards not only Islam but all religions. He had also been misled, he wrote, to believe that the Tudeh Party was independent from the Russian Stalinist line and had as its goal the true political independence of Iran. Little by little, he had begun having his doubts about the Party. But, what had finally revealed their traitorous nature to him was the shameful way in which they had treated the Monarch, the symbol of the country's independence, forcing him to leave the country in disgrace.

Uncle J. had always been a master of rhetoric. Hence, his great admiration for Sa'adi, the master rhetorician of Persian literature's golden age. He knew the importance of the correct tone. In the first draft of his letter, instead of the words "the Monarch," he had written "His Majesty." But he had decided that in the mouth of even a repentant member of the Tudeh Party that would sound false. In the second draft, he had changed the words to "the Shah," but this had sounded lacking proper respect and decorum, especially when one's life was at stake. By the third draft he had got it exactly right: "the Monarch, the symbol of the country's independence." That was exactly the right tone, the right amount of bait, the Colonel's speed. He did not give an address. He only said that he was in hiding, not from the Savak, but from his former comrades, who might try to harm him, fearing that he might divulge any information to the authorities. He would contact the Colonel again, when he knew he was safe from them.

After mailing the letter, he went and hid in the basement apartment of a cousin, along with his wife and infant daughter, letting his beard grow. Now, all he had to do was wait. In time the Savak agents would smell their way out to him, being probably in possession of the names and addresses of all his relatives and friends. They might not look for him for some time, because with the Coup on their hands, they had more urgent fish to fry. Besides, this letter would put their minds to rest about him, for a while. In good time, they would want to find him, get whatever information he might have, and to see whom he could lead them to, especially, if they uncovered some evidence that he was more than a simple misled party member, who had now cried uncle.

For the next few months, Uncle J. managed the best way he could. He found a menial job in some bazaar office for small wages. His boss, probably guessing that he was a Tudeh party member on the run, did not ask any questions or seek any references, being only too glad to hire for pennies a highly qualified engineer, fluent in both English and French, to run his import-export correspondence.

Uncle J.'s situation wasn't unique. The whole country was flooded with high talent on the run. Soon he found out that a whole army of former Oil Company comrades had escaped the Province at the same time he had, and for the same reasons, using him as a model and his barometer as a guide. They searched him out, all looking for a guru. Maybe Uncle J.'s luck would last a few more years and keep their fat out of the fire. Maybe there was some truth to his having connections in the Savak. After all, hadn't he resigned and left in a hurry, just two days before the disaster?

Anyway, now Uncle J. had a little army of former comrades, all looking up to him for guidance and leadership in those times of terror. Old Man Mosaddeq was under house arrest since the triumphant return of the Shah. His top assistants had been jailed and, those who had been free with their tongues about the Royal Family after the Shah's escape, had been summarily executed. Among them only Fatemi, the Foreign Minister, whose wife had been allegedly raped by a gang of soldiers on the night of his arrest after the second Coup attempt, and who had blasted the Shah in strong words publicly the next day, had been severely tortured and had died unrepentant. Karimpoor Shirazi, the outspoken newspaper editor, who had publicly called the Shah's sister a harlot, had been jailed, tortured, and set on fire in a Savak dungeon.

The Parliament had been dissolved under the State of Siege, and those members who had stood with Mosaddeq in the final few days, had been beaten and jailed or worse. Everybody on the Radio talked as if the Constitution of 1906 was dead and buried, and the Shah was once again the Absolute Monarch as in the olden days. Worse, they talked as if the Constitution had never come about, that the Constitutional Monarchy of about fifty years had never happened, that the Constitution had never said anything but that the Shah was the Absolute Ruler, and that the Constitution and the Parliament and Mosaddeq had all been part of a conspiracy by the foreigners and Communists to traitorously limit the absolute powers of the Shah and "weaken" the country. By grace of God, now the Army had foiled these satanic designs and His Imperial Majesty was back on the Peacock Throne, and that was that. And the mullahs, who had once wholeheartedly supported Mosaddeq's National

Front, were now once again in the front, along with a mob of paid thugs and whores, supporting God, King, and Country, i.e., whoever had won the battle, as long as their lands, their tax-exempt status, and their system of raising revenue through tithing remained safe.

There were mass arrests and roundups of Tudeh party members by day, and shootings of young Communists breaking the curfew to write slogans on the walls, by night. The real prize the Savak was after, however, was somewhere else. The Tudeh party had infiltrated the armed forces and the Savak on a large scale and the Savak's priority was to dig out the Army-Savak Organization of the Party. As long as that organization was intact, they could not sleep peacefully. And the usefulness of small-fry party members at this time was limited to what they could reveal under torture that would point the way to the bigger fish. The long held suspicion that some of the members of the Central Committee of the Tudeh Party itself were agents of the British, what Mosaddeq called the "Oily Tudeh faction" versus the "Stalinist Tudeh faction," had now been confirmed.

The evening papers were filled with page after page of "confessions" of ex-Tudeh Communists, admitting their treasons against God, King, and Country, repenting their sins, and begging His Imperial Majesty's forgiveness. As long as those arrested were the young and the small-fry, the Tudeh Party Central Committee stood fast in their order that the members should rather die under torture than sign such "confessions." As bigger and bigger fish were caught, the Central Committee reversed itself overnight and ordered the arrested members to save their skins by signing "confessions," if they must, but not revealing anything else. It was then up to the Savak to decide how much each member knew, how truthful he was, and how far the torture should go before a mere published "confession" would do. Hence the flood in the evening papers of such "confessions," what the language of the street referred to as "crying uncle and eating crap."

That was when Uncle J. and his ex-comrades decided they had waited long enough. They enlisted whatever support they could among their establishment friends, came up with as much bribe money as they could for the Savak generals and colonels, to soften the blow, and then turned themselves in en masse. Uncle J. led the way through his contact with "his Colonel," who was now "his General," after having got his brigadier's star. He wrote to ask whether he could come to Abadan to turn himself in to the General in person, "as one servant of God to another." Uncle J. was the kind of guy who stayed with a winning number, as long as it hadn't stopped winning.

The General agreed. After all, it would be a feather in his cap too, to catch so many "Oil Company" ex-Communists in one swoop. Why should he let the Tehran office get the credit for all those Abadan Communists? If Uncle J. could bring with him the small army of ex-Oil Company engineers he had mentioned, all ready to confess, sign, and sing, maybe there would be a major general's star in it for him.

Uncle J. had also mentioned that they had some money to spend, not for the General of course, who as a true patriot and a devout servant of God, would not hear of a bribe; but to grease the itchy palms in the Savak and army, of those who would not help their own mother without a bribe. This, too, seemed promising. After all, the General had to recoup the two-hundred thousand he had paid in bribes, to get his brigadier's star, and find two-hundred thousand more for his major general's star. Although now that he had got that one star, and with the Second Department sniffing everywhere for any sign of the Tudeh Party's Army Organization, those fancy pants colonels and generals in the Personnel would know better than trying to milk a Second Department Brigadier. Maybe he could get his second star for free.

Uncle J. rode the night bus to Abadan and reported to the designated Savak safe house. From there he was handcuffed and blindfolded and driven in an army Jeep to a destination about an hour away. When his blindfold was removed, he found himself in the familiar room where he had once said his prayers. He was fully prepared to repeat the performance, keeping close track of the time for the prayers, this time having brought his own Imam Hussein's prayer seal and rosary. This was a secret he had not yet shared with any of his comrades, considering the risk of exposure, or the danger of someone else trying the same ruse and blowing his cover. He was finally met by *his General* who, even though somewhat aloof, again gave him a bear-hug, kissed him on the cheeks, and called him his son and his Moslem brother. Uncle J.'s task wasn't really that hard. He signed the form "confession" and gave the names of all his former comrades who were ready and willing to turn themselves in and "pledge cooperation," which was a code name for turning informer. When asked, he also gave other names he knew in the leadership of the Provincial Branch of the Party, figuring that by now they had all been either arrested, or killed, or that they considered Uncle J. a renegade, a traitor, or an actual undercover agent of the Savak. He tried to minimize his own leadership role and maximize the role of his top assistant, the man who had tried to topple him, who had started the rumors about him, and who had in fact been promoted to the rank of the Provincial Secretary after Uncle J.'s resignation.

Resourceful as usual, he concocted a story that even though on the books he was the First Secretary of the Tudeh Party for the Province of Khuzestan, he was really nothing but a simple low-level party member. The real Provincial Secretary was the number two man, and Uncle J.'s only role in the party for years had been to provide a cover for this man, so that he could be free to move around and do the real party work. The story seemed fantastic, but plausible. It explained the absence of Uncle J. from those important party meetings raided, where Uncle J., having been warned by his Establishment friends, had been the only reputed leader missing.

The General took out his pocket *Koran* and asked Uncle J. to put his hand on it and swear that what he said was the truth, and may his soul burn eternally in the deepest hell of the infidels, if he said anything but the truth; a task which Uncle J. performed flawlessly, adding to it a personal touch of his own, to the effect that, "May my ancestor the Prophet, blessings of Allah be on him and his descendants, not intercede in my behalf on the Judgment Day, if I am not telling the whole truth." This impressed the General even more who, as a descendant of the Prophet, had always counted on such an intercession in his own behalf on the Judgment Day. And it furnished another amusing anecdote for Uncle J. and his close friends for years to come.

The next day Uncle J.'s small army of ex-Communists rode the night bus to Abadan and turned themselves in, all repeating his performance, some even vouching that they had known all along that Uncle J. was only a dummy Provincial Secretary, and that the number two man was the one carrying the ball. They all swore on the *Koran*, signed "confessions," "pledged cooperation" with the Savak in every way they could, and paid up whatever money they had brought with them.

With their surrender and nominal "arrest," and the arrest of those few leaders unknown to the Savak until that day, the Tudeh Party's back in Khuzestan was broken. Uncle J. was not worried about being contradicted by his former top assistant. By the time the torturers were finished with him, he would be either dead or ready to confess to anything, including Uncle J.'s version of the story.

The General's report to Tehran, indicating that the Tudeh Party in Khuzestan was finished and done with, and that the former brain trust of the Oil Company's Communist organization was all in custody, ready to sign, sing, and dance, hit the Savak Headquarters like a tornado. The news was relayed up the Savak and Army hierarchy, all the way to the Shah himself, who was impressed. He sent for and personally read the Brigadier General's report, reviewed Uncle J.'s Savak file, and ordered that "the Brigadier and the leader of the Oil Company engineer group" be brought to him at once. The General was ordered to fly to Tehran right away, in an air force jet, with Uncle J. in tow, and be prepared to immediately report to the Saad-Abad Palace.

Uncle J.'s first response, when the excited Brigadier General broke into the room, where he and his friends were kept, was one of fear and confusion. The Brigadier was in a spick-and-span ceremonial uniform, talked in a frenzied state, and barked like a real general, with no hint of familiarity in his face. He curtly told Uncle J. to get ready to leave in fifteen minutes, without saying where he was going. Uncle J.'s friends were even more alarmed. It sounded like real trouble. Maybe Uncle J. had overplayed his hand, or had exaggerated his closeness to the General. Maybe things had misfired and the matters were now out of the Brigadier's hands. Maybe the Brigadier himself was in trouble now, and that meant that their connection, their hope, and their money, were all gone.

Uncle J. was picked up exactly in fifteen minutes, was handcuffed and blindfolded again, and led to what felt like a soft and comfortable sedan. He and the General rode in the back, while a guard rode in the front with the driver. Hardly a word was spoken throughout the long trip, which took almost an hour. They passed through several checkpoints, where Uncle J. could hear the clicking of heels, and could tell that someone was checking ID's. Finally, when his blindfold was removed, he found himself on the air field in an air force base, surrounded by the General, two plainclothes agents wearing sunglasses, and an air force captain. The General was quiet as a mouse, but still in an obviously excited state of mind.

After a few minutes, the captain indicated to the General that everything was in order, and they rushed to a small air force commuter jet ready to take off. One of the agents stayed behind, while the other walked ahead of them, along with the captain. The General was firmly holding on to Uncle J.'s right arm, as if he couldn't trust him out of his reach. Once the agent and the captain were far enough ahead of them, and the other agent was far enough behind, the General, no longer able to contain his excitement, brought his mouth close to Uncle J.'s ear and shouted over the noise of the jet engine, that they were going to have an audience with His Imperial Majesty. "It could mean either my head, or a major general's star. And, remember, if my head goes, your head goes."

Suddenly, Uncle J. felt a deep sense of dread and awe. Many times in his younger days, he had written slogans on the walls in red ocher, denouncing the Shah, while his friends kept a lookout for the police and army curfew patrols. *Death to the Traitorous Shah*, they had all read in large exquisite letters. His friends joked about how Uncle J.'s slogans could be spotted from miles away. He was the only one who took pains in writing his slogans, as if they were penmanship class assignments. His penmanship was so unique, they jeered, that he might as well sign his slogans.

Once in Amjadieh Stadium, during the athletic celebrations on the Shah's birthday, and at the very moment when the Shah had started pinning the medals on the athletes' uniforms, Uncle J. and five hundred party faithfuls sitting on the bleachers across from the Royal Lodge, had begun chanting *Death to the Traitorous Shah!* Dodging the clubs of the policemen and the MP's and the rifle butts of the soldiers immediately attacking them, and running to avoid arrest, they had kept up the chant in an ever-widening circle, waving their fists at the Royal Lodge. At one point, in the midst of fear and confusion and dodging of the clubs and rifle butts, Uncle J. had looked toward the Lodge and caught a glimpse of the Shah in his field marshal's uniform and sunglasses, arrested in the act of pinning a medal on a weight lifter's uniform, looking at the crowd and the commotion with what seemed like surprise and slight irritation.

Except for that one image, everything else about the Shah had always been an abstraction for Uncle J. And now, he was going to meet this abstract entity in person, not as *the traitorous Shah* of the party slogans, not even as *the Shah*, but as *His Imperial Majesty*, who with a snap of his fingers could have him and this mighty Savak brigadier general shot on the spot. And he wasn't going there to receive a medal for athletic prowess, or a commendation for penmanship, but as a "confessed ex-Communist traitor," who could only beg forgiveness by His Majesty's grace. His feeling of dread was like nothing he had ever experienced before. Nor was his feeling of awe. The remotest feeling he had ever had akin to this experience was when, a few years earlier, he had been informed that he would have to go to Tehran to meet a member of the Party's Central Committee. He was never told who the member was, and the meeting had never materialized, anyway.

On the plane the General ordered the two airmen accompanying them to take off Uncle J.'s handcuffs. He told him to act as if he knew nothing about where he was going. And they never spoke again until they reached Tehran. Throughout the trip Uncle J. tried to visualize his audience with the Shah. He felt as if he was reliving his childhood fears in the presence of Mullah Mostafa, or later of the school principal, whenever he was called in for punishment. Although, he had an inkling that he was not being called in for punishment this time. The Shah must have been impressed by something about him and wanted to look him over. Could it have anything to do with his being the brother of the Chief Justice of the Supreme Court?

In Tehran, en route to various Savak and army offices, he was variably cuffed or uncuffed, blindfolded or not, treated like a criminal or a celebrity. The army and Savak generals in Tehran were highly suspicious of the whole affair. They would give their right arms to have a special audience with the Shah, which would mean the high visibility often resulting in fast promotions. If somebody in the Imperial Court liked your smile or the twirl of your mustache, that could make a big difference in your fortunes. Young officers always dreamed of being transferred to the Imperial Guard and fantasized about becoming a Royal Princess's lover. Colonels dreamed of a brigadier's star, every time they got a chance to kiss His Imperial Majesty's hand. The older generals, however, knew that the closer you got to the powerhouse, the faster you could lose your head, too. Never stay too close behind two things, the commander in chief and the mule's kick, was their saying. And yet the way they treated the Brigadier, you could tell they were green with envy. A brand-new brigadier general and a Tudeh Party renegade having a private audience with His Majesty! Unbearable!

At one point a major general had barked at them, "Brigadier! Why isn't this criminal in handcuffs?" To which the Brigadier had clicked his heels in salute and said, "I'll take full responsibility for the prisoner, Excellency General!" He had then whispered in Uncle J.'s ear, "He's green with envy, the pimp! If all goes well, maybe I'll have my second star and his desk, in short order!"

Uncle J. had suddenly experienced a strange feeling, as if the two of them had long been in a kind of conspiracy together. Now his years as the Provincial Secretary of the Tudeh Party seemed ages away. Here he was, still considering himself a devout Marxist at heart, telling himself that everything he had done in the past several months had been tactical maneuvers, rather than ideological changes of direction, in league with a Savak brigadier general who had tortured and killed many of his comrades, on his way to a private audience with *His Imperial Majesty The Traitorous Shah*. It seemed so absurd and yet so real, and even somewhat exciting.

On the final leg of the journey to the Palace the General gave him a few last tips about how he should proceed inside the Imperial Court. He told him of some items in his Savak file, by now probably reviewed by His Imperial Majesty, including the item he had entered, about his being a devout Moslem and as such unlikely to have been a devout Communist. Obviously, the General felt it was in his own interest that this prisoner do well in the audience. The Shah, of course, had the reputation of being a very religious man himself. Uncle J. had watched him once on the television; right after a prime minister had been assassinated by the Devotees of Islam. He had looked weak, haggard, and afraid, obviously trying to appease the more fanatical elements among the clergy.

The Shah had told the people that he led a charmed life. On the eve of his ascension to the throne, he had said, his ancestor the Prophet, blessings of Allah be on him and on his descendants, had visited him in a dream, telling him that he would always protect him from evil and harm. He had then rambled on about an event in his childhood when, making a pilgrimage to Imamzadeh Davood shrine as the Crown Prince, he had fallen off the mule and had been grabbed in midair by a hand from the world of spirits. He had turned to his servant and said, "Did you see that?" And the servant had said, "Yes, Your Imperial Highness! It was the hand of your ancestor the Prophet, blessings of Allah be on him and on his descendants, saving Your Highness from a fall!"

Uncle J. remembered his own exact reaction at that moment. "The son of a bitch!" he had burst out in furious disbelief. "Taking for granted the stupidity and gullibility of the masses. Charmed life, my foot! His ancestor the Prophet!" And then he had fully appreciated Lenin's comment that religion was the opium of the masses.

And now, he was on his way to an audience with this man. He felt less in awe of him, though, of this great King of Kings, as he called himself, remembering how haggard he had looked that night. He, too, smelled of mortality. He, too, had had to lie and cheat and play false and play devout. He too had known fear. He had no more piety than Uncle J. had. He wasn't this gullible old workhorse brigadier general, who said his prayers punctiliously five times a day, and made a pilgrimage to Mecca every other year, with all his shavehead devotion, to store credit with God against the Judgment Day, when angels would measure his good and bad deeds, and when he hoped his ancestor the Prophet, blessings of Allah be on him and on his descendants, would intercede in his behalf.

But this could also mean trouble for him. Had the Shah seen right through him, through all his ploys, his sham prayers, his oath on the Brigadier's *Koran*, the anecdote about his ancestor the Prophet interceding for him on the Judgment Day, his concocted story about being a simple party member, a dummy Provincial Secretary, a cover for the Party's real Provincial Secretary? Was he going to call him in, pull him aside, and whisper in his ear, "Look fellow! You might have fooled that stupid old workhorse brigadier. But you can't pull the wool over my eyes. I have been in this game too long for this amateur bullshit. I have dealt with real pros. What's your real racket? Maybe we can make a deal."

At the gate of the Palace, before he turned him over to the Imperial Guard officers, who treated him as a criminal and the Brigadier as a suspicious outsider, the General warned Uncle J. that he should fall to his knees and kiss His Imperial Majesty's boots, if he knew what was good for his health. And he didn't seem to be speaking metaphorically, either. Nor did it sound like a fatherly advice from one servant of God to another. It sounded very much like an order.

The General whispered to him that His Majesty, despite his Swiss education and his enlightened appearance, was at heart as old-fashioned as the Late Majesty, his father. He liked his hands and feet to be kissed, despite his weak protests on camera, especially when foreign journalists were around. The General had known people who had lost their heads for not kissing His Late Majesty's boots, for having tried to get away with just kissing his hands. And they were ministers, courtiers, and former royalty, not ex-Communist renegades. With this royal son of his, luckily, you could get away with kissing just the hand. But, in the predicament that Uncle J. was, he had better go for the boots.

Few people have ever heard Uncle J. give a thorough account of that audience with the Shah. As he had been inspected and frisked by extremely mean-looking Imperial Guard sergeants, as he had watched the sheepish look on the face of the Savak General, also being inspected and frisked like a common criminal by a Guard captain even after having turned in his revolver, Uncle J. had perceived what a forbidden world he was entering.

They had walked across huge mirrored galleries, with him tightly flanked by two erect, oversized, mustachioed Guard sergeants, each holding a firm grip on one of his arms. When they had first taken away his handcuffs, he had thought that it was a matter of decorum not to have someone in handcuffs in the presence of His Imperial Majesty. But feeling the firm grips of the two oversized sergeants, he had understood the real reason. Handcuffs were not necessary. Once, when he had turned around to look at the General walking behind him, flanked by two Guard captains, his escorts had given a hard jerk to his arms, to let him know that the slightest move out of order would not be tolerated.

He had been stopped at several points and subjected to more questioning and scrutiny. Several foppishly dressed courtiers had asked why Uncle J. was not dressed in a morning coat. Who did he think he was having an audience with, a village chief? Each time the answer had been provided by the Brigadier General, that His Imperial Majesty's orders had been to bring the man to the Palace immediately; that he had been flown in straight from detention in the Savak Headquarters in Abadan; and that there had been no time to prepare a morning coat. The answer had not seemed satisfactory to the courtiers, but it had had to do.

Uncle J. had been given strict instructions about every move he should make in the presence of His Imperial Majesty. He was to watch for quiet signs and hints from his now two civilian escorts in morning coats, to know exactly when to stop, walk, bow down, and finally, throw himself at His Imperial Majesty's feet and kiss his boots. At one point he had felt enraged and made the drastic decision that, come what may, he would not throw himself at His Imperial Majesty's feet and kiss his boots. Whatever it was His Majesty was about to dish out for him, he had to do it without any boot-kissing, thank you. But from the moment he had entered the Imperial audience hall and caught a glimpse of the Shah on his throne at the very far end, surrounded by courtiers and officers standing erectly at attention, he had felt electrified and he had moved like a marionette, in strict response to the signs and hints of his civilian escorts.

Having bowed low on entering the hall and several times across the hall, in sync with his civilian escorts, while literally feeling the breath of the sergeants walking behind him down his neck, he finally had been given the sign to proceed the last few steps on his own, to throw himself at His Majesty's feet and kiss his boots. At that moment, he had proceeded without any hesitation, resistance, or will of his, as if glad to follow signs rather than think on his own, and had thrown himself at the Shah's feet, kissing his shiny black boots smelling of new leather, fighting back a vague and confused emotion akin to tears, glad that it was all over and done with. He had again recalled, as if in a dream, the Shah's faraway face on that day in Amjadieh Stadium, when he had shouted an abstract slogan at an abstract man, and had wondered.

After a few minutes, the Shah had coldly said "Get up!" and Uncle J. had felt the firm grip of the same military hands on his arms, lifting him to his feet and walking him backwards from the throne. He had caught a glimpse of "his General" standing at attention a few feet away, among erect Guard officers and civilians in morning coats. He had stood straight and looked at the Shah, who was scrutinizing him with what seemed like a mixture of curiosity and contempt.

"So," the Shah had said finally, "this is what a Provincial First Secretary of the Tudeh Party looks like, who also happens to be the brother of Our Chief Justice!"

Uncle J. had remained silent, standing at attention, not knowing what to say. He spotted one of his two mentors, now standing behind the throne. There was no help coming from him. His tutoring was apparently over. Now, sink or swim, he was on his own. Maybe no answer was called for. Anyway, it was safer to remain silent. The stakes were extremely high.

"You seem to be an interesting man, Mr. Engineer!" the Shah said sarcastically. "We have read your Savak file. We are not sure We believe all that is written in it. But you must be a very shrewd man, if you were a party member for twenty years and went to jail only for three days. How did you manage that? How did you escape long prison and torture? Maybe We should re-organize Our Savak, get smarter people to deal with the likes of you."

The Shah looked at the Savak General to gauge the effect of that last comment on him. Uncle J. was just beginning to pick that *We* business. It was the *Royal* We, not the first person plural. His brother was not the country's Chief Justice, but His Majesty's Private Imperial Chief Justice. The Shah's tone was beginning to sound amused. Was he playing with him, the way a cat plays with a mouse? Did that mean he would be eaten at the end? But now he was feeling more sure of himself. They were entering his medium, the field of rhetoric, where Uncle J. was an old hand. He hadn't copied Sa'adi's *Orchard* for nothing.

"For example, We don't believe this fantastic story that you were *not* the Party's real First Secretary for the Province of Khuzestan, that you were a kind of dummy Provincial Secretary set up to protect the real one. You were the real Provincial Secretary, weren't you?"

Uncle J. felt a shudder run down his spine. If he said "Yes," he would be instantly destroying the credibility of "his" General and that whole Savak file, which was his only hope of survival. He would be handing his own head over on a silver platter, not to mention his General's, too. He remembered the General's warning, "If my head goes, your head goes." If he said "No" when the Shah's question seemed to imply "Yes" for an answer, would he not be calling into question His Imperial Majesty's shrewdness? What was the punishment for calling into question His Imperial Majesty's shrewdness? He couldn't treat the whole thing as a rhetorical question, could he? He didn't even know he had said it, until he heard himself saying:

"Would Your Majesty believe me, if I said that I was not the real Provincial Secretary?"

"No, We would not," said the Shah.

"Then I should not say what Your Majesty would not believe."

He could see his mentor moving his lips, trying to remind him that he should say "Your *Imperial* Majesty" and not just "Your Majesty." This wasn't just a king. He was a King of Kings. But he could also clearly see that his answer had amused, if not pleased, the Shah. His Majesty must have been somewhat pleased that His shrewdness had not been called into question. He had a reputation for outsmarting all his ministers and courtiers and generals. He had to. How many assassination and coup attempts had he survived?

From this moment on Uncle J. was truly on his own. He had not been abandoned by, but graduated from, his mentors. He would look for no more hints. He would think on his own and think fast. This was no longer a game for those fancy pants courtiers. It was a game for real kings and real provincial secretaries. Although, he had to remind himself constantly that his adversary was not a bantering military governor or a praying workhorse brigadier. He was a King of Kings, a nominally Constitutional Monarch who had made himself an Absolute Monarch overnight, and who wished to be amused. He remembered the old ball game played by ancient Mayans of Mexico, in which it was the captain of the winning team who was beheaded in sacrifice.

"And what about this business of you being a very devout Moslem?" asked the Shah. "We had never heard of a Marxist Communist being a devout Moslem. We, too, have read Marx. Are you really a devout Moslem?"

"Like Your Majesty, I am a descendant of the Prophet, blessings of Allah be on him and on his descendants," Uncle J. heard himself saying again, without forethought. "I grew up in a very devout Moslem family. Sometimes, it is very hard to rise above our early childhood experiences." Now he was playing the psychologist. Had His Majesty read Freud, too? He studied his Royal adversary's face to see whether he had bought his explanation. But His Majesty seemed to be still waiting for an answer. He was not yet amused. Uncle J. had to do better. This was not a penny ante game. The stakes were extremely high. He had to try harder. To keep up the ambiguous bantering, he might even have to tread on dangerous ground. He again heard himself saying:

"If Your Imperial Majesty allows me to presume to say so, I am possibly as devout a Moslem as Your Imperial Majesty is." He became aware that he had said Your "Imperial" Majesty for the first time, and twice in the same sentence. He must have been aware that he was taking a very big risk, to keep the game going. He studied his Imperial adversary's face for effect. He thought he saw the Shah swallow. Apparently he was not amused at all. But he did not let on.

"And how do you know how devout a Moslem We are?"

That meant the game was still afoot. He had neither lost nor won as yet, not even knowing which would send his head to the block. But, in any case, his head wasn't on the block yet. He was given one more chance, by His Majesty's grace. Maybe that word "Imperial," and twice in the same sentence, had saved him this time, had blunted the effect of the presumptuous double-talk. Maybe His Majesty watched out for that word Imperial as meticulously as the Protocol Chief did. Maybe He counted it too, counted how many times people had or had not used it in one audience. It was a winning number. He had better stick with it.

"I once watched Your Imperial Majesty on the television, telling of Your Imperial Majesty's pilgrimage to Imamzadeh Davood shrine as the Crown Prince, of how Your Imperial Majesty fell off the mule and was saved in midair by the hand of our ancestor the Prophet, blessings of Allah be on him and on his descendants."

That was good, that *our ancestor* business. He had better stick with that one, too. It seemed to be the only thing he and His Majesty had in common, except for the fact that probably neither of them believed in God. That common ancestry of theirs was also as dubious as that of anybody else who claimed he was descended from the Prophet. He knew how his own prophetic lineage had come about, at least on his father's side. A local mullah in Tabriz had once encountered his father in the marketplace, hugging him and kissing his cheeks and publicly declaring that his ancestor the Prophet, blessings of Allah be on him and on his descendants, had visited him in a dream the night before, and had said "Mullah Jaafar! Mullah Jaafar! Mirza Hashem in the Weavers' Alley is also one of us, one of my descendants. Let him know that. And let everybody else know that, too." Of course, there was nothing strange about that kind of incident. It was quite a customary way for people to learn about their holy lineage.

Uncle J.'s father had then given a feast to celebrate the occasion, with Mullah Jaafar as the guest of honor. Even as a child, Uncle J. had wondered whether Mullah Jaafar had not made up that dream, so that he would get invited to a feast. His father had a reputation for giving lavish feasts. And if that worked, what would keep a mullah from doing it over and over, for anybody who gave lavish feasts, unless they would not want too much holy competition running around. And couldn't a mullah, for a flat fee, say for five Qajar gold sovereigns, be persuaded to dream that somebody else was also descended from the Prophet, blessings of Allah be on him and on his descendants?

Uncle J. did not know when His Majesty's prophetic lineage had come about. Was it possibly during the reign of His Late Imperial Majesty, the man who would have you beheaded if you didn't lick his boots properly, even when he was only the Army Chief, or the War Minister, before he made himself the King of Kings? How many Grand Ayatollahs would have gladly dreamed then that His Imperial Majesty was also descended from the Prophet, blessings of Allah be on him and on his descendants, if only to keep their heads, let alone their titles?

His Majesty was still looking at Uncle J. with a doubtful look, as if reading his thoughts. He did not seem satisfied. So, what if Uncle J. had watched Him on the television? Had he believed that cock and bull story or not? Since when did Marxists believe in that kind of stuff? And what did he mean by that "possibly as devout a Moslem as Your Imperial Majesty is?" Was he needling His Majesty, implying that He was not devout? And how dared he compare His Majesty's devoutness with his own, a godless ex-Communist renegade? And how dared he to presume to put himself in the same category as His Imperial Majesty?

Uncle J. had to do better, and he had to do better fast. He had better try again.

"If Your Imperial Majesty had not been a devout Moslem," Uncle J. heard himself saying again, "I am sure that the blessed Prophet would not have saved Your Imperial Majesty, being his descendant notwithstanding." The Shah looked like someone who knows something is being put over on him, but has no choice but to go along with it. He was looking around at the attendants to gauge the effect of Uncle J.'s remarks on them. They seemed to have totally missed the rhetorical trick, the presumptuous "as . . . as" clause of the previous sentence, as surely as they were missing the new rhetorical trick being used in this sentence, whatever it was. But they were nodding their wholehearted sycophantic approval, of the idea of His Majesty's devoutness, as well as of the truth of His story of falling off the mule, and His ancestor the Prophet's miraculous acrobatics. The Savak brigadier seemed genuinely impressed by it.

"If We pardon you and your gang of traitors" said the Shah, "and give you responsible government positions, can We depend on you to do good work for Us?"

"Yes, Your Majesty!" said Uncle J., for the first time with conviction. "No matter how misled we had been, following the Tudeh Party, no matter how much we have missed the opportunity of serving Your Majesty, I and my comrades have always wanted to genuinely serve, or thought we were serving, the country." The conviction with which Uncle J. spoke at this time seemed to have truly impressed the Shah.

"That's the first thing you have said, Mr. Engineer," He said, "which We are inclined to believe. You Marxists are traitors, but you are not thieves. We are surrounded by thieves. Our ministers are thieves; Our courtiers are thieves; Our generals are thieves; Our high civil servants are thieves. They are all thieves and liars."

"That's what turns people away and sends them to Communism, Your Majesty," said Uncle J., becoming aware that he was no longer using that "Imperial" epithet, now that he was giving honest answers. Would the Shah see through that too, concluding that all his other statements had been either false or evasive?

"We are inclined to believe that too," said the Shah. "And if We did trust you, and let you serve Us, would you always tell Us the truth?"

Uncle J. seemed more and more in his own medium, now:

"If I was convinced that Your Majesty always wanted me to tell Him the truth," Uncle J. had said, "I would always tell Your Majesty the truth."

"We do want you to always tell Us the truth," the Shah had said, now sounding serious and ominous, and no longer bantering. "And you can begin by doing so right now. Were you or were you not the real First Secretary of the Tudeh Party for the Province of Khuzestan?"

Without intending to, Uncle J. had heard himself say, "I was, Your Majesty!"

"So, there was no 'dummy' Provincial Secretary?"

"No, Your Majesty!" Uncle J. had heard himself say again, as if he had totally lost control over his own mind, or as if he no longer cared to play the game. The game was over with that first admission, anyway. And since he didn't know whether it was the winning or the losing that would send his head to the block, why bother any more?

"The only 'dummies' were in Our Savak, to have bought your cock-and-bull story?" the Shah had continued.

"Yes, Your Majesty!"

"Do you hear that, Brigadier?" the Shah had shouted, sounding most ominous.

Uncle J. had looked sideways and seen the Savak Brigadier standing at attention, visibly shaking and sweating. He had genuinely felt sorry for him. He, Uncle J., had got him into that mess. And what if he was sent back to the same dungeon with him? How could he face him, now? What stories could he come up with this time? That was assuming that the Brigadier did not lose his head, let alone his job? It would be probably a different torturer Uncle J. would have to face, if he was sent back to prison. And what kind of favors could he expect from the new man, who no doubt would know what had happened to his predecessor?

"Give Us another honest answer, Mr. Provincial Secretary, now that you have begun!" the Shah had said to Uncle J. "Is this Brigadier a very smart man?"

Surprised as Uncle J. was, that the game had not ended, and that the Shah was still in humor, he knew that he had taken the bait and had to run with it. His own fate would probably be decided at the end of this audience, making the Savak General's or his successor's pleasure or displeasure irrelevant. But now he felt less concern for his own fate than for the fate of this old soldier, this old "servant of God," for whom he was suddenly feeling genuine compassion and affection.

"No, Your Majesty!" Uncle J. had said, reluctantly.

"But," he had added, just as the Shah was about to thunder at the Brigadier again, surprising both himself and the Shah with the boldness of the uninvited comment, as well as with the genuine compassion and sorrow in his tone. "he is a very pious man, Your Majesty! And his piety makes him gullible."

He had looked at the Brigadier's sweaty and helpless face and had discerned a hint of gratitude there. Whether it did or did not do him any good, he was at least trying to pay back some of his debt, trying to get his fat out of the fire, if he could, no matter what happened to himself. For himself he no longer felt either sorrow or fear. In fact, he felt surprisingly good, almost proud of himself. Even if they hanged him now, at least he had had the pleasure of having bantered with a king, of having bandied words with him. He had looked him straight in the eyes and told him.

"Is he a thief, Mr. Provincial Secretary?" the Shah had asked.

"No, Your Majesty!" Uncle J. had answered, firmly, and proudly, as if the General was his handiwork. "That I know he is not."

"We believe you," said the Shah. "Brigadier!" he then shouted out. "This man has fooled you. But at least you have been fooled by a very shrewd man. In fact, he almost fooled Us, too. And if We don't watch out, he might fool Us, yet."

For a moment there was total silence, while everyone stood breathlessly still, waiting for the Shah's next move. The ax would fall now. The question was who would get it first.

"We also believe that you are a pious man," said the Shah. "We wish We had more pious men like you serving Us. You are doing Us more good with your gullible piety than all those other smart thieves are doing with their smart thievery. And however you did it, you have done better with this shrewd man who has fooled you, than you have done with those others you have tortured to death. At least, you managed to lead him to Us, alive, so that We may have a chance of getting the truth out of him. And without torture."

Was this an occasion for the Shah to pat himself on the back, for having been so shrewd himself, wondered Uncle J.? Was he showing off to his attendants? The more shrewd he painted Uncle J., the more shrewd he himself sounded for having bested him. It was true that he had managed to ferret him out, and without torture. On arriving at the Palace, if somebody had told Uncle J. that he would be spilling all the beans in the presence of His Imperial Majesty, he would have chuckled with amusement. He had underestimated the awe one feels in the presence of an omnipotent King of Kings.

"Brigadier!" The Shah had boomed again. "Consider yourself a major general as of today. And We want you moved to the Headquarters of the Savak in Tehran, so that We may keep an eye on you."

The Brigadier had clicked his heels, still shaking, even though you could read in his face that he was greatly relieved. There was much less tension in the faces of the men in attendance now. The storm seemed to have passed for the time being. The Shah was no longer angry. An angry Shah might lash out in all directions. They would all be at risk. The attention seemed to have turned to Uncle J. now. The ax could still fall, there. But they were obviously not concerned with that. His Majesty's anger at a Savak general might spill over to engulf them. But His anger at a renegade Communist, who had almost fooled His Majesty, would have no consequence for them.

Uncle J. also felt that the next judgment pronounced would be on his head. Judging by the Shah's expression, he liked to think that the worst was over. If the Shah was that pleased with the Brigadier, how much displeased could he be with him? Although, one could never be sure. What did he know about this business of kings of kings? Hadn't He just said that he had almost fooled Him, too? What was the penalty for "almost fooling His Imperial Majesty?" Was he the captain of the winning team, to be sacrificed now, for the benefit of all those who might ever think of fooling His Imperial Majesty?

"As for you Mr. Marxist Engineer!" the Shah's voice boomed through the hall with obvious sarcasm, having resumed its bantering tone after those ominous suspenseful moments. "We have not quite decided what to do with you, yet. The smartest thing would be to have you shot right now, so that you would not have the chance to cause Us any more mischief and fool any more of Our generals. But you intrigue Us. You can be forthright and truthful, even when your life is at risk. It might be good to have someone like you around, to listen to once in a while, instead of always listening to all these kiss-asses."

At this point Uncle J. had bowed down impulsively, feeling genuine gratitude and relief.

"General," the Shah had shouted again, addressing the Brigadier as "general" for the first time. "We want this man brought back to Us tomorrow. You will be held personally responsible for him." Uncle J. had heard the clicking of the General's heels behind his back, and the Shah had waved his hand, indicating that the audience was over.

They had all bowed down and walked backward out of the hall, bowing down in sync exactly as many times as they had bowed down coming in. They had been escorted by the Guard officers to the inner gate of the Palace, behind which the Savak limousine was waiting for the General. As soon as the gate had closed behind them, the General had embraced Uncle J. and kissed him on both cheeks, shedding childlike tears, as he had done on the day of the afternoon prayers.

"I forgive you for having made a fool of me," the General had said. "You handed my head to His Imperial Majesty on a platter. But you made up for it by winning it back. And you got me my major general's star. You stood by me when I needed you, and I will never forget that.

Even though after today, I dare say you won't need my help any more. You have got it made. Who knows what His Majesty has in mind for you? A cabinet post, I would wager."

On the way back to Savak, Uncle J. had wondered whether the General was right. And what if he was right? Could he accept a position like that? It sure beat the firing squad, or the hangman's rope, or the torture chamber. But wouldn't that lend credence to the previous rumors that he had been an agent of the Savak in the Party? But what did that matter now, anyway? The guys who had made up those rumors, or believed in them, were probably dead already, or would be soon. And he was alive. Who knows whether they might not have accepted a dogcatcher position, if it was offered them? Anyway, all the ex-comrades whose opinions still counted were now with him; in jail. They would be the first to encourage him to accept such a position, if offered. To help them, if not himself.

Hell, it didn't have to be a cabinet post. The General was probably exaggerating. The Directorship of a small department would do. It sure beat working for an illiterate bazaar merchant for pennies. He had an infant daughter to think of now. And he was getting tired of his wife's nagging, that she had married a *Mr. Engineer*, only to wake up one morning and see that he had turned into a bazaar clerk. Wouldn't she like to be a cabinet minister's wife, to ride in a chauffeured limousine? And wouldn't that put her relatives in their place? They sure had been quite contemptuous of him lately, ever since he had had to live in their basement. Not to say anything about their constant bragging about their aristocratic and princely lineage. If one rounded up all the people who claimed their lineage back to the Qajar dynasty, there would be nobody left in the countryside to till the land. And how could Agha Mohammad Khan Qajar have had such a huge offspring, being a eunuch and all? But wouldn't it be strange, if it came to pass, to go from being the Provincial Secretary of the Tudeh Party to being a cabinet minister of the Shah, almost overnight! What would Marx say about that? He would turn over in his grave. And could one really change color that fast?

Uncle J. had finally decided that there was no point in worrying about his chickens before they were hatched, trying to resolve a hypothetical conflict arising out of a pious but not very smart general's wild wager. His fate would be decided soon enough, without any help or choice on his part, by a man of variable mood, unpredictable mind, and unlimited power. All he had to do was wait. And wait he did.

He had spent that night in a comfortably furnished room in a Savak safe house, enjoying all the luxuries of a hotel room but a telephone. Two armed guards had been posted at the door, with strict instructions that no one could either enter or leave. The General had made it known to everyone in the Savak Headquarters that His Imperial Majesty had made him personally responsible for the prisoner, until tomorrow. Just as he had let them know that, by His Imperial Majesty's order, he was now a major general, and he had been transferred to the Headquarters in Tehran. Regardless of how displeased or jealous his superiors were, nobody was about to argue with a man who was on his way to have a second audience with His Imperial Majesty in two days. And no one seemed pleased that they might have lost their Communist victim as well.

The next day the General had knocked on Uncle J.'s door bright and early, with his major general's stars already shining on his uniform. They had brought Uncle J. a morning coat to wear to the Court, but Uncle J. had refused to wear it. Wasn't he still a prisoner, he had asked, watched by two armed guards at night? Hadn't His Majesty said that he might still want to have him shot, so that he wouldn't have a chance to fool any more of his generals? Wouldn't it be presumptuous to dress up in a morning coat a prisoner, especially one who might have to be shot? He had insisted that if His Majesty had found no fault with the way he was dressed yesterday, he would not mind seeing him dressed the same way today. The General had finally given in.

"You are smarter than I am," he had said. "Besides, we'll see what those fancy pants courtiers would have to say about it."

CHAPTER THIRTEEN

At the Palace Uncle J. had had to repeat the same arguments with the courtiers, who emphatically wanted him dressed in a morning coat, and he had prevailed. How could you force an ex-Communist renegade prisoner to wear a morning coat, even if he might be a future cabinet minister? Anyway, this would be a good way to have His Majesty displeased with him and ruin his chances for advancement.

He and the General had arrived at the Palace very early and had to wait several hours, before being granted audience. At times, they wondered whether they had not been forgotten. Maybe the events of yesterday were a joke played on them by His Majesty, for His Majesty's amusement. Some said His Majesty did play such jokes. Uncle J., of course, would not be disturbed, if the whole thing turned out to be a joke. But with the General, it was quite a different story.

If he did not go back to the Headquarters with something more solid than his own humble words quoting His Majesty about his promotion to major general and transfer to the Headquarters in Tehran, with no other witness but a godless ex-Communist traitor, now that he had already paraded his major general's stars around the Headquarters, those major generals and lieutenant generals back in the office would get his hide. In fact, his supervising lieutenant general had said to him that he had better have something on paper from the Army Personnel saying that he was a major general, or he would be in big trouble. Nobody was happy to see him promoted to the rank of major general, only three months after he had been made a brigadier, and without paying anybody off. But once he was granted an audience with His Imperial Majesty in a major general's uniform, there would be no questioning his promotion.

A few times the General had approached the major of the Imperial Guard attending them, to see whether anyone should be reminded about their audience with His Imperial Majesty. The major, without even bothering to look up from his desk, had said, "Don't be too eager, General. You'll be admitted when His Imperial Majesty wishes to remember. No one reminds His Imperial Majesty of what he should remember."

It turned out that sometimes people had waited for days, and had gone home and returned to wait for more days, day after day, until one day His Imperial Majesty had finally remembered them. Sometimes, also, His Imperial Majesty had plumb forgot, and nobody had dared or wished to remind Him. And why should those fancy pants courtiers and officers, who had been called thieves and liars and kiss-asses by His Imperial Majesty, want to help him become a major general, just because he was honest and pious and gullible? And why should they want to help a godless ex-Communist traitor land a cabinet post, just because he was good at bantering with His Majesty?

Luckily, His Majesty did remember, shortly before noon, and they were finally granted audience. They were admitted to the same hall, with the same bowing routine, but escorted by two different courtiers. And the first question put by an ominous and extremely displeased Shah was:

"Why isn't this man dressed in a morning coat?"

The Shah's voice had boomed across the hall like a thunder and everyone in attendance had tensed up with dread. They would all be held responsible for this. They would all have to pay for this ex-Communist traitor's stubbornness. They should have kicked his ass and made him wear a morning coat, whether he liked it or not, instead of listening to his smart alecky arguments. Even Uncle J. had started sweating. Maybe these fancy pants courtiers and generals knew their business better than he did, when it came to dealing with kings and princes. What did he know about these things? All his life he had dealt with the poor and the hungry, preaching the equality of man. He had remembered, with significant discomfort, the Shah's earlier words about having him shot on the spot. But he had kept his cool. Since it was his decision not to wear a morning coat, and since nobody else seemed to dare to respond to the Shah's question, he had presumed to answer.

"Yesterday Your Imperial Majesty had not decided whether to have me shot or not." Uncle J. had said quite somberly, thinking of the possibility that His Majesty might decide to do exactly that after all, the General's "wager" notwithstanding. "And since there is no indication that Your Imperial Majesty has pardoned me yet, and I am still a prisoner, I thought it would be presumptuous for a prisoner who might be shot, to appear before Your Majesty in a morning coat."

"*You thought? You decided?*" the Shah thundered again, as ominously. "And where the hell were Our Court Minister and Our Protocol Chief, when you were doing all this thinking and deciding for them?" He turned his head to observe the effect of his comment on the Court Minister and the Protocol Chief, whose trembling bodies immediately bowed down to His Imperial fury, and remained bowed down, as if that was their only defense. Uncle J. recognized the

Protocol Chief as one of his two escorts of yesterday, and the man who had emphatically argued with him today about wearing a morning coat. The Court Minister's face, he remembered from the pictures in the newspapers.

The Shah turned back to Uncle J., as if asking him to witness that he was not able to get any words out of those cowed bodies. The bodies returned to their erect position, as soon as the Shah's face was turned. But they immediately went back to their bowed position, each time the Shah's head made the slightest move in their direction. The routine was repeated two or three times and Uncle J. almost chuckled at the comical effect of the scene, when he felt the Shah's piercing gaze on himself, again. Apparently, since nobody else was ready to do so, it was up to him to supply the proper answer or amusement, whichever His Majesty was seeking.

"Your Majesty!" he volunteered again, thinking it strange that he had become the apologist for generals and courtiers. "They did try to persuade me. The fault was with my obstinacy, thinking it improper to dress a prisoner in a morning coat."

The Shah's face remained impassive for a few moments, then slowly opened in a reluctant smile. He was amused. He had probably resigned himself to the fact that this man was the only one in the hall with whom he could carry on anything resembling a two-way conversation.

"You may be a prisoner, Engineer!" he said amiably. "But you already talk like a courtier. Maybe we should make you Our Court Minister, or Our Protocol Chief."

With that comment the Shah turned around again and looked at the same two bowing figures, who had straightened up and were sneakily trying to wipe the sweat off their flushed faces. They immediately resumed their bowed down positions, perceptibly trembling. Uncle J. wondered how well he would fare as a Court Minister or Chief of Protocol. Physically, it seemed like a very strenuous life, literally back-breaking. And, obviously, His Majesty had a habit of making the people around him sweat and tremble constantly, feeling the danger of possible disgrace and downfall any minute.

"Do you even have a morning coat, Engineer" asked the Shah, looking at Uncle J. with an amused smile?

"No, Your Majesty."

"Have you ever worn a morning coat?"

"No, Your Majesty."

"Maybe you didn't want to wear a morning coat which wasn't tailor-made for you." They seemed to be back to bantering again. The game was on. And Uncle J. didn't lose any time.

"That wasn't my problem Your Majesty," said Uncle J. "Ready-made clothes fit me fine. I am a perfect size forty!"

The Shah laughed with great amusement. He looked around at his courtiers who, with the exception of the Court Minister and the Protocol Chief, were laughing like trained seals. The officers were more restrained, merely smiling dutifully. Only the Savak General was standing at military attention, without even the trace of a smile. The Shah picked on that immediately.

"Brigadier, I see you didn't lose any time to become a major general. You mean you had already bought those extra stars?"

"It was Your Imperial Majesty's command, Your Majesty," barked the General, clicking his heels.

"You mean they actually let you wear those stars on your word alone, without any papers from the Army Personnel?" The Shah's tone was amused again.

To everybody's surprise, the Brigadier shot back an answer. "They did say, Your Imperial Majesty, that I would be in big trouble if they did not get the papers from the Army Personnel very soon." After all, if he did not get some tangible proof of His Majesty's orders soon, those generals in the Savak Headquarters could make life a bigger hell for him than His Majesty could.

The Shah laughed loud and said, "They'll get it, General. They'll get it. Don't worry!" He nodded to his military adjutant, as a sign that he should do something about it.

The Shah had then ordered Uncle J. into a private audience room with himself, with no one else present but two oversized Permanent Guard sergeants posted in the corners. He had asked him many frank and pointed questions. Was he really a true Moslem, was he really no longer a Marxist, had he really turned away from Communism, did he really intend to keep his "pledge" of cooperation with the Savak, or was this all a tactical ploy to fool a few more generals and buy some time? He had warned that if he even suspected that Uncle J. was lying, he would have him shot immediately.

Uncle J. had answered the questions truthfully. No, he was not a true Moslem. He did not even believe in God. But he did believe in common human values such as honesty, decency, loyalty, and honor. Yes, he was still somewhat a Marxist in sentiment, but he no longer intended to do anything to promote Marxist goals. If Marxists and Communists ever came to power, he would be one of the first they would hang as a traitor. Besides, he had a wife and an infant daughter now, and he would like to provide for them and live a comfortable family life, if he was given the opportunity.

He certainly had turned away from the Tudeh Party, he said, because he had found them as corruptible as any other party, and as fanatical as any. There had been too much hero worship there. He had watched their Youth Organization members going around mouthing off Stalin's praise, parroting the Russian propaganda that, according to measurements by Russian doctors, Stalin's brain was much larger than average human brain, a sign that he was a genius. The Party's line certainly had been a straight Stalinist line. The Red Army was invincible and nobody in Russian Communist Party could ever do anything wrong.

For a long time he had suspected that some members of the Central Committee of the Party were traitors. (He did not define the word traitor and was glad that the Shah did not ask him to do so. The Shah understood it as meaning traitor to the Shah, and Uncle J. had meant it as being traitor to the country, the agent of the British foreign intelligence, what Mosaddeq used to call "the Oily Tudeh Communists.") He had found his comrades to be as much ruled by the human frailties of vanity and envy and jealousy and rivalry as anyone else. There, too, were men who would walk over their mothers to get ahead, and who were as greedy for success, and as hungry for power, as any of the Shah's generals, courtiers, or ministers.

After years of dedicated Party work, he had found himself the target of vicious rumors that he was a Savak agent, rumors started by the man second to him in the hierarchy, and most likely to benefit from his downfall. He had begun having difficulties in the Party, because he had not been ruthless enough to eliminate his adversaries, by branding them traitors and Savak agents and whatnot. He had suspected that, sooner or later, his more ruthless rivals would get him, bring him down, maybe even eliminate him. After all, hadn't Stalin done that with all his rivals? He certainly meant to keep his "pledge" of working with the Savak, simply for the reason that the Communists would have less love for him now than they did for His Imperial Majesty.

The Shah had now given Uncle J. permission to sit down and be comfortable, before asking a great many questions about the structure, the hierarchy, and the organizational lines of the Tudeh Party. Who were the members of the Central Committee? Who were the members of the Executive Committee? He seemed quite knowledgeable and, at times, Uncle J. could not tell whether he was testing his veracity or really seeking information. He had wanted to know which of the Savak methods to infiltrate the Tudeh Party had been effective and which had not, and why the Party had managed to infiltrate the Army and the Savak so successfully, while the Savak had done the reverse with very little success. When Uncle J. had answered that the Party members were more dedicated and honestly believed in their cause, while the Savak agents were in it for money and power and rank, the Shah had grunted with displeasure.

The conversation, then, had become more personal and bantering again. The Shah had asked whether Uncle J. had written any slogans on the walls about him. Uncle J. had admitted that he had done so long ago, and had volunteered the joke his comrades routinely made about his penmanship. The Shah had said laughingly, that he must have seen some of his slogans, since he remembered some that were elegantly penned. Uncle J. had felt comfortable enough to even volunteer the account of the Amjadieh demonstration in which he had participated.

The Shah had asked how he had managed to fool the Savak General so completely, and how a man who did not believe in God could have prayed so flawlessly. Uncle J. had told him of his years in the Koran school, the story of Mullah Mostafa, and the canings he had got over memorizing the daily prayers. They had shared a few hearty laughs at the expense of the poor Savak General, who was still standing at attention out there in the audience hall.

The Shah had then asked what Uncle J. had meant by saying that he was "as religious as His Majesty," when he knew full well in his own heart, and he might have well guessed that the Shah knew it too, that he did not even believe in God. Uncle J. had again felt a shudder run down his spine. He had realized why those courtiers and generals trembled and sweated so often and so easily around His Majesty. This King of Kings could become very familiar and very friendly, could make you feel quite comfortable and safe, and then with one word or one question, let you feel that your head could still go to the block.

Uncle J. had nervously fidgeted around, trying to dig himself out of that hole. "But Your Majesty," he had said, "I said that in the context that I *was* a religious man. At the time I said that I did not have the slightest inkling that I would be making a confession to Your Majesty about my disbelief in religion."

The Shah would not take that kind of sophistry for an answer. He had insisted to know whether Uncle J. thought that He, the Shah, was a religious man. After some more fidgeting and sweating, Uncle J. had found it safest to say that he did not really know. The Shah had asked whether Uncle J. had believed that story about the Prophet saving him in midair. With that fearful shudder shooting down his spine again, Uncle J. had admitted that he had not. Did Uncle J. think that the majority of the people believed that story? The uneducated and religious-minded people, Uncle J. had said, especially in the countryside, probably did, while the educated people, especially in the cities, probably did not. Now the ax could fall! Or, his neck could be spared.

When Uncle J. left the Palace that day, he was the Chairman of the National Planning Organization, with the rank of cabinet minister. He had been given a free hand to hire in the Planning Organization those of his former comrades who were genuinely repentant, or to recommend them for high government positions in other departments and ministries, with the understanding that his neck would be the guarantee of their correct behavior, and of their fully keeping their "pledge" of cooperation with the Savak, to dig out the remnants of the Tudeh Party, and especially, its Army-Savak Organization. From time to time, Uncle J. would be called to the Palace for confidential consultations, as a special advisor to His Imperial Majesty.

With the passing of months and years, Uncle J. became the Shah's most trusted friend and confidant. The Shah used him as a barometer to check the veracity and credibility of all his yes-men, and as a gauge to feel out the senses and sensibilities of the common people, even long after Uncle J. had ceased to be one of the common people, had become a courtier of sorts, an extremely rich man, a little king. He had become a fallen archangel among a host of fallen angels, his former comrades, all of whom had now become deputy ministers, and directors general, and big time government contractors, all very powerful and very rich, and all still considering themselves Marxists and revolutionaries at heart, as Uncle J. did. Soon, even Uncle J.'s four and then five and then six year-old daughter, who was chosen as the exclusive playmate for the Shah's younger daughter of roughly the same age, became a courtier of sorts, a little princess.

Uncle J.'s wife, Aunt Sarah, fitted nicely into the picture. She had always considered herself one of those pale princesses filling the countryside, all allegedly somehow related by blood or by marriage to the defunct Qajar dynasty, that had been overthrown by the Shah's father some forty years earlier. You often heard some lady or other vouch solemnly in the course of a cocktail party or dinner, "Yes, Ma'am, my grandmother was a princess! We are related to the Fakhreddowleh's on my mother's side"; or "Yes, Ma'am, my grandfather was a prince! We are of the Farmanfarmaiians!" And most of these people were usually as poor as they were princely, without a pot to piss in. Aunt Sarah was one of them. Not much was known about her grandparents. Her father, who could hardly read or write, had been in the household of A'alam family, the Court Minister, and as such had once been made the governor of Mashhad, the capital of Khorasan Province.

It was quite common in those days for the big feudal landowners to get their household menials appointed to the positions of Mayor, City Governor, or Provincial Governor. This gave them maximum opportunity to flaunt the law. These governors could hardly read or write, but they were courtiers at heart, knowing all the Protocol of dealing with the Royalty, the art of bowing forward and backward, of kissing hands, feet, and other private parts, and of doing the "Yes, Your Highness," "No, Your Highness," "Yes, Your Excellency," "No, Your Excellency," routine. They could bow and walk backward better than most men could walk forward straight. And they had a habit of confusing themselves with a different generation of city governors and provincial governors, who in fact had been of royal blood. Often, these pale princes and princesses traced their lineage to Agha Mohammad Khan-i Qajar, who, with over two hundred permanent and temporary wives, was a eunuch; a very dubious lineage indeed.

Nevertheless, Aunt Sarah, who did not really have much of an access to the Court, Uncle J.'s relationship with the Shah being of a more personal nature, had jumped with both feet into her new role as an honorary courtier. She would lose no opportunity to ride up to the Royal Palace in Uncle J.'s chauffeured limousine, with or without her daughter, whenever she was given the slightest chance. A sentence beginning with "Yes, ma'am, the other day at the Royal Palace" made excellent conversation at cocktail parties. It was a big hit with the ladies, anytime, anywhere, no matter how the sentence ended. She would not have to tell them that she had been allowed only as far as the gate of the inner garden, where she had had to wait in the car behind the locked gate for two hours for her daughter, until the Royal Princess had given her permission to leave. After all, how many cars had their license plates registered in the Palace and had permission to go as far as the inner gate? What mattered if she was stopped ten times en route, to explain once more to another tall, handsome, young Guard officer, that "Yes, I am here, by the order of the Royal Princess, to pick up my daughter who is in Royal attendance."

She would feel her own mouth transfixed by the wide open eyes of the wives of her husband's ex-comrade friends. They would hang on her every word. As the wife of the Provincial First Secretary of the Party, she, of course, had always been a "princess" of sorts among that crowd. And now that the husbands were all rich high government officials, she still had her distinction. She wore enough diamonds to make walking cumbersome. She had always had a weakness for diamonds. At her engagement, and then later on her wedding day, she had not been given a diamond by her husband, who at first was too poor, and then was too busy donating all his money to the Party cause, to set an example for the rest, and who considered diamonds quite *bourgeois*, anyway. So, she was getting even now, buying as many of the largest diamonds she could get her hands on, and with the perfect excuse: the

Royal Palace. As if they weighed your diamonds at the gate, before you were allowed entrance.

The game of guessing how many carats of diamond Aunt Sarah had hanging on her, was always a big hit at the evening parties. It was like guessing how many calories were in a fruit basket, except that here, if you guessed right, you would not get the diamonds as a prize. And if sometimes she cheated and threw in some big imitation diamond, among all the genuine ones she had on, what was the harm, and who could tell the difference?

Aunt Sarah's other weakness was furs. She started with owning a rabbit, and graduated into a fox, a raccoon, a mink, a lynx, a leopard, and then a tiger, in that order. Then came variations on the themes. Every time she took a trip abroad, she left the country diamond-less and fur-less, and came back loaded with diamonds and furs, without paying custom duties, of course, pretending that she had been wearing them when she left. And who could question a cabinet minister's wife, whose husband played poker with the Shah, and whose daughter was the Royal Princess's playmate?

To Uncle J., who himself was not an extravagant man, it all made sense somehow, not because it was an easy way to make a lot of money fast, but because it was a "good investment," with the special nuance the word investment had for him. Uncle J. was always for a "good investment," whether he was talking business, sentiments, or metaphysics. Even before he became a businessman that was a favorite metaphor with him. Whenever he did someone a favor, it was an "investment." He probably did not believe in Heaven, simply because it was not a *sure* investment, the way diamonds and furs were. Anyway, even after the UN conventions and state laws prohibited the sale, import, or export of furs of wild animals in many countries, Aunt Sarah and Uncle J. still managed to find some store or factory outlet somewhere in the world, whether in Manhattan or in Kuala Lumpur, where they could buy as many new furs as they wished, to add to their collection.

One of the highlights of a tour of Aunt Sarah's house, more a palace now than a house, was a "fur tour" for the ladies. The walk-in "fur closets" looked like hunters' lodges, or butcher shops where they sell exotic meat. Sometimes, Uncle J. accompanied his wife on these tours with equal pride of ownership, cracking a joke or two if it was a more intimate group. His favorite joke was "The only fur you don't find here is that of a jackass, only because my wife is prejudiced against jackasses"; to which Aunt Sarah would invariably answer, "I don't need the fur of a jackass, because I have a live one for a husband." Uncle J. was not the man to have the last word on anything with his wife.

The absurdity of the whole business had never hit anyone, until the insurance company canceled their policy, because the value of the furs in the house had reached an astronomical figure. The only way the company would continue the insurance policy was, if the furs were moved from the house and kept in a vault under a separate insurance policy, or if a secure vault was built for them in the house.

After all, anybody could pull up a truck behind the house one day and steal ten million tomans worth of furs. Who could tell when a domestic servant would go bad, when you were talking that kind of money? But moving the furs to a vault would mean that Aunt Sarah could no longer conduct her fur tours, which made them really of little practical value to her. Often enough Tehran was not cold enough for furs, and Aunt Sarah rarely wore furs, anyway. So, even though the insurance remained canceled, the furs remained in the closets in the house, until years later, when Uncle J. did build a vault for them in their new mansion. But the buying of furs was at least halted, if only temporarily.

What was becoming more and more obvious was that Uncle J. had joined the gang of very corrupt government officials. Where would a Chairman of Planning Organization, even one with the rank of cabinet minister, who played poker with the Shah, find all that money to buy furs by the truckload and diamonds by the bucket. The Planning Organization was, of course, the outlet for spending the country's oil money, where all the big government contracts were handed out. Obviously, Uncle J. had joined the practice of getting a big cut for every contract awarded, and with good reason. He had to be a business success, now that he had become a turncoat Utopian idealist, and with the perfect rationalization that there was no way he could change the government bureaucracy. After all, he was a minister, not a prime minister.

Even if he had been a prime minister, he would not have been able to change things. Mosaddeq had tried it and he had got it from every side. Even the Tudeh Party, which should have been glad to see him carry out reform and halt the looting of the public treasury, had savagely attacked him, with the excuse that his reforms would only lengthen the life of the Capitalist system and postpone the Socialist Revolution. How could he, Uncle J., change the system, even given the help of the small army of his ex-comrades, when every Royal prince and princess had his or her own organization, to milk the country dry, not to mention every Army, Police, and Savak general, and every minister and deputy minister and governor and mayor.

To survive in any position, it was taken for granted that you had to steal an amount commensurate with your rank; so much to kick up to your superiors; so much to kick further up to the Imperial Court; so much to bribe other officials who could get you in trouble; so much to keep as an insurance for future bribes, when you would invariably get in trouble, with the police, with the Savak, with the courts, if and when you happened to displease anyone; and last but not least, so much to keep for yourself. If you tried to budge from the system, let alone to reform it, you would be the one to be dragged out into the marketplace and hanged as a corrupt official, for the eyes of the world to see.

Uncle J.'s optimism about having the ear of the Shah had also vanished soon enough. He had quickly realized that when the Shah talked about fighting corruption, he did not mean corruption in the Imperial Court and among the Royal Family. That he knew all about and didn't mind. He did not want thieves, but only among the government officials. Of course the officials had to steal, but only for the purpose of kicking it up to the Royal Family. For themselves, they had to remain content with the power they had, a power which was of dubious value, since at any time they were likely to alienate one source of power or another, and then be disgraced, jailed, or even killed. Little by little, he became convinced that the Shah was not partial to truth either, and that he preferred to be lied to and flattered, even by those he wanted to keep as barometers of the truth. Not to say anything about the fact that by now, Uncle J. had become about as distant from the truth as the Shah was.

Somewhere along this line the Alex affair happened. Alex had always looked up to Uncle J., using him as a role model. He had been Uncle J.'s favorite nephew. Uncle J. liked to think that it was due to his influence that Alex had joined Tudeh Party's Youth Organization and become a revolutionary. He considered Alex the most sensible in our family, the most logical, the most systematic, a miniature Uncle J. So, when Uncle J. left the Tudeh Party and became a turncoat, he could not understand why Alex struck out on his own. He had figured that Alex, like all his ex-comrades, would just follow him out of the fold and pray in his new church. When Alex did not do that, Uncle J. felt a great pang of rejection. He attributed it to Alex's youth and inexperience. "In a few years," he said, "you will change your tune and come round to my way of thinking."

But Alex did not change his tune. He did not come round to Uncle J.'s way of thinking, and they kept drifting farther and farther apart. But for a long time Uncle J. kept trying. As long as Alex held out, Uncle J.'s new ideological position seemed to remain questionable. Alex had to be won over. Uncle J. was not the type of man to argue with you, if you were not more or less of his persuasion already. But with Alex, he would take any excuse to initiate a new argument. His usual line was that Dad had asked him to talk to Alex. That was generally true. Dad was very worried about Alex and what he was up to. But both Uncle J. and Alex knew that Dad was only an excuse. There was something more basic involved, something that went to the heart of the identities of the two men.

It was true that the Tudeh Party was on the decline, ruthlessly persecuted by the Savak, but even more importantly, dynamited from within. Members had turned tail, turned coat, turned yellow, had broken down under torture, and all of this had taken its toll on the Party Organization. It had taken three years to uncover the Army-Savak Organization of the Party and to root it out. And with that the Party's back had been broken.

The Party's strict Stalinist line had been denounced by as many on the left, as on the right. Interestingly enough, it was the old Stalinists who changed color first. The popular saying was that there were now more Tudeh Party leaders working in the Savak than in the Party. But the youths' need for a cause, for a Utopian ideology, had not been superseded. New independent leftist organizations were mushrooming all over the place. Isolated groups of young men and women were discovering the revolutionary fervor all over again. The old ideological dogmas were breaking down and new pragmatic approaches were being tried. New sociopolitical combinations were now being rediscovered: liberation theology, Marxist theology, Islamic Marxism, Democratic Socialism, Islamic Socialism. Young men were taking to the classrooms, to the mosques, to the woods, to the hills. And Uncle J. did not seem to comprehend that there were new revolutionary idealisms preached, of which he knew nothing, because they had not been preached in his mother church.

Everyone in the family knew that Alex had struck out on his own. But no one knew where his new church was. When he left the Youth Organization, he did not even tell Uncle J. Now he kept everything to himself. It hurt Uncle J. that Alex would not even tell him what group he worked with. This called Uncle J.'s Marxist revolutionary orthodoxy, his credibility, his sincerity, his integrity, his very identity, into question. It reminded him that he was now the Shah's cabinet minister, that he now worked with the Savak, although only in name, he alleged, another one of his brilliant evasive tactics, something he could later joke about with the future generations of revolutionaries.

"Don't you trust me any more?" he would ask Alex.

"I do!" Alex would say, impassively.

"Do you think I could ever betray you, reveal your secrets?"

"No!" Alex would say.

"Then why would you not at least tell me which group you work with?"

Alex would point out that he trusted Dad too, that he trusted me too, that he did not think that we would ever betray his trust either, probably not even under torture, but that did not mean he would tell us all his secrets. Uncle J. did not like the analogy. It was not fair. It was not quite to the point. He would ask Alex whether he was putting him and Dad on the same footing. Dad was the Shah's Chief Justice, had always been the Shah's Chief Justice, all those years that Uncle J. had been eating dirt, living a revolutionary Marxist's life. It seemed quite unfair that he should be compared to Dad. He had forgotten that Dad too, very long ago, almost before Uncle J. was old enough to remember, during the older Dark Period under the Shah's father, had been a revolutionary. He did not think that his being "the Shah's cabinet minister" was quite like Dad's being "the Shah's Chief Justice."

I, of course, did not count. I was a mere kid. I had to remain ignorant of secrets, for my own protection. Dad had made Alex promise that, no matter what he did, he would never let me get involved with politics. Mom had made Alex swear to that. Uncle J. had strongly advised it. And Alex himself wanted me not involved, to protect me. "You are my kid brother," he would say. "I want you to live to a ripe old age. I want you to be around to take care of Mom and Dad, if anything happened to me. And if something happened to me, I want you to be around to know, maybe write a couple of those silly poems of yours about it."

Everybody wanted to protect me. I was the family's irreplaceable jewel. I seemed to have a Providential purpose in life. I was the witness to be spared the tragedy, someone to tell the world what happened to everybody when everything went puff, the only one left who would know the story of the big hole in the ground. I had the feeling that I was deliberately allowed to be present at all of the arguments between Alex and Uncle J., as if in a metaphysical discussion to continue for all time, I would be the ultimate witness, the ultimate jury. Uncle J. was not the type to give the same sermon twice, or to preach in somebody else's church. But somehow he felt that he had to win this argument with Alex.

There seemed to be a rivalry between them, as if it was intolerable for Uncle J. not to be the arch-revolutionary in the family, the last word on Marxism, on Communism, on Socialism. He could not bear to see that Alex was the new standard-bearer. This would make him not only the ex-champion, the guy who retired from the ring, but also something indefinable, a renegade, the guy who went to the other side, and, "the

Shah's cabinet minister." It would bring back the rancor of the old Party rivalries.

"But the game is up, don't you see?" he would say.

"But for me it is not a game," Alex would retort. "And, anyway, the Tudeh Party is not the only game in town. They don't have a monopoly on revolutionary idealism."

But for Uncle J. the Tudeh Party was the only game in town, and for him the game was up, because he had tossed his cards and pulled out. He could not bear to think that a game was still going on, and he was not considered worthy of it.

"In today's world, in the Third World countries, no group can win unless it is backed up by either Russia or America. And unless the Russians back up the Communist or the Socialist movement in this country, it remains kid stuff. The Tudeh Party is still the only Communist/Socialist movement in this country that has the support of the Russians, whatever is left of it."

"Then why did you leave it?" Alex would ask. The question made Uncle J. swallow hard. He was not used to being pressed hard. This would be his cue to pull out of the argument with his usual "I had my reasons!" But he couldn't hide behind that formula now. That would be tantamount to accepting defeat, something he could not afford in this case. He had to win this one. He would try to hide behind experience, the prerogative of age.

"When you reach my stage of life, you will know that there is a time for everything. A time comes when you feel you have done your share and there is not much else you can do."

"So, revolutionary idealism is a four or five year hitch, like compulsory military service? You do your hitch, and you retire? Even if that were true, you must admit I have not reached the retirement age, yet. And when you do retire, where do you retire to, the other camp?"

Uncle J. would swallow harder. He was not used to arguing with people who did not think he was right. He had not expected Alex to be hitting so hard, Alex who had always looked up to him, had admired him. But that was exactly why Uncle J. had to win this one. His identity was on the line. He had to regain Alex's esteem, in order to regain his own self-esteem. Now he would head for philosophy, for psychology, for anything that might give him a new handle.

"It's a matter of priorities. You look around and there are other responsibilities, there are other people depending on you, a wife, a child."

"So, revolutionary idealism is only for bachelors, eh, those who don't have a wife and a child? What about mother and father and brother and sister? What if your brother or sister disappears in the middle of the night, never to be heard from again, to die alone in some dark dungeon? What is the revolutionary idealist's task then? To wait for the Russians to strike a deal with the Americans? And what if the Russians decided to sell out one country at one time or another for a bigger geopolitical gain? It has happened, you know. Then all the revolutionary idealists sit on their hands and accept it? How come the Russians didn't lift a finger to keep Mosaddeq from going under, refused to pay him a penny of their war debts, but turned over seventeen tons of gold to this murderous gang after the Coup, when everything was lost?"

"You are mixing everything up now," Uncle J. would say passionately. "It is a matter of the infrastructure. Until you change the infrastructure, nothing else you do is worth much. Mosaddeq was another bourgeois, he wanted to save the Capitalist system, his loyalty was to an insipid 'liberal democracy' within the context of the Capitalist system. The Russians could not support what was not a genuine Socialist-Marxist revolution. They paid off this regime to keep their foothold here."

"O. K. Mosaddeq was not a Marxist. He was not a Communist. He was not a Socialist. But at least he stood for Constitutional Democracy. He tried to take the authority over the Army away from the Shah, and put it under the elected government, to make it difficult for the Shah to run a military coup any time he wanted. Until that was done, nothing else could be done. He even made the Tudeh Party legal again. Not one man, woman, or child were tortured by Mosaddeq's order. And see what we have now. Torture and murder and disappearance by the thousands. And we didn't raise a finger to help Mosaddeq, to back him up. The Russians didn't. The Tudeh Party didn't. They denounced him as a stooge of the Imperialists to the bitter end, the usual slogans that have lost their real meanings. And on the day of the Coup, what did the mighty Tudeh Party do, with their powerful military organization in the Army, the Air Force, the Savak, the National Police, and with half a million Party members and sympathizers in Tehran alone? They ordered all their membership off the streets, so that, as they put it, they could not be blamed for anything. Well, they had their wish. They are not blamed."

"You have bought that naive liberal line. Mosaddeq legalized the Tudeh Party, hoping that they would let down their guards, come out into the open swinging, and expose their military organization, so that they could be crushed then. That has been the standard Imperialist tactic everywhere. When they found out the Party was too smart for that, they had to go the military route."

"And what was the use of the unexposed military organization of the party, if they wouldn't do anything when the time for military action came?"

"Obviously they thought the time was not ripe. You have read Lenin's *One Step Forward, Two Steps Back*, haven't you? It's all in there."

"And how many steps backward is it now? Or have we stopped counting?"

"Well, the battle has been lost. That's what I've been trying to tell you."

"What battle?" Alex would say with amused surprise. "Did you see a battle? I didn't. I thought they were still waiting for the right time. When would have been the right time?"

"One can't always foresee the right time with accuracy. Sometimes one is wrong about the timing. They did not have the strength to win a frontal attack by the Army."

"But if they had come out swinging on that day, with the populace behind Mosaddeq, with Mosaddeq's Palace Guard defending him, the Army would have been divided and defeated, Shah's authority over the Army would have been forfeited, Mosaddeq would have remained, some kind of elected pluralistic government would have remained, and they would have remained."

"That's where you are disregarding the basic question again, the question of the infrastructure. They wanted a genuine Marxist-Leninist revolution. They did not want to bail out Mosaddeq's liberal bourgeois Government. They wanted for everyone to see the liberal bourgeoisie for what it was, to see the *petit* bourgeoisie for what it was."

"And they ended up by letting everybody see the military dictatorship for what it is, themselves first. You talk as if the question of thousands and thousands of people jailed, tortured, and murdered is irrelevant, as if the only relevant question is the abstract question of economic infrastructure, as if people didn't exist except in abstract metaphysical systems, as if all jailing, torture, and murder was beside the point, that it might even be justified with the right kind of abstract infrastructure."

"I didn't say that. You are distorting what I said." Uncle J. would say. He was hot around the collar now. He was sweating. He was starting to take it personally. "I am not defending the Tudeh Party. I am defending the Marxist-Socialist theory."

"You were just defending the Tudeh party as the only game in town. Which is a good argument, if you follow it by one that says, and since that game is up, let's not play at all."

"Again, you are distorting what I said. I said no Communist or Socialist party in this country can win if it doesn't have the support of Russia. And the Tudeh party is the only one that does have the support of Russia. That doesn't mean I am still defending the Tudeh party. There have been treasons in the Party. Even then I suspected that there were traitors in the Central Committee of the Party. I am not defending them. You're forgetting that I left the Party."

"Yes, but not for those reasons. You left before you knew, as you say, that the game was up. You left before you knew whether the Party would fight it out or not. You left when the price became too high. And quite an army followed you. And now they are all living very respectable lives, as high officials in the Shah's Government, and as rich businessmen in the Capitalist system. And their only excuse is that there is no other game in town. They don't wish to remember that the reason the other game folded was because they left it."

"You don't win a revolution by a cadre of local party leaders. You win it by the mass of people."

"The mass was still there, when the cadre of local leaders pulled out and ran for the tall grass. They were still writing slogans on the walls, getting shot at, going to jail, and being tortured and murdered rather than 'confessing' and naming names. And the leadership was applauding them as heroes. Only when the cadre of local party leaders began to be caught, the Party said it was all right to 'confess' rather than die."

"What do you want me to do?" Uncle J. asked, somewhat irritated. "You still want me to go write slogans on the walls? Take to the woods? When we all know that the game is up?"

"I am not the one who is saying what you should do," Alex said. "I am not the one who is doing the prescribing. You have chosen a way of life which makes sense to you, which answers your needs, at this stage of your life. You want to be the Shah's cabinet minister. You *are* the Shah's cabinet minister."

"Do you really think I wanted to be the Shah's cabinet minister?" Uncle J. would say with righteousness. "You don't know what the alternatives were."

"Oh, I know what the alternatives were," Alex would say. "And you chose this alternative. And I am not the one who is trying to talk you out of it."

"Well, I won't be that for long," Uncle J. would say, as a last resort. "I have made my plans. I would be leaving the Government soon."

"You mean you have set up your own companies, to do business with the Government, from the other end? At a higher rate of profit? You mean you have decided to be a Capitalist, rather than a Capitalist's lackey? To buy cabinet ministers for a change? What about the infrastructure? What about the Holy War against the Almighty Capitalist system? I knew the business of America was supposed to be business. I didn't know the Tudeh Party's business has also become business. So, you would be a businessman, a merchant, if you please."

Now Uncle J. was genuinely upset. "I resent that comment," he would say. He would plead his status as an uncle. "It's a rude and mean thing to say, to call your own uncle a businessman, a merchant, especially someone who has lived the life I have lived."

Alex would apologize. He had not meant it as a derogatory comment. He was using the terms for discussion's sake. Any word can be made to sound dirty. Didn't some comrades manage to make even *intellectual* sound like a dirty word? Hadn't the word *liberal* become a dirty word? This wasn't meant to be an *ad hominem* discussion. But the discussions were becoming more personal, more bitter. Uncle J. and Alex were drifting apart, irreversibly. Their last discussion ended on a sad note.

"I may not be able to save you," Uncle J. had said. "if you get caught, whatever it is you are involved with."

"I wouldn't want you to save me," Alex had replied. "I hope I wouldn't create problems for you."

Uncle J. looked at him, really stung. Was that what Alex thought, he must have wondered, that his concern was for his own position at the Court, his cabinet post, his connection with the Savak? They never had another discussion. Alex went underground shortly after that. And Uncle J. hardly ever came back to visit us. Maybe he was too embarrassed to come to our house in his official chauffeured limousine, or in his personal luxury Mercedes.

"When you get mixed up with the Court," Dad would say with resignation, "all you worry about is whether the way you smile is going to displease someone."

When Alex was caught, Uncle J. was allowed to see him once, accompanied by his Savak General friend. Alex's face was badly bruised from heavy beatings. His swollen eyes could hardly open and his toothless and smashed mouth looked like a bloody hole. When Uncle J. had tried to persuade him to talk, to name names, and save his own life, Alex had looked at him with a contemptuous smile and said, "They got you to do their dirty work for them again, didn't they?" Uncle J. had barged out, never attempting to see him again, no matter how much Dad begged. After Alex was dead, Dad tried to get Uncle J. to help him recover the body for burial. But Uncle J. would have nothing to do with it.

"What the hell do you want with the body, Old Man?" he shouted at Dad. "Even if you managed to recover it, which you won't, it would be in such a shape that even crows wouldn't wanna peck at it." He obviously knew more than he was willing to tell.

Dad did try to get the body on his own, but with no luck. He had tried to save Alex before, when he was still alive, with as little luck. He had tried to get the Minister of Justice to intervene. His old friend had looked at him incredulously over his spectacles and said, "My dear Shadzad, where have you been living all these years? On the far side of the moon? You really think I can save your son?" He had written groveling petitions to the Shah, pleading his gray hair and his long years in the service of His Imperial Majesty in the cause of justice, begging that his son's life be spared. His petitions had gone unacknowledged. Then he had written to the Court Minister, who had responded that the Chief Justice would have done better to plead with his son not to become a traitor to His Imperial Majesty, after all the privileges his family had been showered with by His Imperial Majesty's grace.

Uncle J. attended Alex's sham funeral, but no one could tell whether he was there for Alex, or on official orders, so that the rumors would be quelled. It certainly was one of the best publicized funerals in the whole country. Dad had been ordered to make it as conspicuous as possible. After the burial, Uncle J. briefly hugged Dad and me, shook hands with Mom, rushed into his official limousine, and disappeared. I saw him back there one more time only, right after Dad's stroke, and just before I left the country. I did not see him again for a long time. When I saw him next, abroad, he was a totally changed man. Everything about him had been transformed. For one thing, his neck seemed to have disappeared. His head now seemed to grow straight out of his body, which had become much heavier. No matter from what angle he looked at you, his eyes seemed to be looking down.

CHAPTER FOURTEEN

Uncle J. left his Government post shortly after Alex's funeral. Whether he lost favor with the Shah, or Alex's death subjected his equivocal identity to a further crisis that made it impossible for him to carry on business as usual, or he simply considered that an auspicious time to go into business for himself, as he had intended, nobody knew. But once more he showed his genius for timing and his knack for survival. Recognizing that no one's luck in that corrupt bureaucracy lasted forever, for years he had set up his own dummy companies headed by his cronies, had established the necessary contacts and credentials for them to obtain favorable Government contracts, and had placed his friends in key civil service positions to ensure the flow of those contracts. When he left, he had created a small business and financial empire for himself.

In a short time after that, he had established himself and his local companies as representatives of and partners in many multinational conglomerates. He had the means and the willingness to buy anything from anyone, and to sell anything to anyone, at any time, during peace or war, famine or flood, embargo or revolution, for a mere ten-percent minimum commission. Sometimes, by the time a transaction had been concluded through his chain of companies, and through a host of countries, his percentage would have amounted to several hundred percents of the original transaction. And the price would be anything that the traffic could bear, padded by any government official who could be bought, in any country of the world. And everything as legal as selling apples on the sidewalk. Nobody ever went to jail for anything Uncle J. did. You could bank on that.

He was now on the other side of the fence, not a corrupt government official, but a force corrupting governments. His contacts and influence spread far beyond one border and one country. He lived more and more abroad, in the many fortified mansions he had bought, but mostly on *Cotes d'Azures*. He traveled in his personal jet, or on his personal yacht. His phone calls could come from anywhere, Paris, London, Zurich, St. Moritz, Cannes, or Venice; from his car driving past, from his jet flying over, or from his 200-foot yacht cruising by. He had become an international institution, not belonging to any one country. His chain of holding companies was now too big even for the Shah and *his* empire.

Now it was Uncle J. who cut the Shah and a host of enterprising Royal Princes and Princesses into big international deals, and gave them commissions.

Rumors about him were flying fast and furious, that he was in the Holy of Holies of the Freemasons, that he was one of the Illuminati, that he was a Knight of Malta, that he was a member of the Trilateral Commission, that he was a heavyweight in the international arms trade, that he was a top CIA man, with his companies as conduits for channeling CIA money around the world. There was no telling his net worth. Sometimes you would hear him crack a joke at someone who was "showing off his pathetic hundred millions."

He was becoming less and less accessible, even to the family, although the signs of his presence were everywhere: a huge basket of fruits or flowers, or a gigantic tree too big to carry indoors, arriving on Christmas, or the Persian New Year, or the American New Year, or the Jewish New Year, or the Chinese New Year, or on all these occasions, depending on the makeup of the family at the time. No birthday cake would be cut before Uncle J.'s present had arrived, usually at the last minute.

Who could tell when the little box might not have a one-carat diamond in it? And when it didn't, what a disappointment! The real honor was if Uncle J. called in person. Presents were sent by his "boys," or "girls." But if he called, you knew that he had remembered, or that someone had remembered to remind him to remember. If someone got married, the biggest item of speculation was what kind of a gift he would get from Uncle J. Weddings always went big with him. They went even bigger with Aunt Sarah, *the Princess*. If she liked you, you would always get a better gift from Uncle J. And if you had crossed her, you might as well forget the whole thing.

If someone had an operation, there was always a huge bouquet of flowers waiting in the recovery room. Kids always got those huge life-size stuffed animals from Uncle J. Once a kid had received a gift from Uncle J., there was no more pleasing him. Anything you gave him or her would be a waste of time. One could spot Uncle J.'s presents at the door as they arrived, without having to open the card. The card hardly ever said anything, anyway, and it was never in his handwriting, or that of Aunt Sarah, or the *young princesses*, Mini and Mo. In short, Uncle J. had become like God. He was nowhere, but the signs of his presence and bounty were everywhere. Uncle J.'s *boys* and *girls* were the most efficient in the world.

Uncle J. never knew how he was affecting the lives of his relatives, friends, and acquaintances. People had become conditioned to organizing their lives around him. If he was arriving in a town, the word of his arrival would go from mouth to mouth. People would disrupt their lives, cancel previous engagements, decline invitations, miss weddings, miss funerals, change their vacation plans, to be present at the airport, to fight to be the first in line to greet him, and to greet Aunt Sarah, and the princesses, Mini and Mo.

The same applied if Aunt Sarah or the princesses were coming on their own. They were more accessible. They had less to do, not having all those deals to cut. All they had to do, was to travel, and to shop. Anyway, pleasing Aunt Sarah was more important than pleasing Uncle J. And pleasing the princesses was more important than pleasing Aunt Sarah. Or rather, not displeasing Aunt Sarah was more important than not displeasing Uncle J., and not displeasing the princesses was more important than not displeasing Aunt Sarah. Uncle J. feared Aunt Sarah, but he doted on the princesses.

But trying to please the princesses, Mini and Mo, did not help with anything. They were so used to everybody trying to please them that they no longer even noticed it. But if you did *not* try to please them, or if you did something that displeased them, and almost everything displeased them, they noticed that. Then they would whisper something in their Daddy's ear, or make a long distance call at two in the morning half way around the globe, to let their Daddy know that you had not tried hard enough to please, or that you had tried to displease, or that you had said this or that, or that you hadn't said this or that, or that you had done this or that, or that you hadn't done this or that. They would ask their Daddy to be displeased too, and to no longer do for you. Of course, they had no idea what their Daddy had done for you, or if he had done anything for you. They simply took it as an item of faith that their Daddy had done for the world. Why else would he be constantly traveling around the world? And what their Daddy had done, they had done.

If there was a famine in Ethiopia, they were sure their Daddy had done for Ethiopia. If there were boat people from Kampuchea, their Daddy certainly had done for Kampuchea. If there was a war in El Salvador, their Daddy had certainly done for El Salvador. If there was a revolution in Nicaragua, their Daddy had certainly done for Nicaragua. If there were demonstrations in Poland, their Daddy had certainly done for Poland. And if you presumed to ask what was it that their Daddy had done, and for what, and for whom, and for which side, and to which side, that displeased them. That implied that their Daddy might have picked the wrong side, that the side their Daddy picked would not by definition be the right side, that their Daddy could not do for all sides. That implied that their Daddy might not know what he was doing, which implied that they might not know what they were saying. And then they would tell their Daddy that you had not done your best to please. And that their Daddy never forgave or forgot.

If you wanted to give a dime to a beggar in the street, they would persuade you not to do it. The man must be simply beyond help. If there was anything to be done for him, their Daddy must have already done it.

Take Alex for example. After all their Daddy had done for him, he had gone and got himself killed. He had cost Daddy so much, had caused him so much grief. He had almost caused Daddy to lose favor with His Majesty. Daddy had stuck his neck out for Alex. But Alex had been too stupid to listen to Daddy, to even save his own life. After all, Alex had learned everything from Daddy, everything about Revolution and Marxism and Communism and Socialism and everything. Daddy had been the Provincial First Secretary, didn't you know? And now Alex trying to teach Daddy about Revolution! Trying to make Daddy feel ashamed for being a Cabinet Minister and a friend of His Majesty. And this after Daddy had saved so many Marxists from getting jailed, tortured, and killed; after he had helped so many of them get high Government positions and become rich.

He would have done that for Alex too, if he had not been so stubborn. What he did to Daddy was inexcusable. Trying to make him feel bad about being very rich. As if there was anything wrong with being very rich. Everybody should be very rich. Those revolutionaries, they are not against being very rich. They just don't want others to be very rich. They want everybody to give them all their money. And if Daddy wasn't so very rich, how could he possibly *do* for so many people?

Only *they* could make Alex sound so decidedly stupid, so ungrateful, so cruel to Uncle J., so inconsiderate of him and of his position, as to go and get himself tortured and killed, after Uncle J. had told him not to do so. And if you said a word in defense of poor Alex, that displeased them immensely, because that implied they did not understand Marxism, which meant their Daddy hadn't been a Provincial First Secretary, or that they were not princesses, which meant their Daddy wasn't a Cabinet Minister, or that they did not have royal blood in them, which meant their Mommy didn't, or that they were not rich enough, or that they were too rich, or that they were not stupid enough, or that they were too stupid. And then they would be displeased. And they would tell their Daddy to be displeased.

On the authority of their Daddy, they took part in any and every discussion, and they had an opinion about everything. They knew everything not only about Marxism and Socialism and Idealism and Revolution, but also about political theory, economics, philosophy, literature, music, engineering, physics, chemistry, astronomy, astrology, and medicine. It wasn't only that their Daddy had read Marx, and copied Sa'adi's *Orchard*, but that when you *do* for the world, you learn all about the world. And if you dared to imply that there might be an organized body of knowledge in any field, that might require some expertise that their Daddy might not have, or that they might not have, they would be displeased. And when cards and telephone calls and gifts and checks ceased to arrive, you knew that the displeasure had reached the source.

And for so many relatives, friends, and acquaintances who had organized their lives around those cards and telephone calls and gifts and checks, to live otherwise would be inconceivable. For example, if you had got married with the expectation that you would receive a fat check from Uncle J. on your wedding day, figuring that Uncle J. would do for you at the same rate he had done for your brother or your sister, and the check didn't arrive, because you might have said something to displease Aunt Sarah, or the princesses, Mini and Mo, that would never do for your marriage.

Or if Uncle J. did for your education, and Uncle J. loved to do for people's education, for that meant he had made them what they were, in other words owned them, and then the check for your tuition did not arrive, because you had said something to displease the princesses, Mini and Mo, that would never do for your education.

Or if you were jobless and had got used to not looking for a job, or not finding one, especially if you had also got used to eating high on the hog, and then the monthly check did not arrive, because you had not shown your face at an airport on a certain day, or had forgotten to send a card or a bouquet of flowers on a certain occasion, or had said or done something in a certain gathering to displease, that would not do for your eating.

And now that I had not done anything that should endear me to Uncle J., anything that should endear me to Aunt Sarah, anything that should endear me to the princesses, Mini and Mo, in fact, now that I had done everything in my power to displease them all, why was Uncle J. so eager to keep me from going back and, as he put it, get myself killed in a hurry.

"You're just like Alex," he finally said. "Headstrong, stubborn, wrong."

Only then I realized why Uncle J. could not afford to see me go back and get myself killed in a hurry. It would remind him too much of what had happened to Alex. It would stir up the old feelings in him. It would open up that old split. It would call into question his integrity, his very identity. (True, he was no longer the Shah's right-hand man.

Nor was he the Ayatollah's man. Now the Shahs and the Ayatollahs of this world worked for him, seeking his help to get their oil through the high seas, to get spare parts for their airplanes, ammunition for their tanks, food for their soldiers.) Uncle J. was not really arguing with me, but with Alex; not even with Alex, but with the ghost of his own old self. I felt sorry for him. I felt I had to give him that satisfaction, for his sake, for Alex's sake.

"Uncle J.," I said, "this decision will be the first authentic existential act of my life."

There was a silence on the other end of the line. I thought I could hear Uncle J. swallowing.

"Come again!" he said, in a hesitant tone.

I amended myself. "Whether I decide to go back, or decide not to go back, this would be probably the first decision in my life I have made on my own. On my own, you understand? Not because I had promised Dad, not because I had promised Mom, not because I had promised you, or Alex, or Cyrus, or Sam, or someone else, dead or alive."

"Who is Sam?" he asked.

"Just a figure of speech," I said. "Some people say Tom, Dick, or Harry. I say Sam."

"I see," he said.

"All I am saying is that, regardless of what I decide to do, whether to go back or not to go back, whether to stay there or to come back here, this would be the first time in my life I have made a decision. And to take three days to do that isn't a long time, is it?"

"At least you are beginning to make sense," he said. "What were those big words you used earlier?"

"My first authentic existential act."

"Right! And this is what that means, yes?" he asked. "To make a decision on your own?"

"Roughly speaking," I said.

"And the first authentic existential decision of your life has to be something that more likely than not will get you killed? It can't be anything less than that, something that would give you only a broken leg or a broken arm or something? Skiing, or mountain climbing, or hang gliding, or something like that?"

I was missing the barn door by a mile again. I had to try harder.

"Uncle J.," I said. "let me try harder. I haven't been able to do anything on my own for thirty three years, because I have always been too busy trying to do something else, which I had promised someone, dead or alive. All my life I have been running to get away from wherever I was, just to be somewhere else, because I had promised someone. Somewhere along the line, I have missed the boat. Now, I've been trying very hard to figure out where I missed the boat. And my best educated guess is that I missed it back there somewhere, long ago. I have been like a guy who has lost the key to a door, but who has been so afraid of the dark that instead of looking in the dark, where he lost the key, he has been looking in the light, where he knew there was no key. If I go back, I don't know what I would be looking for, I don't know what I would find, I don't even know what the risks would be, but finding out, maybe, is the key I am looking for."

There was a long silence. I wasn't paying for the call. But even if I was, I wouldn't have minded it. It was the most eloquent silence I had ever heard. Uncle J. was not a man to be at a loss for words. When he came back, it wasn't with the same question.

"And the dead will have to wait for their burial, until you have made your authentic existential decision?" he asked, no longer challenging.

"They wouldn't mind it, I'm sure," I said. "I have waited for the dead for a very long time. They can wait for me for a change."

"How much money do you have?" he asked.

Now I knew I had won this one; for Alex, and for myself. That was always Uncle J.'s last argument, when he didn't have any other. He offered you money when he was doing for you. But he also offered you money when he had no better argument. The two weren't the same, but they hurt the same way. It hurt if you accepted the money. And it hurt if you didn't. You felt bad when you didn't take it. You felt guilty when you did. Uncle J.'s money seemed to have been dyed in guilt. No matter how you touched it, or how it touched you, you came out feeling the worse for it, you came out feeling like a loser.

If you asked Uncle J. whether he had two fives for a ten, or if you asked somebody else that, in the earshot of Uncle J., he would pull out his billfold, throw a hundred-dollar bill at you and say, "Here is a hundred. Change it at the bank," which didn't really solve anything. If you asked where the nearest bank, or the nearest American Express Office was, Uncle J.'s immediate response was to reach for his billfold. If you talked about anything having to do with money in Uncle J.'s earshot, he thought it related to him. It was like asking in Caesar's presence, whose likeness was on the coins. And whether he offered you money, because he thought you had meant it that way, or he took offense, because he thought you had meant it some other way, it was always a no-win situation for you. And when he offered money, it hurt you if you took it, and it offended him if you didn't. And that was another no-win situation for you. And everything was that much worse, if the princesses, Mini and Mo, were around. Because they would always insist on putting their two cents in, and they could twist anything and everything around, and make something out of nothing. And Uncle J. doted on them.

If you were in Helsinki and you called Uncle J. in Paris to say hello, and he would be very displeased if you were in Helsinki and didn't call him in Paris to say hello, he would immediately ask, "When are you coming down to see me?" If you mumbled, or gave excuses, such as not having time, or being on a three day conference, or not having vacation, or having to return to school, or having to return to work, or being on a special charter flight, or whatnot, he would always end up by saying, "How much would that cost?" or "Fly down. I'll pay for it." Or "Take a Concord." Your time didn't matter. Your plans didn't matter. Your work didn't matter. Your vacation didn't matter. Let alone trying to explain that you had a girlfriend with you, who was sleeping in the same bed with you, who liked to continue sleeping in the same bed with you, while you were on this trip. In Uncle J.'s mansions, even if you were allowed to take a woman who was not married to you, you didn't sleep in the same bed with her. Now try to explain that she was also married, and to someone else.

"Take a Concord," he would say, regardless of whether Concord flew there or not. And when you accepted the ticket, or the bill, or the check, you felt cheap, you felt sold out, you felt you had lost a lot in that bargain, even if the princesses, Mini and Mo, were not there to look down on you with the daintiest kind of disdain, seeing that their Daddy had done for you again. And if you didn't accept the ticket, and so, couldn't go, because you couldn't afford it, Uncle J. would be offended. And if you went, but insisted on not taking the money for the ticket, Uncle J. would be offended. And if you didn't call at all, then somehow the princesses, Mini and Mo, would hear that you were in Helsinki and didn't call, and they would tell their Daddy to be offended.

"How much money do you have?" Uncle J. asked again.

"Two dollars and thirty-five cents," I said, "in small coins."

"I'll send you a check," he said.

"No you won't!" I said. "I'm on my own now!"

"With two dollars and thirty-five cents in small coins?" he asked in an amused tone.

"Right!" I said. "I'll manage somehow."

"And you're going to pay for your ticket to Tehran with that, too?"

"No! I haven't decided to go yet. But if I do, I'll think of something."

"And what will you spend while you are down there? With the war and the inflation, your monthly payment from your Dad's trust fund wouldn't buy your bread for five days."

"Yes," I said. "I know. I'll have to do something about that too, won't I?"

"I'll give you the telephone number of some of my boys there, to help you out."

"No, thanks," I said. "I'd be glad to say hello to anybody for you, but no help, please."

"You want to go it alone," he said, "don't you?"

"Yes," I said.

"Like Alex did, eh?" he said.

"Go it alone like he did? Yes." I said. "But not going the same way as he did."

"Good luck!" he said. And I am sure he meant it. And I am sure I needed it.

I took a cold shower after Uncle J. hung up. I don't know why, but I did. I hate cold showers. Long hot showers, I really like. But I don't know why now I felt like taking a cold shower. This was the third time he had called me this weekend and I thought the last time. But I was wrong. As soon as I came out of the shower, the phone rang again. I looked at my watch. It was two-fifteen in the morning. Only Uncle J. calls in those hours. He never seems to know what time it is anywhere else, except where he is. And with the prices he pays for the long distance calls, and with the things he does for you, who is to complain?

"What are you doing?" he asked.

"I just took a cold shower," I said.

"Are you drunk?" he asked.

"No," I said. "I am unusually sober. And what is funny is that the more I drink tonight, the soberer I get."

I was surprised at what I said. I had always made a point of minimizing my vices with Uncle J., or what he might consider my vices. And drinking, he considered a vice. In fact, never before had I admitted my drinking to him. But suddenly I felt I didn't give a damn what Uncle J. considered or did not consider a vice. I think if I had been screwing at that moment, and he had asked me what I was doing, I would have told him exactly what I was doing, and given him the full detail of the position I was in, too.

"I must ask you some questions," he said.

"I'm listening," I said.

"I want absolutely straight answers," he said.

"You'll get 'em," I said, surprised at my own cold-blooded tone of voice. I don't think I had ever talked in that tone of voice to Uncle J. I don't think I know anybody who had ever talked in that tone of voice to Uncle J.

"Do you really hate very rich people?" he asked.

"Yes," I said.

"Why?"

"Because they make me think of people who are very poor, very hungry, very cold, and very humiliated," I said.

"Even those very rich who try to give to the very poor, and very hungry, and very cold, and very humiliated?"

"They are most humiliating when they do that," I said. "Usually what they give is nothing to them, but they want to take everything in return. They take so much for granted in other people."

"And those who don't do that?" he asked.

"They would never be very rich, or remain very rich," I said. "Have you read Shakespeare's *Timon of Athens?*"

"No," he said.

"I didn't think you had," I said. "Anyway, no one has any business being very rich."

"Do you blame me for Alex's death?" he asked.

"No," I said. "Alex's death had nothing to do with you. You like to think that Alex's death had everything to do with you, that Alex's life had everything to do with you, that whatever Alex did had everything to do with you. You like to think everything anybody does has everything to do with you."

"I made Alex what he was," he said. "Alex followed in my footsteps."

"You made nobody what he was," I said. "Alex and you walked the same road for a while, and then Alex went on to become what he was, and you went on to become what you are."

"And what am I?" he asked.

"Don't you know what you are?"

"Yes, I do," he said. "I just wanted to know what you think I am."

"Well," I said. "If you know what you are, you shouldn't really care what I think you are. You shouldn't care what anybody thinks you are."

"Alex and I were exactly alike," he insisted.

"Wrong," I said. "Cyrus and you are exactly alike. You both buy and sell, and you both need to be well-liked, and you both desperately need approval."

"And Alex?" he asked.

"He had a vision," I said. "Whether right or wrong, he had a vision. And he paid for it, with his life. You haven't paid for anything, with anything, with anything worthwhile, in your whole life. And you think you own the world. And your wife thinks she owns the world. And your daughters think they own the world. If you made anybody, you made them, I grant you that much."

"You hate me, don't you?" he asked.

"No," I said. "I used to love you. I just don't care for you any more. You have nothing now I want or care for."

"You're really determined to burn all your bridges this time, aren't you?" he asked.

"I don't need bridges *there*, where you are," I said, "because I will not be crossing that river again, not there."

"You don't think you'll ever need my help again, eh?" he asked in an ironic tone.

"That's where you and I don't communicate," I said. "You feel you have given me so much, and all for nothing. And I feel you have given me so little, and have taken so much in return. That's where the very rich miss the boat. You have given me things, objects, scraps of paper stamped with kings' and presidents' heads, things which were nothing to you. And you never understood how much it cost me to accept them, because you never understood what it was I gave you in return. Then things stopped costing me so much, because I stopped caring for them, because I stopped caring for you. They balanced out. You gave me what was nothing to you. And I took what was nothing to me. And that made us even. That's the mistake you made with Alex, too, when you warned him that you might not be able to help him any longer, not understanding that he couldn't possibly care for the kind of help you could offer, where he was. And when you offered to help him out of that dungeon, after what he had gone through, it just showed you still didn't understand the price he would have to pay to accept your kind of help."

"So, I have given you nothing!" he said. "And what is it that I have asked from you? What is it that you have given me?"

"At first, I accepted whatever you gave me, out of love. And I offered you all of me, out of love," I said. "But you thought you had all of me, because you had paid for it. And when I felt you didn't know the difference, I took back all of me, because you had paid for nothing. That's what I like about being poor. The poor can only offer themselves. And that's what I hate about the very rich. They never offer themselves. They think people appreciate their money better. And people often do. They forget that price is not the same as value. Value comes from our love for things, and from our need for that love. Price is what we pay in the market place. It has nothing to do with love."

"Can you put it in simpler terms, so that even a very rich man could understand?" he said.

"Sure!" I said. "We are both snobs. But I would rather be a very poor snob than a very rich snob."

"I think Cyrus is the only sane one in my brother's family," he said, his last word on the subject.

"Yes," I said, my last word on the subject. "He values everything you have, and he values everything you are. He is the man you desperately need. He is your identity. Blessed are the rich and they shall inherit the earth. Amen."

And that was the end of me and Uncle J., I thought. His cool or hot millions were no longer my care.

PART FIVE

CHAPTER FIFTEEN

Waterloo, Iowa
Saturday, January 14, 1984
2:30 a.m.

Sam just called. He is on his way down to see me. He sounded even more depressed than his usual, if that were possible. I have the feeling that he is at the end of his rope. He hasn't been able to sleep for forty-eight hours, he tells me. Catnaps now and then, but no real sleep. He can't drink any more, because of his ulcer. He is in bad shape and he shows it. His eyes have never been so bloodshot, baggy, sunk. I have been watching him deteriorate, emotionally and physically, getting closer and closer to the cliff. He has been talking suicide for ten months now.

Often I have felt that I am the only thing standing between him and the act, as if he needed my approval, my confirmation that he, indeed, has nothing to live for. He seems to need my complicity in his act. I just hope he does not intend to do it tonight. I am in no shape to try to stop him. Besides, if he does, it would be another ill-boding omen for me, another deadly coincidence. Then I would know that all the Fates have conspired against me tonight, that it is the end of the line, the last act of the drama, with the curtain going down on Oedipus's bleeding eyes.

I have not told him about my mother's death, but I suspect he already knows. I am afraid to tell him that I might go away. He might take it as a sign that he must act now, as a gesture of leave-taking. And yet I cannot keep it all a secret from him. If I decide to leave, I must tell him. I can't leave without saying good-bye to the only friend I have had for years, the only one with whom I have shared Alex and Mom.

He *must* know that my mother is dead. He was here when the telegram arrived. And I am sure he knew what that meant. I had often told him that one day I would receive a telegram on Alex's birthday, and that would be the news of my mother's death. I was that sure of it happening that way. And not only because Dad had also died on Alex's birthday. Well-mannered and sensitive as he is, he left before I had opened the telegram, to leave me alone in that initial private moment of my grief. Only after I had read the telegram once or twice, I realized that Sam wasn't there.

3:30 a.m.

Sam has just left me, on his way to start on that long lonely road. The ill omen I feared has come to pass. It is true then: the Fates *have* all conspired against me tonight. In one night, in one fell swoop, I am losing everything that was left to me: Mom, Clare, and now Sam. Only Alex would remain, because ghosts are the most faithful. They have nowhere else to go. Sam has had at least ten months to kill himself, yet he must wait until tonight to do it.

I couldn't have asked him, could I, to put it off one more week, until I was gone! And I couldn't give him one convincing reason why he shouldn't do it. How could I convince him, when I cannot convince myself, when I don't know which way I will jump. I had to be the goddamn honest Joe I am, the man who couldn't tell a lie, not even to save a friend's life. When he asked whether I might not commit suicide one day, I said I had not ruled out the possibility. That went big. That certainly was a convincing reason why he shouldn't do it. And my attempt to repair the damage, by telling him that I would stick around for as long as the world would let me, just to see how it would turn out, didn't go over very well, either.

I feel terribly guilty that I did not, could not, try harder to discourage him. I care much more about my friends' lives, than I do about my own. But, much as I wanted to, I could not be a total hypocrite. For years, Sam and I have talked about authentic existential acts. And now, when he tells me that his next authentic existential act is to end his life, what could I say? He does not have my perversities to keep him going. He cannot be a voyeur in this world. He cannot take the whole world as a stage, as I can; distract himself, as I can; play games with himself, as I can; play games with the world, as I can. He cannot laugh my painful belly laugh.

How could I have continued to dispense hope, when I had none left to dispense. I have done that for ten months. I have done that for five years. There is so much vacuum in Sam's life, and I have so little to offer to fill it with. He has been on the brink so long, he has totally exhausted himself. After months of discouraging him, tonight I quietly listened, as one by one he proposed and disposed of alternatives to killing himself. I said little to oppose him. I only asked whether in all honesty there was no other way left. And when he said there was none, I said nothing.

Was I, too, finally convinced of the inevitability of his suicide? What a twist, when he asked whether I was not committing suicide myself in a round-about way, by going back to a country caught in the grip of mass murder and war and famine, with the excuse of attending my mother's funeral. I hadn't looked at it that way, I said, with a chuckle. Others will see it that way, he said. He may well be right. Is that the way Uncle J. sees it? Is that the way Cyrus sees it?

Behind all our talk about authenticity, is it the old angst that lurks, the old death-wish? Could Sam be right? Could I be doing in a round-about way, what he is doing up front? Are the problems of the two us really the same, no matter how I lumpen it? Aren't we both left with no roots to feed our branches, to make us even hope for a greening? For years, watching our roots dissolve in the thin alien air, haven't we both worn ourselves so thin that we are leaking through, to death?

If I had to pick a symbol of alienation in our time, to put in a cage and hang up on a hilltop for the world to see, I would take Sam. A Palestinian by birth, a Syrian by passport, a legal resident of Lebanon by myth, a refugee in the United States by accommodation, he is considered a coward and a sell-out by his friends; branded a traitor and a collaborator with the Jews by the Palestinians and the Syrians; despised as a Palestinian outsider by the Lebanese; suspected as an Arab Nationalist by the Israelis, and as a socialist by the Americans. Even his name is a myth. Sam, as a legal entity, does not exist.

How ironic that the identity of Subhi Abdul Maaroof, the great homeless Arab poet, should have been reduced to the abbreviation S.A.M., and then further reduced to a one word name, *Sam*, not mythical and heroic, like Macbeth or Macduff or Gatsby, but anonymous, common, a nickname. What could be more common than Sam? His enemies made use even of that, punned on it. Sam, they said, lives on handouts from his Uncle Sam.

A sensitive poetic temperament, crippled by private and public grief, seeking personal salvation in a world that denies its possibility; unable to forget a traumatic love affair after twenty years of mourning it, in his poetry as well as in his life, a love affair which might have been his only refuge from a world dominated by evil, greed, and violence; deprived of his attachment to his only object of sustained distraction and devotion, a journal of Arabic poetry which he published and edited, what alternative does he have?

Could I have agreed that he was a coward, because he would not pick up a gun and fight, I who am so pigeon-livered myself, having a dybbuk and a Hecuba closer to my heart than he has to his? Could I have argued with his misgivings about the course of the best of revolutions, when the torch is passed from the visionary to the gunman;

the idealist's dream becoming the pragmatist's nightmare; the purist's stream of clear water disappearing in the massive mud of the flooding river, in the whirlpools of private ambition and revenge, or in the cesspools of greed, mendacity and prurience?

Could I have blamed him for killing the Journal, after fifteen years labor of love that had made it the most celebrated journal of Arabic poetry in the world, when he found out that the humanitarian foundation subsidizing it was a front for a certain intelligence organization? Could I have blamed him for his refusal to sell, refusal to condone prostitution anywhere, but least of all in the world of art and letters, I who have been accused of being such a purist myself?

Are our peoples so very different, a generous innocent breed, starved, exploited, manipulated, corrupted, reduced to a barefoot motley crowd of infighters, backbiters, back-stabbers, who would sell their mothers for profit or for bread, and who, bent on destroying themselves as well as their enemies, would tear the heart out of innocence itself, for revenge? Our poor innocent peoples, show horses put to carrying dung, songbirds who have sold their voices, while we both perversely cling on to the myths of gutted-out homes, of gutted out cities, that no longer exist, not even in the mind's eye.

4:30 a.m.

Sam stopped by again and then left for good. He has done it. He has launched himself into the Great Unknown. He has swallowed sixty Doriden tablets, made a farewell cassette for me, written three farewell letters, and has by now gone to bed to take a very very long nap. Steeled as I was to face him, I lost my voice, as soon as I opened the door. I felt a dull pain in my chest as he handed me the little package, the last gift of his life, and hugged me tight, with tears running down our faces. He reminded me of my promise to keep his secret until Monday morning, when it would be too late to do anything about it. He has done his research. He is a man who knows his pills, and how long they take to do a man in. He tells me that by Monday morning, even the doctors won't be able to do anything, and I believe him. Yet, I am held to my promise of keeping his secret until then.

Why the hell suddenly everything has to wait until Monday morning, I'd be damned if I know. What's so goddamn special about Monday mornings all of a sudden? I can't see Clare, until Monday morning. Cyrus can't know what I am going to do, until Monday morning. Uncle J. can't know what I am going to do, until Monday morning. I don't know what I am going to do, until Monday morning. My mother can't be buried, until I know what I am going to do, on

Monday morning. And no one can do anything for Sam, until Monday morning, because I can't tell anyone anything about Sam, until Monday morning. And even if they could do anything for Sam on Monday morning, it wouldn't do any goddamn good anyway, because he would try it again another early Saturday morning.

He has left three letters for me to mail, guess when, Monday morning. One is to his old mother in Beirut, Lebanon. As I read the address I find myself asking questions, from no one in particular? Are they still delivering mail to Lebanon? Are people still living in Lebanon? Is there still a Lebanon? Or is Lebanon a dead figment of this dying poet's imagination? Might the mailman just find a hole in the ground in Beirut, where the old Mrs. Maaroof used to live? Might he just throw the letter over the dead woman's shroud, as jets are dropping their bombs, and explosives go off in parked cars, and machine guns sing their daily hosannas of praise? Wouldn't it be a Providential act of mercy, for this old woman to be hit by a cannon ball, just before the mail delivery, to be spared the news of the death of his only son and surviving relative, by suicide?

The second letter is to an "associate" in Paris, the fellow poet who worked with him on The Journal for fifteen years.

The third letter is to a woman in England, *the* woman in his life, his "pale lady," his "Helen of Troy," his homegrown version of Maud Gonne. Is it another poem to her, the ritual that consummates the sacrifice? Will she feel just a little bit guilty? Will she be content now? Will everybody be content now? Will his friends now believe that he was not a coward? Or will they consider this even a bigger act of cowardice? Why, they would say, didn't he commit suicide by throwing his wired body under an enemy car, by driving a truckload of explosives into the enemy barracks? Will his people now believe that he was not a traitor, a collaborator, that he had not sold out to any one? Is it only by death that innocence can be proved? Will his enemies know now that he was not a spy, an agent, an agitator? Will the world be just a little bit ashamed?

....

I have just washed my hands of the guilt of Sam's blood. Let them add Pontius Pilate to the long list of my names. I will not try to save him. I cannot. He is determined to die and he would try it again. I would only drag out his agony and lose his confidence and friendship, which have been left intact even unto death. They would lock him up in an asylum for a while, where his misery would be only heightened. He would fool the doctors and get out in thirty days. The law would let him go. Then he would do it again, without telling me. And he would die, even lonelier, deprived of the one friendship still left to him.

Yes, I will honor the heartrending promise extracted from me by love, long ago. Had I known then that this day would come, that this was no drunken philosophic speculation? I will wait for the Monday mail, for the letter informing me officially, of Sam's suicide, before I inform the police. By that letter Sam has meant to hide my complicity in his suicide, to exonerate me of the charge of prior knowledge, as if that is what worried me. Poor Sam. He doesn't know that what I need is not exoneration, but absolution, and not from my sins, but from the sins of the world. I, too, am a man more sinned against than sinning.

Until Monday I will contemplate in my mind's eye his sleeping face, as it loses the semblance of sleep and takes on the hues of death. I will tiptoe into his room and watch his body deteriorate, as I watched his mind do so over months and years. The dull pain in my chest will be my covenant with Sam, a constant reminder that Sam is turning into a vegetable, that he is growing roots. What a metaphor, what an irony! Sam finally sprouting roots in death. As for me, I will simply add his death to the long list of my grievances. I will be burdened with yet another corpse.

....

Now I have to listen to Sam's tape. Correction: Subhi's tape. I have to stop calling him Sam. He is no more Sam than I am Fink. Sam is no more Sam than Fink is Fink. Let's do away with Sam. I know pretty much what is in the tape. (Sam and I know each other as we know the palms of our hands.) And yet, I fear the minute I hear the tape, I will feel like an accessory to a crime, a murder, if you please.

Has Subhi picked this night, the night of my mother's death, the anniversary of my father's death, the anniversary of my brother's murder, the night of my lover's betrayal, the night when I finally have to square my accounts with the world, to plant himself, as if he too should want to test the limit of my endurance, as if Friday January 13th wasn't already a fully booked date for me? Why should all the Shadzads choose this day for birth or death? Alex didn't know that his birthday would be the beginning of a new calendar. He should disappear on this day. Dad should die on this day. Mom should die on this day. Well, maybe Uncle J. and Cyrus and I will also keep faith and choose to die on this day. And now, even the non-family have got into the act. Clare should choose this day for fornication. Subhi should choose this day for suicide. Who knows, maybe Beth is at this moment being made with child. Maybe this will become a day on which all the acts of the human drama will be played out, at my expense.

But looking at it from a different angle, nothing is surprising at all. It is not all sheer coincidence. There is a tragic thread that leads from one human act to another. Mom had to die on this day, as if it was written. Clare had to choose this day for fornication, because she knew I would go on a three-day binge and be no good to her, one way or another. Her being with me would have only caused her more pain. And as for Subhi, maybe it is not he who has added his burden to mine, but it is I who have added mine to his, by sharing with him my cumulative griefs, and then putting on his back the last straw, the threat of my leaving, and leaving him alone in the face of the whole world.

But how could I have kept my mother's death a secret from him? He has always been with me on Alex's birthday, helping me celebrate, while trying to keep me from drinking myself to death. Subhi and I have always shared our grudges against the world. We have been in the habit of validating each other's despair.

Invariably on such evenings, we have carried out a drunken discourse on the meaning of life and death, the absurdity of the human condition, and the reductio ad absurdum of all human experience, taking turns to quote from the Bible: *Vanity of vanities, says the Preacher.* Playing roles, he of the blear-eyed pessimist, I of the cock-eyed optimist, we have been forever engaged in an eternal argument.

He, Subhi Abdul Maaruf, the fifty-two-year-old distinguished Arab poet, the translator of Yeats, the authorized biographer of Kahlil Gibran, the editor of the celebrated but now defunct literary journal, *Al Edebiyat*, a Palestinian by birth, a Syrian by passport, a Lebanese by myth, an American by refuge, subsisting on a handout from a university fund subscribed to by dubious organizations, still mourning the loss of his one great love, dead some twenty years ago, arguing on the side of Thanatos, asking for one good reason why he should not commit suicide.

I, the thirty-three-year-old gentleman actor, amateur dabbler, Cynic-Idealist, Stoic-Epicurean, Nominalist-Realist, permanent student, permanent alien, permanent drunk, with no known identity, known country, known family, known occupation, known ambition, known conviction, arguing with admirable eloquence, but questionable sincerity, on the side of Eros, giving no sufficient reason for living but sheer curiosity and mulish obstinacy.

Listening to him, in fact, I had often wondered how he had managed to postpone his suicide for so long. As a poet, he had long felt written out. He had no more desire for translating. Translating Yeats' *Selected Poems* into Arabic had been an act of immense personal significance and effort, which could not be repeated. In Yeats' ambiguous and ambivalent relationship to the politics of Ireland and to the English language, he had mirrored his own attitudes toward his Palestinian and Arab identities. In Yeats' great and enduring passion for Maud Gonne, he had re-lived his own unfulfilled love for his lost nameless "pale lady," who had been the subject and argument of all his poetry.

The writing of Kahlil Gibran's biography had been his attempt to root himself in Lebanon, to adopt and be adopted, to persuade himself that he belonged, somewhere. When that too failed, he threw himself wholeheartedly into the publication and editing of *Al Edebiyat*. His decision to kill the journal, rather than sell it for a handsome sum, to those who had misled him for years into accepting possibly unclean money, left him not only utterly penniless, but also without any occupation, pre-occupation, or aim in life.

The disintegration of Lebanon was the last nail in his coffin, his last connection with the world to be severed. When he accepted the invitation to come to America to lecture on Arabic poetry, he did not come so much to make a living, as to make a dying. Suspected by all camps alike, he did not have any friends, he did not seek any friends, he did not want any friends. Disillusioned even by poetry, he was left with nothing but an empty bag. When I met him five years ago, he had already picked his own epitaph, "Subhi Abdul Maaruf, Arab Poet without a home. Suspected by friend and foe alike." And underneath it a line from W. H. Auden, "For poetry makes nothing happen."

And all these years he hung on to the promise, extracted from me by love, against my better judgment, that when his suicide came, I should accept it as an authentic existential act, by a man who no longer wished to live in this kind of a world. He gave me the privilege of holding his last will and testament, a single-page handwritten document in a sealed envelope, making me its executor. I, his only friend, am to receive his only worthwhile possession, a meager library of mostly autographed books, his old gramophone, and a few worn-out Arabic records, which were his intimates unto death. A life insurance of three thousand dollars is to take care of his burial, in a site to be chosen by me, preferably in potter's field. On his grave, preferably alone, I am to read W. H. Auden's poem *In Memory of W. B. Yeats*, which includes the line "For poetry makes nothing happen."

I am used to people dying on me, leaving me their dirty secrets with their last breath, emotionally blackmailing me, extracting from me promises they have no business extracting from anyone. I am used to that. I am the confidant of the dead. The dead don't care what they do to the living. They just pile it on and dare us not to take it. We can't even be angry with them. They have already paid for their lives, for their follies. But they must leave me their dirty secrets and their last cruel wishes, just to add to my burdens.

And yet, I can't help feeling grateful that, if he must do it, Sam has chosen to do it now, as a final act of sharing, as a final act of love, before I go back for my mother's funeral, or just go back, to try and pick the non-existent thread of meaning in my life.

But is it possible that Subhi is calling my cock-eyed optimist's bluff, having suspected my hypocrisy all along? Is it possible that he had not believed my solemn promises, expecting me to break my word now and save him? We had played the conscious-unconscioussemiconscious wish-to-die wish-to-be-saved game, and had decided that it was for the birds. It is only I who am still playing that game, by delaying, by putting off the certain knowledge of what has happened, and my feelings of helplessness and guilt and loss. Subhi has done his part. I have had my cue. The rest is up to me. And now I must listen to the tape.

....

Subhi's Tape

Farhang, my friend, my only friend, my friend to the bitter end! I am recording this farewell to you, not because of any illusions of leaving relics behind, but because it is easier to say goodbye through a machine, that cannot look back and show pain. It will be little consolation for you to know that if I had not known you, I would have ended my life much sooner. Your friendship, your intellectual, artistic, and emotional kinship have lengthened my life for several years. But it is inevitable that I should end my agony now. When you hear this, Charon has already begun ferrying me over the Styx, a useless metaphor, but habit of poetry, like other habits, is hard to break.

I know you will live up to your promise and let me die in peace. By now I should be in deep sleep, catching up with my many sleepless nights. You have the key to my room. You may visit, to say your farewells, as often as you wish, as long as you do nothing to disturb my sleep. I have much need of rest. You may even bring your bottle and drink at my bedside, if it can deaden your pain.

As for the world, but for my old mother and you, there is no one left for whom I care, or who cares for me. My relatives have all either died or been killed, bombed in, or bombed out. Even my mother may be dead by now. Every time a bomb has gone off in Beirut, I have wondered whether her name was not written on it. I haven't heard from her for over a month. But the mail from Beirut now takes a very long time to arrive. All the friends I once had, have either renounced me or been renounced by me. For my enemies, I do not care, though I wish them no harm.

My admirers have long forgotten me, since I have had no more love poems for them, to send to their sweethearts, in red heart- shaped chocolate boxes, on Saint Valentine's Day. If I could recall my books from all the libraries and strangers' bookshelves, I would do so. I have no use for all that Auden wished for the dead Yeats; that my death be kept from my poems by mourning tongues; that I should become my admirers; that I should be scattered among a hundred cities and be wholly given over to unfamiliar affections, or be punished under a foreign code of conscience. I was scattered among only a few cities in my life span, and God knows and you know how little I relished it.

My publisher in Lebanon stole from me long enough, while I was alive, pirating my works and not paying my royalties. And he will do so after I am dead. He will not miss me; though, he may play up my suicide, so that he may rekindle interest in my work, and put more money in his pocket. As the executor of my will, you will never see any of that money. So, as you see my friend, there is no reason for me to change my mind and wake up from this already very deep and very peaceful sleep.

Don't be too sad over my death. Even though neither of us believes in another world, a better or a worse one, do believe that I am suffering less now. It is the living who grieve for death, and I know you have had much death to grieve for. If I could have waited until after your possible departure, I would have done so. But I was already hard put to come up with a good excuse to continue. I cannot bear loneliness as well as you can. I lack your courage to be amused by painful reality. I cannot live my life as you do, with a wide-eyed yet cynical innocence, as if you were the master of ceremonies at someone else's party. I have lost my taste for alcohol. Not only my mind, but my body has finally said enough to that. I never had your taste for human flesh, except with my one great love.

I know you appreciate the emotional and spiritual depth of my one great love. You would not be the poet you are, if you did not. But I cannot understand the range and variety of your involvement with women. You too can deeply love one woman, and yet transfer that love with ease, from the one to another and then to another, to say nothing of all those others you can enjoy with the lust of a goat in his one happy rutting season, and with your "fecund maximum." You may plead Blake's words about "the lust of the goat [being] the bounty of God," and "the nakedness of woman [being] the work of God." But do you worship woman's naked flesh with Blake's mystical piety? Is your goatish lust a measure of your physical and mental health, or is it an example of "regression in the service of the ego," obscenity in the service of sanity?

If I may scold you a little, you are the eighth wonder of the world; Idealist, Nominalist, Cynic, Skeptic, Stoic, Epicurean, rolled into one, if such an animal can exist. Is Fink your way of Hathayoga to physical well-being, while you in your own person seek Karmayoga and spiritual union? Does Fink, with his varied masks, do your dirty work among the swines of the herd of Epicurus, so that you in your own person can live on the level of pure intellect? I envy the way you can embrace the animal in you, to kill the pain of being human. I envy the way you can modulate your sensibilities along such a wide range, from the angelic to the beastly, from the sublime to the ridiculous.

I don't know whether you have been taken in by your own masks, the way others have. Do you really believe Fink is not you? Do you actually not experience him physically and emotionally as yourself? Is being Fink so painful, that even Fink has to create other masks to hide behind? Does your Poor Tom really have a separate existence? Does this clown *Prince Omelet* really exist by himself? I wish I could imitate you, if that is what it takes to numb the pain. I wish I could borrow your masks, mimic your clowning, the best defense against suffering. How do you do it? I could never master that art. I was never good at laughter.

Sense of humor has always remained inaccessible to me, even when it has a tragic lining. Maybe that is why I do not appreciate Shakespeare as well as you do. But you always had the gift of belly laugh, even if you had no one to laugh at but yourself. Who else but you could berate Hamlet for his lack of a sense of humor, for not allowing for the possibility that his ghost was nothing but a joke played on him by his fraternity brothers?

But having berated your Fink, I remember that I have had Sam to hide behind, about as long as you have had Fink. How long did it take me to realize that I was not Sam, but Subhi Abdul Maaruf, an Arab poet alienated from himself and from the world, forced into a false identity, out of a desperate need to belong? Much as I would have liked to convince myself that it was all a matter of convenience, to have a nickname like everyone else, as if really there was nothing to a name. Maybe your Fink is more lucid than my Sam, even in his own self-ironic deprecation.

But having granted you this much, must you always carry things to such an extreme, to attain *reductio ad absurdum*? Have you really no consciousness of yourself when, as Fink, you let yourself be dragged into those orgies of booze and sex that masquerade as acts of love, even if we allow for drunkenness as an excuse? Are you not really conscious of the time you spend in the company of that low life you call McFart and the Twelve Peers and what not. Are you really serious about your admiration for them, because they have no sense of shame, because like Diogenes they have succeeded to live like a dog?

Diogenes as such, was a poetic construct, an ironic fiction created by a poetic imagination. The poet who conceived of that fiction could not have lived it. Yet, you have set yourself the task of at once conceiving such a dog-like life as the most heinous species of human existence, and living it, too. You have, indeed, stood Blake's words on their heads and chosen dog for your schoolmaster. If this is a price we must pay for curing ourselves from the duality of being human, is it really a price worth paying? Your intellectual being cries out no. Your cumulative physical actions under your collective names seem to say yes. If this signifies courage on your part to continue living, and not a mere perversity of purpose, I can only choose to envy you.

I know you are not a coward. I know you do not fear death. I know you would rather choose to die than knowingly hurt another human being, or steal, or cheat, or play false. So, I must think that it is courage that keeps you going, despite your feelings of despair and loss, which are as great as mine. Unless, it is indeed your stated infinite curiosity about the world that makes you want to stick around at whatever price, to see how it all turns out; even if you have to make up apocryphal sayings by dubious ancient Greek philosophers about an observing eye in the rear end of an ass. Maybe this world deserves such an unclean metaphor. Maybe to be amused at such a world, with all its ugliness, beastliness, and lack of compassion and generosity, is an ultimate act of courage, if not of piety and, to borrow from our friend Yeats, of radical innocence.

I am sorry if what began as a loving farewell has turned into a diatribe. I am sure that with your unique gift for nuance, you will manage to extract from this diatribe all the tenderness and affection I feel for you. Maybe I have to be critical and harsh to be able to take leave. I would not begrudge you any sardonic amusement you might avail yourself at my expense. Maybe this farewell might prove too much for you too, and you might have to hand the reins over to Fink, to kick some dirt in my face. I have seen him perform at the extremes of your pain. He is good. He is very good. He has the best gallows humor I have ever known. You see, I am beginning to appreciate this fellow Fink, although a little too late to do me any good. If we had world enough and time and all that Jazz. But by this time, I am past hearing Time's winged chariot behind my back. I am on it. And it is downhill as far as the eye can see, with no prospect of a hill or a tree trunk stopping it.

All that remains to be said now is that you have my will, my epitaph, my keys, my trust, and my love. I have your love, your friendship, and your promise. Keep the world from my door, until my sleep has become permanent and my body has turned into a vegetable. Let no one attempt to awaken me unless it is a dubious God upon the fields of Asphodel.

Among the books that I have left you, you will also find the notebooks containing my unfinished poems. I thought of burning them, but that seemed too much of a hackneyed or dramatic gesture, attaching too much value to them. The only value they have is in their having been personal, just as my books and my records have been. In strange hands, I would be insanely jealous if my poetic ideas were put to any use, for fame, fortune, or prurience. But you may do with them as you please. You may burn them, or bury them, or turn them into poems, yours or mine. Maybe you will manage to give me more immortality than I myself did.

Some of the notes are in Arabic, a language you have not mastered. You once told me that whenever you thought of suicide, you thought of all the languages you had not yet learned, and immediately embarked on learning a new one. That is how I know you must have thought of it often enough, if you have tried to master twelve languages. Maybe my Arabic notes and my death put together will make you more serious about learning Arabic. When we meet again, shall we converse in Arabic? Maybe that punster Fink can pun some Arabic jokes on me. You see, the prospect of death has definitely improved my sense of humor.

I did not choose the place to be buried, because that would have implied that I cared, even if this places the task of finding a grave for me on your shoulders. If I did not have such a dread of being put on fire, dead or alive, I would have opted for cremation as the simpler and cheaper method. But things being what they are, I prefer rotting away at slow speed, having the appearance of being asleep. Potter's field would be ideal. The place does not have to look permanent, nor the grave marking give the impression that once you leave, any one else would remember or care to visit me. Anyway, what you read over my bones will be more significant than where they are buried. Let me share some Yeats and Auden with you in death, as I did in life.

This seems a good place to end this long farewell. I embrace you one last time. If you look in on me, see whether death has mended my face. Water my plants in the window, if you stop by. Knowing that in the next few days, on my way to becoming earth again, I will briefly pass through a vegetable state, has increased my affinity and affection for them. Let them do for flowers on my deathbed, and then let them die with me. You will never remember long to water them, anyway. And plants seem to take their death with much less fuss than we human beings do. And on this note, farewell friend and brother, and better luck to you.

PART SIX

CHAPTER SIXTEEN

Let me level with you: there is an extra joker in this deck. And I am not to blame for it. Yes, I do accept responsibility for anything I do or say. You can hold me accountable any time of day or night. I am a respectable, law-abiding, tax-paying citizen, with a hundred-thousand-dollar life insurance on my back. No, sir! I take no risks.

But, this other character, this extra joker in the deck. Beware of him. He is a low-down yellow dog. He eats with his knife, appears in public places in his pajamas, and doesn't give two peanuts for respectability. He is a gate-crasher, a kitten-drowner, and a welfare bum.

There is nothing you can do to a creature like that. He will eat your bread, drink your drink, and for all gratitude, pardon the expression, it is his, fart in your face. No, there is decidedly nothing you can do to a creature like that; except, maybe, to disassociate yourself from him. And that I cannot do, not in the narrow sense of the word. I am too involved with him.

He considers himself the co-author of my books, which, of course, is an abominable lie. We, the two of us, are definitely not a kind of Beaumont and Fletcher. Ours is a marriage of inconvenience. We are a pair of curious bedfellows, "yoked by violence together," as the late Dr. Samuel Johnson so aptly put it. We are like a ripe cherry and a worm, condemned to live together, while one leaches on the life of the other. Need I say which one of us is the cherry and which one the worm?

I repeat, there is nothing I can do to this worm. He is my nemesis. He is my Fury of divine retribution. He is the chigger under my skin. He hounds me. He apes me. He impersonates me. He forges my signature. He collects half of my royalties and gives a receipt in my name, because he has no name. He has no name, no identity card, no birth certificate, no social security number, no permanent address. For convenience, his convenience, he lives in my room, and sleeps in my bed, which means I have to leave my room and bed, for which I pay rent, to him, whenever he is around.

Now, you would think a degenerate bum like that would be only too content with such an accommodation, too glad to let me write my books, as long as he can enjoy the benefit of half of my royalties and free room and board. But that shows how little you know him. He insists on his clownish romps through my pages, like an inspired idiot. In fact, he claims it is he who supplies the inspiration for my books, the circumcised dog!

Time and again, I have tried to persuade him to take a walk, when I am at my typewriter, and still collect his half of the royalties. Take seventy-five percent, I said. Take it all, I said. Blackmail money, sure. But do you think he agreed? Oh, how little you know him. Not he. He said he did not want any "unearned income." The dog! Yes, he did in fact say that to me. He who has never earned an honest buck in his whole infamous life, did in fact say that to me. Besides, said he, (and try to beat him for delicacy if you can) it was not a question of money; it was a question of "identity," *his* identity. He who has no father, no mother, almost no brother, no name, no permanent address, not even a driver's license, and who refuses to get himself a social security number, so that I should be obliged to pay taxes for even that half of my royalties which he collects, having the audacity to talk to me of identity, of *his* identity, as if the only place where he could find his scandalous identity were between the covers of my books.

But I have finally capitulated, considering that any kind of open dispute over the subject within the pages of my books would only alienate you my delicate and respectable readers. The only thing I can do is to disassociate myself from this creature in a broad sense, as a man disassociates himself from the rats in his cellar, of which he cannot rid himself. He can only show his good breeding to the company by warning them that there are rats in the cellar. I do not want to have to ever apologize for this creature again. When he is on the scene, I am off. I will not even wait to excuse myself or to finish the sentence.

There is only one saving grace. Much as we are, this joker and I, implicated together in the public eye, as elephants and peanuts are, we are as unlike as elephants and peanuts are. By no stretch of the imagination can the reader confuse the two of us, even when he is impersonating me. I am decent, orderly, and kindly. I think systematically, discourse logically, punctuate properly, indent the paragraphs, use capital letters, avoid obscenity, and at all costs try to spare the feelings of you my genteel readers. He, on the other hand, is indecent, disorderly, insubordinate, and vicious. What he is pleased to call his thought, is chaotic, without rhyme or reason. He lacks style and he lacks class. He speaks to himself, and he doesn't care what he says. When he is on the scene, the Republic of Letters is a free-for-all.

The confusion may only arise when he impersonates me, which is, incidentally, quite often. But I give you a tip as to how you may recognize him in such occasions: watch for the ass's ears sticking out from under the lion's skin. Anyway, you have had your warning. *Beware the dog!*

CHAPTER SEVENTEEN

Item: Prince Omelet is alive and drunk in Waterloo, Iowa, operating a motor vehicle on an expired poetic license, living on a joke a day.

Item: Jesus Christ is loose and drunk and still going strong, walking to and fro i' Waterloo, Iowa, seeking absolution from the sins of the world, dragging behind him the whole rogues' gallery out of the Old Testament and the New Testament and the Pig's testament and the Ass's testament, living on a joke a day.

Item: Poor Tom is alive and drunk, living incognito in Waterloo, Iowa, looking for his lost name, living on a joke a day.

Call me Prince Omelet. Call me Jesus Christ. Call me Poor Tom. Call me 'most anything. I'll Baa. I am the spirit that baa's. I don't know who I am. I don't know what I am. I don't know where I am. I don't know my name. I don't have a name. My name is lost. I have no father, no mother, no wife, no sister, almost no brother. I am not anybody's father, and I'm certainly not a mother. Yes, I was of woman born. I was once somebody's son, and somebody's brother, but that was in another time, in another country, which no longer exists.

Yes, I am an actor, in more than one sense of the word. I play in one person many people, and at the time I play those people I think I know who I am. But even then I have a nagging feeling that thinking I know who I am at a given moment does not make it true. What is true is that I have lost the continuity of being who I am.

I have no country, not even in my mind's eye. For a long time I thought I had one, from which I was exiled, to which I was forbidden to return, or had no wish to return; which I loved, or hated, or missed, or did not miss, or care about; of which I kept a mental picture, a fantasy, an illusion. But all that has ceased to be true. That country, wherever it was, in reality as well as in memory, has ceased to exist. It has vanished into thin air.

And now I don't even have an excuse for being without a country. I have been offered one and I have turned it down. I live here. I have lived here for a very long time. So, that should make this my country. But it doesn't. I don't belong here. I don't belong there. I don't belong anywhere. I am not a citizen. I am not an immigrant. I am not a tourist. I am not even a wetback. The official designation for me, and one that defines me best, is a *permanent alien*

Up to recently the definition amused me. How could anybody be a permanent alien. I certainly was not that by choice. Nobody would choose to be that. In fact, for years I had tried to become anything but an alien, temporary or permanent. I had petitioned agency after agency, submitting affidavit after affidavit, to convince the officials that I deserved to be something better, something less alien and more permanent. My money kept many a lawyer in oats. But finally, when the lawyers began earning their fees, when the officials caved in and agreed to make me something other than an alien, namely a citizen, I had cold feet. I felt I could not go through with it. I couldn't be anything *but* a permanent alien. And this after years of going through those tiresome procedures.

To begin with, I had been obliged to have many photographs made of me. Photographs that could not be too old, or too large, or too small, or had to show certain profiles only, with the right ear included, or the left, I forget which. I am not much for photo taking. For one thing, I am not photogenic. For another, I hate cameras. I have never owned one and never will. And to show you how much I dislike cameras, suffice to say that I don't have one Japanese friend, for the simple reason that they all have cameras. They always want to take your picture, or want you to take their pictures, while they do something silly, like hugging a stone lion, or throwing a coin in a fountain, or pointing at nowhere and smiling. For me any picture that cannot be retained in the mind's eye is not worth retaining.

These photographs had to be signed and stamped and verified, as if anybody would want somebody else's picture for his own. Then form after form had to be filled and notarized and covered with official stamps, much more expensive than postage stamps, and much uglier. There were so many inappropriate questions on those forms which I really don't care to discuss. Suffice it to say that I was asked whether I had ever known, loved, cared for, aided or abetted, associated, cohabited or copulated with, borrowed money from or lent to, bought a lunch or a drink for any leftist, communist, queer, pederast, whore, pimp, gambler, pusher, junkie, boozer, rapist, or defrocked priest. The only break was with the Fascists. They didn't care to know about them. I volunteered to give details about all the Fascists I had known in my life. But the officials were not interested in that. After all, what I had done with Fascists was my business.

I then had to get bank statements to show what monies I had or didn't have and why and where and whence and wherefore. Did my money come in big chunks or in a trickle of dirty small bills? I didn't know, I said. All I knew was that there was never enough of it to last me through the month, with all the tax I had to pay on booze.

I then had to find witnesses to appear in my behalf, to testify that I was who I said I was, and that my parents were who I said they were, as if anybody would forge himself or his parents. I had to have witnesses to pledge that my character was as simon-pure as I had claimed, as if people could really tell about your character by just having been around you. Character, Sir, I said, is not what I have, but what I play. They didn't understand.

And I had to pay, again and again and again, dues, and commissions, and fees, to the State, and to the court, to the gentlemen of the bar, and the gentlemen in the bar, to the middleman, the solicitor, the lawyer, and the CPA, and to the porter, and the cabdriver. I was finally told to go home and wait until my number came up. Don't call us, they said, we'll call you. Which was fine with me. Why would I want to call them?

Then, after months and months of waiting and drinking, my number finally came up. A terse three-line letter by registered mail informed me that I was to appear, sober, it was understood, on a certain day, in a certain place, to take a certain oath and, if everything I had said still obtained, and my parents did not change, and my character held, and my witnesses stood firm, to cease to be a permanent alien, and become a citizen. On the designated day, having abstained from booze for eight hours while asleep, with two shaky hands and a shaky mind, and decked in my one best suit, I drove to the appointed place, a well-decorated high school, all dolled up to receive me as a new citizen.

They had the school band playing, and the school choir singing, and all the young freckled high school girls dressed up like junior Miss America's, or like cheerleaders without their pom-poms, all for my benefit. They had congressmen making speeches and soliciting my vote, and Daughters of American Revolution giving me buttonhole flags of America and a map of the best fishing and hunting spots in the county. The hall rang with the message of about-to-be-attained freedom. They even had a special event: they had made a grade school teacher from England a citizen of America a day earlier, so that she could write and read me a poem about how free she had felt in those twenty-four hours.

You see, I didn't know they had been torturing and murdering grade school teachers in England. That's how naive I was. Hers were very fine sentiments and extremely bad poetry. It would have still been okay, if she knew when to stop. But she didn't. After she was finished reading her own, she decided to read to us the poems her second graders had written about her feeling so free on becoming a citizen. I have to admit their poems were much better than hers.

Finally, they played tapes for me, messages from several great men, about liberty and freedom. They played Lincoln's "As I would not be a slave, I would not be a master," a brilliant message that brought tears to my eyes; and John Kennedy's "Let the word go forth..."; and Martin Luther King's "I have a dream." I was deeply touched. Then the time came for me and my fellow-gooks, I mean fellow-aliens, to step up to the platform and take our oaths and our citizenship papers and, yes, be free. And it was then I felt I did not wish to be free, that I did not wish to be anything but a permanent alien.

This almost caused a ruckus. No one on the platform knew how to deal with the situation. The officials had had no precedent for such an occurrence, that anyone should wait for months and years to become a citizen, go through all the trouble and the expense, show up on the platform, and then have a change of heart. It was a crisis, which had to be dealt with. And deal with it they did.

First, the official from the Immigration and Naturalization Service took the matter in his own hands. In a grave avuncular tone, probably meant to impress the Congressman more than me, he warned me of the serious consequences of my act. But when pressed for specifics, he could not come up with any. He said that if I did not go through with it, my number might not come up for a couple of years again, which I didn't mind. I told him I had never cared for numbers. I had flunked arithmetic in school and had never played the lottery. Asked whether because of my refusal to become a citizen, I would lose my status of permanent alien, he admitted, rather reluctantly, that I would not, which was all I cared about.

Then the Congressman volunteered to straighten me out. He put his arm around me, called me "son," and reasoned with me. As a permanent alien, he pointed out, I could not vote. I said I didn't care; I had never voted in my life and didn't intend to do so now. Politicians were all crooks everywhere, I said. Where I grew up nobody voted. They just stuffed the ballot boxes with old newspapers and read the names off the official list. It was cheaper and more convenient that way. He paused and scratched his head.

As a permanent alien, he began again after some musing, I could not volunteer to serve in the armed forces of the United States. I asked him whether I looked stupid enough to want to volunteer in any armed forces. He agreed I didn't. But, he added significantly, I could be drafted, even as a permanent alien, to fight in a war. And wouldn't I want to have a voice in deciding which wars I wanted to fight in and which wars I didn't. I said I didn't want to fight in any war. *There never was a good war or a bad peace*, I declaimed in my best oratory. Who said that? the Congressman asked. Well, Benjamin Franklin, of course, I said. The

Congressman took a notebook out of his pocket and made a note of that, to use in one of his speeches against war, if it ever came to that.

Besides, I added, beginning to warm up, any army who wanted to win a war would know better than to draft me. He scratched his head again. He mused for a while more, looking for a new angle. He finally asked them to play the tapes for me again, which they did. He studied my face, as I listened to the tapes, and as tears welled up in my eyes. He asked what I thought of the speeches. I said they were fine speeches, but that, listening to them a second time, it had hit me as slightly ironic that all the three great men were so free and so dead at the same time, all dying before their allotted time, and through no choice of their own. He said that was a cynical way of looking at it. I didn't deny that. He gave up in despair.

Then the Daughter of American Revolution decided to take a crack at me. She showed me on the map all the nice hunting spots and the pictures of all the fine game I could shoot. I told her I was opposed to hunting. Was I a vegetarian? she asked. No, I said. Didn't I eat steaks and poultry? I did, I admitted. But I didn't like to do the killing myself, I said, especially of the wild animals. She asked whether I liked to eat fish. I said I did, if it was quite dead already, and prepared properly. She then showed me all the nice fishing spots in the county I could enjoy. I said I didn't mind eating the fish, but I didn't care for doing the fishing myself. There were plenty of professional fishing boats, already more than the sea could bear. But when I said that I had always found it incomprehensible that a bunch of grown-up men would sit for hours on their asses on a riverbank with a pole between their legs, waiting for a fish to take a nibble at an inedible worm, to catch a mostly poisoned and inedible fish, she also gave up in despair.

Finally, they asked what was it I really wanted. I said I wanted the privilege of remaining permanently a permanent alien. At this point the Congressman blew his top and shouted, "To hell with the son-of-a-bitch! We don't have to beg him to have a country," and told them to throw me off the platform; which they did, and which was fine with me. I have to admit though, that as I walked through the porch, I cast a hungry and nostalgic glance at the doughnuts stacked on the table, intended for the first free Gook-Citizen breakfast we were meant to have at the end of the ceremony. I could imagine the kind of violent response from the Immigration man and the Congressman, if they caught me munching doughnuts on my way out, after I had turned down the gift of freedom. I didn't want to give them an excuse to deport me after what I had done to them.

While we are on the subject of freedom, I don't mind confessing that I am not one of those silly intellectuals who consider freedom a subjective state of mind. In short, I do not consider myself a free man. I once was a free man, or I thought I was, but that is no longer true. And I am not talking about political or social or economic or sexual freedom. Those things do not bother me. You might think that I am talking about personal attachments, and since of these I have none, then I am free. That's what I used to think, too. In fact, it was to this end that I made it a deliberate study of my life not to have any attachments. I never sought any, and those attachments I was born into, through no fault of mine, literally died on me, including the culture into which I was born. What? Cultures do not die, you say? Well, in my case, even that happened.

My problem is something else, namely, that everything has become irrelevant to me. I don't have anything. I don't need anything. I don't want anything. I don't believe in anything. Am I a Cynic? On Tuesdays, Wednesdays, and Thursdays. On Fridays I am a Stoic. On Saturdays I am an Epicurean. On Sundays I am a Nominalist. On Mondays I am an Idealist. From a family of materialists, of ten-percenters.

Am I afraid of anything? Yes. *Of the eternal silence of these infinite spaces.* And of this grave that keeps opening before my feet. And of having bad breath in my old age; because nice people wouldn't tell me about it, and nasty people would, and I wouldn't believe them.

Do I believe in a personal God, the Great Geometer, the Arch-Pope, the Head Caravaneer, the Chairman of the Committee on Committees? Yes, as a metaphor. God is a great metaphor, I always say. Our language could not function without him.

Do I believe in the Ten Commandments? Not in all of them. I do not believe in killing. I renounced hunting when I was seventeen, after killing one sparrow. I saw a lamb butchered once and I became sick to my stomach. I almost became a vegetarian, except that I like meat, when it is well-done. So, my believing in not killing has nothing to do with humaneness, or humanism, or humanitarianism, or whatnot. I have a weak stomach. I throw up easily. I don't believe in killing, the way I don't believe in stealing, or cheating. I haven't got the guts to try it. I cheat a little in love. But then once I read an old Greek who said that on the perjuries of lovers gods themselves laugh. And what was good for Greeks is always good enough for me.

There is one commandment I always break, sober or drunk. It has to do with hankering after women. I do plenty of hankering. You see, for me a woman is the one thing in life that passes the Cartesian test, my one clear and distinct idea. Once I hankered after and made love to a woman who was somebody's wife, and somebody's mother. We didn't feel we were taking anything away from anybody. She said her husband hadn't touched her for ten years. Did she love her husband? She said she did and I believed her. She was so concerned about his not getting his dinner that she rushed back home to cook his favorite meal. Was she faithful to him? In a way. She said what she gave me, he would not miss, and I believed her. She said the only time he noticed her was when he was hungry. Was she cheating him? She said the question had never come up between them in fifteen years of marriage. Was I cheating him? How could I? I did not even know the man. How could you cheat someone you don't even know? The man was nothing to me. We had no contracts, social or otherwise.

You would think that I must believe in something. Everybody does. I once did, too. I once believed, not in God, not in country, not in motherhood, but in becoming a Great Man. One day, at age eleven, I found a book in my father's library, written by a Greek or somebody, entitled *Of Great Men.* There and then I decided that I would be a Great Man.

I never read that book. I never found out what it was that a great man was supposed to do. But I did believe I would be a great man, anyway. To this day, I still don't know what a great man is or what he does. I know all kinds of people who are not great men. My father, for one. He had the book. He had read the book. He even wanted to be a great man. But he was anything but. So, obviously reading that book wouldn't make you a great man. That is probably the reason I never read it. Now, if my father had been a great man, or if I had thought he was a great man, I would have read the book. But things being the way they were, I could never bring myself to read that book.

So, what am I? I don't know. Who am I? I don't know. I am a man who has no fate. I live in endless possibility. I will never materialize. I can define myself in a thousand negative ways, all the things I definitely am not. But that won't tell me what I am. Am I a rogue? No, I am not a rogue. I am not dishonest, even though I take no pride in being totally honest. I am not proud. I am not humble. I am not envious, because I want nothing. I am not jealous, because I love no one. I am not brave. I am not cowardly. I am not magnanimous. I am not generous. I am not mean. I am not petty. I am not rich. I am not poor. I am not terribly funny. I am not a grouch. I am not a sadist. I am not a masochist.

Believe me, I am not playing a subtle game with you. True, a lot of things I say I am not, are opposites to you. But your opposites are not my opposites. I do not say, "I am not this, *yet* I am not that." I say, "I am not this, *and* I am not that." Not being one does not make me the other. You see, I have told you so much about myself, and yet I have told you nothing. Not that I am devious. In fact, I can assure you I am not devious. I simply don't have that much to say about myself. Except that my name is lost. I am nobody.

Am I not fit to live? Why don't I kill myself? Sheer curiosity. I like to hang around a couple of thousand years and see how the world turns out. I once read a Greek philosopher who said that if he were reduced to nothing but a seeing eye placed in the posterior of an ass, from where he could just observe the world, he would choose that existence over killing himself. And what was good for a Greek philosopher is always good enough for me.

CHAPTER EIGHTEEN

Earth, yield me roots. Not to eat, but to plant. To pierce through this asphalt parking lot surface, you need roots; deep tap roots; unambiguous unequivocal roots. I have my space; but that is not enough. I need anchor now, something to hold me down, something to ground me. Oh, that magnificent Indian chief, looking at the dead bodies of his braves, spread on the land stretching from his horse's feet. My land, he said, is where my dead are buried. Everywhere he looked, the land held him up. He had no use for ambiguity. No ghosts rode his night. But my nights are ghost-ridden. Uncle Ezra, you said ghost frightens no honest man. I am honest and I am plenty frightened by ghosts. You said, Nothing counts save the total sincerity, the precise definition. You left out the dead, the dead that hang on and corrupt the air of the living.

What is my precise definition? I am one who plays, in one person, many people. And when folks say, Young man! What might your name be? I says, 'Most anything.' I is Poor Tom. I is Prince Omelet. I is Jesus Christ. I is Pontius Pilate. I is Dizzy Gillespie, the Clown Prince of Bebop. I is Joe-Shit-the-Ragman. I is a horse's ass. *The precise definition. And no sow's ear from silk purse.* No usura. No gold. No roots.

I am one who has no mother, no father, almost no brother, but has many wise uncles: Uncle J. the Billionaire and Uncle Timon the Pauper and Uncle Walt the Wanderer and Uncle Wallace the Insurance Man and Uncle Karl the Lumpen and Uncle Sigmund the Jew and Uncle Ezra the Jew-baiter and Uncle Ludwig the Jerry and Uncle Billyum the Oirishman, the senator, and the great great-Uncle William the Englishman, the actor.

I am full of other people's wisdom, none of my own. I hear voices, ambiguous equivocal voices. Uncle Wallace says, The prologues are over. Now is the time for final belief. Uncle Ludwig says, Unsayable things do indeed exist. Nuncle William says, Put money in thy purse. Put but money in thy purse. Uncle Ezra says, Gold is inedible. Nothing counts save the quality of the affections. Uncle Karl says, The problem with you is that you is a lumpen; you ain't got no class. Uncle Sigmund says, Look under your Mamma's skirt; you'll find the answer.

And now she dead. And there's this here ghost that rides my night and says, Omelet! I am thy brother's dybbuk, doomed! Revenge my unnatural death! And this other one that says I am thy father's dybbuk, doomed! Revenge my natural death! And this other one that says I am thy mother's dybbuk, doomed! Cry for me! And what do I do? I play. I look for definitions.

But we must have definitions, clear, distinct, and free of contradictions, before the night is out, before we sober *down.* Again, who am I? I am a dreamer, a whory dreamer. Where am I? Well, in the world. What is the world? The world is everything that is the case. *Oh, Das ist Onkel Ludwig. Die Welt ist alles, was der Fall ist.* Sounds more germane in German. Now would someone please tell me what the hell that means. That means, The world is the totality of facts, not of things. *Die Welt ist die Gesamtheit der Tatsachen, nicht der dinge.* Whatever that means.

What are the facts? These are the facts. Fact: Alex is dead. He has been dead a long time. Dead but not buried. Fact: Mom is dead. Dead but not buried. Fact: Dad is dead and buried. Sam is neither dead, nor alive. Slowly turning vegetable. Cabbage, maybe. Beth is married and gone. Almost married, but gone. Sorry maybe, but gone. Unhappy probably, but gone. Clare is not gone, but going. About to do the beast with two backs with the deputy sherr'f.

Well, these are the totality of my facts. This is my world. Where in this world do I belong? Hell, all over it. Over every inch of it. I dream my world. I inhabit my world. I cohabit my world. I make love to my world. I people my world. I *play* my world. Here's my space. Every inch an actor. When Dad plays dybbuk, I play Polonius. When Alex plays dybbuk, I still play Polonius. When Uncle J. plays Polonius, I play Prince Omelet. When Mom plays Omelet's Mother, I play Coriolanus. When Cyrus plays Iago, I play the Moor. When Beth plays Ophelia, I play Laertes. When Clare plays Cleopatra, I play Mark Anthony. When she turns whore and subtle whore. Well, I still play Mark Anthony.

I love playing Mark Anthony; and Prince Omelet, and Othello, and Iago, and Richard the Second, and Richard the Turd, and Richard the Fart, and the Fifth, and the Sixth, and Timon, and Coriolanus, and Shylock, and Lear, and the fool, and Romeo oh Romeo, and Jesus Christ, and Pontius Pilate, and Joe-Shit-the- Ragman. I love playing. I love playing anything. But I most love playing Mark Anthony, especially with Clare. What is she playing now? Cleopatra, of course. She always plays Cleopatra. Oh Cleopatra, oh sweet Cleopatra, oh most anything Cleopatra, almost most absolute Cleopatra, the Holiday Inn Cleopatra. *She makes hungry where she most satisfies.* Would I had never seen her! The greatest soldier in the world turned a jealous whoremaster.

Hast thou affection, eunuch, and letst strangers plough her while she crops? Art thou a man? Yes. *But I love long life better than figs.* Do bravely Clare! Do precisely Clare! Do it with open eyes and open legs. I know what you're doing is just a physical thing. Right? I know you care nothing for him. Right? Just trying to get even. Right? Just trying to get over your hang-ups, right? I know you only love me, right? Jealous? Hell, no! The greatest soldier in the world, jealous? What we have is so mystical, so mental, so spiritual, so unique, nothing can violate it. Compared to what we have, what's a little touch and dip? It's like shaking hands, right? *Nothing matters but the quality of the affections. The total sincerity.* The total openness.

Back to my tables. Where is my world? Well, not here. Not there. Sufi says I belong nowhere. I am a lumpen he says, caring only about my creature comfort, my sensual pleasure. Right, I says. I lumpin' and I humpin'. I live my life a lump at a time, and a hump at a time. He says, I am a clown, too. Right, I says. He says, I suffer from the malady of the bourgeoisie. Right, I says. I is the Booboisie. He says, I am a disgrace to the heroic memory of my brother. To think that Alex's blood runs in my veins! I says, Right you are!

My psychoanalyst says I suffer from intense self-hatred and intense ambivalence, from aggressive orality and erotic anality. He says, I blame myself for being alive, while Alex is dead. And because I hate myself so, he says, I hate the world so. Right! I says! I suffer from an acute case of Timonitis. Item: *If Alcibiades kill my countrymen,/Let Alcibiades know this of Timon,/ That Timon cares not. But if he sack fair Athens,/ And take our goodly aged men by the beards,/ Giving our holy virgins to the stain/ Of contumelious, beastly, mad-brain'd war;/ Then let him know, and tell him Timon speaks it,/ In pity of our aged and our youth,--/ I cannot choose but tell him that I care not,/ For their knives care not,/ While you have throats to answer,/ Be Alcibiades your plague, you his,/ And last so long enough!/ But yet I love my country; and am no/ One that rejoices in the common wreck,/ As common bruit doth put it.*

Oh, Nuncle Timon! You lumpen, you Timon. You Timon, you lumpen! You ain't got no class! You as bad as Alcibiades is! You as bad as Coriolanus is! He who never cared for the mutable, rank-scented many, for the beast with many heads, who hated the breath of garlic-eaters, who never showed his dear mother any courtesy while she lived. Where is your compassion? What about all them mothers who lack sons, eh? What about all them sons who lack mothers, eh? What about all the dead carcasses of unburied men that corrupt my air? *Wouldst thou have laugh'd had I come coffin'd home?* Yes, Uncle Karl was right. You ain't got no class! You lumpen you! Precise definition.

Sufi says I have turned traitor to my people. And Sufi is an honourable man. Who is my people? I ask. Alex was my people. And he dead. And for what? For that beast with many heads. Sam was my people. And he dying. For that other beast with many heads. My people. Once they had a sceptered butcher, now they have a turbaned one. The beast with many heads still butting away. You fear the one, I the few. Said John Adams to Thomas Jeff. But good old John was a pale monarchist. He might have taken a crown, were one offered him. And Thomas Jeff kept his faith and kept his slaves. As for me, I fear the one, and the few, and the many.

Sufi says, I am a traitor to Alex's cause. He oughta know. He shared Alex's cause. I didn't know what Alex's cause was. But he did. And Alex is dead. And Sufi is alive. At what price? And Sufi says I am a traitor to Alex's cause. And Sufi is an honourable man. And now that he is dead, everybody has appropriated Alex's cause. Everybody has appropriated Alex. It is easier to embrace a dead man than a living one, embrace their faults, attribute to them virtues they never assumed to have. For this crowd, everyone is a traitor, except those who have been murdered. As if only by death innocence could be proved. *The best lack all conviction, while the worst/Are full of passionate intensity.* That's Uncle Billyum, the Oirishman, the Senator. They lumpened him to death, too. They called him a traitor too.

Yet, if Alex had not been murdered then, they would have murdered him now. The mutable rank-scented many. Those who have no use for the total sincerity, for the precise definition. *In the name of their God. Each in the name of its god.* Well said, Nuncle Ezra, which didn't keep you from rooting for Il Duce. What are you doing for your people? Sufi asks. I ain't got no people, I says. He says, that's worse than being a lumpen. Not only you don't know your class. You don't even know your people. Right! I says. I ain't got no class! I ain't got no people! What are you doing for the memory of Alex's vision of a just world, he asks? I suffer, I say; for the memory of Alex's vision of a just world. That's the only thing I know how to do.

My analyst says I have a martyr complex. I enjoy suffering, he says. I like to roll in self-pity, when I am not clowning, when I am not good and drunk. So be it, I say. I am a tragic man, with a comic lining. He says, I have confused my theatrical roles with my real identity.

Wrong, I says. My theatrical roles are my real identity. My illusions have become my realities. I am not what I play. I play what I am. Timon, Coriolanus, Othello, Omelet, Mark Anthony, Lear, Poor Tom, the Fool, Pontius Pilate, Jesus Christ, Shylock, Joe-Shitthe-Ragman. I play them all. But he don't understand. He thinks *Oedipus* Trilogy was written by Sigmund Freud.

Sometimes I think suffering is the only decent thing left to do; that the world is divided into two camps, those who suffer and those who make suffer. And I would rather suffer than make suffer. Sufi says, An ass suffers too, under the burden. What are you doing for their suffering? Nothing, I say. I suffer with them. I partake. I dream. I imagine. I think. I drink. I talk to myself. Right, he says. A hell of a lot of good that does them. You just fool yourself. You don't want to face the truth.

The truth? *The Truth?* Now that's a mouthful. What truth and whose truth and in which of man's seasons? *On a huge hill/ Cragged, and Steep, Truth stands, and he that will/ Reach her, about must, and about must go.* That's Uncle Jack. No, not Kennedy. Donne. Jack Donne, John Donne, Undone. That's not in Sufi's tables. Sufi's text is Uncle Karl's. I say to him, Sufi, the Truth is a little larger than Uncle Karl. No matter how you lumpen it. But he don't understand. He don't have the gift of metaphor. He is not a cunnilinguist like I am.

My analyst doesn't use the word "Truth." He calls it "*Reality.*" *Sense of reality. Testing of Reality. Coping with reality.* Now "reality" is a mouthful, too. But it is a smaller mouthful than "the truth." And what is Reality, Socrates? It is something you mix up with something and get something else. It is that exact. Whatever it is, he says, I don't want to cope with it. Do you know what reality is? he asks. Yes, I say. It costs two dollars a minute; hundred dollars for fifty minutes; five times a week; and it hurts. You love to sandpaper people, he says. And now you are sandpapering me! I immediately apologize. I love to apologize. I am good at it. Every time I apologize, it costs me two dollars.

I like "the truth" better than "reality," though. It is more mystical, more slippery, more lumpen. It leaves more room for ambiguity. There is not just one truth, but many truths. Everyone has his own. Now, which is my Truth? I have none. I have many wise uncles, but no Truth. Like Mr. what's his face in *Barchester Chronicles*, on all important issues, I have no opinion. In all significant matters, I have no conviction. *Truth, Sir, is a cow, which will yield such people no more milk, and so they are gone to milk the bull.* Well said, Uncle Samuel. That's uncle Samuel, the other Englishman. The Doc*tor*. So much for my Truth.

I live and die with my great great-Nuncle William the Englishman, the actor. That's because he is a switch-hitter. His truths always come in pairs. For every Othello, there is a Iago. *Put money in thy purse.* For every Juliet, there is the nurse. Take any moral issue and you'll find Nuncle William squarely on both sides of it.

What is my goal? To singly defeat proud death in living like a dog. But that ain't really my goal, either. That's Fink's goal. That's Joe-Shit-the-Ragman's goal. What's my goal? I have none. I play. Do I have a center of enthusiasm? No. Do I have a necessity? No. Yes, ass and boobs. Shut up, Fink. Shut up, you goddamn ass. That's what I said, ass. Shut up you damn punster, you obsessive-compulsive sensualist, you male chauvinistic pig, who have raised your leg in sin against half of the sisterhood of this town, sober or drunk. It's you Clare is getting even with, not me. It's you Beth left, not me. It's you Shay left, not me. It is you Sam abhors, not me. It's you who have scandalized all my decent friends, have given me a black eye all over this town. You keep out of this, you hear? This is not your circus. We must come up with some precise definitions, clear and distinct, and free of contradictions, tonight, before the sun rises, before we sober *down.*

Now, he's gone, I'm myself again. I repeat the question. Do I have a necessity? Yes, booze and sex. Shut your mouth Fink! Shut your big frigging mouth. You boozing cunnilinguist, who stick your mouth into anything. We're not talking about you. We're talking about me! Me! And what is me? And who is me? And where am I rooted? Not here, not there, not anywhere.

I repeat the question. Do I have a need? No! Denial, says my analyst. Denial, repression, and suppression. Obsession and compulsion. Orality and anality. Those are your needs, he says. Bull! I says. Another denial, he says. Another Bull, I says.

That's the problem with you, says Clare. You don't need anyone. You don't let anyone come near you. But I thought you said I let too many people come near me, I says. Emotionally, I mean, she says. You are a great lover, in bed. But you never let anybody touch you emotionally. You've got a six-inch armor plate around you, says my analyst. Why does everything has to measure six inches? says Fink. Shut up, Fink! says I. You don't let anyone *give* you anything, says Clare. It bothers you to have to depend on others, says my analyst. You don't love me, says Beth. You don't love anyone, says Clare. You just love yourself, says my analyst. But you just said I hated myself, says I. That too, says he. You love yourself and you hate yourself. Bull, says I. Another denial, says he. Another bull, says I. You always must have the last word, don't you, says he. I pay for it, says I. Why are you complaining?

Now, I put the question to myself. Do I love anyone? Yes! Three dead souls and a living one. Two dead men, one dead woman, and a living one. Even though she has turned whore and subtle whore tonight, doing the beast with two backs with the deputy sherr'f. You don't love *me*, she says. You love this imaginary idealized perfect woman who is a combination of Beatrice, Ophelia, Sappho, Saint Clare, and Marilyn Monroe. You love this composite image of an intellectual-artist-saint-angel-whore, who doesn't exist, except in your mind, and who no one can live up to. Shay couldn't live up to it. Beth couldn't live up to it. I couldn't live up to it. No one could. You know what? You are a Pygmalion. You should sculpt your own woman. Hey! That's not a bad idea, I says. I may do just that one of these days.

And talking about me playing the subtle whore, she says! What about you? What about me? I says. Of course, there's nothing subtle about your whoring, is there, she says. You don't even try to hide it. You have scent-marked only half of this county. What about all your floozies? What about all my floozies? I say. I have no floozies. They are Fink's. Don't Fink me no Finks, she says. It's you who have raised your leg against half of the women of this town, sober or drunk. Not me, I say. That's Fink's necessity, to hit the bottle, to jump the babe. That's Fink's madness, not me. *Was 't Hamlet wrong'd Laertes? Never Hamlet:/ If Hamlet from himself be ta'en away,/ And when he's not himself does wrong Laertes,/ Then Hamlet does it not, Hamlet denies it./ Who does it, then? His madness.* Oh subtle Uncle William. You were somepin' else. You had an answer for everything. For myself, I'll live and die in your text.

Yes, says Clare. Turn everything into a joke, into a play. All the world is a stage and all that crap. Your problem is that you don't want to take responsibility for anything. That's funny, I say. That's what my psychoanalyst says. And you don't even charge me hundred bucks an hour. Maybe I should go into analysis with you. Free. You can take it out of my hide. That's what Cyrus says, too. That's what Beth said. You're afraid to commit yourself to anything, she said. Except to adultery, said Fink. Shut up Fink, said I.

Of course I would like to be married someday and have a couple of kids, said Beth. What's wrong with that? And what is it you want? Nothing, I said. That's right, buster! You said it! You want nothing. You want nothing bad enough. Yes, I have no center of enthusiasm, I said. Center of enthusiasm, my foot, she said. You have no center, period. And now she writes to say she is unhappy, to say there is a deeper part of her that nobody but me has ever touched. I say, Not me. That was Fink. He is the one with the deep touch. He is the one with the long pole.

So, I have no center. No center. No periphery. No roots. No usura. No gold. No money. That's perfect. How come everyone knows so much about me but me? What's this me everyone knows but me?

Do I believe in anything? Yes, love. Like Uncle Billyum did. He too loved, but did not marry. He too remembered and remained faithful all his life. No matter how many times good old Maud did the beast with two backs with others, she remained his Helen of Troy. Just as Clare will always remain my Cleopatra.

Do I love Clare? Yes. Did I love Shay? Yes. Do I still love her? In a way. Did I love Beth? Yes. Do I still love her? In a way. You and your in a ways, says Clare. You love the whole world, in a way. In your own funny way. But the world needs more than that, thank you! She says I only loved her when she was another man's wife, and I didn't love Beth, *until* she was almost another man's wife. I love to love almost another man's wife, I say. Maybe it is my fate to love another man's wife. You don't know what love means, says Clare. Funny, I say. That's what my analyst says, too. For a price. Always for a price.

To love the way I have loved! Yet Clare says I love no one, and Clare is an honourable woman. Sufi says I love no one, and Sufi is an honourable man. My psychoanalyst says I love no one, and *he* is an honourable man. He says I love only myself. Now, is that something nice to say to someone who pays you hundred bucks an hour five times a week? I can get insulted at the local bar for much less than that, for the price of a beer. I can let Dirty Tom do it. Shit in my face, and for nothing. I can let McFart and the Twelve Peers do it, fart in my face, and for free. And what is this love everybody knows about, but me? Would someone learn me this love? Where do I go to school for it? Where do I apprentice? I have even listened to this "Professor of Love" in California, on the tube, and I haven't learned nothing. Except that he is a faggot.

Sometimes I love the whole world, every man, woman, and child, every animal, every tree, every rock, every river, every bridge, every leaf of grass in it, the way Uncle Walt did. That's where I went to school. And if that's not good enough for the world, well, the world can lumpen it. And sometimes, I hate the world, the way Uncle Timon does. And if that's not good enough, well, they can lumpen that too. I Timon the world and the world Timons me. Intellectualization, says my analyst. Rationalization, says Clare. Bull, says Fink.

Let someone learn me this love. My analyst says that I should be willing and able to give myself, to one woman, or man, or child. Not dead, but alive. And Beth says, If you don't want to marry me, then you don't love me. And if you don't want to have my child, then you don't love me. And Clare says, No child for me. We will adopt. A Cambodian, a Salvadoran, a black South African. And Beth says, definitely a child of my own; in fact, two. One boy, one girl. Till death do us part. And Clare says, Only as long as we love each other, no longer. And I says, Amen. And Fink says, You know you are in love, when you lose interest in all other women, including the one you love.

Now mark me, how I will undo myself:/ I give this heavy weight from off my head,/ With mine own tears I wash away my balm,/ With mine own tongue deny my sacred state. With this ring I thee wed. Till death us part. And what would that prove? That I love? Would that prove what nothing else seems to do? And how many married couples live a life of quiet desperation? Ah! That's uncle Henry, who wouldn't even take Hell on trust, until he had arrived there and seen it with his own eyes. And for honeymoon, a trip to Love Canal, the Home of the Hooker Company. And we will bring forth a multitude of deformed children fed on PCB's in the shadow of nuclear power plants. Another intellectualization, says my analyst. And rationalization, says Clare.

Don't give me that *Liberace*, she says. I am as much a liberal as you are, as much against those things as you are. Besides, who said anything about having children? We'll adopt. Hell, we don't even have to do that. But I will bring my cats. No, thank you! I say. They would shit in my bathtub every time we go away for the weekend. And they would sleep on my tummy at night and purr and keep me awake. And they would meow when we make love and distract me. Face it, she says. You just can't commit yourself. To me or to anyone or to anything. You don't want anyone distracting you, but yourself. You are your own best distraction. You are your own best friend. You are your own only friend. You live in a dream, says Beth. You live in an abstract world, says Clare. You live in a world of illusions, says my analyst. You live on words, says Cyrus. God forgive me, I says. I do.

Everybody wants my love. *Gimme gimme gimme*, they all say. But how can you give what you don't have? How can you love when you feel you're drifting in the space? Sometimes I wonder what the whole thing is about. I feel I am reaching in the dark for a handle which isn't there. *Give me but one firm spot on which to stand, and I will move the earth.* Good man Uncle Archimedes. Coming to rescue in good time. Another intellectualization, says my analyst. Another rationalization, says Clare. Amen, says Beth. Bullshit, says Fink. I say, look fellows! Don't gang on me! I didn't say that. Uncle Archimedes said that.

You and your uncles, says Clare. You are nothing but a walking dictionary of quotations. You got nothing original to say. What can I do, I say, if everything original has been already said once or twice before? Don't give me that, she says. You just don't want to think on your own. To think on your own, you have to take responsibility. And you don't want to do that. You don't want to *do* anything, you don't want to *be* anything, you don't want to *love* anything. You just want to playact your life away.

Sufi says, what are you doing for the hungry masses? I am not Christ, I say. I can't turn my flesh into bread to feed the world. I can't walk on water. Every time I do that I sink. I am not waterproof. I, too, smell of mortality. I don't have a daddy up there to look after me. I am a seer. I just see things. I am not a doer. Alex was a doer. He was undone. And for what? For that beast with many heads butting away out there. A drunken soldiery now can leave the mother murdered at her door. And not in Oireland alone either. Too long a sacrifice, Uncle Billyum said, can make a stone of the heart. And I certainly have a stone of a heart.

Ahmad says, what are you doing for our Revolution? Nothing, I say. It is not *my* Revolution. It is not even *a* revolution. It is a riot led by a turbaned mob. If it is your Revolution, I say, what are you doing here, walking around in a ski jacket and a designer jean, instead of being out there, where men stand in line to buy frozen kangaroo meat or get shot, whichever comes first, and women are herded back into the caves, to be chattel once again. Don't judge true Islam by these false pretenders, he says. True Islam has the highest regard for the place of woman in the society. Don't give me that bull, I say. Where is that true Islamic society, where a woman is highly regarded? In Kuwait? In Saudi Arabia? I haven't seen it, anywhere. We'll make one, he says. Here in Iowa? I ask. He says he is *doing* things here. He is *organizing*. Not with my organ he ain't, I says. If he is organizing people like me, it won't do him any good. I would drag down any revolution I joined. *The problem after any revolution is what to do with your gunmen*, said Uncle Ezra. That is why they all go sour. The gunman takes over where the seer and the prophet leave off.

And Beth says, what have you ever done for *me*? The only rose you ever brought me died in two hours. You must have snatched it from a funeral parlor. When did you ever send me a card on any occasion? When in three years did you ever remember my birthday, even though it is right on Valentine's Day? Jesus Christ, I say. What makes you think I would remember Valentine's Day? It's just another racket to sell cards and candies and jewelry. As if Christmas and New Year and Thanksgiving weren't enough for that! And as for birthdays, I don't even remember my own. The only birthday I have remembered in seventeen years has been Alex's. I am better remembering the dead than the living. Go live with the dead then, she says.

All right, I say. I confess. I am absentminded. My memory stinks. But is that reason enough to treat a man like they are treating me? Walking out on me because I don't remember the Valentine's Day? Ditching me because I don't remember birthdays? What's so special about birthdays, anyway? Every time there is a birthday, someone dies on me. I wouldn't have remembered Alex's birthday either, if all those years I didn't have to watch candles grow on a dead man's cake; if everybody I knew didn't pick that day to die on me.

And Clare says, what are you doing for the two of *us*? I don't know what you want me to do, I say. I've told you I can't walk on water. You want to have children, but you don't want to bear them. I can't get pregnant for you. I can help you with it. But I can't do it for you. I have nowhere inside me to keep the baby for nine months. I can keep him later. You take the first nine months, I'll take the next ninety nine years. I know you think it is wrong for women to walk around for nine months swollen up like pumpkins, looking like fat cows. I don't want to make excuses for God. I didn't make this world. And what's the big deal about looking like fat cows, anyway? There are plenty of people out there, man *and* woman, who look like fat cows. And they aren't even pregnant. You think you can do it, you do it. You make me pregnant, I'll carry the baby. You come on top, I'll lie on my back. I can afford to look like a fat cow for nine months. Maybe even for ten, in case the baby is late. And I didn't say biology is destiny, either. Uncle Sigmund said that.

Alright, says Clare. You made your point. There's no need beating that dead horse any more. We'll adopt. I say, Wait a minute now! What about Kant's *Categorical Imperative*? If it's wrong, it's wrong. If you shouldn't walk around looking like a fat cow, no woman should walk around looking like a fat cow. The point is, she says, they do anyway, whether I like it or not. And they love it. Ten millennia of slavery has done it to them. But there are plenty who can't take care of their babies, once they are born. The world is full of unwanted children. I know. I was one of them. There are so many, you can pick 'em off church steps, out of garbage bins. My mother would have put me in a garbage bin, if she was sure she wouldn't get caught.

Wait a minute, I say. I don't want to pick my baby off a church step, or out of a garbage bin. How do I know he hasn't got syphilis, or AIDS, or some strange thing like the foot-and-mouth disease? Foot-and-mouth is a disease of the cattle, she says, not babies. I wish you would get your diseases straight. Unless you keep saying that just to irritate me. Besides, who said we have to pick our baby off the church step, or out of the garbage bin? There are plenty of adoption agencies, both in the States and abroad. One can pick a nice kid, preferably after he has been toilet trained, maybe even older, like five or six. No way, I say. By then they have learned all the dirty tricks. Farting up a stink in the back of the car, peeing in the swimming pool, hiding under the steps to peep at women's crotches, hiding frogs in the teacher's desk drawer, licking candies and putting them back in the box. No, thank you!

What a wild sick imagination you have, says Clare. I'm just bringing up a point of logic, says I. You think it is wrong for women to get knocked up, but you want to encourage it by taking their babies off their hands once they have gone and done getting knocked up so that they can go and get knocked up again. You want other women's babies, and only after someone else has taught them not to shit in their pants. You want to live with me, but you don't want to call it a marriage. You hate the "connotations" of being married. You don't like the assumptions people make about a married woman. What connotations, what assumptions? Do people assume married women get raped by their husbands every night?

Don't think it doesn't happen, she says. Plenty of married women get raped by their husbands. So, what's the difference, if they get raped by a man who lives with them? I ask. He can go to jail for it, she says. So can a husband, I say. Ha! she says. Try to convince a jury that a wife can really be raped by her husband. Ha! I say. Try to convince the same jury that a woman who lives with a man without being married to him is of such a moral character that her accusation of rape should be believed! You have a point there, she says. I'm surprised that you, of all people, with that male chauvinistic trait in you, should have thought of that. Jesus Christ, I say! You just hate to say you agree with me, even when you agree with me.

What are we bullshitting about, anyway? she says. You haven't asked me to marry you. You haven't asked me to live with you. I know, I say. I haven't said I wanted your baby, either. We are just having an intellectual discussion. You and your intellectual discussions, she says. That's all we ever have, intellectual discussions, whenever we are not screwing.

It is nice to discuss these things, I say, to be prepared, in case we ever decide to do them. The point I am making is that, if we were going to live together, it would make more sense to be married. We don't have to have a priest or preacher or rabbi or mullah or judge tell us that. But we should be prepared to tell ourselves that we are married. We can get married the way doves do it. The way geese do it. The way the ruffed grouse do it. Yes, she says. Ruffed grouse is a good stand-in for you. You would be good at that, beating your pouch.

And if we were going to have a baby, I say, it would make more sense to make our own, rather than take somebody else's leftovers. Unless I was gelded or you were fixed, which we ain't. Unless you preferred a surrogate mother. Yes, she says, a nineteen-year-old blonde that you would insist on humping every night, until the baby's head was out. For God's sake, I say. Not after I was sure she was pregnant. Forget about the surrogate mother, she says. O. K., I say. Besides, it would be cheaper to make our own baby. It is in character with you to think of it that way, she says. We would be doing our own dirty work, I say, and would be having our own fun, too. Well, she says. There's your bottom line, having your own fun. And your fun always seems to be in the bottom. Anyway, when I see your completed and signed application for marrying me or living with me or having my baby, I'll consider it.

And my analyst says, what are you doing for *you*? And I say, I get drunk every night and get laid, as much as the traffic bears. And he says, I thought Fink did that, I thought Joe-Shit-the-Ragman did that. And I say, ha ha ha, now the shoe is on the other foot. I thought you said Fink didn't exist, that my imagination had created Fink, that Fink was *me*, and that Fink's imagination had created Joe-Shit-the-Ragman. He asks whether I concede now, that Fink is me. I do no such thing, I say. Fink is a dirty low-down yellow dog, who lives like a dog, and whose ambition is to be a dog. He is a leader of a gang of low-down yellow dogs that include Joe-Shit-the-Ragman and Nasty and Dirty Tom and McFart and the Twelve Peers. They live on strong water and women's pubic hair. They smell like strong water and women's pubic hair. They look like strong water and women's pubic hair. I, on the other hand, am a handsome gentleman, a scholar and actor, the interpreter of Aristotle's *Posterior Analytics*, the expounder of the works of Hermann the German, and the sole scholar in the world on Geoffrey Chaucer of Monmouth.

And Sufi says, you can't hide forever behind women's skirts. And I say, I bet you I can try. And Beth says, you can't hide forever behind that excuse about the suffering masses. And I say, but I can't help it. And Clare says, you can't hide forever behind the Dictionary of Quotations. And I say, but I can't help loving my uncles. And Cyrus says, you can't hide forever in school. What did you want to go to college for, if you didn't want to get a degree? Just to be in the McGuinnis book of world records for being an undergraduate for sixteen years? Never mind the three point grade point average. With all the bullshit courses you take, you should have a four point. You are an A-plus bullshitter and no-hitter.

And Sam says, You can't act forever, as if nothing in this world mattered. How can a man as serious as you live a life of masquerade and debauchery? How can a man as sensitive as you live on sex and booze, day in and day out? How can an artist and intellectual like you throw away his brain, his imagination, his wit, and his company, on that low life you call Dirty Tom and McFart and the Twelve Peers and whatnot? What do you *see* in them? What attraction do they hold for you? They are my penance for my sins, I say. That Dirty Tom is my Father Confessor. He is my Horatio, when I am Hamlet. He is my Diogenes, when I am Alexander. They have succeeded, where Diogenes failed, to live a life of no shame, like a dog.

And my analyst says, but you are not a dog. You have an Oedipus and a superego. In fact, you have more than your share of it. You can repress and suppress and deny and intellectualize and rationalize, but you can't get away from your superego. And all the sex and booze in the world won't change that. All the repetition neurosis and sexualization of anxiety in the world isn't gonna help. You can't ditch your superego. A dog can, but you can't. Your guilt is killing you. Don't you wish it had been you rather than Alex? You wanted to go to the woods with him, didn't you? You would have rather died with him, wouldn't you? Alex had no right to spare your life, right? Your Mom and Dad had no right to make him promise that, right? Well, Alex is dead and gone. And there is nothing you can do to change that. You just have to come to terms with your enormous sense of guilt. You can't take on your shoulders all the sins of the world. You have to accept that you are not Jesus Christ, that you cannot walk on water. You have to get over your narcissism. That's a ten-buck speech, I say, all this supercargo and schmedipus stuff, and all at my expense.

Funny that Cyrus, the football player, the insurance salesman, says that too. You can't hide behind the dead forever, he says. You can't live off the dead forever. You can't have your head in the clouds forever. It's better than having it up my ass, I says. Is that supposed to refer to me? he says. No, I say. It's supposed to refer to me. It's a metaphor, see? Like, *Put money in thy purse. Put but money in thy purse.*

And Cyrus says and Sam says and Sufi says and Ahmad says and Clare says and Beth says and Shay says and Uncle J. says and Uncle William says and Uncle Billyum says and Uncle Ezra says and Uncle Timon says and Uncle Karl says and Uncle Sigmund says and my analyst says and Clare says and Sam says and Beth says and Ahmad says and Uncle J. says and Cyrus says and Sam says and Clare says and Beth says and Sufi says and my analyst says. Sweet Jesus, deliver me from all these voices. I can't take it any more. I can't hack it any more. Take over Fink! Please take over Fink! For God's sake take over! A joke! A joke! My kingdom for a joke. My Finkdom for a joke.

CHAPTER NINETEEN

Hi there! You don't know me yet. But you will, by and by. I've been watching you being taken in by this babbling lush, this penurious pencil-pusher, this piss-poor penny-a-liner. He won't be any more use to you tonight. He has sobered *down*. He is dead drunk. And that's where I come in, when he is good and drunk. He has had nothing but corn whiskey and black coffee for three days. And he is out cold. You won't have to put up with him any longer. Leave him to me. I'll take care of him, even though by tomorrow he won't remember me.

I put up with him, though. I let him have his innings, simply because I pity him. He is a very touchy character; terribly insecure. Did he tell you about his irregularity, which he calls "colitis?" Of course not. He was too busy abusing me. He does have irregularity. He is full of gas. When he is not terribly constipated, he has a terrible case of diarrhea. With him it is a classic case of feast or famine. And he has got B.O., body odor.

He likes to think of himself as an author. But all he really is, is a scrivener. *I* am the author. I am the one who supplies the inspiration. I crack the whip, he pushes the buttons. He likes to think of himself as the tragic, the sublime, the elevated style; and of me as the ironic, the satiric, the comic relief. And I let him think that. I can use him. We were made for each other. I absolutely hate drudgery, and he is so good at it. You should see how patiently he sits at that typewriter, finger-fucking for hours, while his constipation, excuse me, his "colitis," gets worse and worse. So that he would have to go sit there for more hours and strain, shitting a ribbon at a time. Pathetic. I wouldn't be caught dead doing that. I don't write unless inspiration comes to me. I get attacks of epiphany, and when I do, I get lots and lots of paper, spread them on the floor, and then let go of myself, just like that. Cover sheets and sheets in a jiffy.

His hobbies are various forms of drudgery. He is constantly doing things to make him smart, mark him as an *intellectual*; such as, say, comparing Ovid's *Amatory Arse* with that of Andreas Cappelanus. He fills notebook after notebook with crap, which he picks out of dusty old library books. His floor, his desk, even his bed, are always covered with dusty old books. It's a miracle he hasn't picked up AIDS from them. I bet you didn't know that the AIDS virus grows inside dusty old books. It does. Believe me, I know.

My hobbies, on the other hand, are all fun and fuckery. I drink for pleasure, hump for venery, and compose books for my own private amusement. To be brief, I am an aristocrat, a gentleman of the old school; while this killjoy, this lumpen, is a peasant. He believes in the perfection of work. I believe in the perfection of life. He specializes in Ovid's *Amatory Arse*. I specialize in myself. Ironically, he thinks I have no class, and he is the classy one. He wears these expensive pointed Italian shoes, to give him class. But have you seen his socks? You know what color they are? White. Expensive black pointed Italian shoes and white socks. Now, how can anybody who wears white socks have class is beyond me.

He suffers from twelve different kinds of mania, including the persecution and grandeur manias. For example, you will never catch him walking around the apartment without slippers, for the fear of picking up germs. He would never take a shower without wearing thongs, for the fear of athlete's foot. He would rather die than do that. He is horrified at me, because I walk around barefoot everywhere, and I shower without thongs, and I crawl into bed with dirty feet. I love that. But why waste my time talking about him? It is obvious why he says those awful things about me. He is jealous of me. Why? Because he is a drudge and I am a free spirit. He has colitis and I don't. He has irregularity and I don't. He has B.O. and I don't. He has problems and I don't.

And why don't I have any problems? Simple. When I do have problems, I drink 'em up and they disappear. My motto is: when depressed drink! When anxious screw! I have ways of drawing circles around my problems. I play games with them. I dart jokes at them. I laugh them to death. They'll never get the better of me, my problems. They'll never drag me down, the way they do this character. He is always down, always depressed, always in despair. And I have to bail him out constantly. You heard him call out for me a minute ago. Take over Fink, he said. That's all he can say when he is in despair. Quick, Fink! Say something very funny. Ha, ha, ha!

Incidentally, that's my name, Fink. And yours? Pleased to meet you. My card! Jackass of clubs! Now we are properly introduced. No, my name wasn't always Fink. I wasn't born a Fink. I became a Fink. I was born Farhang Shadzad. That's Persian. That's what I was: Persian. You probably haven't heard of us. We used to keep an empire, until empires went out of fashion. But when they were still in fashion, we kept one and fought like hell over it with every Greek and

Roman and Arab and Mongol and Turk and anybody else who would give us a run for our money. Finally, we gave it up, first to the Arabs, and then to the Turks, and eventually to the British, who kept it for a while, until they couldn't afford it either. But all this has nothing to do with my name.

It's a strange name, my name is, I know. My first name, Farhang, means "Culture." Think of that, anybody calling his son *Culture*. My last name, *Shadzad*, means "happily born." Now, isn't that funny, for someone to be called "Culture Happily- born," or "Happily-born Culture," or something like that? Especially, since I wasn't at all happily born. And for that matter, no one in our family was very happily born, or even died happily.

As to how I came to be called Fink, well, that's even a curiouser story. One day I had this hot date with this gorgeous blonde chick Stephanie. And it turned out into a short date, with headaches and all. So I came back at nine-thirty, carrying my tail between my legs, trying to sneak past the lounge in the Mayflower, that's where I live, without getting caught by the gang, of McFart and the Twelve Peers, Dirty Tom and Nasty, Butch and Wildass Bill, etc. If they caught me, they would skin me alive. They would crucify me. They would make cheap sausage of me. It was a sacrilege with them to come back from a hot date at nine-thirty, and with a zilch report card. They all had the hots for Stephanie and they would insist on a report card.

I had almost made it to the elevator, when they winged me. I was nabbed and lifted by the crotch and carried to the TV lounge, where McFart held his court, to stand trial. First came Dirty Tom's third degree catechism. Did you dick her, my son? No, Father! Did you lick her? No, Father! Did you cop a feel? No, Father! Did you kiss her? No, Father! Did you even try? No, Father! And then the Grand Jury indictment:

Inasmuch as this gook, this wop, this spick, this airab, this nigger, this honkie, after having taken out tonight the purtiest, cutest, littlest blonde chick on this campus, has had the audacity to come back at nine-thirty, with his dirty little tail hanging between his legs, and a zilch report card, with no attempt at dickin', nor lickin', nor feelin', nor fingerin', nor kissin', nor nuthin', he hereby stands indicted and ordered to stand trial, by the order of the Honorable McFart, curses of Allah be on him and on his descendants.

And then the trial: Gentlemen of the Jury (of McFart and the Twelve Peers)! The Prosecution will prove beyond any reasonable doubt, that this non-dickitive non-lickitive gook is a virgin, in every hanging apparatus and sucking aperture and hole of his body. And furthermore, that this gook is guilty of misfeasance, malfeasance, and non-feasance.

The Prosecution will demand that this gook be shortened by the dick, and furthermore, that he be hung in a cage as a relic from the past, as a living symbol of non-gratification and stupidity, as a lesson in timidity and non-humidity, for the instruction of the coming generations of healthy red-blooded vaginable males, as a warning that they should not sink into this low state of moral dissipation and dissolution.

Do you confess, gook?

Alright! I confess! I'm a gook, I'm a wop, I'm a dago, I'm a greaseball, I'm a mick, I'm a Mex, I'm a Packs, I'm a Jap, I'm a Chink, I'm a Dink, I'm an Injan, I'm a Nigger, I'm a honkie, I'm every goddamn thing under the sun: An Airab with the Jew, a mick with the Spick, a kike with the mike, a Jap with the Packs, a Packs with the Chink, a Chink with the Dink, playing fiddle with the infidel, infidel with the fiddle, I'm the spirit that baa's.

What's your name, gook?

Call me Prince Omelet! Call me Jesus Christ! Call me Pontius Pilate! Call me Poor Tom. Call me 'most anything, I'll Baa.

Your real name gook? You lie, you die.

Farhang Shadzad, Your Honor!

What? Are you shitting this court? What deduce kind of gook name is that? What this gook needs is a nickname. Let's give him a nickname. Fink! This gook is a Fink.

Fink! echoed the Courtroom.

And then came the summation:

Gentlemen of the Jury. This maledicktive malelicktive gook is innocent. The Virgin was a tease. A non-dickable, non-lickable, non kissable tease. A non-copus-feelus, a non-fingerato. Therefore, he should be pardoned and released on his own concupiscence, to continue in his state of moral dissipation and dissolution. He should, however, be put on probation and condemned to watch The Lumberjack Match between Ricky "The Dragon" Steamboat and Jake "The Snake" Roberts, in the company of this distinguished uglyass court, of McFart and the Twelve Peers. Curses of Allah be on them and on their descendants.

So, I was christened Fink and everybody cheered and patted me on the back and congratulated me and agreed that Fink was a damn good nickname for me. And I said to myself: Farhang Shadzad! That's a damn good nickname for you! That's the damnedest best nickname for you anybody has ever come up with. And that's the damnedest best nickname for your whole goddamn family. And I wish to God that Dad was alive and Alex was alive to hear your new name. And I wish Uncle J. was here to hear it and Cyrus was here to hear it. They would all be so damn proud of your new name. I repeated it to myself and loved the sound of it. A Fink reminding himself that he is a Fink.

So, there you have it. I am a Fink and proud of it. And that is that. But this lumpen? Well, he is a Fink too. And he ain't so proud of it. Or rather he was a Fink, when I was not. Since I gave up being Farhang Shadzad and became Fink, he gave up being a Fink and became Farhang Shadzad. But whether I am Fink and he is Farhang Shadzad or he is Fink and I am Farhang Shadzad, it don't really matter. It is the Platonic Idea, the *Eidos*, the Finkhood of it that counts, and that we've both got. We are a pair. And what a pair.

You saw it. After all the abuse he dishes out, all the blame he piles on me, I didn't do this, I didn't do that, Fink did this, Fink did that, now he has the nerve to call on me to save his ass when he is in despair. I have to make up a joke for him to make him laugh. I am His Highness's *joke person*, his clown, his fool. He lives on a joke a day, and I am the joker. He does not like ready-made jokes, the kind you can buy for a quarter at any drugstore, the kind you can find in the joke library in any decent family's bathroom. So, I have to make up original ones for him. I could have been a millionaire, selling my jokes to Johnny Carson. But what do I get from him? Abuse, and more abuse.

So far, I have made up eight hundred and seventy two jokes; one hundred eighty six about Louis XIV and other crowned heads of Europe and Asia, one hundred and forty four about the Pope, sixty nine about Oral Roberts, two times sixty nine about Jimmy and Tammy Bakker, and the rest about Anthony and Cleopatra. These last are my favorites. You wanna hear my latest Anthony and Cleopatra jokes? Here goes. You know how Anthony won Cleopatra's hand? Give up? With his Ace in the Hole. Ha ha ha! That's why they call it stud poker. Good, ha? What did Julius Caesar and Mark Anthony have in common? Give up? The same fishing hole. Ha ha ha! You know where Mark Anthony and Julius Caesar played ball? In Cleopatra's balls-room. Ha, ha, ha, ha! Good shit, eh? I hear a smile!

Making jokes, of course, is not all I do for this guy. I get drunk for him, I pimp for him, I take the blame for every disgraceful behavior of his. In short, I Fink for him. What would he do without me? Simple. He would kill himself. He is that type of character; no good. He has no self respect, no dignity, no grace. He likes to whip himself silly, feel guilty for anything. In his better days, he likes to think of himself as a saint. But he is more a sucker than a saint. He is sicker than a saint. He sees ghosts. He talks to them. He talks to himself. He oughta be locked up.

When he is down, he is down. He loses all sense of humor, becomes sulky as a crab, dyspeptic as a goat. He loses his appetite. His dirty dishes pile up in the kitchen sink for weeks. His dirty laundry piles up. His deodorant runs out and he doesn't go out to buy any. He can't get his pecker up. He can't enjoy himself. I have to do all that for him. I have to eat for him, drink for him, screw for him, (which I don't mind. His floozies are the best in town. He has the best meat on the block.). In short, I have *to do* for him. This is the kind of guy who cuts his face with an electric razor. That clumsy.

You know what his idea of fun is? Calling the Greyhound bus depot and listening to the recording of all the buses going east, west, south, and north. He even says "thank you" to the recording. Or, he calls the telephone company's number for time, just to listen to a cutesy voice telling him about all the advantages of long-distance calling, before giving him the time of day. He says "thank you" to that recording too. Or walking down the street and carrying on a conversation with lamp posts. Correction, not a conversation, but a "critical discussion"; in which he takes turns to speak for himself and for the lamp posts; say, on the nature of the Shakespearean tragedy, the number of children Lady Macbeth had, the homosexual tendencies in the Tragedy of the Handkerchief, the incestuous feelings of Lear for Cordelia, whether Shakespeare really had a son called Hamnet, and why Shakespeare left his wife his "second-best" bed in his will. He particularly likes lamp posts for an audience, because they meditate a long time before they answer. They are patient and polite. They never talk back, and they never point out the flaws in his arguments.

Or, he discusses the philosophical translations and elucidations and marginations and evaginations of Herman the German. Or, he expounds Aristotle's *Posterior Analytics*. (He is good with that. He is good with posteriors, anybody's posterior. He is basically an anal character.) Or, he discusses the poetry of Geoffrey Chaucer of Monmouth, on which he is the only authority in the world. He likes to be thought of as an intellectual, even by lamp posts. You know, he is a terrible snob. An intellectual snob, which is the worst kind.

For myself, in any discussion I need the personal touch, the human contact. You wouldn't catch me dead talking to lamp posts, or to telephone recordings. My favorite audience are unemployed Mexican farm workers, who don't speak a word of English. They are the most receptive audience in the world, and the kindest. Once I see one, I immediately cross the street. I begin by asking a legitimate question, like the way to the post office, or the nearest bank. As soon as I hear that telltale "me no English," I go to work on him. I let him have it. I pile it on, first my Anthony and Cleopatra jokes, then my Louis XIV jokes, then my Pope jokes, then my Oral Roberts jokes, and make an end with Jimmy and Tammy Bakker.

I keep talking and the man keeps saying "me no English," until he finally gives up, fascinated with my fascination with whatever it is I am telling him, stands there hugging himself with folded arms and nodding, patiently listening to me with an amused smile, the way you would listen to a retarded relative out of sheer kindness. If there is a bench nearby, he points it out to me to sit down, so that my feet wouldn't get tired. He sits down by me and turns sideways on the bench, so that I wouldn't have to twist my neck around. He looks at me with keen interest, nodding regularly, to make sure I didn't think that he wasn't really listening, that he was just pretending. When I finish, or get tired, or stop, because I am merely ashamed of myself, he waits a few more minutes, to make sure this wasn't a temporary break, that I had really made an end of it. Then he gets up and hugs me, kisses me on the cheeks, as if I were an unfortunate younger brother, or a handicapped cousin. He tears up for my unfortunate condition or openly begins to cry. I watch his stooped back as he walks away from me, slapping his forehead as he goes.

My second favorite audience are bank officers on lunch break, the Rotarians, the junior business executives of America, the traveling salesmen, any stranger who makes the unforgivable mistake of addressing me on the sidewalk with a meaningless and uninvited comment such as, "It's gonna be a nice day today," or "Sure looks like it's gonna rain," or "You sure look happy today," or any other comment that wouldn't cost him money. But that's my cue. I immediately approach him and reach out to shake hands. He reaches out with a "nicely met fellow" smile, expecting to shake hands on the run. But I hang on to him, and keep shaking his hand, while coming up with more of the same crap.

"It sure is a nice day. The best we have had in three weeks. How long do you think it's gonna last?" As soon as we have exhausted the variations on his original theme, and as he tries hard to pull his hand away and run, I offer him a fresh bait.

"How do you think the Stock Market will behave, in the face of the President's urinary tract infection and impending prostate operation?" That usually plays for a good two minutes, while the man scratches his head or his ass with his free hand, trying to look important, now that his opinion has been asked, worrying about his stocks, remembering that he hasn't checked the Wall Street Journal today, wondering whether he should take advantage of the President's urinary tract infection and make a killing, would that be patriotic?

When that subject is exhausted and the man is desperately trying to get away, I ask him whether he has the latest quotes on next year's pork belly market, or next spring's unplanted beans. At which time, he jerks his hand out of mine and rushes away, grumbling to another passing-by bank clerk or fellow-Rotarian that, "This guy is crazy as a loon. Stay away from him. They oughta lock these people up, instead of letting them run loose. No wonder the crime rate is so high.

My least favorite audience is *him*, this snob, this *pseudo-intellectual.* He is a phony, a fake, a book louse, a scrivener, a workhorse. It is all a cover, this intellectual stuff, for his insecurity, his inadequacy, his irregularity, his impotence. He is the only man I know who has gone to college for sixteen years without getting a degree. He has had eighteen majors and twenty six minors, including twelve different languages and literatures, among them pidgin Latin and Swahili, philosophy eastern and western, theology and religion eastern, western, southern and northern, history, biology, psychology, anthropology, physics, metaphysics, astronomy, and astrology.

His are not studies, but obsessions. For example, while studying English literature of the Middle Ages, he becomes obsessed with the works of say, Geoffrey Chaucer of Monmouth. Suddenly everything else goes overboard. He eats, drinks, dreams, speaks, shits nothing but Geoffrey Chaucer of Monmouth. He ignores every other subject, until they kick him out of the Department of English as being no good. Then he goes to philosophy and gets hooked, say, on Aristotle's *Posterior Analytics*, or on the medieval works of Hermann the German. Suddenly, everything else goes overboard. He eats, drinks, dreams, speaks, shits, you guessed it, nothing but Aristotle's *Posterior Analytics*, or Hermann the German. In short, he is an anal character.

Take sex. He likes to think he is a ladies' man. In fact, thanks to me, he has got that reputation. The truth is that, left on his own, he can't even get it up. He is usually too depressed to do that. And when he is not depressed, he is too boring to interest any woman. So, he has to call on me. He has to borrow my charming and bubbling-up personality, and I would have to woo and win for him. And then I have to lend him the rest of me to accomplish the task. If I left it to him, there would be many a damsel in distress, who would have to depend on her own magic fingers to finish the job, and then leave in disgust. Sometimes, when he has been especially mean to me, when he has been badmouthing me, I get back at him by doing exactly that, by cutting the power on him, by leaving him in the middle of the act, just short of the finish line. And when I go, everything goes.

He is slow as a two-toed sloth when he is down, and quick as a barnyard rooster when he is up. And all because he is too wrapped up with his ghosts and dybbuks and Geoffrey Chaucers of Monmouth and Hermans the German, even when humping. The only magic that works for him consists of three words "Take over Fink," and like the giant out of Aladdin's lamp, I have to rush to the rescue with my pecker pointing like a compass needle, and save the day. And while his reputation enhances at my expense, I eat the dirt of anonymity and, instead of credit, take abuse, around his "puritanical" and "intellectual" friends.

And if you think he is weird, you should see his friends. Take this upside-down bird, Sam. That's not even his name. His name is Subhi Abdul Maaroof. He is an Arabian brown babbler, who knows all the ninety-nine names of Allah, and the second and the third and the fourth rings of power, but can't pick his own nose. Yes, he was born under a rhyming planet, a shrimp of a poet. Now, what would you expect from a guy called Subhi Abdul Maaroof, especially one who goes around calling himself Sam? What would you expect from a guy who hasn't been laid for twenty years? You heard right, twenty. He is still hung up on a broad who ditched him twenty years ago for a London supermarket manager or dog astrologer or something.

He doesn't even have hands-on experience, can't jerk off, except in his mind. He is good at that, mental jerking off. He calls it poetry, but take my word for it, it is mental jerking off. I've heard some of it. *Lady!/Camera loves you!/The world loves you!/I love you!/Your shit smells lilac!* Nobody who gets laid properly would go for that kind of stuff. Anyway, twenty years ago when she left him, he kissed his pecker good-bye one night before going to bed, and he has never heard from it again. He has never vaginated or extravasated since.

Even before that, I assure you, he wasn't much of a lover. I bet you when he humped this gal, she felt like someone was drilling her teeth, she felt like tossing and twisting as if she was in a dentist's chair. I bet you he never made her ooze, made her flow for him. He probably wasn't even smart enough to use his mouth, I mean properly, instead of mouthing off poetry to her. He should have let his mouth do what his pecker couldn't. She, of course, knew what could be expected of a man, not having busted her cherry in his bed. She dropped him for this supermarket manager or dog astrologer or whatever, who probably had a dick like a horse and that Midas touch, a solid short stocky fellow with a fantastic dick and a fantastic lick, who went at her, balls like a bull's. No more of that dentist stuff for her. No more "late supper" and ballet, watching Nijinsky screw a silk scarf.

This fellow Sam, he hates me with a passion. He can't stand me for getting laid every night. He is green with envy of me, for the way I can enjoy myself, the way I don't let anything drag me down, depress me. He calls me an animal. He calls me a swine from the herd of Epicurus. He is jealous of my sense of humor. He calls it sick. He is jealous of my drinking. He says I'll get water on my brain. He is a master of jack-assery, and he wants his pal, this fingerling fellow, this triune jerk, this yellow-bellied sapsucker, to be like him too. He wants him to renounce all fun and fuckery and join him for a continuous orgy of mental jerking off. They consider each other intellectuals and artists. And they look down on us chickens, on me, on Joe-Shit-the-Ragman, on Nasty, on Dirty Tom, on Wildass Bill, on McFart and the Twelve Peers. They look down on the world. All they can talk about is their Uncle Williams and Uncle Billyums and Uncle Ezras and Uncle Karls and Uncle Ludwigs and what not. A Heathcliff curse on them both.

This guy Sam, he'll end up killing himself, mark my word. *He,* of course, will be very sad over it, heartbroken. He will lose his appetite again, lose his sleep, lose his temper, lose his pecker, and become dyspeptic. And I would have to do for him again. I would have to eat for him, drink for him, sleep for him, screw for him, even shit for him. So that he can have his cake and eat it too. So that he can be the highfalutin mourning intellectual and artist, weeping and mouthing poetry over the grave of his intellectual-poet friend, while I do his dirty work, the work that keeps him alive.

As for me, I wouldn't care if Sam dies. I wouldn't mourn for him. After all the abuse and insult he has piled on me for years, trying to get his pal to dump me, get rid of me, lock me up, even kill me. Why should I mourn him? Why should I return kindness for abuse? He calls me a dog. He calls me low life. He calls me a Fink. Hath not a Fink eyes? hath not a Fink hands, organs, dimensions, senses, affections, passions? fed with the same food, hurt with the same weapons, subject to the same diseases, healed by the same means, warmed and cooled by the same winter and summer as a Sam is? If you prick him, doeth he not bleed? if you tickle him, doeth he not laugh? if you poison him, doeth he not die? and if you wrong him, shall he not revenge? No, I will not mourn for Sam. Let him look to his bond. I will get drunk on his funeral and get laid. I will get drunk on anybody's funeral and get laid. So much for Sam.

I do all this for *him,* of course. I am His Highness's whipping boy. He never gets drunk, humps the babes, sits and shoots the shit with Nasty and Dirty Tom and Wildass Bill and McFart and the Twelve Peers. He never watches soap operas, Dallas and Dynasty and How the Hole Turns and The Little Whore on the Prairie and Rockie I & II & III & IV and all that low-class lowbrow stuff. I do it for him. He never watches the pro wrestling matches, how the whatchamacallit beats the shit out of the what's-his-face, kicks him in the crotch and grinds his balls into the mattress, wipes off his ass with his face, pulls his eyes out and shoves them up his ass.

No sir! Not he. He does not enjoy that kind of stuff. He wouldn't admit it. He is too sensitive, too weakhearted. He is too good for all that. It's Fink who does it. That's what he tells Sam. He doesn't tell him he makes me do it, so that he can get his kicks. He doesn't tell his *intellectual* friends that. They might not have a very high opinion of him, if he did. Just as he doesn't tell his *girlfriends,* the *nice* ones, the *intelligent* ones, the ones he might one day want to marry, all five or six of them, that he humps all those floozies in town at all hours of day or night. It's Fink who does that. It's Fink who is the whoremaster. And he doesn't tell them *nice* ones that the one who humps them too, who starts them on and gets them off and never stops until their juices are all aflowing, is also this low-down lowbrow Fink. He doesn't tell them that he himself is impotent, can't get it hard enough to poke a hole in a bowl of margarine.

But that's all right with me. I prefer floozies to his constipated spiritual and intellectual brides, anyway. When I am with a broad, I want her to hump me with her bod, not with her mind. When I want to exercise my mind I go to the library. When I want to exercise my mouth and my hands and my pecker, I go to bed. And I don't school where I screw. And who does he call floozies? Nice red-blooded healthy women who want to be properly laid, no matter what excuses they give. They are my cup of tea.

And you know the one thing all these women have in common? They all scent-mark their territory, whether they know it or not. Not one of them ever leaves without leaving something behind, a watch, a necklace, a bracelet, a stocking, a bobby pin, a safety pin, something to come back for, something to be reminded by, something to warn rivals with. Bless their hearts. And to call them floozies? Now, really!

Why do I stick around and take all this abuse? Pure goodness of heart. One of these days I will leave him, strike out on my own, become my own man, take my floozies with me, maybe even get married, go to a meat market and pick me a rare wife, a real two-breasted woman. If Emperor Hadrian could find himself a proper wife in a circus, couldn't Fink find himself a rare wife in a meat market? If she would be well done, she would be well done by me. Definitely no intellectual wife for me. No meat in the head, just enough meat on the bod. I am an ass-and-boobs man. Not too much of an ass. But must have an ass. No half-assed wife for me. And if she has no boobs. What shall I do with her? No, she must have boobs. Not too much boobs, though. No flabby stuff that flattens out like pancakes, when she is on her back. That's not for me either. I want it crisp as French toast.

What? That's not much of a wife you say? It would be better than those tight-assed frigid non-dickitive non-lickitive snobbish bluestocking bluenose bluetits he falls for, those no-ball thin-lipped ribbon-tailed birds of paradise, impenetrable from all sides, those duck-footed fag hag hat persons, all fuss feathers and perfume, who, being terribly adult about it, wouldn't fuck for fear of pain pregnancy or putrefaction, who would rather get laid in the head than in the tail, rather hiss poetry than kiss, rather be kicked than licked; in short, the kind who don't like me, who don't appreciate me, who find me vulgar. All I can tell them is, at least I do my own dirty work, don't depend on someone else to do it for me. And once I am gone, we'll see how long they'll stick around him. *Adios.* You will no longer have Fink to kick around.

PART SEVEN

CHAPTER TWENTY

Waterloo, Iowa
Monday January 16, 1984

It is seven in the morning. I have just come back from a long walk through a cold winter day, watching the sun rise on fields of snow. After three days on a diet of corn whiskey and black coffee, my body feels purged and my mind is clear as a bell. I have emerged from a fourteen year binge. I have shed a skin. I am a new man. What I have done, what has been done to me, over the past fourteen years, seem as remote to me now as the far side of the moon.

My mind is a blank. Hard as I try, nothing comes to it, but the American Indian's battle cry, "It is a good day to die!" Not that I want to die. Indeed, I have never felt so alive and so eager to live as I do at this moment. I have never felt so unencumbered, so free. I feel like Adam on the first day of Creation, ready to name things. I look out on a wonderfully unfamiliar world.

I have finally taken stock of myself. I am thirty three years old, and I have never known who I am, what I am, or what I want out of life. I have always fulfilled other people's expectations of me, none of my own; have lived other people's visions of me, none of my own; have lived up to my promises to others, none to myself. I have never initiated anything in my life, only followed. I have never acted, only reacted. I have never taken any risks. My choices have always been negative ones, not to be somewhere, not to be something, not to do something. I have never *gone to a place*, but only *run away from* a place. Today, I have squared my accounts with the world, reckoned with the living and with the dead. The dead have finally let go of me. The ghosts have finally let go of me. The fool and the clown have finally let go of me. Now I am my own man.

Fourteen years ago I came to America, not knowing what America was. America is a state of mind. America is an idea. America is what you bring to it with yourself. Dad never had an America. He never knew an America. He only had a dream, a vision, of America as a place where the future would be shaped, where the last battle would be fought.

He never lived his America. He waited for others to live it for him. And they failed him. Alex had an America, even though he didn't know it. And he died for it. Cyrus came to America to sell. He sold America. I came to America to escape. I skipped America.

Today, I know enough about myself, to go looking for my America. I am going back to start looking where I began, where I missed the boat in the first place, where I lost myself. I came to America empty-handed and I leave it empty-handed. I brought nothing with me and I take nothing with me. When I come back, I will come with my arms full. And when the Lady with the Lamp, in the Harbor, says to me, *Give me your tired, your hungry, your poor. I will take care of them.* I will say. No, Lady. You give *me* your tired, your hungry, your poor. *I* will take care of them. This time I have come back with my arms full.

CHAPTER TWENTY-ONE

I left Waterloo for New York, via Chicago, on Wednesday January 18, 1984, headed back for my mother's funeral, not knowing whether my telegram had arrived in time, not knowing whether anyone had even bothered to postpone the funeral, until I arrived. I landed in New York and slept most of the four-hour stop I had at the Kennedy Airport. I finally boarded a British Airways flight for London and fell asleep again as soon as the plane took off. I slept most of the way over the ocean and woke up only to eat. My body seemed to be doing its best to recover all the lost sleep of the previous week. And with my desire for alcohol gone, I was recovering a healthy appetite.

At London Heathrow Airport I had to wait a long eight hours before boarding an Iran Air flight for Tehran. I had been lucky in finding a seat on the flight on such a short notice, now that with the war, and with the Iraqis' threat of shooting down even civilian airplanes, Iran Air was the only airline still flying between London and Tehran. I had been warned that I would have a long wait in London, that the arrival time of the flight was unpredictable, and that the takeoff might be delayed for hours. Apparently the flight route was kept secret, and the arrival and departure times were kept deliberately irregular, because of the Iraqi threats.

There was a long line of people ahead of me, waiting for the same flight, almost all Iranians. I recognized most of them from the New York BA flight, except that their appearance had undergone a sea change. Women had totally changed their looks, covering their naked arms and shoulders in long-sleeved jackets, their low-cut necklines in turtleneck sweaters, their hair and foreheads in "Islamic head cover." The lips that were rouged and shiny red on the BA flight, now looked chastely pale and unadorned. The exotic perfumes had worn out and had not been refreshed. Men had removed their ties, but kept their shirts buttoned-up, to give them that "holy" Islamic *bazaar look*; especially those who had also had the foresight to grow a full beard. They seemed like a line of actors having just gone through costuming and makeup. Mine seemed to be the only unrehearsed part.

I was the only man in the line wearing a tie. Funny that this was the first time in fourteen years I had worn a tie, the only one I owned, which had belonged to my father. I wondered why I had worn it even today.

Was it a tribute to the memory of my father, a lifeline to the past? Was it a need to hang on to my only link with him; having already sold the other link, the antique silk Kashan rug, the family heirloom, to pay for my trip? Or was it another perverse attempt to be different, to wear a tie where no one else would, to do in Rome as no Roman did? I impulsively reached for the knot to open it, to remove the tie, but something stopped me. Why should I? I was through with trying to please the world. I was through with even caring what the world expected of me. If wearing a tie meant non-Islamic Western decadence, so be it. Although my face, not having been shaved for a couple of days en route, must have begun to assume that holy bazaar look, despite myself.

When they announced the time for boarding, everybody suddenly was in a big hurry to get on, as if afraid that they might be left behind, as if the seats were not pre-assigned. And everybody had positively too much hand luggage, with extra bags and objects hanging from their shoulders, their hands, their wrists, and their necks, bumping into each other without being unduly courteous. I seemed to be the only one in no hurry to get on, and with only a small handbag. And luckily for me, because by the time I got on, there was not one inch of empty space in the overhead compartments.

On board the plane, I was struck by the unfamiliar "Islamic head cover" of the stewardesses, (no doubt the same *chic* set of the Shah's airline, having got religion lately,) and by their manner of calling everyone "Brother" and "Sister." I chuckled the first time they "brothered" me. But soon I got to like it and began "brothering" and "sistering" everyone in return. We were, in a sense, a brotherhood and sisterhood, of teetotalers, alcohol being forbidden on the flight.

At times, I had the feeling that I was outside reality, as if I were on a new and different stage, acting in a totally unfamiliar play, in a role totally uncharacteristic for me; a character in a passion play maybe, say, the martyrdom of Imam Hussein. At other times, it seemed so natural that people should all look alike, with no fancy clothes, or distinguishing hairdo or adornment, calling each other "Brother" and "Sister." But then, I would remember the looks of these same people on the BA flight, and could guess what they might look like again tonight, behind closed doors. I had heard of wild parties going on all over the town at night in the privacy of homes, with music and dancing and drinking, with the booze fermented in basements and closets, away from the watchful eyes of the Revolutionary Guards. Sometimes the parties got raided, and then it was a matter of interrogation and public whipping and jail and whatnot. And on that note I fell asleep again.

I woke up to the Captain's announcement that we were making the final descent for Tehran. I peered out of the window, nostalgically looking for the brightly lighted and colorful look of the sprawling city, as it had looked on the night I left it fourteen years ago. But all I saw was a huge darkness, behind which the war-ravaged city was hiding from enemy's rockets and bombs.

We disembarked in almost total darkness, in a blacked out airport. Things lighted up only after we were inside, behind the drawn curtains. I hardly recognized the old building. It looked run-down and in disrepair. Balconies and staircases were cordoned off. Whole areas were shut out to the public. There were no signs of shops or even the old cafeteria. The old colorful commercial look was gone. The chic sexy posters were replaced by morose "revolutionary" ones, where all men appeared darkly bearded and all women chastely covered. Where life-size pictures of the Shah and his queen hung before, now there were huge turbaned pictures of the Ayatollah.

There was none of that air of excitement one associates with airports. Everything had a somber and gloomy look. Was that a reflection of the country's new mood, with all the blood that the Revolution had spilt; or was it the war, with its new horrors of death and destruction? We walked through armed guards, of the regular police, of the army, of the Revolutionary Guards. The uniformed police looked bored and insignificant, as if they felt their alertness was no longer required or rewarded. But the Revolutionary Guards' bearded faces beamed with pride of youth and authority and vigilance, backed up with submachine guns.

In the immigration and customs lines, I could no longer tell apart the immigration police, the customs' officers, and the secret police. Invariably, it was the bearded man out of uniform that had the ominous look of ultimate authority. I was stopped at a counter by a young bearded man, who told me to open my small suitcase, while he himself unceremoniously turned my handbag upside down and emptied its contents on the counter. He rummaged through my personal effects indelicately, unfolding my shorts, T-shirts, and sweaters layer by layer and shaking them out, unrolling my socks and meticulously examining them. Then he began flipping through my books and scanning them. He scanned the English books first and in a hurry, but became more interested and meditative when he came to the Persian volumes. He picked up Ferdowsi's *Book of Kings* and peered meaningfully into my eyes.

"What's this?" he asked.

Surprised that any Iranian might not know the greatest and most popular book of epic poetry in Persian literature, I hesitated to answer at first.

"I thought everybody knew Ferdowsi's *Book of Kings*," I mumbled, trying not to be offensive.

"Oh, I know the book, all right!" he said, sarcastically. "That's why I'm asking. Book of *Kings*, right?"

The way his intonation emphasized the word *Kings,* I realized for the first time where he was coming from. Had the greatest work of classical Persian literature been banned, simply because it was a "Book of Kings?" The man held up the book with a grin and showed it to another bearded man, somewhat older than himself, who stood a few feet away. The other man, more portentous looking and seeming to have more authority, wielding a carved wooden stick like an officer's pointer, came over and took the book. After some meditation, he also peered meaningfully into my eyes.

"What do you do?" he asked, rather suspiciously.

"I'm a student," I said.

"Student of what?"

"Of literature, among other things."

He looked up from the page he was scanning, even more suspicious.

"Aren't you a little too old to be a student?" he asked cynically.

"I didn't know there was an age people had to stop being a student," I said, sounding a little sarcastic.

"Twelve-year-old boys are running in front of Iraqi machine guns and being martyred, to defend the country and the true faith, and you think this is the time for grown-up men to hide in America, to drink and dance and party, and study literature, 'among other things?'" He now sounded quite ominous. Apparently, their search of my luggage was not just a customs' inspection.

Now they both began rummaging through my books, with zeal and energy. They exchanged another meaningful glance over the *Divan of Hafiz* and gave me another significant stare. Had Hafiz fallen from grace too, I wondered. They must have taken all his talk of wine and women literally and missed everything. Over the *Rubaiyat of Khayyam* they shook their heads ruefully. But with Rumi's *Divan*, they could not quite make up their minds. After they were done with the Persian works, they returned to the English books with new interest. They reached for the big volumes first, seeming to recognize the works of Shakespeare, judging by the contemptuous indulgence in their smiles. But with Yeats, they seemed lost.

"What's this?" the older man asked, flipping the cover open with his pointer.

"Yeats," I said. "English poet."

"The English *Book of Kings*?" he asked, sarcastically.

"No," I said, contemptuously. "Lyrical poetry. Like Hafiz, more or less."

He looked up to see the expression on my face, as if he had picked up my contemptuous tone. Unable to decipher my deadpan expression, he recovered his superiority and his contemptuous smile. When they were done with the books, they asked me to empty my pockets. I emptied the contents of all my pockets on the counter. The older man quickly reached for the miniature leather bound Shakespeare Sonnets.

"Is that a Holy *Koran*?" he asked with excitement, as if willing to give me a last chance to redeem myself.

"I'm afraid not," I said guiltily. "It's Shakespeare's Sonnets."

He ruefully shook his head.

"Carrying all this rubbish around," he said, "and not one copy of the Holy *Koran*. No prayer seal. No prayer rug. No rosary. What are you, a Bahai, or a Jew?"

I shook my head.

By this time, the younger man was examining my identity booklet with interest.

"He's a Twelve-Imam Shiite and is supposed to be a descendant of the Prophet," he said with disbelief and gross sarcasm, pointing something out to the other man. They looked at me with new curiosity.

"Is your father a descendant of the Prophet?" the older man asked.

"He was," I replied. "God be merciful to him! He is dead." "My mother was a descendant of the Prophet, too." I volunteered with hesitation.

"How come you've dropped the title of *Seyyed* from your name, then? Are you ashamed to be a descendant of the Prophet, and on both sides, too?"

"I didn't drop it. My father did," I said defensively. "He did that at my birth, when he got my birth certificate."

"You mean *he* was ashamed of being a descendant of the Prophet?"

"No," I said. "Rather, he thought that was a private matter between you and the Prophet and God. He saw no point advertising it. He didn't want to get anything for it."

"You know how many people would give a right arm to be a descendant of the Prophet, and on both sides, too?"

"I'm sorry," I said. "I had nothing to do with it. It was my father's doing. And he is dead and gone. Whatever his sins, he'll be judged up there."

"What did your father do for a living?"

"He was a judge," I said.

The older man rolled my father's name several times around his mouth, as if by filtering it through his taste buds he could revive my father's flesh or summon his soul, to get to know him, or know him better.

"Sure he was a judge!" he finally said with recognition and a victorious ring to his voice. "I remember him now. He was the Shah's Chief Justice, wasn't he?"

"He was the Chief Justice of the Supreme Court during the Shah's reign," I admitted guiltily. "But he was not 'the Shah's Chief Justice,' as you put it."

"He sure was!" he said bitterly. "He was the Shah's Chief Justice, all right, during all those years when our young devout brothers and sisters were being tortured and martyred."

"You know he had nothing to do with that," I said reproachfully. "The courts never dealt with political prisoners, you know that. It was the Savak. And my father had nothing to do with it."

"I sure don't recall him ever objecting to any of it," he said with more sarcasm. "I sure don't recall him resigning over it."

"He tried," I said. "They wouldn't let him resign. He stayed home for the last three years of his life and refused to set foot in the court. There was nothing else he could do. He was nothing but a figurehead, anyway. The Chief Justice was a joke, you know that. The whole judiciary system was a joke, when it came to political prisoners, you know that. The judges were only allowed to deal with petty thieves. And since you recall so much, you might also recall that his own son was killed under torture, when he was the Chief Justice."

"Sure I recall, now that you mention it," he said sarcastically again, with another victorious grin of recognition. "Alex was his name, wasn't it? Alex Shadzad. He was one of the Fedayin, wasn't he? He was a Communist."

"If that is the case, you seem to know him better than I do," I said, no longer able to contain my sarcasm and anger. "All I know is that he fought against the Shah and he was killed by his men, under torture. And that sent his old man to an early grave, too."

"I bet you he didn't even say his daily prayers," he said contemptuously, "your father, I mean, the descendant of the Prophet. I bet you he had even forgot the words. I bet you he never observed the fast."

"No, he didn't!" I said, now defiantly. "But let's not talk evil of the dead. Let's leave them to their heavenly judge."

"And didn't he have a brother also, now that I think of it," he went on vengefully, unwilling to give up his advantage, "who was a cabinet minister of the Shah, his Chairman of the Planning Organization?" He seemed to have been a revolutionary historian of sorts. At least, he seemed to know the history of my family quite well.

"Yes," I said sadly, sounding no longer defiant, but bored. If I am to be interrogated, I thought, I would rather they did it in a private room and gave me a chair to sit on, too. My body was reminding me that it had been traveling for nearly forty-eight hours now, and that it could surely do with a little bit of rest.

By this time the younger man had discovered my diary and was scanning it with great interest. He pointed out certain passages to the older man and they both grinned from ear to ear.

"And what is this?" the older man asked, as if they had discovered new evidence of my and my family's guilt, probably enough to declare us all *corrupt on earth*, fit to be hanged.

"My diary," I said, nonchalantly. "I don't think you would be interested in it."

"We'll be the judge of that," said the older man. "You seem to be a very interesting fellow. This should give us a very good idea of how you have spent your time in America all these years, 'studying literature among other things.'"

Now they both began reading and paging through the diary, seeming alternately amused and shocked by what they read.

"You seem to drink a good deal of whiskey," the older man said, "and quite proud of it, too. Not to mention the ample evidence of fornication."

"All imaginary," I said. "I make things up in my diary to amuse myself, as if I were writing stories."

"And sacrilegious and profane, too," the younger man put in his two cents, as if they had not heard my last defense, or had found it too pathetic for a response.

After a while the older man got either bored or angry and shut the diary abruptly. He waved his pointer in the air and two machine-gun toting Revolutionary Guards ran over. "Take this man to Room 120," he said to one of them, while handing the other the evidence of my *corruptness on earth*, *the Book of Kings* of Ferdowsi, the *Rubaiyat* of Khayyam, the *Divan* of Hafiz, the *Divan* of Rumi, and my pathetic diary, the record of my boozing and fornications. I reached for my passport and my identity booklet, but he indicated that they would be hanging on to them. The Guards firmly grabbed me by the arms, as if the mentioning of that room number had already pronounced me guilty, armed, and dangerous.

They walked me up a short flight of stairs and into a room, where a police captain and a heavyset bearded man sat at a large desk. The way they sat, it was obvious that the bearded man considered the desk his own, and the police captain only a second fiddle. He was full of his own self-importance and everything about him showed it. The police captain sat somewhat to the side, almost straddling the corner of the desk. A buzzer sounded and the bearded man went to the adjoining room, where I could see my former interrogator briefing a middle-aged mullah in black robe and turban and wire-rimmed glasses. The mullah's head was bent and he was looking at me over the wire-rimmed glasses riding on his nose. Apparently, my case had entered a new phase, where not only bearded but also turbaned authority was required.

The new bearded man joined the briefing. The mullah listened intently and nodded ominously as my former interrogator gravely laid out my case. The new bearded man soon began his own nodding, in sync with the mullah's. Apparently they were reaching a consensus about the gravity of my case, possibly my *corruptness on earth*. The police captain looked up at this time from examining his nails and saw me looking with apprehension at the scene in the adjoining room. He looked back and forth several times, first at my face and then at my judges in the adjoining room, and nodded almost imperceptibly, as if sympathizing with my predicament. He seemed tragically human and apparently quite aware of his own insignificance. With a sad look in his eyes, and an almost helpless gesture of the hand, he pointed to a chair.

"Sit down, son!" he said. "Rest your feet. They'll be with you soon enough."

It felt good to be called son so informally, after all that formal and ominous *brothering*, and to know that someone else cared about my tired feet. I also noted that he had kindly excluded himself from the collective body of my judges. I sat down gratefully.

My new interrogator finally returned to his desk, carrying with him the stack of my books and documents. He gave me a harsh look, as if surprised and offended that I had taken the liberty of sitting down. I looked sheepishly at the police captain, silently asking for his guidance or intercession. The captain, as if he had read both our minds, casually vouched that he had told me it was all right to sit down. By this time, I had already stood up impulsively, wondering whether the captain had not exceeded his authority in offering me a seat, and unwilling to get him in trouble. The bearded man, as if content that both I and the captain had acknowledged his authority over people's right to be seated in his office and in his presence, now imperiously waved me to sit down again.

"You are already in big trouble," he said gravely, "even before we have begun interrogating you."

He briefly reviewed the list of my crimes *already known*: Being in possession of condemned and immoral books such as the *Book of Kings* of Ferdowsi, the *Rubaiyat* of Khayyam, and the *Divan* of Hafiz. Not being in possession of a prayer seal, a prayer rug, a rosary, or a copy of the Holy *Koran*, with every implication that I did not follow the Commandments such as saying my daily prayers and observing the fast. Admission in my own words in my diary that I regularly drank whiskey and committed fornication with women, some even married; although, in America, he added gratuitously, all women were fornicators, whether married or not. Having dropped from my name the title of *Seyyed*, ashamed of being a descendant, and on both sides, of the Prophet, blessings of Allah be on him and on his descendants. Having had a *corrupt on earth* father, guilty of numerous crimes under the damned Shah. Having a *corrupt on earth* uncle, guilty of numerous crimes under the same damned Shah. And having had a Communist and *corrupt on earth* brother, his having been killed under torture by the Shah notwithstanding. This much, he let me know, was a given, beyond any dispute, going into the formal interrogation.

The purpose of his interrogation was to see whether I was guilty of any more crimes. What had I done in America for fourteen years, wasting the *Moslem Populace's Purse* and badly needed foreign exchange? Why had I not returned sooner to discharge my obligations to the Islamic Republic and to His Holiness the Imam, when the Holy War against that infidel Saddam was declared? And why was I returning now, in the middle of the war, when the tides where turning in favor of the Islamic Republic? There was every reason to suspect that I was a spy, either for The Great Satan America, or for its murderous stooge, that damned and infidel Saddam, curses of Allah be on him and on his descendants. Why else would I be returning now, knowing full well that I would be drafted and sent to the front forthwith? Unless, it was my mission to be drafted and sent to the front forthwith, so that I could carry on my spying in the field."

"But I've come back to attend the funeral of my mother," I said sheepishly, afraid that even this might not be an adequate excuse, given the long list of my crimes.

"Hmmm!" the man mumbled, as if this insignificant and unforeseen piece of information had created a problem for his whole line of argument. "How come you never mentioned this earlier?"

"I wasn't given a chance," I said. "I was confronted with my and my family's list of crimes from the word go."

"When is the burial?" he asked, doubtfully.

I mumbled that I did not know exactly. It had been originally scheduled for last Saturday, I said guiltily, but I had sent a telegram asking them to postpone it, until I arrived.

"When did your mother die?" the man asked, looking baffled beyond belief. Even the police captain looked up with alarm.

"Last Friday," I said.

"Your mother died last Friday and you wanted them to postpone the burial of the dead until you arrived a week later?" the man shouted with rage and amazement, as he jumped to his feet. "What kind of Moslem upbringing did you have in the household of two descendants of the Prophet, that you don't even know how long a dead body can be kept above the ground, before it is buried? Didn't you even get religious training in the middle school?"

I felt quite embarrassed to admit that I had no remembrance of how long the Moslem law allowed a dead body to remain above the ground, before it was buried. Was it until the next sunset, or until the body began to smell, given that refrigeration, let alone refrigeration of dead bodies, had not been invented yet in the seventh century, at the time of the Prophet, blessings of Allah be on him and on his descendants? In my asking to have the burial postponed, apparently I had committed another sacrilege, which would no doubt be added to the list of my crimes. And, obviously, my mother had already been buried, even before my plane left Waterloo, and my excuse of having returned to attend her funeral no longer obtained.

"Do you even know how to say your daily prayers?" the man asked, suspecting now that my religious foundations were even shakier than he had assumed.

I wondered whether I should lie and answer in the positive. And what if he asked for a demonstration? Could I bluff my way out with that one sentence I remembered from the *Koran*: *In the name of Allah, the Compassionate, the Merciful*? Would they give me a few days to prepare for the test?

"No," I said, with disarming honesty. The police captain looked up again from the examining of his fingernails and stared at me, presumably wondering at either my innocence or my stupidity. What kind of Moslem upbringing, indeed, had I had in the household of two descendants of the Prophet, if I didn't even know how to lie? Didn't Islam itself excuse *Taghieh*, lying when one's life was in danger? And didn't I know that my life was in danger?

"Are you proud of it?" the man shouted again with rage and disbelief, falling back in his seat. "A descendant of the Prophet on both sides, and not even knowing the words of the daily prayers?"

I remained silent. I recalled how eloquently Uncle J. had argued against my coming back. Did he know how long the dead could remain above the ground, unburied? Would I really find now the key I had come looking for?

"Maybe the brothers at Evin can straighten you out," he added calmly, indicating either that his interrogation was over, or that my case was beyond hope.

"Evin?" I echoed him, shocked, having heard of the dreaded Evin Prison. "You mean the prison?"

"Yes!" he said. "You'll be *interrogated* there at first. There, they have all the necessary files on you and on your family and all the necessary equipments. It may come to prison, or it may come to worse than prison. They might hang you as a spy, or they might send you to the front. If you clear even one Iraqi mine with your miserable body, you'll be saving one devout Moslem brother's life. They'll decide all that. Anyway, I'd start remembering my daily prayers fast, if I were you. And I would get hold of a prayer seal, a rosary, and a copy of the Holy *Koran*."

He rang for the Revolutionary Guards. "This brother will be going to Evin," he said menacingly.

CHAPTER TWENTY-TWO

I was handcuffed and driven up to Evin Prison by two Revolutionary Guards, just before sunrise. The streets of the city were blacked out and empty. The only cars on the road seemed to be those of the police and the Revolutionary Guards. In the pre-dawn darkness, I tried to re-orient myself and reconstruct the map of the old city in my mind. But I was doubly handicapped. There were new streets and new squares, and the old streets and squares had new names. To the best of my determination, Shahreza Square and Shahreza Avenue were now called Liberty Square and Liberty Avenue. And Pahlavi Road was now called the Prophet's Vicar Highway. I could not read the names of any other streets in the dark.

We reached Evin Prison grounds at daybreak. We passed two check points manned by submachine gun-toting Revolutionary Guards, circled the sinister-looking Prison itself, and came to a stop in front of what seemed to be a row of administrative offices. I was led into a long window-less room, empty except for a wooden bench. A pitiful 25 watt light bulb hung from a very tall ceiling, barely lighting even the center of the room. I was told to wait there and I heard the key turn in the lock.

I sat on the bench and held my head in my handcuffed hands, too tired to think. I had an eerie and detached feeling, as if I was suddenly placed outside time. Was this all a dream? Was Mom really dead? Was she already buried, without my having had even a glimpse of her? Where was I? Was I really some ten thousand miles away from Waterloo? Had I really buried Sam three days ago? Had I really hugged and kissed Clare for the last time and said good-bye to her for good? Luckily, I fell asleep very soon and did not wake up until a couple of hours later, when they came to take me for interrogation.

My handcuffs were removed and I was led into a large office, where a bearded army colonel sat behind a desk under a huge portrait of the Ayatollah, absorbed in reading. He pointed to a chair with his right hand, while waving the guard out with his left, without lifting his eyes from his reading. I sat down and began massaging the sore spots on my wrists, where the handcuffs had pinched. I began orienting myself to the contents of the room. It was quite bare. The desk was stacked with piles of folders. I tried to study the face of the colonel, who was still absorbed in reading. Then I recognized the book in his hand. It was my diary. I was really in for it.

I tried to guess how far he had reached and what he was reading at that moment. Was it the Jimmy Buffet song: *My head hurts/ My feet stink/ And I don't love Jesus?* Or was it one of my fornications he was so absorbed in? How considerate of me to have brought along my own evidence of being *corrupt on earth,* my own invitation to a quick hanging, to save the Islamic Republic time and money.

When the colonel looked up finally, I almost jumped out of my skin. It was my old ham-actor Savak colonel of the Shah-Reza Avenue office, Colonel Sobhani. I felt an unexpected sense of pleasure, as if I had met an old friend, whom I had not heard of for years, or had assumed was dead. I stood up impulsively, ready to step forward and shake his hand, as soon as he gave any sign of recognition. But he studied my face with a somber and impassive expression and without the slightest hint of recognition. I sat back on the chair, with a vague sense of disappointment and loss.

"We have very serious charges against you, brother," he said. "very serious, indeed. Against you and your family. Your family seems to have been a nest of infidels and traitors against the country and against Islam, despite the fact that you are a descendant, and on both sides of the family, of the Prophet, blessings of Allah be on him and on his descendants. Not even counting what is in this diary, in your own words, which by itself is enough to justify declaring you *corrupt on earth* and hanging you."

As he stood up, I could see the rosary that he held in his right hand, moving the beads along, presumably counting silent prayers. I examined his face again, to see whether I had made a mistake. He looked older than my ham-acting colonel, but that was only to be expected. It was fourteen years since I had last seen him. But the resemblance was unmistakable, even with the beard. And the insignia on his collar was that of the legal branch of the Army. Could he be a twin brother, a first cousin? The Colonel turned his back on me, as if to avoid my closer scrutiny of his face. Now he held the rosary in both hands behind his back, counting the beads in silence.

"First," he said, twisting his head around, "there was your father, the arch-traitor, the highest judicial officer of the land, the Chief Justice, whose responsibility was to protect the lives of our innocent Moslem brothers and sisters, during the tyrannical reign of that damned and infidel Pharaoh, the Shah. But instead, he remained silent while thousands of our devout brothers and sisters were tortured and martyred."

Now there was no doubt in my mind that it was my old friend the ham-acting Colonel. That unmistakable cross-eyed look came over him as he twisted his head around to look at me. Soon, he was in his own old element and up and at it, walking around his desk and along the wall, maneuvering between the empty chairs, his squinting eyes fixed on that imaginary spot to the left of his nose, his hands waving in the air, shooing imaginary flies.

"Then, there was the other arch-traitor, your uncle, the Chairman, the Cabinet Minister, that infidel descendant of the Prophet, who was first a godless Communist, and then turned coat and became the Pharaoh's confidant and poker partner, robbing the *Moslem Populace's Purse* and squandering it on the Pharaoh, on his whorish queen, and on that whole host of whorish princesses. Then there was your brother, another godless Communist, one of those misled and infidel Fedayin, enemies of the true faith, who was tortured to death by the Pharaoh, and it served him right. Otherwise, we the servants of His Holiness the Imam would have had to do it.

"And now we have you, a godless, irreverent, sacrilegious, boozing, whoring, fornicator, who doesn't even know his daily prayers, who doesn't know how long a corpse can remain above the ground unburied, who has had the audacity of dropping from his name the title of *Seyyed*, ashamed of being, and on both sides, a descendant of the Prophet, blessings of Allah be on him and on his descendants. And after fourteen years of squandering the *Moslem Populace's Purse* and precious foreign exchange in the Sodom and Gomorrah of the Great Satan, now you have returned to spy on us for the Great Satan and for its stooge, that infidel and damned Saddam, in the middle of our Holy War. But you may let your masters know that the Islamic Republic, under the guidance and command of His Holiness the Imam, will trample that snake the Great Satan, crushing its head, and will smash the jaws of its damned stooge Saddam."

I admitted to myself it had been wrong of me to call my colonel a ham-actor. He was a true and genuine actor, the most original I had ever seen. For myself, I had never played any part so convincingly as this man played himself. He *was* his role, which he changed only every decade or two, with each new regime that came to power. And all the makeup and costuming he needed, was a uniform, a beard, and a rosary.

Soon, we were back to that business of Duke of Cornwall "*Why Dover? Let him answer that!*". The Colonel emphatically wanted to know why I had chosen this particular time to return, and for what purpose. The fact of my mother's death and funeral had been already erased underneath my crime of not knowing how long a corpse could remain above the ground, unburied, if there had ever been a corpse.

The easiest thing for me to do now was to admit that my mother had never died, that her corpse had never remained above the ground, that there never was a corpse, and that the whole thing was a hoax, an excuse for me to return to the country in the middle of our Holy War, to spy for the Great Satan, and for that damned infidel Saddam, and get hanged or shot, or whatever it was they did to the *corrupt on earth.*

If the Colonel had really forgot his office on Shahreza Avenue, if he had really forgot those interrogations of me he had conducted under the life-size sceptered picture of "the Pharaoh," His Imperial Majesty the Shah-in-Shah, instead of under the turbaned picture of His Holiness the Imam, what could I possibly say that would shed any light on anything? No, it was positively easier to confess and be hanged once for all. But the Colonel, in his excited ham-acting, would not hear of it; he would not hear that I was ready to confess and be damned. He had better methods to deal with the likes of me. There were those he could set on me, who could make me talk, who could uncover the whole Satanic plan.

And with that threat or promise, I was buzzed out, delivered to my submachine gun-toting keepers, handcuffed again and sent back, not to my nice old quiet waiting room, where I had so soundly slept, the pinching of handcuffs notwithstanding, but to that sinister and ugly prison. As I was marched down the steps of the administrative offices building and around the block of adjacent buildings; as the gloomy and hideous looking prison itself loomed larger and larger; my heart began to sink within me. I was back in real time and real space. This was no longer Waterloo. It was not even the world of my ham-acting *Duke of Cornwall* Colonel. We had now passed the limbo and were descending into the first circle of Hell.

We stopped behind a huge black steel door, where we were inspected through a peephole before being let in. I was handed over from submachine gun-toting bearded men, to six-gun-packing bearded men. I was marched down several long ugly corridors, inspected through more peepholes, until I arrived in a huge dark hall with heavy stone columns and a tall ceiling that looked like an ancient Roman bath. The air was subterranean and musty, as if sunlight had not pierced through it for ages. The heavy silence seemed filled with sinister conspiratorial hummings and whispers, coming from behind many a closed door. Once in a while a distant word or cry would reach the hall, as if from the far-out space

After a short stop there, while my guards changed, I was led through another steel door, down another long dark musty corridor, and into a foul-smelling window-less cell, faintly lighted by a tiny light bulb hanging from an extremely high ceiling. My handcuffs were removed and I was left alone. As I heard the door lock behind me, I slowly let myself sink to the ground in a corner. It was a relief to be by myself, no matter how foul the cell smelled, no matter what else was in store for me. Even the semi-darkness of the cell was a relief. I was about to close my eyes and try to take a nap, when a sudden movement in another corner of the cell startled me. A dark human shape bowed down from a stiff standing position. I was not alone. A dark bearded man was saying his prayers in the other corner.

I felt intruded upon and irritated. Now I could not possibly take a nap. I had to deal with this stranger first, and I could not do that, until his prayer was finished. I began studying his dark form, backed against the wall and facing me at an angle. He was a young man, about my age, considering that the beard makes you look older. He seemed absorbed in his holy task, as if totally unaware of my existence or intrusion. I watched his face as he prayed standing straight, as he bowed down, as he went down on his knees and prostrated himself. It seemed like a choreographed dance. I remembered I had done that dance once, twenty-odd years ago, to please my mother, the descendant of the Prophet, blessings of Allah be on him and on his descendants. I remembered that I had once even memorized the words that went with it, in the religious education class in the middle school. How remote all that seemed now.

But why was he praying *there*? Why was he there at all? If I was there because I was a *corrupt on earth*, coming from a clan of *corrupts on earth*, why was this pious praying mantis put there? Was he there to spy on me, to draw me out in conversation to learn my secrets, to listen to me in my sleep? Or was he there to make sure I would not hang myself and rob the hangman? As I was meditating these questions, and as my eyes were getting used to the semi-darkness of the cell, I noticed a toilet ewer in another corner of the room, next to a water tap in the wall, and a grating in the floor near it. I crawled over on my hands and knees to investigate. It was the can. And that was what the foul smell emanated from.

I crawled backward on my hands and knees, as if I had no energy to stand up, or as if the new existence I was condemned to, obviated the necessity of walking on two legs, of being human. Crawling on four seemed like what the situation asked for. When I reached my corner again, I lay back and stretched my legs, feeling quite in my element. Now the presence of a chair or a sofa would have shocked me beyond measure. I stretched farther down and lay on the ground, to test it for my nightly sleep. This hard floor obviously was my bed. With my hands folded under my head for a pillow, it seemed reasonably tolerable. I sat up again, as it looked like my companion was finishing his prayer.

He picked up his prayer seal, kissed it three times, put it in his pocket, and then looked up at me for the first time.

"Peace be upon you," he said piously, bending his head reverently and amiably.

"And upon you," I said, returning his courtesy.

We stared at each other for a few minutes in silence, sizing each other up, as if we had nothing more to say. He had a sympathetic look and seemed quite at peace with himself. He did not look like a spy. I wondered whether his silence was not because of his suspicions of me, wondering whether I had not been placed there to spy on him.

"Morad is my name," he said.

"Farhang is mine," I said. I wondered whether he was giving only a first name, as it was usual with the Fedayin or Mujahedeen, as a kind of *nom de guerre*.

"And why is a pious man like you here?" I asked. "I thought this was a place for the *corrupts on earth* like me."

"Are you a *corrupt on earth*?" he asked.

"That's what they tell me," I said, with amusement.

"Are you a Bahai or a Jew?" he asked, kindly.

"A Twelve-Imam Shiite, believe it or not," I said. "And a descendant, and on both sides, of the Holy Prophet, to boot, blessings of Allah be on him and on his descendants."

"You don't look it," he said.

"I know," I said. "That's part of my problem. The title *seyyed* was dropped from my birth certificate by my father, when I was born."

"And they hold it against you?"

"Yes! Among other things."

"Are you a believer in Islam?"

"I'm not a believer in anything," I said. "That's my real problem."

After I had said that, it occurred to me that I might have already said too much. If he was placed there to spy on me, I had made my first confession to him, before I had ever found out why he was there, with his beard, his Imam Hussein prayer seal, and his pious praying.

"But why are *you* here?" I asked, to regain the initiative. "You sure seem to be a believer."

"I am," he said, sadly. "A true believer. I am a Mujahed. I have the same sap and root as these pretenders to Faith. We led the Revolution together, to set up a just Islamic society. But now we have become the victims of the just society we fought for. We were sold out. The country was sold out."

"And you still believe?" I asked.

"In these turbaned mullahs? No!" he said. "In Justice? Yes. In true Islam? Yes."

I looked at his face. He had the looks of an honest man. And his piety did not seem feigned.

"But they had been talking about true Islam, too," I said, "hadn't they. And they still do. And see what their true Islam turned out to be like. Why should people believe that yours would be any different?"

"I take it you don't believe in any religion," he said, indulgently.

"I told you, I don't believe in anything."

"Do you remember how to say your prayers?"

"No, I have forgotten," I said. "That is another one of my crimes."

"Any others?"

"Oh, many!" I said. "I booze, I fornicate, I don't own a *Koran*, or a prayer seal, or a rosary. I read Ferdowsi's *Book of Kings*, and Khayyam's *Rubaiyat,* and Hafiz's *Divan*. My father was the Chief Justice, under that cursed Pharaoh, the Shah. My uncle was a cabinet minister of that cursed Pharaoh, the Shah. My brother was tortured to death by the men of that same cursed Pharaoh, the Shah. And they are all my crimes."

"Is your last name Shadzad, by any chance?" he asked knowledgeably.

"Yes," I said, quite taken aback.

"And was your brother's name Alex?"

"Yes," I said, no longer surprised.

He got up and walked toward me. "Can I embrace you?" he asked gently. I let him embrace me and kiss my face.

"He was a true hero of the Revolution, your brother was," he said. "I am sorry for what happened to him."

"Did you know him?" I asked.

"Not face to face. But I knew him. Everybody knew him. He gave us courage to go on, when the going was tough. A pity he did not live long enough to see the Shah fall. But maybe he was lucky not to live long enough to see what they did to our revolution. If he had survived, these people would have surely killed him."

"What's gonna happen to us?" I asked.

"They'll hang us," he said matter-of-factly.

"When?" I asked, resignedly.

"In a couple of weeks," he said, with equal resignation. "When they brought me here two weeks ago, there was another Mujahed brother here. They took him out two days ago. They said he was going home. But we knew they were gonna hang him. They have a long record of that. None of our brothers has left this prison alive. Once they invited in the families of a whole lot of them, to see their loved ones. And then they hanged them in the courtyard before their very eyes. I figure I have one more week. And I know they are hearing me say it right now."

"You mean the cells are bugged?" I asked.

"That's what I mean," he said. "So, don't say anything here you don't want them to hear."

"I've got nothing to say that everybody can't hear," I said. "That's really my biggest problem. And how long do you think I have got, before they hang me?"

"I'd give you two weeks also," he said, "if you are Alex Shadzad's brother. Unless they think you know something that they must find out, and you won't talk, and they think they can make you talk. Then they'll torture you for as long as it takes, or for as long as you can take it."

"Have they gone through that with you?" I asked.

"Yes," he said. "But with us they know where they stand. They know we would gladly drink the nectar of martyrdom rather than talk. So, they don't waste too much time with us. We hang easily."

There was a cynical but graceful smile on his face. There was not much else left to talk about, and on that cheerful note we stretched out, each in his corner, and went to sleep.

CHAPTER TWENTY-THREE

When I woke up next, I was totally disoriented. I found my bearings only when I recognized Morad's dark figure praying in his corner. There was a tin bowl of cold sticky rice lying next to me. I had no idea of how it had got there. I had no appetite, anyway. I waited until Morad finished his prayer.

"Good morning," he said, when he had finished.

"Is it morning?" I asked, impulsively looking at my wrist, for the watch that wasn't there. They had taken it away with all my other belongings. I could see that he had no watch either. Yet, he seemed to have certain knowledge that it was morning.

"Yes," he said. "You slept through the night like a baby. I didn't want to wake you up when they brought the dinner." He made a contemptuous gesture towards the bowl of rice lying near me.

"Is that the dinner?" I asked.

"It is whatever you want it to be. It is the dinner, the lunch, and the breakfast. That's all you get in a day. And it is better that way. The less we eat and the more constipated we get, the less we'll stink the place up." He pointed to the grating in the floor, while holding his nose.

"And how do you know what time of day it is?" I asked with frustration. "How do you know *what* day it is? It seems like an everlasting night to me."

"The prayers," he said. "I have an inner clock that tells me the time for the prayers: the morning prayer, the noon prayer, the afternoon prayer, the evening prayer and the night prayer. And after each night prayer, I make a scratch mark on the wall with my prayer seal. It might not be very reverent to use your prayer seal that way, but God understands and forgives. That's how I keep count of the days. And that bowl of rice always comes between my evening and my night prayer. That's why I call it dinner. I say my night prayers after the bowl."

I thought how lucky it was for me to have a cell-mate that kept track of time that way. But what if I had to stay there two more weeks by myself, after they had hanged him? What if my next cell-mate turned out to be another *corrupt on earth* like me, who didn't know how to pray?

How would I keep track of time then? How would I kill time in that one long everlasting night? What were the chances that they would give me some paper and pencil to write some more irreverent poems, as a last wish of a condemned man? Maybe they would give me a chance to bring my diary up to date, give a fuller account of my fornications on this earth, for the instruction of the posterity.

During the day I tried to write some poems in my head. Some lines even came to me. I repeated them to myself again and again, until I was satisfied I had fully memorized them. In the meantime, I tried to keep track of the time by following Morad's prayers. I tried to think back to Waterloo, but Waterloo now seemed farther than the far side of the moon.

I thought of Clare and some of our good times together. But it hurt to do that. It made her absence and loss more unbearable. I thought of Mom, but she had lost all presence in my mind, as if she had been dead for many many years. I tried to think of Sam, but it seemed like such a useless exercise. It made everything seem such a waste. I tried to recall some of my Fink jokes, but I realized I had totally lost my sense of humor. By the time of Morad's night prayer, there was nothing else left to think about. Then I tried to recall the lines of poetry I had written and memorized earlier in the day, and I could not remember one single word. And to think that this was only my second night in the hole. That was when I panicked.

I had avoided using the can all day long, waiting to do it after Morad fell asleep, this being the first day that I had finally eaten that inedible bowl of rice. Morad must have been using the same stratagem, not having needed to relieve himself all day. Although, he used the tap water for his ablutions before each of his five daily prayers. I wished I had the same excuse to wash my hands and face. I had no desire to do so. I felt dirty and itchy all over and figured my hands and face were probably my cleanest parts. There was no soap there, and washing without soap somehow did not quite sit right with me.

Morad lay down shortly after his night prayer and immediately fell asleep, judging by his loud snoring. I tiptoed to the grating in the floor, squatted down, and cautiously and guiltily lowered my pants, scared that any minute Morad might wake up and shame me. What if he was not really asleep and was only snoring to give me the excuse to relieve myself. How considerate of him. I felt so self-conscious. Did that mean I would also have to adopt that ploy, to give him the excuse. What a desperate way to be civilized and courteous!

But I was wrong. Morad was sound asleep, with the deep sleep of the righteous. I was the one who had all the difficulty in the world in falling asleep, even after I had relieved myself. The floor that had not seemed so hard at first, was feeling harder and stiffer by the minute. And my mind was absolutely refusing and blocking any thought that might help it relax itself. Even counting sheep seemed out of the question. And the worst was not knowing what time it really was. After what seemed like a couple of hours of tossing and turning I became even more panicky. I felt a desperate need for human contact, an urgent need to talk to Morad. I called out to him, first gently, then louder, and louder, until he woke and sat up.

"What?" he asked in a rather startled tone.

"Will you teach me how to say the daily prayers?" I asked.

"Have you suddenly got religion?" he asked gently, with a smile. "Did your ancestor the Prophet visit you in a dream?"

"No!" I said. "I just can't go to sleep. I can't imagine how I would keep my sanity here for two weeks, after they have hanged you."

"That's a kind thought," he said humorously. "When do you want to start?"

"Right now, if I can!" I said, impatiently. "And not necessarily now, but, I would also like to learn the meaning of the prayers. I would like to learn Arabic."

"Suits me fine," he said, sleepy-eyed. "I may not be the best teacher of Arabic, but I know my *Koran* well enough."

In an instant, I felt I had regained my cheerfulness and my sense of humor. I remembered what Sam had said in his tape, about our meeting on the fields of Asphodel: "When we meet again, shall we converse in Arabic?"

"I have this dead Arab friend," I said. "We promised that when we meet again down there, we would converse in Arabic."

Morad smiled good-humoredly, after a yawn.

We began the lessons right away. Seeming only too glad to teach, he did not even lose time in translating the lines of the prayers for me. Knowing what the prayers actually meant, made them more purposeful, my lack of belief in their efficacy notwithstanding. I could tell that Morad had been a conscientious student of the *Koran*. After we had gone through the whole set of prayers, he asked me to put on a demonstration, while he listened and corrected my mistakes. When we finally lay down to sleep, I had something to rehearse. And I was totally relaxed. I kept rehearsing the prayers, until I fell asleep.

In the morning, Morad woke me up in time for the morning prayers. In that eternal night of a 25 watt bulb hanging ten feet overhead, I actually felt I could tell that it was just before the sunrise. Otherwise, we would not be saying our morning prayers, would we? As we had agreed, we began saying our prayers aloud, so that I could check the correctness of mine against Morad's. I hardly made any mistakes, thanks to all the rehearsing I had done before falling asleep. And as the day went along, my mind went along with it, further rehearsing the prayers and their translations, which now sounded like a new kind of poetry.

The days now became more tolerable, more cheerful, and shorter. By the third day of the prayers, the jailer brought me a prayer seal, along with our bowl of rice, and called me "brother." Morad had been right. We were being watched and listened to. Otherwise, how would they have known that I had begun praying? It didn't matter, though. I wasn't doing it for them. I wasn't doing it even for God, although I felt a kind of piety doing it. I certainly felt a new sense of brotherhood with Morad. Now my lessons in Arabic had been extended beyond the daily prayers, to embrace any verses from the *Koran* that Morad could remember. It felt like being back in school, and it was fun.

A week after my arrival, as Morad had guessed, they came for him. They told him he was being freed and sent home. For a minute, I felt overjoyed that he was being freed after all. But as he embraced and kissed my cheeks, he winked mischievously and said, "I'm going home, get it?" And I knew that they were taking him away to hang him. My sudden joy at his release turned into sudden despair. He was the only attachment I had left in the world. And now they were taking him away to hang him.

With his departure, the walls of the cell closed in on me. The room began to look dark and smelly again. The bowl of rice became even more inedible. Even the daily prayers lost their poetry and significance. But I kept hanging on to them, if anything, with more of a compulsion. They were the only thing standing between me and total panic, between me and insanity.

That night I could not sleep at all. And not having Morad's inner clock, I had no idea what was the correct time for the morning prayer. I probably began the whole thing several hours too early the next day, because by the time the bowl of rice arrived, it was already a long time after I had said my night prayers.

The next day I even forgot about the bowl of rice and waiting for it before saying my night prayers. By the time the rice arrived, I had already said prayers for two full days. And I seemed quite confused whether I had put the correct number of scratches on the wall. By the next day I had given up trying to keep count of days. I would get up and pray whenever I felt I needed to, which was quite often. Also having to make ablutions before each prayer by washing my hands, feet, and face, gave me a good excuse for the wash. But inside my clothes I felt dirtier and itchier each day.

When they came for me, I couldn't tell for sure how many days had passed since Morad was gone. It seemed they had come a day or two sooner than Morad had calculated. But I was glad that they had come. In fact, I would have gladly gone even a few days earlier, to be hanged with Morad. It would have felt good to have a companion in hanging. Even Christ had two thieves.

However, I was wrong. I was not being taken away to be hanged, but only to be interrogated again. I was led down a long flight of stairs, into a large basement, very much like the old Savak basement I had visited long ago, where I had been given the account of Alex's death. And on reaching the basement, I had the greatest shock of my life. There they were, my old friends, the lieutenant colonel, now a full colonel, and his three assistants, whom he now introduced to me as "Brother Hossein," "Brother Aziz," and "Brother Akbar." The only difference was that they all had full beards now, and looked older. The gold teeth were there, the missing tooth, and the hole in the middle of the smile. But the lecherous wink was gone. The colonel's handlebar mustache now merged with the full beard, and he had a rosary in his hand, on which he presumably counted his prayers.

To my surprise again, nobody gave any hint of recognition. With my ham-acting colonel, I had assumed that the lack of recognition was feigned. But now I began to question even that assumption. I really wondered whether this foursome remembered me at all. Why should they remember, after fourteen years, a young boy they had terrorized and humiliated and lusted after, all in a day's work? Maybe they did not even remember Alex, with whom they had certainly had a more intimate relationship. Maybe we were both two insignificant numbers among many, whom they had "treated" and then forgot.

Again I found myself seated on a chair in the middle of the basement, as the colonel and the "brothers" closed in on me. The colonel was playing with his rosary and mumbling *In the name of Allah, the Compassionate, the Merciful,* as he raised his right foot and set it on the chair next to me. Then he began reciting my and my family's long list of crimes: my father had been the Chief Justice of that "damned and infidel tyrant the Shah," at a time when many of "our devout brothers and sisters were being tortured and martyred," and my uncle had been the cabinet minister of the same "damned and infidel tyrant the Shah," and my brother had been "a godless and infidel Communist," and I was a boozer and a fornicator, notwithstanding my being a descendant, and on both sides, of the Prophet, blessings of Allah be on him and on his descendants. These by themselves were enough to condemn me as a *corrupt on earth* and hang me.

But what he was mainly concerned with was that I was a spy, for the Great Satan America and "its stooge, that damned and infidel Saddam," whom they were going to smash to pieces and send to the deepest hell of the infidels, under the guidance and command of His Holiness the Imam. What he intended to find out was what my exact mission was, who my contacts were, and, had I been drafted and sent to the front in the uniform of the Islamic Republic, what my specific spying goals and objectives would have been. When I pleaded innocent to all the spying charges, he assured me that he had ways of making me talk, and he promised to do so immediately.

He reached out and grabbed an electric cord, naked on one end, which "Brother Akbar," our old "Dr. Azodi, the specialist in electroshock treatment," had kindly made available to him.

"You know what this is, boy?" he asked ominously.

"An electric cord," I mumbled.

"It sure is," he said. "And you know what it does? It sends multiples of 220 volts of electricity right into your balls, until you scream your head off, and beg me to let you talk, and tell me all I want to know."

Was it that they had kindly done away with the "rectal feeding," and "bottle feeding"; that "Brother Hossein" and "Brother Aziz" had been cured of their disgusting infidel habits and were rehabilitated into their new bearded and holy Islamic personas? Or was it that in the interest of time they were skipping a few steps in my "treatment," going straight to "electroshock therapy?"

When I again pleaded innocent to the spying charges, the colonel gave the go-ahead to begin the "therapy." They rolled over a small machine on wheels, connected the cord, tied me to the chair, and unceremoniously pulled down my pants. I closed my eyes and leaned back in the chair, resting on the nape of my neck, feeling already faint and dizzy. I anxiously awaited the dreaded moment of contact and intolerable pain, which was being cruelly delayed, probably to increase my anxiety and dread. Suddenly, as if a reprieve from Heaven had arrived, the telephone rang, and everything stopped. And I wished to God that it was the order for my immediate hanging, to get it done and over with, once for all.

I did not dare open my eyes. I could now stay in darkness forever and do away with daylight and the real world. I could hear the colonel's voice, obviously talking to a superior, someone who could mercifully order my immediate hanging. "Yes, sir!" he said. "Yes, sir! Right away, sir!" The telephone clicked and I heard the colonel shouting at them to put my pants on. So, the order for my hanging had arrived. Allah was, indeed, compassionate and merciful.

I was untied and handcuffed again and led out of the basement. But instead of being led to the courtyard, I found myself being led out of the prison, the same way I had been led in. I was put in a Jeep between two submachine gun-toting Revolutionary Guards and blindfolded. We drove for almost half an hour, before I was led out of the Jeep, still blindfolded, and rushed up a flight of steps, into a building. When they took my blindfold off, I found myself in a splendid looking hall, carpeted with expensive silk rugs and adorned with huge chandeliers. There were many offices, guarded by soldiers and Revolutionary Guards.

I was immediately rushed into a large office, where a bearded army major general sat at a large desk. A fat middle-aged mullah in black robe and a huge black turban sat on a cushioned chair across from the desk. They both looked at me with intense curiosity, as if I was a strange species they had just been discussing.

"So, this is the *corrupt on earth* spy of the Great Satan," the mullah said with contemptuous amusement, "descended, and on both sides, from the Holy Prophet, blessings of Allah be on him and on his descendants."

"It is so, Excellency Ayatollah," said the general, deferentially.

"It shames me," said the mullah addressed as ayatollah, "that such a person should share with us such a holy lineage and with so little desert and appreciation."

"Quite so," said the general.

"Do you think, General," the mullah continued, "that our Holy Ancestor, blessings of Allah be on him and on his descendants, would on Judgment day intercede on behalf of such an unworthy descendant?"

"I don't know, Excellency Ayatollah," said the general, torn by seemingly honest doubts. "Our Holy Ancestor is compassionate and munificent beyond all measure, but even he might have difficulty finding one grace in this worthless descendant of his, to merit intercession."

"Quite so," said the ayatollah. "Even though, I understand that in prison, he has begun saying his daily prayers again, as if our Holy Ancestor, blessings of Allah be on him and his descendants, has deigned to soften his heart, and may yet claim the lost black sheep of his flock."

"Yes, the Holy Prophet is never quite indifferent even to the blackest sheep of the whole flock. Who knows, whether he might not yet deign to visit him in a dream and save him."

"Quite so! Quite so!" said the ayatollah. "Much as we Ulama have the responsibility of seeing to it that the *corrupt on earth* be punished and hanged, do we wish to be the ones to hang such a black sheep, no matter how unworthy, who is a descendant, and on both sides, of the Holy Prophet, blessings of Allah be on him and on his descendants?

What if our ancestor the Holy Prophet stops us on the Judgment Day and tells us that he had intended to bring this black sheep back to the straight path yet, if we had not taken the matter in our hands?"

"He is compassionate and munificent enough to do that, yet," said the general.

"And of course," said the ayatollah, "much as I would like to see the snout of the Great Satan rubbed in dirt and his spies hanged, we do not want to twist the lion's tail unnecessarily at this time, to give him an excuse for further mischief. Especially now, that thanks to the leadership of His Holiness the Imam, we are winning the war against that infidel Saddam."

"Quite so," said the general, ingratiatingly.

"Well, General!" said the ayatollah, getting up to leave. "You deal with the matter as you best see fit, and in the manner we discussed."

"Yes, Excellency Ayatollah!" said the general, getting up to see him to the door. "I get your meaning and am in full agreement. We'll follow the procedure exactly as we discussed it."

As the mullah left, the general returned to his desk, asked the guards to take off my handcuffs, leave the room, and close the door. He sat down and looked at me again with curiosity, before offering me a chair to sit down. I hesitated, suddenly realizing that I was too dirty to sit on such plush chairs. For the first time in a couple of weeks I noted that I had not had a bath, or changed any clothes, in as many weeks. I suspected that my body odor must be unbearable by now, even though I had lost my sense of smell; which explained why the foul smell in the prison cell had disappeared after the first few days. But not to seem rude to the general, I finally decided to brush the dust from the seat of my pants and sit down.

"You are extremely lucky, young man!" the general said after a few moments. "You were about to be tortured and hanged as a spy and a *corrupt on earth*, when I called. Luckily for you, some influential people, such as this powerful Ayatollah, have interceded in your behalf, recommending maximum leniency, considering that you are a descendant, and on both sides, no matter how unworthy, of the Holy Prophet, blessings of Allah be on him and on his descendants."

I was puzzled. For the life of me I could not think of any possible connection I could have had with that or any other fat mullah, except for the dubious holy blood which I shared with them. The general, as if he had read my mind, continued.

"And I myself, have a long friendship with a man who is very near to my heart, and who is very near to you in blood."

Suddenly lights went on in my head. This was my "Uncle J.'s General." And that middle-aged fat turbaned ayatollah was probably recruited to my cause by Uncle J.'s "boys." So, only weeks after I had burned all my bridges with my Uncle J., his mighty long arm had reached through the clouds across five thousand miles and sprung me from the Evin Prison, one step ahead of torture and death. What I felt immediately was not gratitude, but amazement, that at the very moment that I was being condemned to death for the crimes of that *corrupt on earth* uncle of mine, he could reach out and snatch me away from the jaws of death and from the claws of my and his accusers.

"I will be brief," said the General, "since time is short. I must have you put on a Zurich flight that leaves in three hours. Instead of being hanged as a spy, as you well deserve to be, you will be taken to the airport immediately and expelled, never again to return to the Islamic Republic. Once in Zurich, you will be met by your Uncle's men, who will take you to him. If I were you, when I see him, I would fall to my knees and kiss his feet with gratitude. And when you do see him, give him my regards."

The General buzzed and the guards returned, along with an army captain.

"Captain!" the General barked, excitedly. "You are directly responsible to see to it that this prisoner gets to the airport, is put on the Zurich flight due to take off in three hours, and is expelled from the country, with his passport stamped, *Never to return to the Islamic Republic*. Put his handcuffs on and keep them on until the flight is ready for takeoff. If he tries to run, shoot him in both legs, but keep him alive, so that we can hang him." There was not a hint in his voice that he did not mean every word he said.

The captain clicked his heels and we were dismissed. I was handcuffed and led into the hall, where I was blindfolded again and rushed out of the building. I was hurriedly pushed into a waiting car and driven away, with a police siren escorting us all the way to the airport. At the airport, my blindfold was removed and I was rushed out of the car and down the corridors, bypassing the passenger lines and inspections. People looked curiously at this dirty, smelly, bearded, handcuffed VIP, being railroaded through. As I was pushed up the steps of an Iran Air flight sitting on the runway with its lights flashing, I recognized my small suitcase and black handbag being handed to a flight stewardess by a Revolutionary Guard.

Just before they closed the doors for takeoff, the army captain took off my handcuffs and left, giving a series of instructions to the plane crew on the way out. The seats next to me were empty on both sides and I had plenty of elbow room. I sat back, still reeling under the rush and excitement of the day. I was exhausted. The stewardesses were specially attentive and solicitous of my needs. They took turns in stopping by and offering me soft drinks. They were obviously curious, but were curbing their curiosity with great effort. Only when we had landed in Zurich and I was about to leave the plane a free man, one of them asked me what my crime had been.

"I am," I said amusedly, raising my index finger skyward, "a spy for the Great Satan!"

"Oh, my God!" she said, drawing away from me, unable to control her horror and shock.

At the Zurich airport I had no difficulty identifying my Uncle J.'s "boys," and they me. I was the dirtiest, smelliest, bearded passenger getting off the plane, and ahead of everyone else. And they were the most distinguished-looking bunch of chauffeurs and bodyguards waiting to pick up a passenger. I was rushed into a black Mercedes and driven away. I immediately fell asleep and did not wake up until we were at Uncle J.'s Saint Moritz villa. That's where he usually stayed when he wished to be alone, away from everyone, even his wife and daughters. I was gratefully looking forward to seeing him and embarrassed to have to face him and hug him and kiss him, looking and smelling the way I did.

Luckily for me, I was informed on arrival that Uncle J. was taking his afternoon nap and that I had to wait until he woke up. The butler, as if he could read my mind, told me that he would not be up for an hour or two, and that I had plenty of time to shower and shave and change. He also confided to me that my Uncle was a very sick man, in much pain, and that he badly needed his afternoon nap, which was brought about by sedation. He would reveal no more. I had had no idea that my uncle was a sick man.

The butler had already prepared a hot tub for me, and I jumped into it with the excitement of a thirsty man diving into a pool of fresh water. The vapor of the gardenia-scented bath lotion was intoxicating. Up to my ears in warm soothing water, I closed my eyes and tried to shut out every memory of my life.

Shortly after I had finished my leisurely and long bath, had shaved and changed, the butler came to let me know that my uncle was awake and ready to see me. It was late afternoon when I was finally led into his bedroom. I could not believe how much he had changed. He looked very thin and haggard. His neck had re-appeared and it seemed unusually thin and long. And there were dark pouches around his eyes. I was so very glad to see him. And he seemed equally glad to see me. He sat up halfway in bed and let me hug and kiss him. The butler brought us tea in a crystal teapot on a silver tray. He poured it out and left. We took tea in silence for a while, as if in a loss for words.

The room looked very modestly furnished. A silk Tabriz rug covered the center of the marble floor. Two framed Persian miniatures covered one wall, a large anonymous abstract painting another. A large crystal bird stood on a tall black stand in one corner of the room, a large malachite elephant in another. On a small oak bookshelf next to the bed there was a *Divan* of Hafiz and a *Divan* of Rumi. Uncle J. caught my eyes looking at them.

"Yes," he said. "I have been reading Hafiz and Rumi. You were right. There is something there I had missed."

I sipped my tea, not knowing what to say. I was embarrassed to even remember our last phone conversation.

"So," said Uncle J. again, after some silence. "you finally got out." It seemed he was reluctant to think back to that conversation, too.

"Yes," I said. "Thanks to you, and to your General, and to your Ayatollah."

"I'll take the credit for 'my General,' as you put it," he said. "But not for that turbaned tub of guts, who now calls himself an ayatollah. That little 'intercession' of his cost me a quarter of a million dollars. But I wanted the General's back covered, in case something went wrong, to make it look as if the suggestion had been put to him by someone else, and he had just gone along with it. I didn't want him to take all that risk by himself."

"I'm sorry I caused you so much trouble and money," I said. "I should have listened to you and not gone."

"Never mind that now," he said. "You are alive and safely out, and that's all that matters. Did you even get to see your mother's grave?"

"No," I said. "All I saw was the inside of the airport, the inside of the Evin Prison, and the inside of the General's office. The rest of the time I was blindfolded."

"Did you find the key you were looking for?"

"Yes and no."

"Did you learn anything new?" he asked with amusement.

"Yes," I said. "I learned about how long a corpse can remain above the ground, unburied."

"I'm sure you learned more than that," he said with a smile. "You seem greatly changed. You're not the same man I last talked to in Waterloo, only a couple of weeks ago."

"A lot has happened to me, since you last talked to me in Waterloo, only a couple of weeks ago."

"You don't seem as proud as you were."

"I am not," I said. "Nor as self-righteous."

We were silent again for quite a while, while the butler came in and poured some more tea and left.

"You also look very different from when I saw you last," I said.

"You mean I look more human?" he asked.

"No," I said. "I meant you have lost a lot of weight. Are you sick?"

"Yes, I am," he said. "Just between you and me, I am dying of cancer of larynx. This is not for advertising. No one knows it, not even my wife and daughters. I could not take their hysterics, their over-solicitude, their crowding me. They'll get their inheritance all right, and they can shop for the rest of their lives. I just want to have some quiet before I die."

I felt tears in my eyes and a lump in my throat. I looked away to hide my eyes from him.

"I'm very sorry to hear that," I mumbled, fighting back my tears. "I had no idea you were sick."

"Well," he said. "I have done my share of living. I've done more than my share of living. Even a cat runs out of lives some day. We all must die one day. As they say, it's a camel that sleeps at everybody's door. I don't know whether my life has been worth anything. True, I personally and knowingly haven't hurt anyone. I can't even be sure of that. But even if so, is that enough to make your life worth anything? Maybe you were right. Maybe I haven't paid for anything worthwhile in my life, with anything worthwhile. I made a lot of money. I raised a family, but I don't even know whether I did right by them. I spoiled them. I overprotected them. I corrupted them. Or, rather, my money did. Maybe that's all money ever does: corrupt. Maybe it is luckier to be born poor and stay poor."

"Well," I said, "the way I look at it, big money is like a mantle of great office. When it is thrust upon us, it brings some responsibility with it. We can choose to shun the mantle, but if we accept it, we cannot shun the responsibility."

"I wish it was as simple as that," he said. "Anyway, I wish we had understood each other better sooner. And I wish we hadn't quarreled this much, you and I. We probably have more in common than you think."

"Well, I wish we hadn't quarreled so much, either," I said.

"We could have been better friends. We should have been better friends."

"Yes, we should have," I said. "Maybe we were hurting too much inside to do that. You know, an awful lot had happened to us, more than our share. We had to take it out on someone. We weren't the type to take it out on strangers. So, we used ourselves for that."

"Maybe so," he said. "You were too harsh, both on yourself and on me. You expected too much, both from yourself and from me. You wanted me to give the world what I didn't have in me. You wanted me to be what I couldn't be. Alex wanted that from me, too. You were both thrusting a heavy mantle on my shoulders, which I couldn't carry. And I wasn't smart enough to see that, or honest enough with myself to admit it. You wanted me to be what you yourself couldn't be, a savior of the world. You thought I *had* to be a savior of the world, just because I had piled up a lot of money, despite myself. I never wanted to be very rich, or very powerful. All I wanted to be was just a nice guy, well liked by everybody. Anyway, it takes much more than a lot of money to be the savior of the world."

"Yes," I said. "It takes a burning desire and an obsession with Justice."

"Well, then," he said. "I didn't have that. And it takes a lot of self knowledge and humility to know what one doesn't have, to not be flattered by people's wrong expectations of us, not to fall into the trap of a false identity. Instead of accepting what I was not, I tried too hard to defend myself for not being it; first with Alex, and then with you. But we both have learned a lot in a very short time, haven't we. Neither of us are as proud or as self-righteous as we were."

"Seems that way," I said.

We were silent again, for a long time, while we drank more tea..

"How long do you have?" I asked.

"A few months, the doctors tell me," he said. "Less than six."

"I'm sorry," I mumbled again, still fighting back my tears.

"What do you plan to do now?" he asked.

"Catch my breath first," I said.

"And then?"

"Go back to Waterloo."

"Why there?" he asked.

"To have my Waterloo," I said.

"And after you've had your Waterloo, what then?"

"Get down to earth; get some animals for companions; plant some roots; see what I can do with ten acres of bottom land. Try to rebuild the Garden of Eden."

"And your dream of a just world?"

"It will have to wait," I said. "It will have to wait until I have caught my breath, until I have pulled out all the arrows. Anyway, a garden seems like a nice place to begin both dreaming of and building a just world."

"That's a pretty modest plan for somebody who wanted to change the world. If you still want to change the world, and if you still think you can do it with money, I'll give you money. Let's see whether you can do what you blamed me for not doing. Let's see whether you can have money and not be corrupted by it. I'll give you a million dollars, for your dream of a just world. Let's see what you can do with it. Let's see whether you will keep it out of the stock and bond market, and big business, and the real estate, and import and export, and all the things you always pooh-poohed, and still make it work for you. Or whether you'll get sucked into the same trap, of just making more money with it."

"*An empty sack cannot stand straight*," I said. "That's what Benjamin Franklin said. And right now I feel I'm an empty sack. I have to fill me first, with something, before I can stand up, before I can tend to the business of changing the world. Give me a couple of years."

"I'll do that," he said. "I'll give you a couple of years and a million dollars in a trust fund. Just for your dream of a just world. When you think you are ready to claim the heavy mantle, come and collect your money. Let's see whether you can deliver as much as you expected me to do. Fair enough?"

"Fair enough," I said.

"And why only ten acres?" he asked. "Why so modest, even with land, to re-build the Garden of Eden?"

"The way I figure it," I said, "if they divided up the earth, ten acres of bottom land would be a just portion for a just man."

"It's gonna be an awfully crowded garden," he said.

"Noah did it in an ark, save the world," I said.

"And why animals for companions?"

"Well," I said. "I've had a thought. Maybe we've had it all wrong all this time, going on the premise that human beings started as angels. So, we're so disappointed when we see them act like beasts. Maybe, if we begin by seeing them as beasts, and see how far they have to *fall upward* to become angels, we may get somewhere with them yet."

"Well," he said. "You know best. You are the poet and the philosopher. I'm just the guy who bought and sold."

It was time for me to leave and let him go back to his rest. Apparently, his body could take only so much at a time. I had a peaceful sleep in his guest room that night. The next day I said good-bye to Uncle J. and left Zurich for New York and Waterloo. I knew that was the last time I would be seeing him, alive or dead. I knew I could not afford to go to his funeral, especially now that I knew how long a corpse could remain above the ground, unburied. He would be the last of my significant dead, whose burial I would miss again.

As we made the final descent into New York and the plane tipped its wing in the glare of the rising sun, I caught a glimpse of the Lady with the Lamp. I spread out my hands for her to see. I had come back empty-handed again. But I hoped I would not remain that way forever.